NoVA

A NOVEL

James Boice

SCRIBNER

New York   London   Toronto   Sydney

SCRIBNER

A Division of Simon & Schuster, Inc.
1230 Avenue of the Americas
New York, NY 10020

First Scribner hardcover edition January 2009

SCRIBNER and design are registered trademarks of The Gale Group, Inc.,
used under license by Simon & Schuster, Inc., the publisher of this work.

For information about special discounts for bulk purchases,
please contact Simon & Schuster Special Sales at 1-800-456-6798
or business@simonandschuster.com

Text set in Aldus

Manufactured in the United States of America

1   2   3   4   5   6   7   8   9   10

Library of Congress Cataloging-in-Publication Data
Boice, James.
Nova : a novel / James Boice. —1st Scribner hardcover ed.
p. cm.
1. Teenagers—Suicidal behavior—Fiction. 2. Suicide—Fiction. 3.
Psychological fiction. I. Title.
PS3602.O45N68 2009
813'.6—dc22   2008032792

ISBN-13: 978-1-4165-7543-6

To R.

NOVEMBER 2, 1998

Tot Lot—Third Entrance

His name is Grayson Donald and he is dead. His body hangs from the chipped orange rim of a basketball hoop on a full-sized green and red court adjacent an empty tot lot in a clearing in the woods between two streets of habitacles in a high-growth subdivision in an incorporated township called Centreville in Northern Virginia. A black and gnarled path leads from the street to the clearing and it continues through the clearing twisting and splitting where the roots it covers fight against it and opens onto the other street of homes. The subdivision if viewed from above by the angels and demons in heaven peering over the edges of the clouds for sight of the soul due them forms a complex network like a maze, the systematic perfect darg of an exotic species of beetle. The body of the dead boy is seventeen years old. It has more or less completed its sudden morphing from the ungendered body of a boy to the odorous and hairy imago of a man. There is not any chest hair though the legs are quite hirsute, as is the groin. It seems his lower half received his father's barbigerous DNA and the upper half his half-Irish mother's set of fair genes (or those Irish genes could be from his father as no one is sure exactly what his father is—a barnacle accumulated from the itinerant ramblings of European vagrants and mongrels). He is like a half man, half beast from mythology. His shoe size is 9½. The body sways in the November night. There is no breeze. After his feet knocked off of his father's stepladder, his body kicked and fought, his hands went to his neck, the rope dug into it so deep, and pulled upon it. This doesn't mean that he thought it was a mistake once the irreversibility of his death became clear to him and that he resisted it. Rather it is what the body does once it knows it is dying. It takes over the mind and all the God and science within it and becomes its own beast, its instincts quelling consciousness, muscles spasming like worms on pavement after rain. For the reaction of that which is alive when faced with the death ever awaiting it like an old man in black with his hand out is to run and flee, shriek, panic, pull at that which kills it, fight death off, reduced to a frantic shameful critter in the wild.

He took the stepladder one hour ago from the side of the garage where his mother would park the Escort when she came home, removing first the sloppy tangled garden hose caked with old chunks of mud and then the dusty golf clubs on which the hose had been tossed. It is his father's and is metal—thin and aluminum with brown rust in the joints where it unfolds and in the nuts and in the grips of the steps. Now the stepladder lies on its side, still opened. The routous clanging so silenced now. Grayson's eyeballs red. The rope sinking into the fleshy underside of his chin, the browning flesh swelling up around it like risen dough. The rope was hanging on a nail in the garage, white and coiled and untouched since the day his father bought it at Hechinger and hung it there. He weighs 145 pounds, alive. He walked here from his house carrying the things of his deceasing. A distance of a quarter of a mile. His brain is still alive though it is without worth as blood has been denied it for over eleven minutes. His brain is the mulch, is the shoes he wears. The tip of a deep red tongue protruding between two thin nearly colorless lips. His hands hang at his sides. His small feet point down. The rim is durable—two rims welded together, one on top of the other, to form one thick rim off which the ball bounces drastically when shot, mandating perfection or nothing. The purpose is to defend against kids who might bend it by pulling themselves up by the net and hanging off it, doing chin-ups. Its pole too thick to wrap your arms all the way around, painted dark green but chipping, the old red showing through beneath. Curved at the top like a capsized J. Some kids can still shimmy up it regardless. Grayson Donald has never been the sort to climb. Climbing is genetic. One of the biggest reliefs in his life came the first day he walked into gym class at Braddock Park High School and saw none of the climbing ropes that hung from the corner vaults at Catholic school. The rim is strong. It did not offer so much as a creak in protest to the demands his body made upon it without warning eleven minutes ago. There is no one else other than he named with his name in Centreville. There are between twelve and fifteen kids his age named Chris. Ten different Brians, four Bryans, eight Ryans, eleven Matts, seven David or Daves. In his confirmation class when he was fourteen there were three Tims and they all chose the name Joseph. The girls tend to be named Lindsay, Jennifer, Katie/Katherine, or one of the variations on Christine, Kristine, Christina, or Kristina, unless they are Asian. There are leaves on the edges of the court and they are brown and thin. Not long ago they were sussurant and green in the branches of trees. Earlier before he arrived two sixth graders named Chris and Ryan wearing baseball caps with professional sports team logos on them sped down the path, in the opposite direction that Grayson would soon move in, on expensive new Diamondbacks with pegs on the rear wheels, not using their brakes, hopping off any mounds or obstacles before them, speeding home before nightfall from lighting matches and burning leaves and sticks in another set of woods behind the school. Before that there were people wearing barn jackets and walking golden retrievers, plastic grocery bags stuffed in their pockets, here and there a jogger, a mother pushing a stroller speaking to the baby within as though the infant were herself. After the boys there was nobody until Grayson. The tot lot and basketball court are on a plateau rising up in the center of a drainage ditch that when full has Canadian geese floating atop it honking like an extended family of gypsies picnicking on the roadside. The slopes become part of the game. The drainage ditch has a concrete nuke silo sticking out from it. And there is a wrought iron ladder that you can climb down to go into it and light matches and burn things that you might find on the way gathering them up like a glacier and you can be unseen by the adults who look out their windows and wander their bike paths, indeed go about their days and lives with no object other than catching children crouched in woods and sewers burning things. Also in the silo are the several mouths of tunnels extending out from it in all directions like arteries from the heart and if you are a child and crouch down far enough you can crawl through the underworld. Deep within these sewer labyrinths is the best place to light matches and burn your debris. Venture in only if it has not rained and bring a flashlight and a pocketknife for cutting things you might find if you still have yours from Boy Scouts. On all sides around the dead kid are homes. Decks and backyards and gas grills. Portable basketball hoops. They circle him at a distance like wolves. If his eyes were open he would see the lights in the windows like eyes and shadows within rising from kitchen tables and carrying dishes to the sink, rinsing them for the dishwasher, glancing out the window at the wooded area behind their home that they pay an extra lot fee for, the value of the home rising and dropping, they can hear the ticking on the quietest nights like this one. Domestic living. The things of family. Finger paintings on the fridge, three-foot baby gates in doorways to keep the dog out of the living room, the flashing spectral of televisions, the blue fanal of bulky beige computer monitors plugged into the tower with the ropelike cable of a parallel port. Floppy disks, filing cabinets. Recliners and living room sets, sofas torn by the cat. The darkness outside and the lights inside blinding them to the knowledge that outside dies a boy who lived among them but upon whom their eyes have never laid. And they will not know until the morning. They will sleep the night through with him dangling out there under the moon. They will bicker and eat and laugh and brush their teeth, read a few pages in bed. They will lie in darkness thinking about their lives and deaths. In the morning a fifteen-year-old girl named Lindsay Martinez who goes to his school but does not know him will be putting on her bra, hair still wet and sticking to her back, the pink lace curtains of her bedroom window tied open, soccer trophies and academic achievement certificates from elementary school and middle school tacked to the wall, vinyl blinds twisted open, "Torn" by Natalie Imbruglia playing on Z104 on her Aiwa stereo with CD/tape/AM/FM radio and detachable speakers and remote control and digital screen that scrolls the station number across it, staring at herself in the mirror of her vanity as she blow-dries her hair, singing along in undertone but so sleepy at 6:30 AM, dazed and mentally checking that she didn't forget to do any homework, decided that the kind of boyfriend she wants is a NORMAL guy, like Carson Daly only cuter and who wears Samba Classics, the kind of shoes she wears, and she senses something is off and her eyes move to the window and she sees out over her backyard then the playground and sparse woods, the trees naked and spindle-shanked, and the basketball court, and her hand with the brush in it stops halfway through her hair, her head bent sideways so the hair hangs, the hair dryer still going, hot air on her face she does not feel. She squints. She straightens her head. She says, — Oh my God.

In his stomach is chewed-up, partially digested baked ziti and masticated steamed vegetables and what was recently a dinner roll with margarine on it, and Coke. It is now all a pinkish mush in there. This is the second time this week that his stomach has held such contents. His mother makes baked ziti for dinner on average twice a week. She makes chicken three times a week. Normally it is chicken covered with Shake 'n Bake and some flavored instant rice on the side. It is not uncommon for families in Little Rocky Run to set a designated hour of the evening as the time when all members must be home and seated to eat dinner together at the table in the kitchen. Six o'clock is usually this time. The Donalds do not eat together as a family at the same time every day. Dinnertime at the Donalds' is whenever Grayson's mother finally comes home and puts the baked ziti in the oven or covers the chicken that has been defrosting in the sink in Shake 'n Bake. Domino's is ordered every Friday. Grayson normally is the one who places the order if he is home, as his father does not like telephones. Two large pepperonis, two two-liters of Coke. With frozen baked ziti you can drive home from work and take it out of the freezer and unpeel the foil and stick it in the oven before even putting down your purse, and with chicken you can rinse the pieces in the sink and put them in the plastic bag that comes with the Shake 'n Bake with the Shake 'n Bake in it and shake the bag, covering the chicken in crumbs, and put the chicken on a cookie sheet with tinfoil underneath if the Teflon coating has worn away and toss it into the oven before the cold-eyed fatigue of your unending days at last consumes you and your marrowbones turn to jelly upon seeing the sofa and the television just sitting there all for you like a valley of flowers and furry animals. And the ziti and chicken can be cooked and cooled by the time your husband and child begin prowling forth out of their warrens drooling and unforthcoming, sniffing around the kitchen like hyenas for food.

The baked ziti in his stomach now is being broken down by enzymes and acids and moving inch by inch into the intestines. He cooked it himself today, reading the instructions on the back of the package. His lunch was not eaten in the Braddock Park High School cafeteria at 9:57 this morning, the first lunch period. If it were any other day it would have been. It would have been spaghetti, chopped into inch-long bits and covered in a dark red lump goop and eaten with a spork. His lunch has already made its way through the intestine and colon and now takes the form of hot brown shit cooling in the sagging seat of his Hanes boxer briefs. A hard-on protrudes from the crotch of his cargo pants. The cargo pants are very long and baggy and worn low on the hips, the common way of wearing any kind of pants in 1998 if you are a teenager, regardless of your race. There is also a substantial amount of Sprite in his stomach and digested Mountain Dew in his bladder. There is no water in his stomach. The only water he has consumed today was that which he accidentally swallowed while brushing his teeth this morning. If it weren't for the hard-on the bladder would be emptied, creating a large dark stain in the khaki and a drip down his left leg and small pool on the court below stinking like iodine. In his blood is THC metabolite, no cocaine metabolites, nor barbiturates or benzodiazepines. There is mostly caffeine and sugar. No sertraline or paroxetine or anything similar. No traces of the LSD he did when he was fourteen, not even in his spinal fluid. They said to test you for LSD they tap your spine because that's where it goes. No alcohol. No common opioids. His body is warm to the touch with no rigor present. The eyelids are without special note. The conjunctivas and scleras are unremarkable. The corneas are cloudy. The irises are hazel. The pupils are equally dilated and fixed centrally. The skeleton of the nose is intact. The lip and frenulum are atraumatic. The teeth are natural and in good repair. Abundant edema fluid mixed with blood-tinged purge fluid emanates from the nose and mouth. There is a ligature mark around the neck with a suspension point at the back of the neck. There will be a small laceration on the back of the head when he hits his head when he is cut down. There will be no bleeding involved. Two small abrasions on the right side of the neck from the noose. No marks on the hands or wrists. His fingernails cut very short. The toenails are short and clean. The back and buttocks are without special note. The scalp hair is nearly black and overgrown into a helmet of hair that with his beardless face makes you realize how so very young this person is.

Little Rocky Run in Centreville is twenty-five miles west of Washington, DC. The mailing address here is Clifton, the neighboring wealthy quaint bourg in the hills that looks frozen in the antebellum, manses on sprawling plots, a gravel road dollhouse hamlet, deep woods and lakes, old ghost railroad tracks. The quirk is a remnant of the origins of Little Rocky Run when the planners endeavored to market their vicinage to potential residents and did so by suggesting it was located in the desirable and historic Clifton, where Clarence Thomas lives, and that by living in Little Rocky Run you could be more or less living in that idyllic storybook place as well and could spend your days shopping for antiques and your Sundays traipsing through the honeysuckles with your children. Also neighboring Centreville on another side is Manassas, the garish apartment city of malls and fast food places, red lights, car dealerships, lost causes, the middling gray hole of dropouts and divorce. Grayson Donald grew up here in Little Rocky Run in Centreville, mailing address Clifton. His family moved in twelve years ago from Northern California. They bought the home from Tyler Nickerson, a real estate agent still working in Little Rocky Run exclusively who has sold a good portion of the homes here. The home was still being built when the Donalds bought it. All homes on the street were. Grayson wandered through them as a little boy. The air smelled like the third layer of the earth. Migrant workers, their discarded Gatorade bottles and caulking tubes, all that sod rolled up in balls atop the orange dirt, the tar wet and ditches filled with quicksand, loose nails everywhere. All in upheaval. Stray articles of clothing, dormant yellow machines on which to climb. The mud. He lost shoes in the mud. Collected loose nails in his pockets. Little Rocky Run spreads for miles off Union Mill Road where Civil War trenches line the shoulder. A featureless desert of tract homes and new minimanses jammed among each other just going for a thousand acres of well-groomed yards and colorful landscaping and doorbells and 25 mph signs—lives being lived and nothing in the way. There is an elementary school, Twin Lakes Elementary, in the middle of all of this like the church in an Olde English village. In 1998 it overflows beyond capacity and there are plans for a middle school to be built up on Union Mill Road. There are School Zone signs almost everywhere. They pop up nearly a mile away from Twin Lakes Elementary. Stop signs. Children in bikes zoom around. To get anywhere you need a car. There is enough money and no worry about rent or eating. There are commuter jobs and swim teams and braces and standards for how long your grass can be. You will get a note from the Home Owners' Association if your shutters are in need of repainting. Tennis courts, swimming pools, rec centers, retirement funds, report cards, hills, driveways, mailboxes, wood fences, gardens, wind chimes, aluminum baseball bats, video games, Rollerblades, garages, faux brick, blue Southern skies, Blue Ridge Mountains in the distance, Courts and Drives and Ways and Terraces and Circles, a baby factory, a breeding ground, all excess elements of living trimmed away like the hair of the mothers for the sake of creating and raising babies and maintaining the health, physical safety, and education of all, and little else is of value if it is not work or school or doctor appointments.

Off Union Mill Road there are four entrances into Little Rocky Run. At each a rock with a plaque attached to it and the words *Little Rocky Run* engraved in curvy script and the image of what looks like the side of a mountain. You refer to where you live by which entrance you use—the First Entrance, the Fourth Entrance, etc. Grayson Donald lives in the Third Entrance. Technically the numbers are wrong as there is an entrance before the First Entrance but for some reason no one counts this entrance. The First Entrance is where the oldest homes of Little Rocky Run are and also the cheapest and smallest. The Fourth Entrance contains the prefab quasi manors approaching the million-dollar mark already in 1998. Braddock Park High School sits across from the First Entrance on the other side of Union Mill Road backing into Braddock Park and Twin Lakes Golf Course. It has three thousand students in 1998. Trailer classrooms crowd the grounds like mold growth. When it's autumn and perfect like tonight and the trees are bare you can see the high school from the elementary school. There are two swimming pools in Little Rocky Run not counting the smaller one by the town houses which is where the uncounted true first entrance is and where the homes were first built and are sold most cheaply. There are seventeen tennis courts in Little Rocky

Run. This is the only tot lot that has a basketball court too. Though one of the two pools does have a basketball court. How many tot lots there are in total no one can know for sure. Their numbers and nature are forever in flux. They are like the stars above you. This tot lot is in the Third Entrance. The fathers are in the military. They are here because the army, the air force has stationed them to one of the countless government offices scattered around Northern Virginia far enough away from one another that no single bomb or missile would wipe all of them out. The CIA headquarters in Langley. The Pentagon in Arlington. Several others unmarked and unknown. These are greige ziggurats of bureaucracy and secrecy. Fifteen miles east is Foxstone Park in Vienna where the spy Robert Hanssen, who works with some of these fathers in the FBI, meets his KGB handler with a briefcase of documents. Most fathers make the commute every morning with seldom more than a vague emotion of complaint. Men and women of duty. The fathers who are not military are civilian contractors to the military. They are brilliant people who consult in the research of the design of weapons systems, develop fuel cells and the technology of military action. Or they work for Mobil in a middle-management capacity, transferred to that entity's corporate offices. Or they are at AOL in Dulles. They are here because of work. Work is why they breathe this air. The mothers are brilliant too. They have large butts and short hair and wear jeans pulled high with T-shirts bought on vacation tucked into them. The fathers wear sweaters, boat shoes without socks, short hair, nice watches. It is a time before Lasik surgery. The era of DSL and VHS. Definition is not high. The HBOs stop at number three. MTV plays some videos. Clinton is in office, there is no such thing yet of something called 9/11. There is nothing that is called a text message. Hybrid engines can be found only in academic science journals. *Blog* is but an onomatopoeia—the sound of humanity about to sneeze. It is calm and controlled and hardly anybody stands out from one another in 1998 in Little Rocky Run save for the two former NFL players who live here—disgraced former placekicker Steve North and former Washington Redskins legend Donnie Warren, who hangs out in a lawn chair at his sons' Little League games at Carlburn Field signing autographs.

No one can say for sure why it is spelled that way, with the *r* and the *e* reversed. We have our theories. One is that it is left over from the English who originally founded the township in the 1700s. It is even said that John Smith had a hand in its finding on his journeys up and down the East Coast in the first years of the 1600s battling the epic blade of Powhatan, the Salvage king. Though it's easy to dispute this if you know the first thing about the general history of Virginia and Smith, one can still see the little pigeon-toed footprints of Pocahontas stamped in the soil along the Civil War trenches preserved by dictate of the Commonwealth on Union Mill Road. Her phantom perfumes wafting through the nyctalopia like beacons to the moonglow, making them craters of the moon seen from the earth. And John Smith's following after, big and booted. Imagine the daughter of Powhatan sneaking through the woodland to the tent of the enemy, the nubile Salvage princess dozing nude in the captain's tent, shadows from the fire flickering over her shoulders. Smith outside crouched in the dirt picking tobacco from his teeth and cleaning his pistol, his men among him, drinking and smoking, all their balls save his swollen to the size of volleyballs after years of wandering the dankness of this black wilderness without God in it, nudging their leader in the ribs for details, Smith fighting a grin beneath his natty beard and ignoring them, when out doth come she, her hair mussed, eyes puffy from sleep, wrapped in the skin of a bear, floating like Ophelia out of the tent and past them, their conversation stopping and their eyes following her, all silent and staring up at her, the moon on their faces, or it's the light from her, watching her walk down to the water and letting the bearskin drop to the mud and wading into the river like a baptism or a suicide.

The township wasn't officially incorporated until the Civil War. It is said that the first shot—the spark that ignited the conflagration—was discharged here. Until then Centreville consisted of three or four farms and those who worked them. And that was it. We can assume there was some sort of post office. A corner of somebody's pantry perhaps. Which brings us to another plausible theory of the spelling of Centreville—that the man in charge of the paperwork necessary to incorporate the township with the Commonwealth was inebriated at the time he was filling out all the forms. Or he had a brain fart as he wrote what he meant to be *Centerville*. Or he was simply pretentious. He thought perhaps that since the English, the fashion trendsetters and world dominators of the earth—i.e., the U.S.—of the era did things like stick *u*'s all over the place and reverse their *er*'s, then he should do that too in the spelling of something so important as an incorporated township of the Confederacy. Also he may have been doing this paperwork on Manassas Battlefield as cannonballs whizzed by his ear and craniums exploded their brains all over the side of his face, making it difficult to concentrate.

After the war was done and all the bodies buried and the blood in the ground was dried up and blown off in flakes by the wind, and the freed Negroes were sent off their plantations to be ghettoed in Chicago and Detroit and all over the country, in every manner of speaking, and the 1800s turned into the 1900s and the car was invented and the population of Northern Virginia blossomed from ten thousand to over one million, as the 1950s mutated into the warped madness of the earth at the end of the millennium, the people who moved in and began to spawn themselves weren't Southern enough to call themselves Southerners but weren't Northern enough to be called Yankees either. They lost their twangs but still said *y'all*. They regained the *r*'s they once dropped in the North. They were reserved and conscious of themselves like they were in the North though they still hung rebel flags in the rear windows of their trucks. They weren't wealthy nor were they poor. They were famous for no particular type of food. Their weather was hot in the summer but not as hot as Mississippi or Louisiana. The winters were cold but not nearly as cold as the winters of Maine or Vermont. The springs were pleasant and the falls picturesque. What was left when all was washed away was a pink-fresh nobody, white people with occupations called things like Senior Marketing Data Information Analysis Coordinator, making low six figures in pharmaceutical sales by their thirtieth birthday. They drank Miller Lite and drove midrange sedans. Half voted Republican, half voted Democrat. The music they listened to was played at a low volume in the car on the commute, the mix station, whatever was on, the open-format rock stations floundering until giving up and switching over, the country stations, the R & B, and nobody minded that whatever station they chose played the same four songs on repeat because they were songs they enjoyed. And they went to the gym after work and met their friends for happy hour and slept with their friends with condoms and became married at age twenty-seven and purchased a home and ventured forth in procreation. They had no structure to their faces. Their bones morphed into one another. They spoke the same syllables on top of one another, and they were cast out in the middle where they tore the plastic off their new shirts and tossed them in the washer in the year 1998.

You think as you die. These are backroom, fleeting thoughts. It is the kind of thinking one does while shoveling out one's car or scrubbing the burned stuck bits of canned croissants off a cookie sheet whose nonstick coating has baked away over the years. Silly and rampant thoughts released from the abyssal crevices of the cerebrum like the cerebrum's been soaking in detergent, like in a commercial, the screen split and your brain soaking in detergent on one side and your socks soaking in the leading brand on the other side, your dreams and vague ideas and subconscious desires floating up from the socks through the water. See the difference?

It's a lot like dreaming. Your limbs flailing, your arteries contracting like the mouths of unguinous baby birds, your heart in emergency mode, pushing itself high into the red to fight for its every last beat, and all the while you are thinking, Did I pay my cable bill? Or, I didn't buy anything for Mother's Day. Or, what's today? Tuesday? Random, flickering but highly specific images that must mean something or come from somewhere but at first glance appear not to. A trumpet with mistletoe around it. What is it and where did it come from? As for Grayson Donald, this is what he thought about as he died: a great idea for a new kind of thermometer. They should invent a thermometer, he thought, that one can stick outside one's window that instead of simply telling you the number of degrees it is outside, a number that can mean nothing if there is a cold wind or a high humidity, it tells you what kind of clothing you should wear today. For example it might say, HEAVY JACKET AND HAT AND THERMALS or SHIRT AND LONG PANTS BUT MAYBE BRING A SWEATER TOO. A more expensive model will include a moisture sensor and it will also be able to say UMBRELLA. If somebody were to revolutionize the thermometer in such a way, he thought, he would make millions. He might go down in history. The majority of human beings would pay you to tell them what to wear every day, sure. It is a daily challenge that no one since the first weatherman has thought to address. Take an obstacle out of people's mornings. This is the basic principle of business. The interpretation of numerical data—they will pay to have that done for them. They will line up for it. You'd probably go down in the annals of history. Though the guy who invented the original thermometer didn't so maybe not. Unless his name was Thermometer. Greek guy. Socrates and Thermometer hanging out in Athens in their tunics. No—meter means measure, thermo means temperature. Wouldn't it be a hoot if that were his name though anyway—talk about being into it. This thermometer though, Grayson thought, huge spots of eclipsing fanal exploding before his sight, the rope tearing his flesh, kicking and seizing, will save countless people from getting sick from being underdressed after trying to decide if 42 degrees is too warm for the heavy jacket. It will also save them from irritability and even heatstroke from being overdressed on surprisingly warm days. People will feel better overall and more cheerful and comfortable. Imagine a city filled only with that kind of person. Tolerant of the slow and lost on the road, pleasant and nonperspirant on crowded trains. Crime rates will drop, the general mood of humanity will improve. War will end. Poverty will disappear. A love train across the universe.

He thought, Hmm, will the success of such a product threaten the mental health industry (a booming industry) and big pharmaceutical enough that they will take action to . . . *remove* the inventor of the new thermometer before it can hit the market? Would he begin to find threatening notes in his mailbox made from the cutout letters of newspapers? Hear the sound of sticks breaking in his backyard at night? Feel the need to get down on his belly in his driveway every morning and take a peek at the ol' undercarriage? He considered that this could be precisely why the thermometer has remained the same (aside from the invention of the digital thermometer—oooh, Pfizer's really shaking in their wingtips!) for so long, just like the umbrella. Thousands of years probably. No new take on the technology has been made or least marketed because thugs have a death grip on the market, arresting the development of the thermometer. There is maybe a secret sect of high-powered vested parties. They live among us. Mercury distributors, little glass tube makers. People whose business provides the ink for the black dashes. And so on. Think about it. Who else would buy mercury if thermometers stopped needing it? Though digital thermometers don't use mercury. Must have been a deal of some sort there. Kickbacks. The answer to any question in America is a one-word answer: Money. Why did the Founding Fathers declare independence? Money. Why are the Rolling Stones still at it? Money. Then he thought, I should eat fish more often. It's an entire genre of food I have thus far neglected all the time eating baked ziti and Shake 'n Bake chicken. In fish there's probably a whole new world of gustatory experience out there. It will change how I perceive everything.

Then he kicked once more, shat his pants, and died.

The same freakish meeting of the right ions and chemicals and temperatures that mashed together in the collision that gave us life on earth—the perfect levels of fluoride in the water, the right amount of iron in the soil, the proper amount of sunlight with the correct direction of the wind blowing the delicate wafts of toxic emissions from downtown Washington, DC, factories where children of the slaves stabbed one another and black women accepted white cocks into their siccaneous and trembling mouths and old Hispanic men quivered in methadone clinic lines six hours deep, mixed with illegal dumping in the Potomac where condoms floated in the current and oil slicks on Chesapeake crab backs. It all blended to form a cloud that slid west and met with the humidity and spent buckshot cartridges and Civil War bones clad in blue and gray to create concrete and vinyl siding and front yards laid in chunks, child care centers and video rental places. One day there were dirt roads and horses and the next there was one of the biggest counties in America, Fairfax County, hallowed be its name. A barricaded oasis severe and new in a state known for its tobacco and NRA meetings and its agomphious inbreeding. Isolationists hiding in the Blue Ridges in their meth lab trailers with wall safes stashed with weed and coke. Truck drivers and Mennonite sex offenders. The difference is stark if one were to drive thirty minutes south or west. One world ends and another begins. It's like there's a chalk line drawn and—BOOM—people have accents and spouses in prison and sores from picking their face, eight or nine cigarettes hanging out of their mouth, Natty Light deuce-deuce in one hand and a losing scratch-off ticket in the other. In Northern Virginia no one really smokes. The cost of cigarettes is a full dollar higher than anywhere else in the state where in 1998 a pack of Camel Lights costs around $2.50. No one smokes in NoVA except for teenagers and middle-aged men at Fourth of July parties if they've had four Bud Lights and their wives aren't looking. Gas prices are way higher too. Don't even ask about traffic. There is nothing but traffic. It's second only to L.A. The planners must have had a hard-on for traffic. Public transportation sucks if you're outside the Beltway. You have to drive. On 66 East around Manassas the road suddenly doubles in size as you cross into NoVA from the boonies and things EXPLODE. 66 is the main artery of NoVA. It's like the Jersey Turnpike. It goes right into DC. To get into DC from Centreville you get on 66 East and sputter along on someone's bumper and someone else on your bumper going about 10 mph. You pass the Vienna Metro station and pass Falls Church, lurching and braking and drumming your fingers on the wheel to DC101 or Z104 keeping your eyes straight or fiddling with the AC—anytime of day except maybe three in the morning there is this awful, unending constipated traffic—the traffic reaching its peak and all forward progress halting altogether as the Beltway approaches—famous and mighty, enigmatic and impossible to figure out which direction you need to go in because it's a circle—north is south and south is east—and most cars veer off here to sit idle on the on-ramp and you can see the line of red brake lights snaking off in eternity and you've never been more grateful for anything than you are that you don't have to get on the Beltway. And as you pass the on-ramp something suddenly gives and all engines roar like at NASCAR, your car jumps forward, all brake lights vanish, as before you is CLEAR SAILING, the concrete soundproof walls on either side of you, the trees sticking out from over them, the Metro tracks running down between the west- and eastbound traffic, the HOV lane marked with a white diamond phasing out and after a while it chops down to two lanes and there is no stopping you.

The people of NoVA know 66 unconsciously. Like how the Salvages John Smith met knew how to grow victuals. They can cruise along 66 with a blindfold on and talking on their cell phone while programming their radio and hit their exit without even tapping their brakes. 66 is a walk down to the mailbox. The reaching back to flush the toilet.

In NoVA you'll find that most of your life is spent in your car, at red lights waiting to make a left turn, the *tick-tick* of your blinker. Flipping down your sun visor, glancing over your shoulder, changing lanes.

31317 Marblestone Court— Third Entrance

He's decided he will tell her.

As he sits at the L-shaped desk in the swivel chair, in the small room in the corner of the second floor of the house, in which there is a tabletop Xerox machine, with a newspaper clipping still in it, and a bookshelf, with textbooks and books by Thomas Aquinas and one called *On Death and Dying* and another *The Road Less Traveled*, a file cabinet, a bulletin board with a Mothers Against Drunk Driving sticker pushpinned up but otherwise empty, blinds closed, chin in hand, elbow on desk, in sweatpants either dark gray or faded black, brown socks, flannel shirt, other hand manipulating the mouse, worn-down blue mouse pad, eyes dilated wide and focused for distance, his face ghostly green from the computer screen, room silent except for the whir of the computer, checking his e-mail, waiting for porn to download, he decides when she gets home he will tell her.

He will wait as he hears the electric garage door rumbling beneath him then the door opening downstairs and the jingle of too many keys being wrestled out of the knob and the door closing again and her sighing the way you do at the end of a day where you're not sure if lunch happened today or yesterday or in a dream. He'll wait for the clacking of her flat beige shoes on the linoleum floor installed last winter and her responding to the dog's huffing and collar jingling with, —All right, all right . . . then a sound like a terrible scuff being ripped through the linoleum floor, followed by the collapse of a briefcase and canvas bag filled with manila folders and books set down on the table, the clink of a coat zipper against the metal back-meeting-seat part of the chair, then another suction sound as she opens the freezer for a pan of baked ziti and a hollow rattle of the pan being set on the middle rack in the oven, the *beep-beep-beep . . . BEEP* of the microwave timer, the thigh-high dog gate being moved aside and the lowest stair oomphing, then the next, a knee creaking, an irritated sigh as the oomphing of stairs gets higher and closer. By then he will have opened and unlocked the computer room door and put his shrinking and softening penis back inside the hole of his boxers then pulled the waist of his sweatpants up from his knees. He will be able to see, through the wooden bars of the banister, the top of her brown permed head gradually appear, like someone doing the trick where you stand behind a couch and pretend to be walking up and down imaginary stairs. He will say, only slightly moving his jaw, —Hi, and she will sigh, —Hello, though they won't see each other, their voices fleeting and long distance, fading. He will let her go into their bedroom and change in the walk-in closet into her sweatpants and sweatshirt in privacy, so she won't have to deal with him watching her and seeing the pad of fat between her belly and groin that bulges these days against the front of her underwear, let her go to the bathroom, which she always needs direly to do upon returning home, where she can fart and poop if she needs to without feeling him outside, waiting, hearing. Then after he hears the toilet flush and the bathroom door's lock click and the door open he will go in and sit on the bed and say hello and she'll say hello and he'll ask her how her day was and she'll say and she'll ask back and he'll say, but then he'll exhale, pointedly, and perhaps rub his forehead and give a disarming half smile that will make her ask if something is the matter and he'll say, —Actually, yes, there is. There's something I think we need to talk about. Sit down. Do you mind sitting down? And he will tell her.

He'll make a dentist appointment and reseal the deck and get a haircut too for Christ's sake and make a better effort at creating a better social life for himself and he will tell her and cut down on cholesterol and go into her room—*their* room—and tell her because it's important for both of them that he *tell her*.

Not that he buys into those TV therapist types, those daytime talk show *be strong and overcome* kinds of things but what he can be on board with Oprah and the rest of her ilk about is that you have to be honest. And that it takes guts to be honest and it's not always the easiest thing to do but you have to suck it up and be a man otherwise you won't be happy. He thinks of himself definitely not as a pushover or scaredy cat. However, though, the thing is, he's always had trouble engaging in conversation with someone immediately after they've defecated—the toilet still running, their olid stench still fouling the air, their butt still cold from hanging bare over the water, a trickle or two of urine still drying in their underwear. It gives him bad memories of the Pentagon car pool, the shrimp platter . . .

So that's why, when he hears her come home, and sees the top of her head, and hears her go into their bedroom, he decides he'll finish his Jack Daniel's with ice, his eleventh of the day though he thinks it's still his third (started drinking at around two after getting home from Best Buy, though he thinks he started drinking at six). Then he'll tell her. While he's doing this he checks out some more free pictures of girls not much older than his son, nude and fellating and impaling themselves on candy-colored dildos and anonymous and multiple penises, close-ups of their waxed buttholes as they pull their cheeks apart, a penis in their butthole, another one in their vagina, one time two in each, amateur everyday-looking girls, the kind he likes the best because he finds professionals with implants bulging beneath armpits and clown makeup and obvious hazy digital retouching, posing and hamming and all that not a little insulting to his intelligence and normally skips over them on proud principle, another browser window up behind the porn one and slightly to the side so if she or his son happens to walk in unexpectedly—and he listens with one ear for the sound of the hallway carpet being stepped on—he can click on the barely visible slice of the safe browser window (and he keeps his pants on when the door's open, obviously), set to an innocuous if liberally biased *Washington Post* article, concealing the picture set he has up now of a thin tanned blond girl with pink lips and pigtails in the bath shaving off her pubic hair while sucking on a lollipop, so he doesn't have to go back and relocate it once she leaves again. He looks at the girl sticking a finger in her own anus while looking back and winking at the camera then goes back to the main menu, where there's a list of descriptions of picture sets, and clicks on 19 Y/O SORORITY SLUT DOGGY-STYLE FUCKED AND FACIAL. Sure enough there is a person as described engaged in the advertised activity though it is debatable to put it mildly whether or not she is nineteen. If she's nineteen, he's twenty-four, and Clinton's not a louse. There is a variety of thumbnails organized on the page that follows her from dressed and seated on a couch, hands clasped in her lap and smiling at him sweetly, to licking semen off one breast as a deflating wet uncircumcised penis dangles before her face. He looks at this page for two seconds and clicks on the last picture, the one with the semen. Looks at it for a few seconds, then checks his e-mail, a Hotmail account he set up three days ago under a fake name and info, types in the URL of an online dating site in the window with the picture of a girl with semen on her, and the address fills itself in automatically after he supplies the first two letters. No new postings have been added by women in the area, only one by a mentulate black man whose post contains a grainy picture of what looks like an instrument of animal husbandry growing out of his groin. We're talking bulls, equestrians. Feeling suddenly candent and inferior, he checks his e-mail again, deletes an e-mail for mortgage refinancing, then looks at a picture set of a heavy black woman spilling out of a bikini, badly dyed blond hair, fucking a group of eight men of various races and penis sizes in what looks like a movie theater, culminating with a few pictures of her with what seems to be a pitcher's worth of ylem on her face, neck, hair, and breasts. He hears the toilet flush. Clears the history, closes out all windows, feels ill, looks at the little digital clock in the lower right corner on the taskbar, feels guilty and empty, thinks, Time flies when you're looking at porn, opens Explorer again, checks his e-mail, closes it, waits thirty seconds for what's left of his erection to thoroughly diminish, stands up, adjusts his pants, goes down the hall past his son's room—door closed, but you can see a light's on, music playing (so-called—sounds like Bob Dylan with a cold, heh heh heh)—goes into the bedroom, she's coming out of the bathroom and the toilet is still running, he smiles but she doesn't and he puts her hands on her hips like she might break and goes, —Hi Momma, and kisses her, going *mwah*, on the lips with careful delicacy by habit because when his beard scratches her face she complains and it makes him feel lonely.

—Where's Gray? she says.

—In his room I think.

—I have baked ziti in the oven that'll be ready in an hour about, she says.

—Ed Hurkle called, he wants to have an HOA meeting, laughing kind of.

—Fine. I'll put it in the fridge before I go.

—Ed Hurkle, he says, still laughing kind of, shaking his head. —HOA meetings. Okay, Ed. Be right there.

He goes *Argh* and sort of laughs, raising and dropping his arms, then asks her where she's going, and she says back to Mason for another class in an hour and she has to write a paper for it before then. He watches her leave the bedroom and head toward the computer room, takes off his sweatpants and puts on his jeans and tucks his flannel shirt into them, whistling tunelessly, thinking, HOA meetings *suck*, but also eager to go, puts on his tennis shoes he keeps in the closet next to his church shoes, tomorrow he will tell her, tomorrow is the day, puts on his watch, grabs his wallet off the dresser.

GREENBRIAR HIGH SCHOOL

The Greenbriar High School library is famous in Fairfax County for its art nouveau but otherwise senseless glass cube display spiraling in the middle of the library from floor to ceiling like an upside-down tornado made of glass carrels treated in a way that makes them frosted like big freshly defreezered ice cubes.

Recently renovated, the high school is no longer the fortress of imprisonment it once resembled, with its beige stone blocks and angular façade, marquee with peeling paint and missing letters, hallways mephitic with old sweat, hard shiny linoleum floors with so many decades' worth of grime from soles of teenagers' shoes stamped into them that the joke among the maintenance staff, in the years leading up to the renovation which took four years to finish, was the futility of the floor buffer. When one janitor didn't have anything to do, it was always fun to say to the others, —Well maybe I'll go buff the floors.

As third period ended today, Ms. Donald—math department, geometry, Grayson's mother, first name Vicki—watched her students stand at the cluck of the minute hand of the black and white wall clock onto the :03 dash and toss their backpacks over both shoulders in the style that made Ms. Donald feel impossibly out of the loop because the last she heard only nerds and band kids wore their backpacks like that while if you were cool, which all high schoolers had to be of course, you slung yours over one shoulder like you didn't give a single hoot *how* backpacks were designed to be worn you're wearing it *this* way. How do these things happen? she wondered. Is there a secret sect of teenagers in some moldy school basement like Skull and Bones deciding these things? Do they pass out memos, this group, dispersed by means of faux hand slaps and written in a language only those between fourteen and nineteen can understand? She thought, Must be a language of one-syllable noncommittals and evasive generalities. *Shit man like I mean dude fuck like and stuff, you know?* She thought of saying something about waiting for her to dismiss them before they stand up and go but after years of this you learn to pick your battles. And plus she was standing too. As the last one vanished out the door she picked up the messy stack of tests and gave it a good tap on the desk, aligning the papers, and felt a pleasure in doing so. Put the tests back down and took her purse from the big bottom drawer—instinct whenever she leaves her classroom—and made a run down the hall to the Coke machines for a Diet Coke before next period. She is well known in her family for this, the overprotectiveness of her purse. Grayson watches her in the city, sees how she holds her purse under her arm like a football.

She moved down the hall and through the school without really going anywhere. Greenbriar High School is the elder sibling to Braddock Park High School and located a mere four and a half miles away down Stringfellow Road. Vicki's is a world of schools. In 1998 Stringfellow is a skinny two-lane jumblegut with blind curves and potholes and is the quickest easiest route to Greenbriar and the Fair Lakes business parks and deluxe strip malls, chain restaurants, and the prominent and consequential Fair Oaks Mall. Thus Stringfellow is most often very traffic jammed. Especially at rush hour you sit parked in front of the little old houses there waiting for the light, houses inhabited by old or poor people with big barking dogs kept in cages in the back and TV antennas on the roof, Confederate flags in the window and in the back of their pickups, people who have lived there for thirty years, moved out there because it was a quiet road with trees and not much traffic. In the years after 1998 when Stringfellow is expanded dramatically to better accommodate its ochletic traffic, these homes and families will vanish without explanation or interest. A place evolving around nothing but schools. The annual varsity football game between Braddock Park High School and Greenbriar High School is so intense and anticipated no matter the current quality of the programs that the game has its own name: the Sully Bowl. It is the last game of the year. You can buy commemorative mugs and T-shirts and bumper stickers and can coolies at the concession stands at these games with SULLY BOWL and the year of the game. You can wear these with pride if your child's school is victorious. It's taken seriously. Fights have broken out among parents in the stands. Calm, reserved, and respectable NoVA people suddenly shedding all decorum and giving in to the violence bubbling within them. The rivalry developed not only because of the proximity of the two schools but also because for the first couple of years in Little Rocky Run—in 1998 this would be eleven, twelve years ago, when what homes there were were scant skeletons of pine sticking out of muddy mounds wrapped with sod, driveways still unpaved and bedrabbed empty lots on either side, gravelly roads and concrete gutters along the curbs an inch and a half higher than the street—there was no Braddock Park High School yet so the high school–aged kids had to be bused over to Greenbriar. Then Braddock Park High School opened, a new and excellent school in a new and excellent incorporated township, and those students returned to their end of Stringfellow Road. Though neither township could be called downtrodden, there is certainly a class difference between the two which doesn't help with the deep-seated animosity they already feel toward one another. Greenbriar High School's colors are purple and gray and white. They are the Chargers. Their logo is a knight on horseback holding a lance. The football team though eschews the medieval imagery in favor of a little white lightning bolt on a purple helmet. Braddock Park High School's colors are a blue slightly darker than a powder blue, black, and white. They're the Wildcats. Their logo is a paw. Their helmets are this blue with a black paw on it. On a day of inclement weather, be it a vague hurricane watch or exceptionally buldering, there are always rumors that the other has been let out. Another rumor is that at the other school the boys and girls share locker rooms and showers. As Vicki Donald has found herself repeating over and over again in her life to roomfuls of tizzied students, school cancellations are decided by the Fairfax County Public Schools superintendent's office and since both Braddock Park and Greenbriar are in Fairfax County, when one gets out, the other does too. This never seems to satisfy them. They never feel this is correct. There is greater truth to what they have heard from one another.

Vicki Donald has taught math—everything from freshman remedial math for recently arrived children of immigrants coming from third-world countries with hardly any formal schooling to senior advanced calculus, aka Calculus BC, which is worth college credit and is mostly composed of the precocious who speak like grad students and paint their faces for football games, take like twenty hours a week of SAT prep classes, hire college essay consultants, intern at DC think tanks, pad the remaining nanoid white space on their college applications with things like string ensemble, community service work, volunteering for local political campaigns, sleep about three hours a night, and in general live and act like jacked-up corporate lawyers. Vicki's been teaching at Greenbriar High School since the Donalds arrived in Centreville when John was stationed to the Pentagon from Fort Ord in Monterey, California, in 1986. He's a lieutenant colonel, U.S. Army, retired. West Point graduate. Former Green Beret. Onetime sniper instructor. Vicki taught in Salinas for four years back before Salinas turned into Mogadishu. She's just paying her dues, as she sees it. This is only temporary. She means that in a religious sense. This life, all of this, its concerns and occupations—its materials, social relationships, happiness, everything—it's all unimportant. Or at least less important than matters of the soul. The life ever after. The love one has for God. She also means it in the sense that she doesn't plan on being a lifer like most of her colleagues in the math department at Greenbriar High School, not if she can help it. She has greater aspirations. She's tuned in to bigger and truer things. The ultramundane. The eternal. First of all she'll become a principal. Then she'll get into heaven. She'll see her mother there. She'll love the Lord for all eternity. Most of her colleagues are on autopilot careerwise and soulwise, she sees. They have all fallen into the trap of routine. They are grounded, unconcerned with anything beyond themselves. Their workday ends at 2:30 and they get summers off, two weeks at Christmas—er, Winter Holiday—and another week for Spring Break, plus a plethora of other holidays sprinkled throughout the year. Not a bad gig. And most of what they have to teach and how they have to teach it is predetermined by the county, the state, the school board. Others. Standardized testing. They just have to teach to the tests. Not a bad gig at all. Their responsibilities if they are crafty about it can be whittled down to making and handing out Xeroxes and basic babysitting. Any Hillary Rodham Clinton notions they may have entertained when they first entered teaching of reaching that one difficult student in the back of the room and inspiring him, changing his life, sending him on the path to becoming the first black president of the United States or something, or rousing the room with education like in *Dead Poets Society*—that goes away after the first year or two after it becomes clear that parents will complain or administration will scold if you step too far out of line with the approved curriculum. Plus there are serious boundaries to respect when it comes to student-teacher relationships and most of those movies betray them with almost comical flagrancy. For example it's the no-no of all no-nos to bring students into your home. And it's exhausting and frustrating because one finds that most kids just don't want to be reached. And they won't be the first black president no matter how hard you beat your head against the wall behind which they hide. It's not like in the movies. The kids just want to be left alone mostly. After a year or two most new teachers start to feel that in order to survive they must temper that hopeful it-takes-a-village part of their brain and stick to the minimum of what is required of them. And there you have the demilitarized zone between teachers and students. Excluding her Calculus BC type-A go-getters of course. The institution, the machination, this entire *culture* of public education—all these people showing up each day and just going through the motions. It's a farce on education, she believes. Something absurd and creepy out of Orwell. Or worse—out of reality. It is how they will find the real world to be, she thinks. So maybe it's for the better. They will enter the workforce and find life standardized. They will be filed accordingly. Their performances will be evaluated. They will have incentives and quotas. For the rest of their lives, most will just show up and go through the motions. That by definition is the middle. And that will be it. Vicki can't understand it. Most of them will do so without God. She can't understand how they will get through life without God. Without God, what's the purpose? What is the meaning? She's grateful she has the love for God that she has, feels sorry for those who don't. Grayson. She prays for them now. She sees them all as the same—these teachers (these placeholders, these leeches taking advantage of all the holiday time) and these students. Quote unquote. Everything in this culture should be shrouded in quotation marks, she thinks. Vicki though is putting up with teaching only as she climbs the ladder toward administration. She's a very driven woman and isn't afraid to work her rear off to get what she wants, is how she sees herself. She routinely applies to open assistant principal positions that come up around the county but has yet to get beyond the first interview. She has only a master's in education. Getting these kinds of jobs, your personal experience and skill and overall suitability for the job don't have as much weight in regard to whether or not you get the job as does whether or not you hold a doctorate in education. It's just the way it is. You are the degree you hold. Unless you play tennis with someone on the school board or have coached the varsity football team to States. If no one likes you or has any reason to like you, Vicki has learned, not to complain but just observing, a doctorate makes them like you. Thus she's been enrolled in the doctorate of education program at George Mason University, ten miles down 29 in the town of Fairfax, for two years, since the morning after a particularly demoralizing interview for assistant administrator at West Falls Church High School. She has classes to attend three evenings a week, one to teach one night a week (Monday, when she has both classes), twenty-page papers to write more or less every other week, projects to design, lots of reading. In her classes she has to teach, she has to teach other teachers who are like her but younger and wide-eyed and getting their master's. They're still so excited and sanguine about becoming the best educators of young minds hungry for knowledge they can be. Sometimes she wants to interrupt her own lecture to scream at them, —Run! Run away! Run to Wall Street! Run to law school! Run for your lives!

The average salary of your quotidian, run-of-the-mill Fairfax County public school teacher in 1998 is $32,000 a year. You can devote your entire working life to molding the minds, inspiring the lives, safeguarding the well-being of the children of NoVA, forever affecting their futures for the better, and never be compensated more than a particularly fervent Outback Steakhouse waitress. There is an automatic pay increase if you have your master's in education. The system picks it up. It causes a bit of a blip in the computer, the machine reacts, adjustments are automated. Vicki got her master's in the early 1980s before Grayson was born. Teachers are expected not to be human anymore. They are not to live but to grade. They are encouraged to give up their homes in favor of cots in the gymnasium. Bathe in the locker rooms. Lesson plans, homework, tests, Back to School nights, parent-teacher conferences, meetings with administration. If you let it, it can become a 120-hour workweek. A new teacher in 1998 starts at $27,000. A master's boosts you to $30,000. Vicki has been in the system for twelve years. She is department head. She has a master's in education. She's good at what she does. She's great at it. She is an asset to the county. She is talented and devoted. She is paid $44,000 a year. In Montgomery County, the bizaro-NoVA, Maryland's share of the Washington, DC, metro area, teachers start at $32,000. With a master's it's about $35,000. You don't need any degree above your junior high school diploma to understand Fairfax County's epiternal teacher shortage. They'll hire just about anyone who's not a Class A sex offender.

Often there are moments in her life when Vicki, a human being on this planet, one specimen in an endless and impossible perpession, finds herself at the overhead projector explaining cotangents with a washable red felt pen, the projector light blinding her as she looks up, glancing now and again over her shoulder at the pull-down projector screen to ensure the image is aligned properly since one cannot depend on the students to tell one if half of it is on the painted cinder-block wall, the machine's fan whirring like something industrial, puffing air on her wrist, and she'll be explaining cotangents, and writing on the transparency, and talking, teaching, educating, and a student—usually an Asian girl in the front row wearing black Prada and with no eyebrows and the surgically created fold in her eyelids that Asian girls start getting around age sixteen—will speak, raising her hand as she's asking the question, and the sudden tucket of this other voice no matter how meek the voice is will make Vicki jump and nearly drop her washable red felt pen, and she'll have to take a moment to comprehend what is happening, what is being asked and how she is as a teacher to answer, sometimes needing the girl to repeat herself, often then afterward having to rewind and proceed in the lesson from a point already passed, often this is the case, often this is what happens.

Or she'll be at her desk, her students all hunched over their tests, the susurrant etching of thirty pencils, middle of the day, Wednesday, flipping through a textbook she has to read for class, hand in her perm, and the silence of the room will melt into her like the soft but thorough creep of anesthesia and she will be wrapped unawares in a solitude unbroken by the little theater coughs and muttered vulgarities of her students, they will disappear altogether, just her and her textbook, Vicki Donald and the Lord, and at this point in her hypnosis in her nose some crusty lodger will make itself known, and by instinct the hand in the perm will move to the emunctory and a finger will insert itself into the proper nostril and set forth excavating the lodger, but in not achieving success on the first try the finger will burrow deeper, twisting to get the proper angle, her teeth baring, the skin at the entrance of the nostril stretching as the finger goes deeper and deeper, and this is the point that the bubble around her will break and she realizes where she is, and she looks up at her class with the finger stuffed to the last knuckle in her nose, and she yanks it out and goes a little pale, her eyes ranging back and forth with quickness to ensure none of them have seen, and they never have seen, and she is unaware that this is how she thinks of her students, how she refers to her students in conversations with other teachers or in meetings with administration who she knows she is more talented than and will join or replace in time just as soon as she gets her doctorate, yes that is how she refers to her students even in thoughts to herself, clear and legible, the word spelling itself out in her head not in the language of consciousness but in the English language, for that is what they are—they are THEM.

*   *   *

She was a virgin when she married John. He was twenty years old and she was seventeen when she met the polite and intelligent West Point cadet.

How she made it so far as a parthenian, especially coming of age in the late '60s and early '70s, was because she was raised very Catholic by a first-generation Irish mother and a first-generation Italian father who managed somehow to be both overbearing and distant. He kept the oldest of his four daughters on a very short leash by saddling her with the responsibility of helping her mother raise the other three. Her father spent most of his time at his office as vice president of a plumbing parts manufacturer and on the green at the country club where he was president and not only that but also the club's first non-Jewish member. This was in Westchester, New York, just outside Manhattan, in a house that backed into a golf course. At one point her father was, on paper at least, a millionaire. He was a bald short man who spoke without moving his jaw though not in an upper-class yacht club way but rather just like no one he spoke to deserved the energy it would take him to fully enunciate. Plus Vicki attended all-girls Catholic schools her entire life until meeting John. She wore thick dark-rimmed glasses and skirts below her knee and long straight hair that hid her face and double-breasted shirts with a brooch, makeup was not allowed. Not even nail polish. When she first got her ears pierced Grayson watched, chewing on his fist, tiny and fat in a stroller beside her.

Vicki still attends Mass every morning in addition to Sunday. There is nothing she takes more seriously. She rises by habit at first light to fit in morning Mass before getting to school before the first bell at 7:15 and can say the rosary in the car from St. John the Apostle to Greenbriar High School, a drive of ten or eleven minutes, without having to use actual rosary beads to keep count. She knows how many Hail Marys is ten by pure intuition. Like how chefs know when a steak is done by the smell. She teaches CCD on Sundays even though Grayson isn't enrolled (when he was, she taught the classes in the Donalds' living room on Wednesday evenings) and taught his First Communion and Confirmation classes and sees to it that the family is up on time on Sundays for Mass. She believes if you get your family to Mass your job of making a good family is more than halfway done, which used to be no problem at all. Though she still wakes him up so he has the opportunity to go, which is the best she can. Maybe it's not the *best*. But it's her obligation. And there is free will after all. As much as it kills her each week. The soul comes first, you have to be right with God before anything else and nothing matters compared to that and there is no room for negotiations. There is the world and then there is eternity. The laws of man and the laws of God—natural law. Her firm beliefs make it easier to work hard. They make her tough and unfatigable. Whenever she gets tired or would rather just sit down and watch TV, whenever she gets the urge to eat when it isn't mealtime, she thinks of Jesus on the Cross and saints such as Francis of Assisi and all he gave up and it makes her guilty and dislike herself and her human urges, her original sin, and so she trudges on.

Three years ago she and John headed St. John the Apostle's Pro-Life Committee, which consisted of maintaining a small table in the vestibule with bumper stickers that said things like ABORTION STOPS A BEATING HEART and IT'S A CHILD NOT A CHOICE, etc., and pamphlets and a newsletter and pictures of the committee adopting a highway, etc., a small coffee can wrapped in blue paper with a slit sliced in the plastic flexible lid and the words on the ridged red Folgers can, on the paper over it, PRO-LIFE DONATIONS—BUMPER STICKERS $1—BUTTONS $1—PAMPHLETS 50¢. And some other stuff. The idea was you had to give a dollar or two, whatever you felt was fair, in exchange for taking a bumper sticker or anything else. It was an honor system. The idea was Catholics could be trusted in their own church. Vicki and John Donald also staged Coffee and Donuts the first Sunday of every month after the 12:00 Mass. The 12:00 Mass, also called the Noon Mass, was known to be the Mass for the cafeteria Catholics. Strangers no one recognized, pouting kids, babies allowed to cry and cry without being rushed outside, shorts, impatient knee twitches. Every once in a while a Game Boy. She really shot the Game Boys nasty looks. The earlier the Mass, the more devoted the congregation could be counted on to be. Vicki preferred the 8:00 Mass herself.

Coffee and Donuts involved, on Saturday night, driving the Ford Escort wagon to downtown Alexandria, forty-five to fifty-five minutes away depending on traffic—66 to 495 to 395—to the Krispy Kreme and filling the entire back part of the Escort with a dozen boxes of glazed donuts, then, during the Noon Mass, setting up the utility-sized AA-style coffeemakers, hot water, and tea bags, in the multipurpose room, as it is officially called, and putting out a basket for donations (suggested, per a sign handwritten by John in his strange blocky scrawl like that of a child: 25¢ per donut, 50¢ per cup of coffee or tea), which meant having to attend the 8:00 Mass (fine—more than fine actually) or the 9:00 Mass (also satisfactory) and coming back after everyone had eaten donuts and drunk coffee, cleaning up and breaking everything down and loading the leftovers back into the forest green Escort and going home and putting them into the basement freezer at home (for eating by the Donalds—Krispy Kreme can last forever if frozen. You can put Krispy Kremes in the freezer and take them out in a hundred years, defrost them in the microwave, and they'll still be just as good. No one wants to know why) and counting all the money and change using an electric coin sorter that didn't work well, rolling all the coins by hand manually, putting all the money into a little blue zippered pouch bought at Office Depot along with the coin wrappers and coin sorter by the Donalds and not asking for reimbursement, considering it a contribution to the church (Vicki invariably also drops a $25 check in an official church donation envelope into the basket passed around every Sunday Mass), and bringing the pouch to the bank during lunch sometime during the week to put into the account set up by Vicki at First Virginia in the name of St. John the Apostle Parish.

Chartering buses to take parishioners into downtown DC for the Walk for Life pro-life rally and march every January on the anniversary of *Roe* v. *Wade*. Gently prodding Monsignor Crosby, the warted and resticus pastor, for more pro-life slants in his homilies, elbowing with Marcia Willis for more space in the church bulletin—which she, Marcia Willis, treated like it was the fucking *New Yorker*, in Vicki and John Donald's opinion—for weekly news about the Pro-Life Committee's doings and reminders about Coffee and Donuts.

Carpooling and wrangling bodies to get to the Manassas abortion clinic off Sudley Road, ten or so miles away, and getting hold of signs as gruesome as possible of aborted fetuses to hold while walking in a circle in the parking lot outside the abortion clinic, saying the rosary, yelling at cars, volunteering to counsel unwed mothers at what they call a crisis pregnancy center, which is really a pro-life place purposefully ambiguous in the phone book and a few doors down from the abortion clinic in the business strip mall, with dentists and insurance agent offices, etc., set to trap the less sapient, more frazzled of women seeking abortions by letting them think they are indeed in the abortion clinic they are looking for then having them watch an introductory video to tell them about the procedure for which they have come in today that turns out to be basically pornography for the pro-life produced by Operation Rescue and featuring wall-to-wall bloody fetuses being ripped out with tongs from between women's legs, close-ups of the faces of the fetuses, their eyes closed and mouths open, pieces of the baby tearing off inside the birth canal and having to be retrieved, the blackened carcasses of saline abortions, withered like human charcoal, close-ups of dead baby feet and little dead baby hands, aborted baby heads held between tongs like documentation of East Asian barbarism, pink and lifeless baby bits arranged on a sheet of what looks like the paper bibs they clip around your neck at the dentist to form a dismembered but complete baby corpse, a mandatory last step of an abortion to make sure the doctor got everything and no knees or fingers are still in there and floppy dead babies being found en masse in black trash bags in Dumpsters behind abortion clinics, a single piano twinkling dolent notes over all of this, shots and explanations of the blender and vacuum—the instruments of abortion—the female narrator calmly and maternally explaining that this is what you can expect today with regard to your abortion, and also to please know that science proves that your chances of getting breast cancer and becoming sterile can increase as much as 70 percent after an abortion and also that science proves as well that life starts at conception and that what everyone insists on calling the fetus, as if it is the spleen or something, is really a baby no matter what cold, soulless terms of medicine you want to throw over it. There are interviews with solemn parents whose young daughters bled to death after their abortion and the parents didn't even know they'd been pregnant. There are shots of smiling young mothers playing with their toddlers at a playground, pushing them on the swing, the late-afternoon sun hitting just right. It's no-holds barred and is great at breaking young pregnant unwed women and girls down. Then people like Vicki and John come in and give you tissues and gently prod you into keeping the baby, you don't want breast cancer or to become sterile do you, you don't want to kill your baby do you, and they have free pregnancy tests too which is another reason to go there (advertised in the window), and they can help you with adoption ("Adoption Is an Option" is a slogan of the center's—it's also one of the more popular bumper stickers available on the St. John's Pro-Life table) and if you do keep the baby, they give you donated baby items such as cribs and clothes and food and toys and take a picture of you and your baby when it's born and put it up on the board in the back full of mothers with babies they've saved from being aborted. They help you. Things they can't help you directly with are referred to someone who can. If you want to hear about becoming Catholic they can help you with that too and often do without invitation during the counseling session.

Vicki didn't engage in much of the socializing that took place among the Centreville donut-munching Catholics during Coffee and Donuts. She mostly put herself to work keeping the donut boxes pleasantly displayed and open along the tableclothed table and keeping them stocked and making sure the coffee wasn't all out. She ran around in a teal dress with shoulder pads. Her eyes had an uncanny once-a-century way of being magnetically attracted to people who took donuts without donating. She privately resented these people but otherwise did nothing. Cafeteria Catholics. It wasn't that they were evil but that they weren't aware that there even was a Pro-Life Committee and didn't see John's sign and didn't come to Mass enough to know that Coffee and Donuts wasn't just a nice social free thing the parish did for after Mass, for everyone to celebrate having gone to Mass or something. They show up on Easter and Christmas suddenly devout and of faith in their ties and skirts and hair done, praying and singing with great fervor as if they have been showing up every Sunday all year. A lot of them, and Vicki has proof, don't not believe in abortion.

This for a long time was Vicki's weekend.

She still very much retains her beliefs. They are at the very core of her selfhood. There is no Vicki Donald without her faith and sensibilities. She has not fallen, nor has she wavered. She has not weakened. But she hasn't stood in front of an abortion clinic with her family saying the rosary and holding a wroth poster before traffic in two years. She tells herself it is due to the fact that she now has class on Saturday mornings and papers to write all weekend and tests to grade and lesson plans to develop for her master's class. She never sees her family all weekend. She hasn't been to the Walk for Life in three years. Nor does she haggle for space in the St. John's bulletin. And tonight the Pro-Life table is out of ADOPTION IS AN OPTION bumper stickers. The pamphlets are in disarray. One is crumpled into a ball, one about the true ineffectiveness of condoms in the prevention of pregnancy. Its cockled words. If a plane were only 75 percent effective, would you board it? A box of church candles has been left on top of the table. A couple church bulletins tossed there without thought by yesterday's late Mass parishioners making their exodus as though the bulletins were some flyer handed to them at the top of a Metro escalator. A pamphlet telling the story of St. Agnes of Rome, the patron of virgins, who as punishment for refusing to give up the chastity she'd vowed to the Lord was gang-raped and slain. This pamphlet is currently balled up now with a hardened wad of watermelon Bubble Yum in it. A used tissue crusted with the snot of a tyke. A leaking almost empty huge purple Slurpee. A toy plastic car. A DON'T BLAME ME . . . I VOTED FOR BUSH sticker stuck to the wall upside down and crooked at about the height of a seven-year-old's hand. A well-worn Royal Purple Crayola crayon. The folded-up business card of real estate agent Tyler Nickerson scribbled on in Hot Magenta is jammed into the slot in the lid of the coffee can which except for a mangled paper clip is entirely empty.

These are the truths of human life that once had to be decried. She once felt impulsed to trumpet them. For they sank if not breathed into with the air of her lungs.

She left her classroom and joined the mad river rush of adolescence in the hallway, an infinite realm of bodies quaquaversal, everybody with backpacks over both shoulders, a race of biology in its natural habitat, and she tried to blend in as much as she could so as to not draw attention to herself but adults here had an undisguisable odor, a damning mark seared into their auras, the corruption of age preceding them like a town crier clanging his cowbell. The students like ground-dwelling rodents as footsteps approach their hole. Impossible to be caught, rarely captured on video. There is no escape being a teacher in need of caffeine and corn syrup walking down a hall. You feel drained from, eaten off of. Lonely and in charge and with a firmer handle on the world than they but at the moment incapable and lacking. The feeling of fame. This little Hollywood. Like the stars it's a love-hate relationship. A mutual foul-tasting life support. There are teachers who take up the vocation for this reason. They need to feel fame, superiority. To walk down a hall and see heads turn, the hundred pinpricks of eyeballs staring into them. Nothing makes up for low pay like vivisection. As you walk down the hall you have the feeling that they're all pulling one over on you. What it is exactly you don't know. But there lingers always the smoke of guilt in the air.

She passed a five-foot-one Hispanic girl with her dark belly showing and a fine line of hair leading down into the front of her, in Vicki's opinion, obscenely tight jeans, and wearing eyeliner and maroon lipstick caked on and something in her hair that made it look both wet and hard, and Vicki listened as she passed to what the girl was saying to another Hispanic girl who was overweight and papuliferous and thus receiving of much more of Vicki's private goodwill since she looked nothing like one of the . . . *people* John probably had met while traveling overseas and . . . well she's not going to think of this right now, not now, don't know when, but not now, because she doesn't know what to do, the lockbox, oh God, oh Mary Mother of God pray for us sinners now and at the hour of our death amen, she is so hungry, her belly rumbling, blood sugar low, and what the Hispanic girl is saying is, —His dick is like bent.

—Nuh-uh.

—It's bent, it's crooked.

—No it isn't.

—For real, it looks like this.

She held out a finger and they laughed. The other one said, —Oh my God. You know who has like the hugest dick? Andy Stephens.

—Nuh-uh.

—Mm-hmm.

—At Braddock Park?

—Mm-hmm. It's like a broomstick.

—How do you know?

—I heard.

—Yeah right, you gave him a hand job in eighth grade.

—Nuh-uh.

—I heard about it. You did.

—What'd you hear?

—That you gave him a hand job in eighth grade.

Vicki a few years ago had a sophomore girl threaten to beat her up. It was over the girl's talking in class. She was a black girl. The girl was asked to leave the classroom and to report to the assistant principal's office. The girl instead threatened to beat Vicki up. The girl was suspended for seven days. She and her mother and a lawyer appealed before the school board but the decision was upheld. Vicki never got beat up. It was something that Vicki was able to let roll off her back, knowing how black girls can be. Black people in general. Such histories. They really have it rough in our society. Raised poor and angry. You can't blame them. It's a vicious circle. And kids that age in general. Their brains don't belong to them. They are these cancerous growths within their skulls. Separate creatures entirely. Their bodies are miswired, necessary circuits are not completed, they are unfinished and animalistic. She thinks of Greenbriar High School in the midst of its renovation. Life is a TV show to these people, with commercial breaks and mood music. And then when it stops pleasing them they change the channel. Find something that does. This, Vicki believes, is due to their being raised by television. She as a parent is guilty herself of being weak and often just sitting Grayson there in front of the TV while she went about her business. They can't see the boundary. And they are basically all walking genitalia. All of them. These appendages and orifices all of a sudden doing strange and incredible things. Freshly hatched hormonal larvae creeping out of the ground and prowling horny and mindless like they've been bitten by zombies. Walking libidos with Tourette's. They frighten her. Their lack of religion, their mercy to their ids. They are beasts. It's like a building full of bulls. But she can't show them that. She clenched her jaw, made no eye contact. Let them know they are beneath you. They could snap at any time. Nothing is holding them back from rushing the teachers and killing the adults, taking over the school then the town then the state. They'd run through her classroom naked, copulating on her desk, disemboweling the gym teachers in the cafeteria, play basketball with their heads. Eat each other. Tribal warfare, hierarchy of the jungle. The girls would rule the raving and horny boys. Sic them onto each other and fornicate with the survivors until they are drained and opiated and enslave them. What's stopping them really? If it weren't for adults, Vicki thought, and teenagers were allowed to follow their impulses it would be utter and nihilistic pell-mell.

Andy Stephens. Vicki knew that name. Andy Stephens, Andy Stephens.

The Hispanic girls veered into a classroom. A tall boy with a pubic hair mustache and a military haircut in baggy jeans hanging off his butt, with a loop on them for a hammer, and a way oversized vertical-striped Polo shirt that looked like it hadn't been washed in two weeks made a joint-smoking motion with his finger and thumb, over his lips, to a skinny boy with a blond shaved head who looked twelve and stank of cigarettes, pants equally tremendous, half the other one's weight being generous, and half a foot shorter, baby faced, standing against the wall before a window on the other side of which was a guidance counselor's office. The tall one after doing the joint-smoking gesture started laughing, bending a little and pulling at his pants at the thigh and holding the other hand in a fist like when you're coughing, over his mouth, then punched his little angry friend hard in the arm, who opened his mouth and covered the spot and went, —Ow *fuck* man.

A very large girl in an extralarge black T-shirt and oversized black jeans and dyed green hair at the tips and an earring in her eyebrow and a bar in the cartilage of one ear, light acne, safety pins along the seams of her pants, toes of her shoes just poking out from the cuffs, a sexually ambiguous shadow lurching from the abysses of public education, stood flanked by a small frail boy with long brown straight hair to his chin and a crooked tattoo of barbed wire around his wrist and what very well could be corpse makeup on his face, eyebrow also pierced but infected, discharging a white goo. He didn't seem to mind this. A group of five black kids stood in a circle in the middle of the hallway and everyone walked around. The traffic parted and reconverged after the circle of black kids. One of them, a boy with a navy blue T-shirt down to his thighs and elbows, very very skinny, all teeth, his T-shirt said TOMMY HIL-

FIGER, all of a sudden without impetus screeched and sprinted off at full speed down the hall, legs kicking with exaggeration and hairless arms helicoptering, neck veins popping out, teeth, holding on to the back of his pants' waist, almost knocking Vicki over and she spun with him and went, —Hey. *Hey.* But he didn't stop and she knew they were watching her and that she needed to follow through and catch him and yell at him as a matter of principle, and he was now shouting something unintelligible as he ran on to the end of the hall by the stairs. She was conscious of herself trying to appear not to notice that he was a black kid.

The kids look at any weakness in the order as a precedent, they are always looking for the first sign of failure in the discipline, the green light to strike.

She considered going after him. Or yelling at him to slow down, act his age. Being cold and humorless to him. Shame him into behaving himself. And doing it in a way that would not look like she notices that he is black. But she really needed a Diet Coke.

She thought, Bring a cooler full of them. Put it in your classroom. Make leaving the room altogether unnecessary.

An attractive white student named Ryan O'Donnell, a junior with a marine haircut with frosted tips, hemp necklace, baggy cargo pants, Abercrombie & Fitch T-shirt, walked alongside a cute blue-eyed brunette with shiny lips also wearing an Abercrombie & Fitch T-shirt. Vicki has Ryan O'Donnell fifth period in her Calculus BC class and she thinks the girl is in one of her Algebra I classes. She's petite and pouty. He's wide receiver or quarterback or something on the football team that lost at States last year but is undefeated thus far this season. He's a popular, well-liked kid. Vicki likes him too and she is invariably happy whenever he strolls in late to class which is basically every day, he brings a certain light to the room, though she would never admit her liking of him because he's always disrupting her class with his one-liners snapped from the back of the room where he sits with his legs splayed and arms draped over the desk pencil-less and sans books, playing dumb when she calls on him to solve the problem on the board in an attempt to bust him when he's whispering to the girl in front of him or otherwise not paying attention. Being nice to him would only encourage him. Because he makes her crack, he knows how to get through these rock-hard fortresses she has built up around herself brick by brick over the course of her entire life.

He had today in the hall his cocky smile and as usual carried no books or pens or backpack, a hemp bracelet around his wrist and Birkenstocks even though it's November, and he stopped when he saw her coming his

way and pointed his chin up toward the ceiling with his arms straight
down his sides then snapped one hand to his forehead letting it quiver in
salute for a moment, his mouth frowning like a bulldog and eyes big and
scared and the girl he was with laughed at him and Vicki when she realized what he was doing nearly sneered such was her effort not to grin or
laugh. He stayed like that until she passed him and then he snapped his
hand down and kept walking, singing, —*Got it made, got it made, got it
made . . . I'm hot for Ms. Donald!*

Vicki clutched her purse under her arm and couldn't help it as she
briefly imagined what his penis looks like. Fat and dark among the tuft of
black hair like a blind seaborne thing emerging from its cave at the
depths. She imagined him sucking on a breast. Not her breast, just a
breast. Feeding on it with his eyes closed like a puppy at the teat. Insa-
tiable hunger. Swallowing, licking the residual discharge off the nipple
and off his fingers where it dripped. Swallowing and gasping and saying,
—Momma . . . and going for more. Then once full getting bored and losing interest in the breast and wandering off wiping his mouth. She imagined him on top of the girl, pulling down on her bra, the top of his head,
on top of Vicki, between the legs of the girl, Vicki's legs. Watching him
eat dinner off a plate and his white butt up in the air bobbing, his back
hunched and mouth open, the girl's head wrapped up in his arms, her
nose in his armpit, Vicki's nose, the smell of boy. He reminds her of her
husband John when she first met him at West Point at a dance. She and a
group of seniors from her all-girls Catholic high school in New York
were chaperoned up there on a bus. She was seventeen. He was older—
twenty. Distinguished and excellent in his gray cadet uniform. Following
her around all night and asking her inane questions about New York—
the history, the chief export, the property taxes, etc.—and being really
fascinated by everything she said, her one-word answers, as though she
held ancient truths that he had long sallied to find. His silly grin. Taking
her punch from her at one point and looking around over her head then
turning his back and spiking it with something from a flask concealed
within his jacket and giving it back to her, not telling her what it was
even though she begged him and hit him on the arm. Calling her
young'un. He put a finger to her lips and said, —Sssshh. Go on,
young'un, take a snort, it's good. Our secret. This is what we do here. You
don't drink in Westchester do you? Well I'm from Wyoming and in
Wyoming the only reason we go to dances in the first place is to drink
booze. She couldn't imagine Wyoming. She saw the plains, buffalos, cow-
boys. She felt like a lady in a movie. Three years later they were married.

She scowled and ignored Ryan O'Donnell, pretending not to be imagining him sucking on a breast or his penis ejaculating. She felt she had to say something sharp in response to his antics, put him in his place in front of this mass of students. But she couldn't come up with anything. Story of her life. If she could give herself one trait, change one thing about herself, not that she would since that would be an affront to her maker, she would give herself a quicker tongue, a more formidable bridge between the thinking and speaking halves of her brain. More like Ryan O'Donnell. And skinny too like Jane Fonda or Mary Hart. Attractive and blond. Athletic, smiley, charming. Bigger breasts. Flatter tummy. She would eat less. Speaking of food . . . her belly rumbles now again and she feels the sting of self-disgust for it. She's so fat. She's so hideous and old. She's trash. She's scum. A self-absorbed sinning ugly woman who is so dumb, dumb, dumb . . . and lazy . . . No, no, stop it, Vicki, stop it . . . She kept walking. Almost all the way down the hall when Ryan and the girl were already on the other end, hundreds of people between them, Vicki stopped and turned and yelled, —Are you going to be on time today? and sort of laughed but he didn't hear, other kids turned to look at her, and Ryan was walking off into the back stairwell with his hand on the small of the girl's back, and the girl was smiling at something he was saying and he was reaching out to grab another boy's shoulder and hold him still while he said something in his ear then hit him on the back and continued.

An Asian boy with glasses and bowl cut sitting against a set of lockers alone, doing the thing where you pinch your nostrils and inhale hard through your nose and take your hand away and your nostrils remain pinched for a moment. His eyes were crossed trying to look down at his own nose to see if it was working and it was.

And outside shiny jeeps and new SUVs and hand-me-down station wagons three years old and enormous gray grandfather cars occupying the student parking lot in which a spot costs $100 a year. You are allowed to paint your spot however you wish. Just so long as there are no vulgarities or references to gangs or drugs or crime or anything else that can be considered by administration to be questionable.

These kids have my number. They are products of the world. The average and secular. They constitute the masses of a godless crowd, because the world is godless and crowds are nefarious and these kids then are nefarious and will grow into nefarious, untrustworthy adults bearing nefarious, untrustworthy children, and my job, why I am here right now, what I do in order to pay my bills and support myself and my child, what I do to keep myself away from home—because I hate my husband, I hate him with everything I have, all the hate I have refused myself to feel all of my life until this year—because Christ didn't hate but loved—I give to John Donald, my husband of twenty-five years—twenty-five years—the purpose of myself here and now is to give these people the ability to do math.

A white boy with glasses and helmet hair and a J. Crew plaid button-down shirt who for a brief second Vicki thought was Grayson made out pornographically with a hundred-pound girl wearing black stretch pants and bracelets and a push-up bra and a purple Express shirt, dark wavy hair and either Hispanic or Middle Eastern of some sort. Indian or something, Vicki thinks. Any other day, Vicki would have broken them up. Making out in the hallway is not acceptable. Her method of breaking up people who are making out is to say, while walking by without breaking stride, —Excuse me, that is inappropriate. Then looking back to see their red faces as they disengage, the male putting a hand in his pocket and smiling with embarrassment and the girl looking at the boy and touching her hair and looking around. Vicki isn't sure why she gets the immense level of pleasure that she does out of catching kids making out and yelling at them for it. It's something that can really make her day. On certain blah days, she'll forgo the Diet Coke and wander the halls hunting them. She'll poke her head in the theater, behind the bleachers in the gym, check the stairwells.

Today though she just ignored them. They felt her wind on them as she passed and disengaged, the boy running a hand through his hair and putting his hand in his pocket, and the girl wiping her mouth and going, —So, um, yeah, and the boy going, —Yeah . . . and both giggling and watching Vicki until she was out of sight then reengaging as though they had never been interrupted.

At last she made it to the Senior Lounge where the nearest Coke machine was. There were nearly a dozen Coke machines in the school but she still wouldn't have minded if they put another one on this floor somewhere closer to her room. She celebrated to herself when she got her dollar in on the first try. She hit the Diet Coke button and the orange dot beside it lit up and no beverage was dispensed. The machine just hummed. Everywhere students were walking around with Coca-Cola products. Signs advertising Coca-Cola in every hallway and all over the cafeteria. She hit the other Diet Coke button and there was a rumbling from within as the product was deposited and her change was dropped with a tappity-tap into the small cave. She slid the coins out one at a time along the bottom of the cave using her index finger. She bent down without bending her knees and after some readjusting dislodged the can from the open compartment below then straightened and somehow managed to pop the top of the can with her trembling extremities, careful it didn't explode, sighing and grimacing like someone with a bad back as she straightened. *Aaaaaahhh.* . . . She makes this sound also when sitting down, whenever she sits down, like it's been days of feckless wandering in a dire nugatory since she last sat. As she bent for the Diet Coke she was unaware of the tall joint-smoking kid passing by behind her and checking out her large middle-aged fernum with her underwear lines visible in her wool-blend pantsuit pants hiked over her bulging pelvis up to her belly button and smiling sordidly. A good way of telling which teachers are on autopilot and more or less just holding their breath until summer and which teachers have ambitions of administration is seeing who wears the pantsuits and who wears the jeans. She closed her eyes and downed half the Diet Coke standing there at the machine, a light brown dribble going down her chin, the scant lipstick she wore coming off the sippy hole, and she swallowed and licked her lips exhaling, her breath coming out in uneven staccato sighs that went throughout the Senior Lounge, a boy fast asleep on the old sofa there, the fever pitch white noises soothing and softening into the background, a cleansing stream washing through her as she was now redivivus, caffeinated, fortified anew, the fizzies easing her friable gut and her wind filling her again, she was able to face the remainder of this interminably unremarkable day.

WEIGHT-LOSS JOURNAL

Nov. 2, 1998

I need to stop eating. I have been "over eating" again recently. Especially food my body does not need (potato chips, "Honey Buns" from vending machine during the day). It is hard because the vending machine is right there in the teacher's lounge & when in there, my "social anxiety" acts up & my first instinct is to go to the vending machine, for food, to give myself "comfort."

This is a weakness that I recognize & need to work towards overcoming. My "shyness" leads to my "over eating" and has ever since my youth. I <u>definitely</u> do not want to return to "that place" again. I see now that if I could be more comfortable in "social" situations, such as the teacher's lounge during my breaks, I could curtail my problems with food. Why can't I just chat and be normal? It is a sign that I am not meant to be <u>just</u> a teacher perhaps. I should <u>embrace</u> this "sign."

I also need to cut down on Diet Coke. I could substitute Diet Cokes with water a lot of the time. This would help with my problems with "irregularities" as well.

I am trying to show more self-control over my appetites but it's been hard lately. I ask You Lord to give me the strength to show more willpower and more "drive" in terms of exercising more and finding the time to do so.

I ask you for Your help in becoming less "shy" if it is Your Will.

I ask You to remind me when I crave a snack such as a "3 Musketeers" to remember You on The Cross & how You had nothing to eat or drink.

Give me the will to remember how You suffered for me. And to offer up my hunger between meals & craving & "social anxiety" for the sins of the world so that they may be forgiven, in Your Name. I know the body is Your "temple" & I feel disgusting after "pigging out." I don't like it and please know I am trying as hard as I can. The body You have blessed me with deserves to be cared for & respected & kept fit. You have blessed me with good health. Please help me to take care of my body and to only eat what my body needs, if it is Your Will.

All of this I ask in Your Name.

GREENBRIAR HIGH SCHOOL

Safe behind the closed door of the TEACHING STAFF ONLY sign during her lunch period, in the math department teachers' lounge, newspapers covered the two round tables and the coffeemaker was burping, the vending machine was stocked with candy bars and Honey Buns, *People* magazines were here and there, a portable radio turned to Z104 played a commercial for Jenny Craig at a low volume.

Amy Gauthier, the twenty-three-year-old gym teacher, sat at one of the two round folding tables drinking her fourth Mountain Dew of the morning and doing that thing where you pinch your nostrils and inhale and they stay pinched. Nobody had any idea how stoned Amy was. Amy's husband is an ex–private first class, United States Army, who is these days a security guard at a First Virginia Bank branch in Falls Church, off 66 exit 72. They got married when they were both nineteen when she went to visit him at his base in Hawaii during her summer break after her freshman year of college. His army buddies literally kidnapped her when she got there in the middle of the night and carried her bound at the ankles and wrists like a battering ram and tossed her head-first into the back of a Humvee where they slid a veil on her head and sped to the beach where Bryce, former Greenbriar Charger tight end, was waiting hands-over-crotch in his formal army wear, beside the chaplain, with his new mustache. What Amy was thinking about as she wed Bryce was how much she hated the mustache. Soldiers get a big salary boost if they are married. The only pressure more intense among young soldiers than the one to get married ASAP to someone is the one to hook up, as they call it, with townie girls. Amy smoked an average of one-eighth of an ounce of weed every day since her first day of college when her parents closed the door of her Virginia Tech dorm room and her roommate unpacked her four-foot-high much-residued glass bong. Amy attended Greenbriar High School '89–'93. This is her second year as a teacher. Once a semester she has to teach a week-long Drug Awareness class to her freshman gym students. She has stood higher than all hell, eyes red as roses and mouth audibly sticky with thick white stuff in the corners of her lips, in front of her Drug Awareness class as a stern-looking freshman boy with a big black hoodie asked in his reedy midpubescent voice, — What does it feel like to be high?

She has responded, her own voice echoing in her head, —I . . . I don't know.

They've also asked her, —Have you ever done speed?

—No.

—Have you ever wanted to?

—No.

—What's it like to be on speed?

Around 87 percent of her male students have self-abused to thoughts of their young gym teacher. Three percent of her female students have.

Amy and her husband live in a town house in Little Rocky Run. The forgotten town houses before the First Entrance. Amy and Bryce have surround sound and a fifty-two-inch TV and an extensive VHS collection of nearly every major studio release of the last four years plus the big indies like *Pulp Fiction*. Bryce's favorites are the buddy comedies where a black guy and a white guy are cops and have to put up with their racial and cultural differences to capture the bad guy. For example, the *Lethal Weapon* series, his favorite. And also pretty much anything starring Martin Lawrence. And they have a couple DVDs as well.

Vicki regarded Amy with wariness as she entered the lounge and not only because Amy happens to be attractive in the sun-kissed and athletic early-twenties way that only girls named Amy can be and how Vicki has secretly always wanted to be, but because Vicki has a strong suspicion about her. It has to do with Amy's lack of experience, being so close to being a teenager herself, and how Amy by temperament comes off a bit flaky and out of it. Plus if there were superlatives among teachers at Greenbriar High School, Vicki believes Amy would be voted Most Likely to Have Her Mug Shot on Local News in Regard to a Student-Teacher Sex Scandal. Hands down. Just look at her. She's practically the same age as they are. You hear things being a teacher. Whispers floating around the ceiling. The essence of conversations makes its way into your percipience. Things you know without knowing you know. Vicki, being Catholic, believes where there's smoke there's fire. She was also suspicious of Amy because Amy's a gym teacher and this was the math department teacher lounge. Amy should have been in the gym department lounge. As department head, she thought of saying something. Vicki was not sure what auburn-haired and freckled smiley Ms. Gauthier was up to, but she didn't like it. Not one bit. She'd keep an eye on her.

Amy still has periods of starvation. They are not linked to stress or powerful emotional episodes. She just stops wanting to eat. She's not hungry. Food repulses her as much as it does after you gorge at Thanksgiving. She goes for days on soda and candy alone. When she's on one of her starvation cycles Bryce doesn't notice her not eating though he compliments her from the couch as she comes downstairs and steps across between him and the supereminent television hooked up to satellite and surround sound how good she looks. She sits there next to him faint and with white spots in her vision watching what he's watching and doesn't know why she let herself get married, it was something she couldn't control, she can't explain it, it happened. In life things happen. She can't explain why, nor can she understand. It's futile to analyze them. Thinking about herself makes her feel stupid. Not in reflecting upon her past mistakes but because the enormity of herself is far too complicated. It's akin to studying economics to most people. It's abstract, tangled, almost meaningless. She never made any of her choices. They are just what happened. If she had to guess, it's her lack of backbone perhaps? The same thing that probably causes her anorexia. Low self-esteem, as they call it. Does she believe in that term? It's hokey. She's tougher than *low self-esteem*. She has self-esteem. She feels fine about herself. She's pretty, she knows it. Funny. Cracks herself up sometimes. She never made a conscious choice to cheat on her husband, it was just what happened. She doesn't consider it cheating. She doesn't consider it anything. Because she simply doesn't consider it. She was, what, nineteen? Twenty? Bryce was doing the same thing. Their marriage wasn't . . . There's a lot of gray. Whatever. She doesn't want to think about it, it's over. She doesn't want to be a gym teacher. She doesn't know what she wants to do and doesn't think she is particularly blessed at any one thing in particular at the level at which she might make a living at it, doesn't know where she wants to be. She's just here. Just Amy. Twenty-three years old. Getting through her days. Going to work, going to the grocery store, going home. After college was over and she and her roommates had to pack up their shoddy Blacksburg apartment, mephitic with stale cigarette smoke and spilled bong water, beer sputum, and overflowing ashtrays (the one they unscrewed from the wall of the stall in the ladies' room at Arnold's Taverna and stole in her purse and brought back home and screwed in to the side of the wood dorm room–furniture couch), Beast keg shells in the bathtub, never functional oven, unidentifiable growth of an earthy hue on the carpet, brown and yellow stains on the walls, broken red cups in the dead bushes out front, shoes hanging from the power lines, after subsisting on nothing but Marlboro Menthol Ultra Lights, vodka crans, Food Lion brand soda, and the occasional DQ Blizzard, she had to go somewhere, so she joined the endless stream of vehicles each packed with possessions like a gypsy caravan that paints the way each May up 81 and down 66 from the green college mountains of Virginia feeding back into NoVA, and she moved into Bryce's parents' house in Greenbriar where she lived alone with them for nearly a month feeling like a young small-town wife in ages past, until Bryce's discharge, and he moved back home with his mustache which she made him shave. He tried selling cars, applied to the Fairfax County Fire Department, was rejected, got a security job at a bank. In his off time he set forth working on a memoir—working title *The Soldier*—based on his four-year enlistment in which the most exotic locale he was stationed to was a six-month-long administrative mission in Hamburg, Germany. Amy has snuck peeks at the Word file on their Dell in a folder on the desktop called "New Folder." The manuscript includes such passages as: "This dark solitude of the soul is no place for the weak. But I will survive because I am a soldier. I crave blood on my fists and the feeling of bones shattering against my knuckles. I want to kill, kill, kill. It feels good to kill. It is a release. Soldiers are warriors. That is why I like to kill." That's taken from the chapter about his mission as an orderly in the base hospital in Jacksonville, North Carolina. Amy copy-and-pasted that passage to an e-mail to her old roommates from Virginia Tech, which they enjoyed with great immensity. For Amy, with her new kinesiology degree, it was either wait tables at an Olive Garden or become a gym teacher. Gym teachers got summers off and were done at 2:30 each day, so there was really no choice at all. Maybe she will wait tables one day yet. Who knows what she'll do. She's been thinking of waiting tables over the summer. Keep herself away. Each year that passes she feels herself changing more and more. Becoming an adult. A teacher. Getting rooted, decided. Does that scare her? Does that give her bolts of panic up and down her arms? Yes. Though today Amy still generally thinks of her job, her marriage, and overall existence as a purgatorial waiting room—the layover to somewhere amazing—which works for her because she is the type who has enough trouble paying her cell phone bill on time each month let alone getting around to a divorce, but she believes it will happen that through choices of her own or the crumbling of the cookie she will wake up one day having become what she really is supposed and wants to be, whatever that is, and her life will not feel like purgatory anymore but *life*, like she was told over and over and from seemingly all directions and sources growing up in NoVA that a special snowflake such as she would one day live, but until then she smokes Marlboro Menthol Ultra Lights in the car on her way out of the faculty parking lot and has been subsisting on nothing but Blizzards, Sour Patch Kids, and generic lemon-lime soda from Giant for the last five weeks.

Vicki sat down across the table from Amy. As Vicki sat at the table, chosen over the other table because it by a narrow margin was covered by the lesser volume of *Peoples*, *Cosmos*, checkout aisle gossip rags, and newspapers, she went, —*Aaaaahh* . . . Other than the radio turned to Z104, the lounge was quiet. Outside the door the cruentous din of thousands of lunatics in riot. At the other table were two women. They were math teachers Juliette Emerson and Heidi Goldfarb. Both prefer Ms.

over Mrs. Ms. Emerson looks and talks like Newman from *Seinfeld* in drag. She struggles with her weight to the extent that—well, she doesn't struggle with her weight exactly since she doesn't really mind her weight, nor does she make any effort to lose any of it—but she is big enough that her arms when in repose never go totally all the way down. She is penguinal, known for inadvertently knocking her students' books and personal effects off their desks when she wanders the aisles of her room in one of the T-shirts she wears every day and turns too quickly. The degree to which she shrinks hallways is significant. She teaches pre-algebra and general math and in the teachers' lounge today was sipping coffee from her mug which says, I'VE GOT EVERYTHING UNDER CONTROL! with the words upside down. One dumplin hand gripping the finger loop of the mug, the other up at her temple, pushed under her straight brown hair which she cuts herself and washes with $1.19 Prell and rubbing in a circular motion. —What period is it? she was asking no one. —What day is it?

Heidi Goldfarb was sitting beside her and also rubbing a temple, pausing long enough now to down a hissing mug of Alka-Seltzer followed by a handful of Advil then a strong pull from a bottle of Pepto-Bismol to wash them down, sighing once she swallowed, —Oy. . . . She is shorter than Juliette Emerson but just as squab, roughly the same age, poofy Jewish mother-in-law hair, teaches general math and pre-algebra and is known for her seemingly bottomless supply of ugly, homemade-looking sweaters with glittery stuff woven into them in the shapes of stars or big suns with faces sewn onto the front, snowmen and reindeer and snowflakes in the wintertime. A Christmas sweater for all seasons. Or several dozen . . . Her mug says I'M DOWN TO MY LAST NERVE AND YOU'RE STANDING ON IT! in upside-down words. A mass-market paperback of *The Perfect Storm* open on the table facedown. All her medicines arranged before her. Both women had their eyes closed, a hand on their mug, and a hand rubbing a temple. They looked like they were working to conjure the dead. They groaned like Gregorians. Heidi Goldfarb whispered, —Hear that? Can you hear them? Oh God listen to them. Do you hear? Of course you do. You do because you always hear them. They never sleep, they never rest. They're out there always. And the thing is they are always out there and always will be out there. You know they will be. You can count on it. Nothing you do matters. You can stay in here for a week. They won't go away. They *never go away.*

She poured a bunch of Advil into her palm and deposited them into her mouth, chewing them like Skittles, washing them down with a hard snort of the pink stuff, never opening her eyes or pausing in the rubbing of her temple. —They're like vampires. How do you kill them?

—You can't, Ms. Emerson muttered. —It's illegal to.

Ms. Emerson's skin, especially her nose, is always oily. Her nose is always red. Hers is the parous complexion of a cold, or childbirth.

—Tuesday? she said. —Is it Tuesday?

—I have like a great big utility-sized industrial nail, it feels like, that has been physically like driven by sheer force of hand, without a hammer I mean, into the base of my skull at you know the soft part right at the top of your neck?

—Mm, Ms. Emerson said.

—I got called a quote unquote fucking bitch today which was a dream come true, let me tell you, by a very enormous black man which is what he is because he's eighteen years old and still in general math. Unbelievable. He'll be released as a certified member of our society soon enough, just so you'll be warned.

Amy Gauthier was eating from a family-sized bag of Sour Patch Kids by the handful, now peering down at a four-month-old *People*. Outside it sounded like someone who was possessed by the devil barreled into the door in the midst of his ghastly and slobbering fit and they all jumped and the creature wailed and seethed at the door then ran off.

—I mean it goes and it goes and it goes, Ms. Goldfarb said. —These Advils are helping but I mean we'll barely make it to Christmas Break er excuse me *Winter* Break because I don't happen to be Christian thank you very much. And then we'll show up in June in casts and crutches and hooked up to kidney dialysis machines but grateful to still have our lives only to have to start all over again in September as soon as we're back to good health and emotional, I don't know, optimism I guess, and so on and so forth. You know what it's like, I've noticed? I like associate them with like they have the ability to regenerate and multiply like little evil I don't know what. They can do this. We'll never win. We are simply in over our heads here. I think it's time we realize and maybe accept or do something about it. I don't know.

—Yesterday was Monday though wasn't it? So today's Tuesday right? But then again I remember having this exact same conversation with you yesterday. Right? Didn't we?

Ms. Emerson looked at Ms. Goldfarb with pleading desperate eyes.

—I don't know, Ms. Goldfarb said hopelessly. —So God help me I don't know I don't know I don't know.

—So then if we did then that makes today Wednesday. Because. Right? Today's Wednesday? Is that right?

Ms. Goldfarb sighed and didn't answer, carried her mug to the water cooler, filled it up, eased back down into the chair which creaked sadly, reaching for another Alka-Seltzer packet from the box in the middle of the table.

—Wednesday's good, Ms. Emerson said. —Two and a half days down, two and a half to go. Wednesday's good. Wednesday I can handle. Wait. What's on tonight?

—I don't know. *Friends*.

—*Friends*?! So it's *Thursday* now? *Friends* is on *Thursday*. Today's *Thursday*? It's *Thursday*?

—I saw the commercials last night for tomorrow an all-new *Friends*, tune in tomorrow because *Friends* is all new on Thursday on NBC, Must-See TV.

—Huh. Thursday . . .

—And which is good though because then that means tomorrow is Friday then so and when today's over which I am not sure it ever will be, I just refuse to believe it at this here and now but hopefully it will, after I've finally gone home and gotten into my sweats and sat through rush hour in the Taurus which makes this noise like I don't know what it is but it comes and goes and I should get it looked at and then when I've made chicken for dinner for Greg it will only be as I think about the next day only one more day to survive before the weekend. I love Thursday night, Juliette, I really do. I'm really starting to appreciate going to bed on Thursday nights and thinking about how there's only one tiny insignificant day to get through before the weekend. Speaking of by the way we should go shopping on Saturday or Sunday because Penney's is having a sale at Fair Oaks.

Ms. Emerson said, —That or I might just curl up into the fetal position from Friday evening until early Monday morning. With the covers over my head and my cat on top of me. Think about how I should have majored in business. My hand hurts.

—I didn't think hands could hurt.

—Well they can because mine does. Hand me the Advil.

—The fingers you mean. Your fingers hurt. You hurt your finger slamming it in a door.

—No. The hand. The actual hand itself.

—Want an Alka-Seltzer too? Or a Diet Coke?

—No just the Advil there please.

The cap on the bottle was already off, which was a small joy for Juliette Emerson, divorced, mother of one seventeen-year-old son the same age of the kids she teaches but he goes to Braddock Park High School. Ms. Donald and Ms. Emerson have chatted enough to make this connection, though her son says he doesn't know any Grayson Donald. It's a big school, Braddock Park is, double its capacity right now, thirty-one hundred students, six hundred alone in her son's class. Ms. Emerson gloated to herself that she was able to bypass lining up the little arrow with the little nub then pry, the cap releasing it a pleasant *pop*, shook four Advils into her hand and tilted her palm mouthward—impossibly thin, hardly colored lips—downing the pills with a swig from her coffee. "Truly Madly Deeply" by Savage Garden was on Z104. Ms. Goldfarb got up again to switch it to the oldies station where something by the Beatles or the Rolling Stones or one of those was ending. Vicki was filling out preliminary paperwork for the vacant assistant administrator position at Woodson in Springfield. The radio sang, *Jer-ry's Ford makes it clear, let the competition be-ware!* Then something happened with the radio and it went to dead air. And outside in the hall as the roar of interemption became louder than ever, someone or thing was picked up and tossed a far distance against the door where it hit, cackled, and scurried off. At the impact all the teachers jumped. The radio came back to a commercial for Blue Cross Blue Shield and Amy Gauthier turned the page of *People* and said just loud enough for the others to hear, a couple Sour Patch Kids stuck to her molars, —Today's Monday.

GREENBRIAR HIGH SCHOOL

We always know room 211 is Ms. Donald's because it says so in the small rectangular window on the side of the door. The small rectangular window has two layers of glass between which is wire mesh. Looking closely around Greenbriar High School, we can see all kinds of similar preventative measures in the design of the school taken more to protect property and avoid expensive and time-consuming lawsuits than to safeguard our health. The cages over the wall clocks in the gymnasium, for example. The rubber strip on every stair in every stairwell. In the cafeteria our spaghetti being served to us cold and precut into inch-long bits. The purple-pink rounded letters in the window that spell out MS. DONALD (period included) were bought by Ms. Donald at the Teachers' Store in Centreville in the Centreville Crossing strip mall at the intersection of 28 and 29, next door to Lone Star Steakhouse, Ruby Tuesday, and across the street from the airportlike Life Time Fitness. The classroom at that moment was empty, the door closed. Ms. Donald was in the teachers' lounge. We were in other classrooms. But they were similar. The desks arranged in six rows of five. No windows facing outside. The desks in which we spend our days are constituted of an orange plastic chair attached to a curved half desk almost always on the right-hand side through there are one or two here and there—normally found in the back row somewhere, in the corner—with it on the left. Below the orange plastic chair, whose butt is curved rather than angular, there is a metal basket designed for the storage of books and notebooks. It is rare that we use the basket. We instead hang our backpack over the back of our chair. The way the desk is designed is to give even the most obese of us enough room to fit and learn. We are often obese. We are tall. We who are tall have found that slouching is difficult in the chairs because the height of the half desk assures that unless we sit uncomfortably and formally straight up then our knees will push against the cork-colored underside of the half desk. As females with the rare exception are too short for this to be a problem, we suspect this was done on purpose to keep the males awake. Sometimes the chairs are blue but mostly they are orange. The half desk is a synthetic woodlike substance painted to look like real wood. We have vandalized them. Drilled away over the course of the year bit by bit like *Shawshank Redemption* with the tips of our pens into the edge facing our bellies until there is a cone-shaped canyon. Etched LIMP BIZKIT, FUCK YOU, DON'T CRITICIZE WHAT YOU CAN'T UNDERSTAND, SEX, FAG, TIT, HI, HELLO, JB, EKL, WHO FARTED, etc. On the wall is a whiteboard ten feet long and four feet high with red, green, blue, and black markers on the silver rutted edge along with the frayed old eraser, all of which were purchased by Ms. Donald at the Teachers' Store with her own money after submitting request after ignored request to administration, for three months, to please supply her with whiteboard markers so she could teach her students. An overhead projector is on a black metal wheeled cart off to the side, its power cord wrapped around it. On the cart are yellow caution stickers with shadow men being crushed by the cart, run over by the cart, chased by the cart, the cart stealing a shadow man's identity and draining a shadow man's savings. A wall clock is also on the wall, with no steel cage over it. We can tell you that the clock is seventeen seconds slow. We know this clock like we know ourselves. It is the clock of our lives. Black and white with a red second hand. Somewhere someone has a stat that every two seconds in the world another dozen clocks like this are produced. In a nuclear attack, the only earthly survivors will be cockroaches, Keith Richards, and these clocks. There are posters. One features a sailboat floating on a serene ocean at dusk and the word FORTITUDE beneath it, all on a black background. We believe it would make more sense if the word beneath it were SAILBOAT. Another one has a close-up of a runner crouched down at a starting line, face down but with sweat dripping off his nose, and it says SACRIFICE. We think it should say TOWEL. These posters were also bought at the Teachers' Store with Ms. Donald's money, along with another poster of a cartoon frog being swallowed by a cartoon stork, with no text or explanation whatsoever. And the alphabet running along the top of the wall all the way around the room, the kind with the uppercase letter and then the lowercase letter, like something in a kindergarten classroom to teach the children how to read. We don't know what the alphabet has to do with math. Another says MATH! and has four children, representing both genders and the major races of the world, their eyes wide and mouths in joyous rapture, peering into a big red book held up before them by the four-eyed Asian boy in the middle. A Greenbriar High School football pennant upside down by the door from the divisional playoff runner-up year of 1991. A bulletin board with pictures of students now long graduated working on homecoming floats in a driveway of a home in Greenbriar in clothes that only we notice are outdated and goofy—turtlenecks under sweatshirts, for example. These were taken by Ms. Donald in 1992 when she volunteered to be in charge of the senior class homecoming committee, something she never did again. In these pictures the girls with crimped hair and ski caps smile with all their hearts clutching crepe paper and showing their glue guns to the camera. Young men with mustaches in stonewashed jeans and unbuttoned denim shirts hold hammers. The unplaceable discoloration and tonal difference of a six-year-old photograph. On Ms. Donald's desk, on the side of the room opposite the doorway, is a white jar of which the top screws off revealing a sponge Ms. Donald touches to wet her fingers in order to help her turn the page of a textbook or the next student's homework off a stack to grade. This Ms. Donald bought at the Teachers' Store with her own money and on the corner is a couple packs of blank computer paper that she bought as well. Also on the desk is a photo of her son Grayson, his ninth-grade yearbook photo in which his smile and his eyes reveal the deep-seated insecurity of that age. We can see how macilent he was then just by his face and neck, his braces, lips self-consciously crowding his teeth. His smile looks fought against and fought for. His hair looks wet. He looks naked to us. We are curious to look at it but we also get the feeling of invasion when we look at it, of cheating. There are Post-its everywhere all over the desk. They have spread to the wall to the side of the desk. Some are blank. The ones on the wall are taped there for reinforcement. Also on Ms. Donald's desk today was a neat stack of completed tests covered by means of the Teacher's Edition of the geometry book we use, a seven-pound tome that is two inches thick and has on the cover a Spanish boy of about fourteen years old wearing bell-bottoms and a tight yellow T-shirt chatting with a black girl in overalls and glasses who is supposed to be fourteen too we suppose but looks to us more like twenty-three. They are on a street corner in East L.A. it looks like. It looks like the fourteen-year-old boy is picking up a whore. There was a framed photo on the desk of a young Ms. Donald, forty pounds lighter wearing tinted tremendous glasses and a beige turtleneck, holding a pudgy drugged-looking baby wearing a beige collared shirt with a single brick red vertical stripe and white collar. Standing behind them with hair covering one eye and eyeglasses also big and dark is a thin man. They all look off over the viewer's right shoulder, smiling awkwardly. We don't feel the light in the room. It is the mere suggestion of light. A misunderstanding of the concept. It comes from flickering, humming tubes in the ceiling that make our skin look greenish and veiny. The ceiling is made up of panels of a Styrofoamish material and have gray pokes in them, brown water stains. The whiteboard cannot be totally erased clean. The indelible traces of lessons of yore remain forever no matter how much she scrubs. Three fluorescent tubes were out. One flickered in its final hours. The floor a cold tile, five-inch squares, beige with brown specks. In Ms. Donald's classroom as in all our classrooms sounds don't travel and organic materials do not decay. There is no temperature or lint. The air tastes of nothing. Odors are neutralized. It is air that has been breathed a thousand times before. A wooden apple on the desk says WORLD'S BEST TEACHER. A poster on the wall has a puppy and the words "DO" IS THE FIRST PART OF "DONE." The door opened, a couple of inches, then closed again. With a rustling, leaving a stink in its wake, something rasorial and shadowy pulled itself along the floor toward the stack of the tests on Ms. Donald's desk.

7145 Springstone Drive—
First Entrance

I wake up naked on top of my sheets with a fucking boner so big it hurts and the shades drawn making my room still dark at three in the afternoon. My forty-seven-inch TV is on HBO, an episode of *Oz* that I have already seen about three times already. My mouth is dry as fuck but I dont feel like getting up to get water and I have to piss too but I dont feel like getting up to piss. I just lie there with my boner trying to decide what to do. Since my dick is already hard I think, Might as well fucking jerk off. So I jerk off, imagining fucking Brooke Burke from *Wild On!* on E!. Just as Im about to come I catch a glimpse of a fucking naked guy on *Oz*. You can see his fucking balls. This really fucks me up but I am able to still come within thirty seconds into my come sock I keep somewhere on the floor. Its Brooke Burkes face I come on, her mouth, not the dudes balls, and Brooke smiles up at me with my fucking spooge all over her face and then she vanishes and Im happy for a second. Im hungover as shit. My brain feels like a hard little knot, dry as a rock. Its pretty amazing I had a fucking boner at all considering how fucking yacked I got last night. Its a motherfucking miracle. I can still feel the bitter drip in the back of my throat and the pasty spit in my mouth tastes like beer and, I guess, fucking tequila, though I dont remember drinking tequila, but who the hell knows. Last night was fucked up. I got shitfaced with my boy Brian and some other peeps in Brians moms basement but didnt get any pussy. Though this one slut Carrie I used to hook up with played with my dick a little after everybody else passed out. I have to shit. But Im also starving so I have a choice to make this morning and I choose SHIT. Then SHIT I do! Loud and stinky like pissing out of my ass. It stings my asshole its so hot. I feel like Im losing half my body weight (185 pounds). Before I flush I take a look just to make sure no organs or some shit is there, and when I see the yellowish brown the water has turned into with a layer of crust around the edges, and peering closer I can see hints of solid shit down at the bottom, I feel happy. I like looking at my own shit. I need a cigarette. I have to wipe my ass like eight fucking times before I get all the fucking shit off my ass. Not to mention I have to flush three times and then theres still skidmarks all over the fucking bottom of the toilet. I look at myself in the mirror and check out my pecs and am pleased with the latest results. Ive been lifting again recently. Im so fucking out of shape. I havent lifted since high school when I wrestled and just joined Life Time last week. I used to be fucking obsessed with that shit but now I just do it to stay in shape. I look good though I have to admit. I pull out my dick and give it a bit of a rub to make it bigger though not entirely hard just so it just looks like I have a bigger dick. I stare at myself like that in the mirror and imagine all the pussies my fucking dick has been in and has nutted in (thirty-seven and counting) and I feel happy.

I leave the shitter which needs to be cleaned but I dont know when the cleaning ladies are coming. I catch a glimpse of my little brother Dwight in his room on his bed in only his boxers like me and hes cleaning a rifle with a dish towel.

I say to him What da blood clot ya faggot. The History Channel is on his TV and he is eating pizza. I say that better not be the fucking last of the pizza you bitch.

And he looks up at me and says whatever.

And I say you fucking fag it is isnt it.

And he goes fuck you.

And I say come over here and say that bitch and of course he doesnt say shit because hes a fag. I pull out my dick and wave it around but he doesnt look so I put it back and go why arent you at school and he says fuck off and I say fuck you you fucking faggot give me a cigarette you fucking nigger and he tosses one at me. Its a fucking menthol. I say what the fuck is this a fucking niggerette? And he just fucking shrugs and mumbles something.

Then I go downstairs and sure enough there is an empty Papa Johns box on the kitchen table, that fucking bitch, so I make a burger on the Foreman grill. Three of them actually. While its cooking I check what else Mom has in the pantry but the fucking bitch has not bought shit. There is NOTHING to fucking eat. What the fuck! Im starved as shit and three goddamn hamburgers arent going to do shit. I go out on the deck while its cooking and smoke that cigarette which is fucking gross and sit on the hot tub and spit on the deck a couple times and scratch my asshole a little because I think I missed some shit and its hardening now and then I smell my fingers and sort of like it and the old bitch next door is out in her yard fucking around and she waves and I wave, smiling, saying under

my breath Hi you stupid fucking bitch. She calls the cops whenever my
parents go away and I have a party, I know its fucking her. I dont know
where Dwight got that rifle because its not one I recognize but I flick my
butt out into the yard but the wind catches it and it lands in my moms
fucking flowers. Fuck it. The suns hurting my eyes so I go in and watch
Maury Povich in my dads La-Z-Boy with it reclined and the footrest up,
fondling my balls, drinking a Coke.

I eat two of the burgers but get sick of hamburgers before the third
one so I throw it away and leave the Foreman covered in fucking fat and
grease because I DONT FEEL LIKE CLEANING IT and the rest of the
patties out on the counter because I DONT FUCKING FEEL LIKE
PUTTING THEM AWAY and my plate on the end table while I watch TV.

I start thinking about how theres no fucking food in our house and
how Dwights a lazy dumb piece of shit. Im still so hungry I cant think
straight. Im fucking sweating. So during a commercial I reach over and
get the phone thats there beside the La-Z-Boy and I call my mom at
work and say what the fuck is wrong with you Im starving to death and
all there is is fucking chicken and soup and Chips Ahoy! which I hate and
you know that. Am I supposed to eat soup? I say, how is soup gonna fill
me up? Why cant you fucking go to Giant every once in a while and get
Fritos and Pringles and GOOD food that I fucking ACTUALLY LIKE?

And my mom says Sorry Ill stop on the way home.

But I dont want to hear it Im in too bad a mood to even want to fucking hear it so I hang up on her in midsentence and go back to my room
and play my new Nintendo 64 for three hours then lie on the couch in
my room and watch MTV on my big screen and take a nap then watch
Donnie Brasco on my DVD PLAYER with SURROUND SOUND until I
hear my dad come home from work. He comes upstairs and opens my
door without fucking knocking and hes carrying his briefcase looking like
a piece of shit but I admire him I guess.

He sighs and goes Hey Trent how was your day?

I say Great! I went to the admissions office at Mason and picked up
some information about registering for classes next semester.

And he says Great. Thats great.

And I say Can you help me with the applications?

And he says Sure Id love to, good for you.

Then he goes to his room and I call my boy Brian on my cell and say
What the blood clot, faggot and he says What the blood.

And I say What the fuck is going on tonight, fuck face? Lets go to
Red Rocks or Shark Club or OTooles or Blue Iguana or lets go to Adams

Morgan or some shit or have a fucking party at your house again tonight.

And he says I cant have a party again here dude because the pantry door got fucked up and my moms mad about it.

And I say Fuck your mom you fucking nigger (I was the one who broke the pantry door). Lets get fucked up Im fucking bored as shit dude lets get some fucking yay from your boy and some E and go fucking clubbing downtown at the Spot.

And Brian goes Fuck the Spot.

And I say The bitches there are fucking hot though and Im trying to get my fucking dick sucked.

And he goes Whatever.

And I go Call that bitch Jen and see what shes doing because Im try-ing to fuck that bitch in the fucking butt (even though she has like no fucking titties) and get fucking hammered dude lets DO something for fucks sake, this towns so fucking boring, Northern Virginia fucking sucks dick.

He says Let me call you back. I was taking a nap but Brians a bitch who has only fucked maybe ten fucking chicks in his life and he fucking falls in love with every one and thinks they love him, two of which were when we double-teamed some sluts in Ocean City.

I tell my boy Brian hes a fag and hang up my cell and am excited about the prospect of getting fucked up tonight and maybe sucking on some titties. Im in a much better mood now. There is nothing I like better than having some plans for the night and the prospect of pussy. Im very outgoing and just like to party and hang out and have a good time and hook up with girls.

I watch *The Simpsons* and pass out for like an hour and Brian still hasnt called when I wake up so I call him again and again and again and leave a voice mail that goes YO WHAT DA BLOOD CLOT? PICK UP THE PHONE YOU SHITFUCK then another one that goes YO MOTH-ERFUCKER YOU SUCK COCK, YOU FUCKING NIGGER!

Then I say fuck it and take a shower and jerk off in the shower so if I do pull some buns tonight I wont shoot my load too quick, having for-gotten I already jerked off this morning until its too late.

I lay out some clothes and finally settle on my new Abercrombie shirt and cargoes. I smoke a couple bowls in my room listening to Wu-Tang and spray some Woods on my balls and put some of my Bath & Body Works gel in my hair which takes about twenty minutes to get right. Then I go downstairs really pumped about tonight and imagining myself pounding shots and pounding pussy too, ha-ha, and making everyone laugh at my jokes and dancing with some fucking big-tittied sluts with a bottle of Dom P in the club and looking good and shit.

My mom is home making dinner and the Foreman is cleaned and the patties are put away, my dish on the end table is gone and so is my Coke can and napkin.

I ask my mom what shes making but its fucking chicken again (the lazy bitch!) and I ask her why she cant cook something fucking GOOD for once Im STARVING I havent eaten in like SIX hours.

She says why dont you get a job? And she says Why dont you get your own place and buy your own groceries and clothes and pay your own cellular phone bill (she really calls it cellular phone)? That way you can eat what you want when you want, youre twenty-two years old for goodness gracious (or something like that she says).

And I say Mom what da blood and shes smiling and I reach around her and give her a kiss, knowing how great I look in my new Abercrombie shirt. I got it at Fair Oaks yesterday when I was fucking bored as shit during the day and wanted to drive my Honda around anyway and check out the new fucking badass subwoofer I got and new rims and shit. Next thing Im going to do is tint the windows and put some fucking fog lights on it or some shit and lower it. Im thinking of having my name painted in tag on the side of it or some shit: TRENT BATCHELOR. Im well known for my car.

So anyway I kiss my mom aware of how athletically I am built and how masculine my voice is and how overall handsome I am. She says where are you going and I say Im fucking going out. She says Dont drive drunk please and I go I never would do that Mom you know me. She gives me $50 out of her purse even though I have her credit card already which is what I used to buy my shirt and cargoes and also a pair of Kenneth Coles that were $300 yesterday because I WANTED THEM.

She says I love you and I say Love you too.

On the way to the driveway at almost 9:30 I am calling my boy Brian on my cell telling him Im coming over but then I see my Honda parked there on the curb under the moonlight and its so stunning and beautiful I dont answer right away when Brian says Yo what da blood clot?

Fairfax County Parkway— Falls Church to Centreville

Today I am on the schedule at First Virginia Bank's Falls Church branch until 1700 hours. In my mind I am prepared to remain on detail until then. Mental preparation is very important. When I say that I mean it. It is important in many things and can be applied to your profession. This knowledge is one advantage I have from my experience in the Army over those who did not go into the Army.

The mind is a very powerful thing. They teach you this in the Army. You develop mental confidence and preparation by running seven miles through mud or withstanding tear gas in Basic.

My time in the Army has sculpted me into a man with many tools for preparation to be utilized in daily life. I think of going into the abandoned house with my company and being told to remove our gas masks and having to obey this order. Then they throw in the tear gas. You cannot leave until they say so. Tear gas burns your eyes and trachea and inner ears like you have swallowed fire. Your saliva turns thick and you cannot swallow. It is the worst pain in the world. But you cannot give up. You must persevere. You and your fellow men must endure. When they finally let us leave we crawled out. We were spitting. Some guys are vomiting. Do <u>not</u> rub your eyes even though you will want to. That will only make it worse.

That was the last time I felt pain.

Today Lindsay, one of the tellers at the branch of First Virginia Bank at which I work security detail, says to me around noon that I can leave if I want. This is quite the surprise. I look at her and say, "But my job is to keep this bank secure."

Lindsay replies sarcastically, "What's going to happen? Someone going to rob us?" She giggled.

"Maybe," I say sternly. "And if they do, my job is to be ready."

Lindsay rolls her eyes tauntingly and says condescendingly, "No one's going to rob us. I'll tell Ethan you are here if he calls. I will tell him you went to lunch."

I am uncertain about giving up my post, but I thank Lindsay gratefully and leave. Lindsay is very cute. I burn for her. She goes to the gym every day. And it shows: Her buttocks are firm. She does not have fat on her waist. I believe she is interested in me as well, despite my silence and solitude. She enjoys my sense of humor and likes my physique. I am very well built and can bench four hundred pounds. I can squat substantially more. Plus, since I was in the Army, it shows how hardworking and responsible I am. I am fearless. I am the warrior.

I would not be against the idea of engaging in three-way sex with Lindsay and my wife Amy. If Amy is accepting of the idea. I believe all women are sexually attracted to other women but do not admit it. All women are 10 percent lesbian. The reason this is more acceptable than men being attracted to each other is that men lose their masculinity by engaging in homosexuality. Women lose nothing. I would like to have a threesome. It is my fantasy. It is what turns me on sexually. I believe Amy as my wife owes me happiness and acting out my fantasy would make me happy. It would be best to have a threesome soon. When Amy and I have a baby and begin our family, I would not be as interested in engaging in a threesome. I do not believe in engaging in threesomes when you have a family. I would be very dedicated to the commitment of family. I take family very seriously and look forward to being a father. I would not jeopardize my family's well being by having three-way sex. Others may have different opinions on the matter. That is just the way I see things. That is just me. I have a unique viewpoint on things.

On the Fairfax County Parkway I begin to feel solitude again. Creed "My Own Prison" is on DC101, my favorite radio station. I realize listening to "My Own Prison" that I have no pain in my life. I need pain. Pain feels good. I cry out for pain. I want to burst and burn. The lack of pain in my life is a source of pain. No pain causes pain. Pain is the only thing that is real. Lately I have had the urge to go on a rampage of total destruction. I wouldn't hurt anybody of course. No one innocent at least. No women or children. I believe anyone who harms women and children is a coward. That is my personal belief. If you harm women and children, I will harm you. Plain and simple. I am the warrior. I will harm you.

I often feel like I am disturbed. Am I crazy?

It's not that I mean anyone harm. I do not want to hurt anyone. Especially myself. I fear myself sometimes. I really do. When I am alone I get very nervous. I wonder what I will do. I am my own worst enemy.

I am a weary soldier. I am battle fatigued, but I am still strong. I want to be an artist. I have a poetic, dazed soul. I want to be a hero. I do my duty in life well. Soldier, worker, husband. I earn my living and support my family, even though right now my family consists only of my wife Amy and I. We will have children soon. I replace my young wife's birth control pills sometimes, just to see if she notices. She doesn't.

The forces of the dark wilderness are against me. I am on trial but I am falsely accused. I am so tired, so worn out from fighting. I can relate to people who have been in wars. I was never in one, but I would reenlist with zero hesitation if given the opportunity. For example if we were attacked by an enemy. I often think about what would happen if my country were attacked. Or if the world were attacked by aliens. I have no doubt we would all unite. All the countries of the world. We would join forces to fight the enemy. We would come together, put our differences aside. I would sacrifice my life. I would fly a plane right into the alien spaceship if it were asked of me in order to save the world. I am prepared to do that. That is my training as a soldier in the United States Army. I would protect the women and children. I want to sacrifice myself. I want to be a hero. I want to reach out and touch the flame. I know it will burn me but I still want to touch it. I have to. I want to take your chin in my hands and scream your name as I watch your beautiful eyes turn away from me and your pretty lips curl into a smile. You betray me and stab me in the back. I am crawling in the dark. Why do you do this to me? Why do you have to be like that? No one can hear me inside my shell. I am an outcast, my insecurities flaunted. Mocked by you. But I feel nothing.

Am I insane? I really wish something would happen, such as terrorists blowing up something close such as the Pentagon or the Washington Monument. That way I would have my chance, and a reason to feel the way I do. My hell is no hell. My pain is no pain.

13762 Bluestone Place— Second Entrance

Ellen Eucker today got her teeth cleaned at her scheduled six-month appointment this morning in Falls Church then stopped at the First Virginia Bank branch there to make a withdrawal via the teller inside, still wary even after all these years of ATMs and drive-through windows, where the security guard made her uncomfortable by standing there at the back of the bank staring at her rear end, this muscle-bound guy with a marine haircut standing there and glaring and staring at Ellen Eucker and Ellen Eucker's rear end as she waited in line waiting to make a withdrawal running her tongue in nervousness over her squeaky-clean teeth. And when she passed the security guard on the way out he was muttering to himself, barely moving his lips, —I am the warrior, I am the warrior . . . And now back at home and dressed after a midday bath the specter of the security was fading at last. Ellen though was already haunted by the new scaevity in the master bath, the tub roomy and cream-colored, Jacuzzi jets and skylight overhead and enough room on the ledges of the tub— almost royal in comparison to the standard carved-out angular block one finds in most normal bathrooms in apartments for example—clean enough to eat off of, no pinkish blotches of mildew around the drain or discolorations on the floor, no black grout in the cracks of the wall tile or blue-black embryonating of petri life in the corners of the soap dish. Her tub is curved like a small boat. She images herself as being in a boat. She closes her eyes and allows herself to float nude and tranquil down a river of soothingness and empowerment toward her happy place. She never does get to her happy place. She certainly didn't today. And she felt today as though thanks to the dreadful, absolute nagging disruption that was currently in the tub right now that she could bathe for years and still never get to her happy place. She stared into the tub, at the scaevity, feeling herself getting depressed and gassy. What a fatiguing endeavor was life. It was no wonder people jumped off bridges.

Good broad ledges that were flat and good for candles and small cute wicker baskets bedded with wood shavings on top of which were placed minisoaps shaped like barnyard animals and seashells and wrapped in plastic and also little bottles of bubble baths and bath salts and boxes of soap beads—to *soothe* her, to *revitalize* her skin—plus a tiny waterproof radio with CD on which she plays either the country station or her Garth Brooks or Yanni CD. An absolute delight of a bathtub. Normally. Enough room for her to stretch out her toes and wiggle them, drifting down her river.

Normally.

The bath had not been the best bath she had taken, in her mind, considering the tremendous pantheon of phenomenal baths taken not just in this tub but in her career of bath takings—she didn't really get into baths until eleven years ago with the birth of her first son—but it was up there. The bubbles had been at a nice level, not so little you had to scoop bubbles out of the water and put on your arms and neck, etc., but not so many you got them in your mouth and had to sit all the way up with your face to the skylight so they wouldn't block your air passages. The main failing of the bath had been something that was really no fault of its own: that it had occurred midday. Everyone knows the best baths are at night. At nighttime Ellen could turn all the lights off in the bathroom and the bedroom and light the candles—tangerine ginger, strawberry waterfall, Arabian princess daiquiri, chocolate dreamscape mist, etc.—and close her eyes, losing herself in being in the dark, her body floating, licked by the proper bubble level—three quick squeezes of the bottle. She likes how she looks in her bathrobe, a purple heavy cotton knit that she bought from Hecht's at Fair Oaks four years ago. She can unwind. She looks forward during her day as she pours cereal for the kids and gets them off to school and goes to either Giant or the nursery for flowers for the yard or calls the air conditioner repair guy or the cable guy or the washing machine guy or to get an estimate on a screened-in porch, depending on the day, to the moment she will turn off the water and remove her robe, avoiding her reflection, and hang the robe on the hook beside the doorway and take that first step into the tub, the water hot and the skin scalding at first but quickly adjusting to it, immersing herself in tranquillity setting afloat down her river.

Midday baths, in Ellen's opinion, are by nature far less wonderful. It's far harder for a bath to please Ellen Eucker when there is a white burst of sun poking through the skylight above her, burning red onto her closed lids, pretty much forcing her to keep her eyes closed at all times. Sometimes while on her river she wants to open them. The relaxing and dramatic effect of the candles is lost in the daylight. And she no matter how hard she tunes it out always hears the soaps and commercials for personal injury and patent lawyers on TV downstairs she invariably forgets to turn off before coming up but she is already settled and relaxed and so doesn't want to deal with getting back up and hearing the water drip off her into the bath and step out, dripping water all over the floor as she reaches for her robe, wetting the robe for when she is done with her bath, pausing the Garth Brooks or Yanni CD or risking that they'll play a song she likes on the country station and she'll miss it, effectively abandoning the bath and wasting the bubbles and beads and hot water and candle wax and time it took to draw the bath and drying off to avoid dripping water through the house to be stepped in later by Ellen in her socked feet. If you ask Ellen Eucker, stepping in water in your socks is truly one of the most miserable experiences life has to offer and is capable of putting her into a panicky funk for the remainder of the day. Don't believe her? Ask her husband. Ask her children. And so she has to settle for a less-than-silent bath, unable to let her thoughts drift and body revitalize because she inevitably finds herself sucked in to the soaps' dialogue and following the plot, or thinking of things she could invent and patent, sometimes losing herself to such a degree that she forgets that she's supposed to be drifting down her river to her happy place and even getting out of the bath to sop naked and careless to the toilet during commercial breaks to pee not even considering the possibility that she might later step in the water she's tracking everywhere in her socks.

The whole pain in the ass of taking baths is one of the main reasons why she is on Wellbutrin.

Now and then when she doesn't feel like floating on her river, she'll read a page or two of her book called *She's Come Undone*, by she forgets the person's name, of which she's read eleven pages in total in the nineteen months since she bought it, the lone work of fiction she has purchased in that time not counting those she has purchased for her children for their summer reading lists.

She peered down into the tub at the scaevity within, her eyes wide, humming with mindlessness the simple tune from the grandfather clock's hourly jingle in the foyer. The tips of her blond hair were drying on the back of a long-sleeved red T-shirt from Hecht's. She wore jeans up to just below her navel and white midheight socks with gray heel and toe. Long straight hair that is naturally brown. She has a stylist who comes to your home and does your hair in your kitchen, washing it in the kitchen sink. Ellen still has to spend fifteen minutes on her hair each morning, after driving the kids to school and coming back and showering in the stand-alone tub on the other side of the master bathroom in front of her side of the mirror manipulating a straightener . . . Ellen has those two thin bands protruding from her lower throat and a bold nose, her shirt makes her breasts look thin, floppy, which they are . . . She and her husband Tim had the tub installed after moving in in 1996. The tub that originally came with the house, which they bought from Oklahoma before construction began, was just unsatisfactory, Ellen found, with grip grains at the bottom where her bare mother-enlarged butt had scraped with pain whenever she changed positions too fast, as she called Tim so many times at work to tell him about that they had a talk about how often she *complains,* as Tim called it, though she called it *communicating,* and they agreed that Ellen would make an effort to *complain*—or *communicate*—less, which she did until the next time she scraped her rear end on the bottom of the tub, resulting not in another talk but in a new marble-smooth tub which she found to be too small so they had to get one custom made. She still by instinct moves with deliberate care when sitting up or scooching down in this new tub, emotionally scarred, wounded from the old tub.

There's pretty much nothing else Ellen can think of that she likes to do besides take baths.

The rear end wasn't always like this. There was a time when the rear end was great. In high school, in college—University of Michigan, Delta, Delta Delta ("Tri Delts Will 'Tri' Anything!"—she still has the T-shirt)—it was legendary, her only saving grace on many occasions. It was something boys could like her for. Men too—elderly professors, the fathers of her roommates when they'd come for Parents' Weekend—she'd catch them checking her out—married men with their children at the grocery store passing her in the condiment aisle and blanching, staring straight ahead not making eye contact. Girls too. Female bartenders would compliment her, give her free drinks. Other pretty girls at parties would like her. That's why she was invited to pledge Tri Delta in the first place. Her senior year the Tri Delts went to Spring Break in Cabo San Lucas and she won a booty contest. It also got her into trouble though. More than once a drunk girl she didn't know at a house party threw her beer on her just because of it. Women are strange, she admits. She's always had a hard time getting along with them. What friendships she forges with them are tempered by a mutual distrust and wariness, blanketed with grins and pleasantries, smeared with rebukes and snipes once backs are turned. In high school she did not have any boyfriends. She was too high maintenance and always scared them off with her demands and expectations. Except for the English teacher who hit on her. And her neighbor for whom she removed her top in his hot tub when her parents were away, his wife there drunk and laughing and topless too. In college the rear end blossomed into an Ass. It might have been the seven pounds she gained. She started wearing cutoffs. She found an endless array of men willing to put up with her moods and rages. She could call them eight times a day, pout until they bought her something, use their cars, live in their apartment. She was never alone. The ass was appreciated especially during sex when the guys she had sex with would grab it, squeeze it, do her like a doggy so they could look at it (Isn't that the term? Isn't there a term? *Do it like a doggy?* Something awful like that. Tim's always saying it). Black men especially. The maintenance man in the building where she had her philosophy class her junior year. Hispanics. Felipe, the cook at the restaurant where she waited tables. Henrique, Felipe's cousin, a busboy. Brazilians, Guatemalans, Africans, Saudi Arabians, Indian bachelors behind the register at the 7-Eleven near her apartment. She did it like a doggy with dozens of local minority men. Even the several Caucasian students who were her lovers were overcome by it. One guy with zits all over his shoulders—a senior, doesn't remember his name—spent nearly a half hour in her dorm room early in her freshman year after a Tri Delt clothing drive for battered women on the quad, on his knees behind her, Loopy or something, that was his name, a Sigma Nu, that was his last name or at least what everyone called him, or maybe he was her pledge master's boyfriend's friend from home, or his little brother, she gets them confused it was so long ago and she thinks of her life as premarriage and postmarriage, two different lives altogether. But Loopy, if it was Loopy, she remembers, spent a good half hour on his knees physically licking her ass cheeks from top to bottom like he was painting a fence until every inch of ass had been licked by his tongue at which point he put his own facial cheek to the ass and stayed there like that making weeping noises as Ellen tried to figure out what she was supposed to do before comprehending the world of endless possibilities opening up before her. The start of her life. But eventually she would exhaust their capacities. As hard as they held to her, soon enough they could hold on no longer and had to let go. Not Tim though. Tim stayed.

But after it's given what you have asked of it, it's tough to maintain that kind of ass—especially when you're thirty-eight—even with somehow managing to squeeze a trip to Life Time Fitness once a week into your schedule.

She's been considering now for over a year joining a belly-dancing class there, at Life Time.

She has thought with great vigor of competing in a local fitness competition.

Or a marathon.

Or half marathon.

Sometimes she tans.

She goes to a salon in Tysons Corner.

Her pubic hair untapered except where she shaves it on the inside of her thighs.

Her breasts 32B with disproportionately large areolae and stretch marks that never completely faded even with the cocoa butter.

That is her body. When not bathing it, her days consist of being on hold with the insurance company, emptying the dishwasher, calling Tim, napping, eating, going to Giant, bringing the car in for service, shopping for picture frames.

Even though Merry Maids comes to the Eucker home on the second Tuesday of the month at the price of $65, Ellen still sweeps and vacuums and changes the Glade PlugIns and by habit cups her hand and runs it along the kitchen table and countertops gathering crumbs and brushing them using the hand off the edge of the counter into the other hand cupped below the edge waiting to catch them.

She doesn't allow shoes past just inside the front door where there is a pile of shoes of all shapes, sizes, conditions.

She smiled now with intense fear into the scaevity. She fought back tears. They were the tears she would get after pageants in her brief and unfortunate stint on the circuit as a little girl in Michigan. She held her breath. The water now cold and the bubbles dissolved into a film of blue violet around the edges. The wicks of the candles smoking still. Wax liquefied but hardening in the pits at the base of these wicks. They smelled not like Absolute Cherry Sindulgence but like burned glycerine. She checked the drain again. The switch flipped beneath the gold and arched faucet not stained with hard water but gleaming. She pushed it up, against its resistance. She flipped the switch and got out of the tub reaching for her towel, dried herself off, put on her robe. While dressing she was overcome with unease. She paused for a moment, one foot stepped in the leg hole of her underwear. She stayed still. She was like an animal. Then she pulled them up and continued dressing. She went into the bathroom, approached the tub with great slowness and peered into it, holding her breath. What horror awaited her. She pushed the switch again. Then again, and again. Harder and harder she pushed.

DC101—101.1 FM

DC101, alternative/modern rock radio, 101.1 on your dial, compressed and formulated, the guitars digitalized and the sound a shiny black tan coming to you on 66 as the afternoon sun hits. The music is the sound of ease, songs you know, comfort, no disruptions and a bolt lights up when a song comes on by a band you otherwise would never have thought about today. You perk up because the song is exactly what you wanted to hear right now, you realize, without knowing it, a song that was a popular inescapable hit last year or the year before, maybe five years before, but it's been cooling off in the depths of the playlist ever since and they bring it back exactly right, and you turn it up, your personal radio.

13762 BLUESTONE PLACE— SECOND ENTRANCE

Another thing is that also it's hard to enjoy a midday bath knowing you have to be somewhere in an hour and a half, which was true for Ellen, as she had to pick up her kids from school then take them to football which she initially did not agree to the boys participating in—their brains are still developing so much and all football is is bashing their heads together—but they and Tim wore her down on it somehow. Time for the bath taker comes in blocks, rounded off and slow moving—an hour and a half carries with it substantial weight. Ellen can tell you this. Time is neither easy nor clear and makes no exceptions for those adrift on the river. Even of course if you don't plan on being in the bath for long because you have to be dry and dressed and in your car's driver seat and back out and join the line of minivans and SUVs etc. driven by moms at 15 mph the six-tenths of a mile to the Twin Lakes Elementary Kiss and Ride—the school is located just behind the Euckers' home, it's literally a stone's throw away, especially if Christopher her oldest were throwing the stone, on the other side of some trees and a drainage ditch, but she won't have her children climbing fences and traversing a rocky, wooded area in order to get home every day, it's not safe, she simply would not be comfortable with that, nor is she comfortable allowing them to walk along the street, it's over half a mile, Brian is five years old, she's not going to be the mother who forces her five-year-old to walk nearly a mile home from school each day with who knows who wandering around out there looking for little boys, she won't be the mother who lets her boys get kidnapped and she doesn't want to think about what else—then wait idle keeping an eye out for your children, the products your ovaries and your husband's semen have made, screaming among the mass of all the other little products of copulation. It's nice stepping into a bath knowing you have as long as you need, though most baths last no more than thirty mins because after that the water becomes cold and fingers have pruned and you've listened to the three good songs on the Garth Brooks CD and you get bored sitting in water staring up at the skylight and get an urge to sweep the kitchen floor or take out the trash. You talk yourself into these urges until you can think of nothing else. This is how time is spent. Excitement is generatable.

Ellen Eucker secretly considers herself a theoretical physics aficionado in the realm of that man in the wheelchair who talks like a robot and is also an amateur forensic scientist, in the realm of Court TV.

She groaned and pulled the sleeve of her red long-sleeve T-shirt up beyond her elbow, *Guiding Light* the soap she watches, her pale freckled forearm with faint blond hairs invisible unless at the right light. She took off her skinny silver watch with no numbers or notches on the face, slid off her gold bracelet, looked under the sink for the chance of there being a rubber glove down there, wasn't one, took off the other gold bracelet, groaned again, whining, as she put the watch and bracelets on the white faux-marble sink counter—two sinks, one for her and one for her husband Tim who worked at the Pentagon with John Donald, Vicki Donald's husband and Grayson's father, before John retired four years ago: her side with lotions and toothpaste and makeup, her mirror bottom splattered with white dots, an orange monkey wearing an umbrella hat, a training manual for how to assemble and fire a .50 caliber machine gun and Tim's side with an electric shaver and spirally cord plugged in and a green LCD light on the body of the razor blinking in rhythm with Ellen's heart, the paint bubbling slowly, imperceptibly on the walls, what was

hours ago shell macaroni—no sauce, just the shells, plain—gathering
for discharge in her colon whenever ready, and as she reached into the
lukewarm water, dirt from her filthy human body with all its crevical vulgarities and haunts, random hairs big and small floating around, nearly
vomiting, she gagged and thought, Why does life have to be so horrible all
the time? Next door Judy Stanley was assaulting herself with the business
end of her twelve-year-old son's Timothy's aluminum twenty-four-inch
baseball bat used in SYA (Southwestern Youth Association) AA ball last
season to hit a home run for the Orioles.

Ellen farted a little and pinched at the drain cover and withdrew her
hand, carefully she pinched because of her manicure, coming closer to
puking, smelled her own fart, wouldn't admit it but kind of liked it, but
when she opened her eyes to peer face-to-face upon the cause of the
scaevity there was merely a single blond hair in her fingers. She hit the
water with her fist but softly so as to not splash, and said, voice croaking
a bit from disuse, —Oh, flippin' great! and carried the single hair to the
wastebasket hanging between her thumb and forefinger and dropped it
in, rubbing her fingers together to make sure.

The thing about home was at home you didn't have to act. Venturing
out for Ellen was a performance. She'd be walking across the Colonnade
parking lot to the electric one-way doors of Giant, avoiding the kid with
the train of carts, and she wouldn't recognize herself. How she walked,
her stride, the tension of her mouth when a Volvo stopped to let her pass
because pedestrians have the right of way.

Ellen looked upon her past as something that had been endured. The off-
campus apartment, the crust around the burners on its stove, the
midterms she'd studied for in the library, the huge parties and tormen-
tuous music, the drunk boys, the bongs and coke and weight-loss pills, the
moving back in with her parents in Ann Arbor and working in Human
Resources for a company that did something with optometry research
until she met Tim who was in the army stationed at the U.S. Army Gar-
rison in Warren whose friend was the new guy at work and they did it
like doggies on the first date in his room in his apartment while his
roommates watched baseball outside four feet from the door. Got married,
she got a new name, misspelled it Uecker more than once on the return
address corner of bill envelopes, moved to Fort Benning, Georgia, when
Tim was stationed there and then Officer Training School, then Oklahoma, then Japan, then Oklahoma again, then Virginia, birthing children
along the way. Here she was now looking for Drano in the laundry room

of her house in Little Rocky Run in Centreville, Virginia. She keeps a bucket of cleaning supplies for Merry Maids in the bucket there in the laundry room, off the family room on the first floor, with a door that opens onto the garage, half-full bottles of blue liquids and white spray bottles, goo caked on the caps, invisible sticky stuff, labels faded, peeling. Wasn't any Drano, collapsed onto the floor and sat against the washing machine, a GE that still maintained its factory fresh sheen on the plastic white knobs, and she saw a dust bunny in the corner under the window as she lowered her face into her hands. What was she going to do? Called her husband at work on the third floor of the Pentagon on the cordless she'd been carrying around with her by instinct as usual.

—Yeah, Tim said after four and a half rings.

—Hey.

—Yeah.

—The tub's clogged.

—I'm busy.

—It's not even like a little clogged, she said. —Like there's no movement whatsoever. At all.

There was an audible sigh on the other end. —I'm busy.

—It's totally and completely flippin' clogged. The darn thing.

Ellen didn't recognize herself on the phone, especially with Tim. When she imagined herself talking on the phone what she imagined was drastically different from what she actually observed when she was actually on the phone and talking. The things she said and how she said them. They weren't her. But she was married and this was the man she married and just a phone call, her family.

—Is there Drano, her husband the man she married said, spacing out every word as though relaying bomb-defusing instructions to a halfwit.

—No. Jesus. There's not. I've looked everywhere. There's no flippin' Drano.

It didn't sound right.

—Just relax, Tim said.

—I'm relaxed.

—Don't take this out on me.

—I'm *not*.

—The drain being clogged is not my fault.

—I *know*.

—There's nothing I can do about it right now to fix it considering I am here at work ready to plunge into this report I've been putting off all morning until after lunch. And now it's after lunch. Everything that goes wrong you come to me and say with this tone of yours, The drain is clogged. Like I did it.

—Tim, darn it.

—*You* clogged the drain.

—Tim I know.

—*You're* the one with all the hair.

—I *know*. I'm *depressed*. That's how I *talk*. I *ache*. I'm on *antidepressants*.

He sighed again and it sounded like he grunted and said, singsong and slow and gentle, —Don't worry about it and I will take a look when I get home.

—Okay.

Tim knew how to deal with her—women were easy, almost like they got bugs in their brains out of nowhere and to get the bugs out they come to men and talk, and the men listen as they talk and talk to get the bugs out and finally the men offer, in as few words as possible, the most obvious basic vague solution to the problem and somehow this exterminates the bugs. Sometimes Tim found he didn't even have to do that. He didn't have to offer a basic obvious solution or to say anything or even think at all, only nod and appear to pay attention as the woman talked her bugs out until all of a sudden the woman stopped talking and wandered off to empty the dishwasher and he could go about his life.

—Buy Drano on your way home, Ellen said.

—Yup. I'm busy though. I really have to—

—And get me an Almond Joy too.

—Mm-hmm. Wait, what if they don't have them.

—They'll have Almond Joy.

—But what if they don't. Sometimes they're out or I can't find them.

—They're right there with the other candy bars. King size. Get king size.

—All those candy bars though. I stand there in front of the cash register like an idiot staring down at all the cash registers and can't for the life of me locate the Almond Joys. Meanwhile there's a line gathering and the cashier looking at me.

—Three Musketeers then. But please find Almond Joy. They're blue. King size.

—Okay, Tim said. —I'll try.

—Okay.

—Mm-hmm.

—Okay.

—How's your day besides?

—Fine.

—Okay.

—Bye.

—Bye.

Ellen was a fully formed grown adult woman who had given birth.

She was still on the laundry room floor, watching the dust bunny. There were two of them now. Her knees were up. She clicked the cordless off with her nose and pushed the antennas down with her big cleaned front teeth with pink receding gums. The dust bunnies were bluish-purple, the color of the film on the water. A square of sunlight fell on them. Ellen let her head roll back against the hollow metal-like front of the washer, where it gave a bit like the hood of a car being sat on, stared up at the ceiling and breathed once and the ceiling had no brown birth-mark stains, which she enjoyed distantly.

She closed her eyes and floated on her river.

TWIN LAKES ELEMENTARY SCHOOL

There was Christopher who is eleven, Michael who is nine, and little Brian who is five. There is everyone this excellent day after school. All Euckers accounted for! And the blue sky clear and buses orange with the stop signs that unfold off them and teachers with whistles around their necks hugging themselves, Mrs. Kittle the principal standing there with the sea of children parting around her like the queen of a city of elves, her arms crossed with both sides of her sweater in her fists to keep it closed, lots of makeup on her face, smiling always, her high black-skunked hair like Marge Simpson's holding up in the breeze somehow, red shoes, black stockings, old, like fifty, a grandma. But where was Mom? They stood on the curb of the Kiss and Ride. Christopher in a hooded sweatshirt looking around for her careful not to show on his face that anything is wrong because he is the oldest and he knows his broth-ers look to him to know how they should react. Where was she? The mad rush of children chirping vanished. All the cars left the lot. The buses with their stop signs that flip out. Even the small one for the handi kids. Even Mrs. Kittle was gone. The afternoon was high and open with the smell of football, wet leaves, and bicycles. The sky nimble and tasty. The mud of the ground. The last of the teachers' cars emptied from the lot. The wind swept an old newspaper bag onto Christopher's feet. Where was she? It was getting cold and the unsettled worry of the day passing you by crept in and the afternoon. They should be home right now. His brothers' eyes looking at him. What do we do? What are we doing? What now? We're waiting for Mom, Mom's supposed to be here like she is here every day. The intercom beeps and Mrs. Kittle says, "All walkers and car riders are now dismissed . . ." Already we have our backpacks on and are lined up along the wall of our classrooms ready to push and elbow each other as we rush and scream out down the hall and down the stairs and through the downstairs to the door, obeying when a teacher says NO RUNNING! out to where Mom's red Grand Cherokee is waiting and we go to it and get in and go home. Then Christopher and Michael go to practice and Brian stays home and plays Nintendo. That's how it is and how everything went right up until now because there's no Mom and we're not supposed to cut through to our house so what now?

—Where's Mom? Michael said.

—Shut up.

—You shut up.

—Jesus.

—Yeah?

—Shut the hell up, Michael, I'm serious.

—Shut the hell up, Michael, I'm serious.

—Fuck you.

—Awwwwwww! I'm telling Mommmmm . . .

—Shut . . . *up*.

Three brothers with the same buzz cut standing in descending height on the sidewalk in front of Twin Lakes Elementary. Here they were, put on earth to wait. Christopher mentally calculated the route home. He knew it well. He was awesome at it. The shortcut through the field behind the school where he ran a 6:31 mile last year, the best in fifth grade, beating Aaron Merten by three seconds (hopes to get his time to around 6:05 or so this year). Then climbing the fence in like two seconds, grabbing hold on the other side and doing a flip off it and landing on his feet, then running down the hill where people sled when it snows, over the drainage ditches and into the woods, through someone's backyard with no fence, and home. It's so simple, he can do it with his eyes closed. Leap over the part of the creek where you have to step on the rock in the middle exactly right. The field behind the school where his team—Orange Team—won Field Day last year with him the anchor in tug-of-war. He's the best at the shortcut, the best at football. Michael is not the best but he can do the shortcut. He's slow and fat and can't climb the fence fast. Tore his pants that time. Brian wouldn't be able to do it. He'd cry. Could he carry him on his back? He wished he had his bike. A Diamondback with pegs. He's a Boy Scout, a forward on the SYA select soccer team, finishes his tests first usually, always reads the most books for Book It, Becky Shapalis has a crush on him he heard from Jessica Farthing, listens to Puff Daddy, Third Eye Blind, Dr. Dre's *The Chronic* even though it's old. He is one of the top three cutest boys in sixth grade, by his own analysis. He's quarterback in football, point guard in basketball, pitcher and cleanup in baseball. Michael is none of these things. Nobody is any of these things except Christopher Eucker.

It had been an hour since school ended. An hour since Michael, fourth grade, swung his backpack at Roberto Morales. And Mr. Jackson saw him swing his backpack and came stomping over with his big beard in the wind holding his thermos and yelled so loud at Michael, —*Yo!* Like a cannon booming. Michael froze and Mr. Jackson made his way through the crowd of children clearing the way for him and he looked crazy, his eyes wild and crooked yellow teeth, yelling at Michael in front of everyone, bending down to get into Michael's face so Michael could smell the black coffee on his breath as he shouted, —Want me to take you over to Mrs. Kittle and see what she thinks about that? Swinging your book bag at people like a thug? You little thug? You want to swing your book bag at me? What do you think? Want to go over there and tell her what you just did? What do you think she'll think of it? Think she'll hug you? Think she'll thank you?

Michael just sort of smiled, his face turned away from the rancid air blasting forth from Mr. Jackson's mouth.

—Think this is funny?

—No.

—Think that's comedy? Swinging your book bag at people like a thug?

—That's subjective, Michael said.

—What?

—Comedy is subjective. He glanced over at Mr. Jackson's red face, a vein in his forehead throbbing. —What? It's true.

Meanwhile Roberto had crossed the crosswalk to the other side of Springstone Drive and was watching. The crossing guard was a woman whose Geo Tracker was always parked there in the morning then the afternoon. It used to be a cop who parked there and told you when to cross. There was a shotgun in his cop car. You could see it inside. Roberto told him about it. He walked home with Roberto one day just to pass it and see. It was bolted in. He imagined what would happen if he stole the cop's keys and took it. Mr. Jackson looks like a Civil War general. He looks mangy and insane. A rural isolationist. Like he had been living here all this time in the woods, a wild remnant of the Southern yore, and Little Rocky Run was built up around him. He dresses in faded jeans and old denim shirts. There are rumors that he was in Vietnam. He has a jar of ears somewhere, is the rumor. He is renowned for taking no shit from the kids. He teaches sex ed to the boys. This is the man who tells them about vaginas and hard-ons. His first name is Jackson. It says so next to his picture in the Faculty section of the yearbook. Jackson Jackson. He always has a thermos filled with coffee on his desk. He pours it into the thermos's lid during class and drinks it black. He listens to talk radio during lunch, shaking his head and cursing under his breath. Every year late in the summer they send you a letter in the mail telling you who your teacher will be that year and Christopher was infinitely grateful this summer that his did not say MR. JACKSON but MR. DENMAN, the other male teacher at Twin Lakes, whom everyone loves, fat and jolly and red cheeked with a balding white head, a pager on the waist of his jeans which are always too big, always tugging up on them during class. Mr. Denman speaks gently. Like the host of a children's television show. He smells like soap all the time. Mr. Jackson smells like beef jerky. Michael thought it was interesting that Mr. Jackson called it a book bag instead of a backpack. Behind Mr. Jackson as he reamed him out, Michael could see Roberto watching from his safe distance, laughing at him and pointing, clutching his belly and doubling over, cutting it out whenever Mr. Jackson seemed like he might turn around.

It had been an hour and a half since Christopher told Stacy Getzle that she had no boobies by way of having Chris Nesbert pass her a note during silent reading time as Mr. Denman sat at his desk on the other side of the room, oblivious and trusting. On the Yankees in SYA AA Little League, Christopher Eucker is the best player on the team, and Chris Nesbert is an easy out, perennial right fielder, number 9 hitter, guaranteed to play only the two innings the coach is obligated by SYA to play each kid. On the note Christopher Eucker drew a girl with his blue automatic pencil, the cool clear kind you have to buy lead for at Giant and compare to your friends' to see who has the best one. The girl he drew resembled

Stacy only in that both had legs and a face. Stacy is a quiet mature type of girl who looks older than most of the other girls in sixth grade and already owns and regularly uses a compact, because her older sister is in eighth grade and lets Stacy go with her and her friends to the mall sometimes. The picture he drew was of a girl with a drastic concave chest that swooped inward like a canoe. He wrote beneath this person: YOU. And he circled the chest with a red colored pencil he borrowed from a nerdy quiet girl named Sofia Hassan who sits next to him and he drew an arrow from the circled concave chest to words he wrote beside the portrait which were

ROSES ARE RED
VIOLETS ARE BLACK
WHY IS YOUR CHEST
AS FLAT AS YOUR BACK!

And he showed the note to his friends Mike Weingartner and Ryan Sullivan who are on his football team though they play safety and tight end respectively because they're not as good as Christopher. They laughed with their hands over their mouths and Christopher passed the note. Every Friday they wear their jerseys to school like they do in high school. It was the ninth time this week that Stacy Getzle has been told she was flat by Chris, Mike, and Ryan. She lives in the Fourth Entrance.

Brian Eucker wore sea-green matching sweatpants and sweatshirt with a little alien playing basketball on the chest of the sweatshirt. Earlier in the day he cried in Mrs. Rosicky's PM kindergarten class because he didn't get a chocolate milk during snacktime. He now clutched his belly and doubled over groaning. Michael and Christopher looked at him.
—What's the matter with you? Christopher said.
—Ooooooowww!
—What.
—Ooooooowww!
—*What*, Brian.
—He's dying, Michael said.
—No he's not.
—Yeah he is, look at him.
—Oooooww!
—Are you dying?
—His appendix burst I bet.
—Brian did your appendix burst?
—Nooooo! Ooooowwww!

He fell to the ground and curled into the fetal position.
—Brian! Christopher was shouting, panicked.
—I . . .
—What! What!
—I have to . . .
—You have to what!
—I have to *poop*!
Michael cackled. —He's gonna poop his pants!
—Oh shit, Christopher said.
—Shit is right!
Christopher looked around cursing. What was he going to do?
Where was his mom?
—Ooooowww! It *kills*!
—He's gonna blow!
—Stay here, Christopher said.
—What if he blows?
—He won't blow.
—But what if he does though?
—Just stay here.

He left them and ran to the front entrance of the school, an all-brick
red building with off-white trim, black doors, trailers on the side, a blacktop in the back with yellow faded lines for dodgeball and hopscotch, basketball hoops. He tried the door. Then the other. Then the other. He
looked back at them. Brian rolling back and forth on the ground, Michael
standing over him, laughing at him, nudging him with his foot. He put
his hands up on either side of his eyes and peered inside against the glass,
saw no one, not even Wanda the janitor in her loose blue janitor shirt and
long red hair. The school was a deserted shell. The floor shiny. He could
see the playground through the back doors, the dominion of his many
dodgeball glories. Beyond the playground was the field, the fence that was
so simple to climb, the creek with the rock that he knew how to step on it
right in the middle. He tried the doors again, banged on them, felt scared,
thought about leaving his brothers and taking off through the shortcut
alone, coming back with help. Maybe something was happening to his
mom. Lying on the floor dead. Getting raped. Go across the street, knock
on doors, explain. Adults help. He imagined his mother with a big ugly
guy on top of her. Like one of the guys who work on the house. Manassas guys. She screaming like on TV. In the kitchen, the guy straddling her,
catching her arms as she flails them, he holds them down. His mother
dead in her car. From now on he would be Christopher Eucker the Boy

Whose Mom Is Dead. And how terrible it would be when his grade goes to Camp Hemlock in the spring and how other kids' mothers would be there to chaperone but not his. He would have to get rides to practice. The other kids would see him and ask him why he had to get a ride, where is his mom, and he would have to tell them she died. He tried the doors again. He went around to the side to try those doors and if those weren't open he'd try the ones in back. *Where the hell was she?*

31317 Marblestone Court— Third Entrance

November 2, 1991

Mom,

Hello from my confinement, my religious persecution. Hopefully you have found this note on the hallway floor after I have passed it beneath the space below my bedroom door. It is my only manner of communicating with the outside world. I've realized in my forced incarceration in my bedroom these several hours that I've spent the entirety of my childhood—indeed, all ten years of my life (minus those I was not sentient or otherwise too occupied by naps, feedings, jingling plastic objects, and the other things of infancy to be aware of my surroundings)—wondering if I would be sentenced to eternal damnation for not following the rules of some vague, evasive institution. This institution constantly belittled me, using fear and intimidation to seek control of my soul. It tried to tell me how to live, how to love. It attempted to make me into one of its many premolded clones, suppressing any creativity or uniqueness that I desired.

I consider myself an independent person. I do not need somebody to control my mind. I detest the fact that someone is trying to control my thoughts—the one thing in this world that is actually mine—by branding certain of my thoughts as sinful or otherwise inherently wrong or bad.

I cannot be who I really could be while following the backward, oppressive dogma of an antiquated and superstitious institution that is anti-freedom of expression, anti-individual, and that maintains itself by infusing inferiority complexes into its subjects.

I find it ironic that a goodly number of the people who watch, in captivated disbelief, Channel 7 News Special Reports about New Age, apocalyptic cults, and brainwashing are actually in no different of a situation.

You made me write this letter to explain why I have decided to no longer attend Mass with you and Dad on Sundays and your CCD class on Wednesday evenings in our living room. You also wanted to know whether or not I believe in God. To answer your last question first, I cannot decide if I believe in a higher power. If there is an Omnipotent Creator of All Things, I do not believe it would endorse a few of its creations to create an institution that uses its name or the idea of its existence to brainwash and coerce the rest of its subjects into sacrificing their greatest gift: individuality.

As for why I shall not be attending Mass and CCD, it's probably due to the same reason that you and Dad do not go to a Jewish synagogue every Saturday or to a Buddhist temple on whatever day is their Sabbath: You do not happen to believe in it. If you want to dismiss my newfound disbelief as an arrogant ignorance (like Dad insists on doing), I have to wonder if you know all there is to know about Judaism or Buddhism. You must since you don't believe in them. Those religions have been around a lot longer than Catholicism, and though we do not have the stats on this, I am willing to bet that more people have subscribed to these religions than to Catholicism over the course of history, so there must be something special about them. You must simply be arrogant and ignorant if you don't believe in them, to apply Dad's argument. What if you were to have been educated about one of those religions, Mom? What if you were taught about Judaism? What if you were born in Tibet and raised and taught by Buddhist parents? Are you obliged to then adhere to Buddhism? Is Truth simply what culture one was brought up in and taught about in one's youth? Or do you and Dad believe that you would be obliged to find your way from Tibet to the nearest Catholic church and convert to your Number One Ultimate and True Religion? Please do not say yes.

I am ignorant about a lot of things. Catholicism is just one thing in a universe of things I am not an expert of. Am I obliged to become an expert in all the things in existence before I can justify my not participating or utilizing them? Who has that kind of time?

For example, what about botany? I am not an expert in botany. Is it not okay that I do not practice botany? Must I learn more about botany before I can justify spending my time on things that aren't related to botany? I mean, honestly.

You and Dad are the latest in a long line of this bumbling heavy-handed effort on the part of the tyrannical to enforce its religion upon those at its mercy. Think about it, Mom. Manifest Destiny, the Spanish Inquisition, the Crusades. History is stained with the blood of tragic and ultimately silly endeavors of which yours is a microcosm. All they have taught us is that one simply cannot force another to believe in something. This principle holds true for religion and extends to anything else: the magic bullet theory, that the moon landing was a hoax, that human life begins at conception. Trying to force-feed your beliefs down one's throat by whatever means you will is savage, barbaric, and ridiculous. And if I did suddenly turn into Charlie Christian b/c of your intimidation, it would be out of fear and spinelessness on my part and thus phony and false. My advice to you is to lay off me and accept the fact that here in America, there is Freedom of Religion. Let me discover whatever I will discover on my own so that it will be real. I'm sorry if your beliefs don't match, but please try and honor my individuality.

We can discuss ceasing my enrollment in Catholic school in favor of public school whenever you are ready. You'll know where to find me.

Grayson

13762 Bluestone Place— Second Entrance

She was in the laundry room . . . The scaevity was there. She listened to it approach the laundry room with the oncoming wind of a traveling vortex. She felt it rise up through the piping and squeeze itself out through the tub's drain and hover up aloft then leave the bath in search of her, trailing her soapy scent. She clenched her eyes shut and focused, focused on floating on her river, getting to her happy place, willing or trying to will away the voraginous thing tumbling down the stairs now in the meandering manner of the undead. Happy place, she thought. Happy place, Ellen. Soothing, revitalizing, empowering happy place . . . It was a goety mass of intertwined blond hairs, stubbly dust shaved off legs, armpits, and outer bikini region all held together by slime, spit, vaginal discharge, anal gunk, phlegm, ear wax, dirt, grime, rank and gelatinous goop, green bacterial buildup, the rust and filth of the modern civilized sewage system—the rejectamenta of society, the repellent facts of human beings—that had been building up for years in the walls of the pipes like in those toothpaste commercials she sees with an animated graphic of teeth and gums showing plaque building up on them or the ads for cholesterol medications showing stuff building up inside your arteries, your death imminent and silent. Fluoride and chlorine, minerals, bath bead residue, lead, the shit of mice, fruit flies washed down and never known, soil from the spring when she planted bulbs in the backyard, lint, toxic emissions from driving. She felt its presence as it entered the laundry room, all the things she had washed from her flesh, stood no chance against them in union and returned against her. It floated betwixt the eyes of the last person to see Grayson Donald alive, hovering there one foot from the bridge of her nose which did secrete a minuscule level of oil caused by the Dove bars she depended on, the Diet Cokes. The scaevity bobbed like it dangled from strings. Still water dripped off it. A long meandering black pube hung astray from the bottom. It had a face. Its eyes were rimmed with calcium and pollen, its teeth from candle wax and the shards of yellowed toenail clippings of yore. It smiled with pitilessness and spoke coughing over the curled epidermises of dead arachnids. —El-len . . . El-len Eu-cker . . . She whimpered and kept her eyes closed, buried her face in her arms which held her knees to her chest and are beginning to develop that jiggling layer of meat on the undersides. The arms of the Ellen Euckers of America. Of the college-educated mothers of three, the white women who live in good neighborhoods with home owners' associations in an area with great schools and virtually no major crime or people of color not counting Asians. They were the arms of presidential elections and evening news broadcasts, inoculations, indignation. Hillary arms. The smiters of Oprah. Constipation arms, child trapped in a well arms. Cancer arms. *People* magazine arms. Her arms are the arms of the blue dress, the rammers of the cigar. The brachials of squeamishness and refusal to look the truth of us in its black nighttime face.

—El-len . . . El-len Eu-cker . . .

Whispering gently as though rousing her from sleep.

Until she peeked open one eye a crack and it screamed, —EL-LEN!

She shrieked and ran out of the laundry room. The scaevity did not follow. Outside unfathomed birds twittered and in the backyard leaves fell from the small weeping willow the man she married bought from Frank's and planted as a sapling when they first moved in. The leaves skinny and yellow. They gathered in the grass in the corners of the fence and blew like sand along the driveway next door. Sticking out halfway from the cracks of the deck. And in the wood rack of the gas grill. Tim has a promise from the United States Army that he will not have to uproot his family, sell his house, take his children out of school again for the duration of his service before his retirement. But you can't trust them. They make their own rules as they go. And so she can't settle in and make friends. That is why she hardly leaves the house except for errands. You can't trust them. They make rules then make new rules that break the rules they made. The leaves were skinny helicopter petals. They spun in the wind, yellow and translucent like the wings of ancient dragonflies. And her family is subject to the whims and bureaucracies of the military of a nation, an olympic facelessness with megafeet that stomp the ants in its path. And there was no noise, so quiet here, the skinny leaves in the driveway next door, you cannot trust them, you cannot trust anyone.

Twin Lakes Elementary School

Who were these boys, motherless and shivering? Where do they go and what do they know?

The leaves golden and brown in front yards and their friends out on their street at home, at football practice. The flower displays were here naked and whimpering as a car or two dribbled home early from 66, but soon Springstone Drive which they watched with utter concentration would be an overflowing passage of a fleet of commuters in white shirts and ties going slow with sun visors lowered, headlights on even though there would be no darkness yet. Little Brian had a tightly packed turd in his Underoos and a dark stain in the crotch of his green sweatpants. Michael had long since gotten bored with chanting, —Brian pooped his pa-ants! Brian pooped his pa-ants! and was now chucking pieces of mulch from the school's landscaping at the yellow crosswalk sign. The sign had two stick figure silhouettes apparently walking across a street. One looked like a mother and one looked like a daughter. Brian had long since stopped crying about having soiled himself and was also throwing mulch chips at the sign. Christopher now watched a red car appear way up the hill on Sandstone Way, connector between First and Second Entrance, the route Mom took to get to Twin Lakes Elementary. He said nothing yet, wanting to be sure. They had many times seen the red Grand Cherokee resting at that stop sign then gliding left easy down Springstone and drifting with turn signal blinking into the Kiss and Ride where Mom would be at the wheel unlocking all four doors with the push of just her own unlock button, windows cracked, reaching into the back and moving stuff around with one hand. Christopher said, —Hey, look. And he pointed at Mom's car and a bolt of hope pumped through the three, an annoyed relief, and all the worry washed away. —Finally, Michael said, the thicker of the three and wearing a blue T-shirt and jean shorts, totally inappropriate attire sea-sonwise. His meaty cheeks were red and his nose was redder and he was on Ritalin. Christopher worried about Mom's reaction to seeing what Bri-an'd done. He was mad at her. He'd been tested for Gifted and Talented but didn't get in. The brothers straightened and watched the red SUV ease left onto Springstone and approach, and Christopher helped Brian with his big empty backpack. They stepped close to the edge of the yellow curb and Michael said he was starving and couldn't wait to play Nintendo 64 and was *The Real World* on tonight? The red car didn't slow with its blinker but kept going, an Explorer they saw now, darker red than Mom's Grand Cherokee. Christopher couldn't understand why Mom inside was so small but still a woman but with short black hair or why Mom's car had changed from a Grand Cherokee into an Explorer and Michael said, — You're retarded, but still the three standing shoulder to shoulder followed it with their entire bodies as it passed, its brake lights tapping on and off as it disappeared around the bend.

PENTAGON—ARLINGTON

Tim Eucker used to work one story below Grayson's dad John Donald. One story exactly. Meaning that if Tim were to have spent an hour or two one morning taping together twelve feet's worth of pencils and driven the resultant stave up into the ceiling directly over his head sitting in his swivel chair at his desk in his cubicle and broke through the Styrofoamy paneled matter and whatever wires and beams were between floors, eventually with enough effort he would have punctured the hard smooth sole of John Donald's left black army officer shoe as John Donald sat in his own swivel chair in his own cubicle. The two men are not necessarily friends, despite Tim's efforts. He has found that adult men in Little Rocky Run do not have many friends. And they are not very open to forging meaningful platonic relationships with other men. Sure they're polite enough. They might wave as they drive by or engage in casual chatter at Little League practice. But as for anything beyond surface pleasantries? Not really. Mostly the men are content to let their wives be the social ones. They tag along to dinners and Christmas parties. They smile and make little jokes. They drink light beer or wine and remain overall quiet and agreeable standing around with the other couples discussing the kids. Fears are not shared, secrets are not confessed. The point of Little Rocky Run is to get away from friends, it seems to Tim. You occupy yourself with your family and work and don't have much interest left over in the lives and perceptions of others. It's exhausting enough just remaining solvent. Your world develops clear and unmistakable boundaries in Little Rocky Run—dirty and clean, safe and dangerous, expensive and cheap, hungry and full, acceptable and not. It might have taken the car pool for Tim to finally face these truths.

It was a short-lived idea of Tim's that he got one of the first days here as he stapled a 678 ream of paperwork for a colonel. The idea hit him hard and fast and made him instantly happy. Bonding with those he lived and worked among, forging the foundations of a community, sharing fears, confessing secrets. Establishing generations of tradition and culture. Having people at work he could stop by and chat with, complain about the bureaucracy, run out with for a burger at lunch, grab a beer with after work. Super Bowl parties. He was already envisioning the Super Bowl parties by the time he finished the stapling of the ream.

Sometimes the silence of the mornings can be too much for Tim. He stands there in the kitchen spreading Philadelphia cream cheese on his Thomas's cinnamon raisin bagel with his back to his family. His family oblivious to him. And as the coffeemaker gurgles he looks out the window over the sink into his fenced backyard at the weeping willow. Its hair blowing like gold in California. He hears a single bird and nothing else. The din of his family fades. All pinpoints around the song of the bird that he cannot see. He wonders how he ended up here. Why houses—drywall and wood standing aright—make it acceptable for people to live on a strange plot of dirt in a certain location on the earth chosen like some omnipotent monster spun it on its axis and stopped it with its hulking medius and said, —There! He lived a stone's throw from a man and they each morning climbed into their little machines and joined the exodus, sitting through an hour of rush-hour traffic each, expending gas, time, and patience, risking their lives in these machines, vital bits of their souls atrophying off like an hourglass, inane voices babbling between hits on the radio—all to get to the place where they work, a location to which they otherwise would not go if a salary were not gifted them in return, and they sat there on top of one another all day then when the day was done they got back into their separate machines and did it again in reverse.

That evening he called the Home Owners' Association on the phone in the kitchen with a thing on it to make it easier to rest between your head and your shoulder when your hands are busy—Ellen put it on— and got them to put a five-line blurb in the part of the monthly newsletter where they list the numbers of all the kids available to babysit for any Pentagon employees interested in car pooling to call (703) 631-____.

Most phone numbers are (703) 631- . . . Only recently have you had to
actually include the (703) every time you dial, due to the fact that so
many people have moved to or been birthed in NoVA that they have
simply run out of phone numbers. The first three digits of phone numbers, after the (703), in NoVA are going to be either 631 or 266 for the
most part. The Donalds' though is (703) 378-____, 378 being tradition-
ally a Chantilly number. This has to do with the Donalds being one of the
first families to set up phone service in Little Rocky Run, before the
phone company designated 266 and 631 and settled for 378 since it was
closest. The zip code has recently changed from 22024 to 20124. But
that has nothing to do with the story. Tim heard back from five Little
Rocky Run Pentagon employees and the car pool was born. They were:
John Donald, Eleanor Kimble, Bruce Whiting, and Richard Batchelor.
Tim asked Richard upon first speaking to him on the phone if he could
call him Dick but Richard said quite seriously, —No. Tim asked him if he
was a bachelor, since his last name was Batchelor. Richard said, not laughing, that no—he is married and lives in the First Entrance on Springstone
Drive and has two children, sons, ages twenty-two and seventeen and
their names are Trent and Dwight respectively. Tim in the duration of the
car pool came to know Richard Batchelor's house as the one with the
pineapple flag that says WELCOME on it waving from a post on the front
porch and an electric company green box in the front yard, this giant
humming power source that seemed cancerous and evil.

Tim's twist upon the traditional concept of the car pool was to decree
that it would be a different member's turn each day to bring in veggies
and dip for the ride. And also that some upbeat music should be played
which Tim would take care of—some rock and roll, like the Eagles or Billy
Joel, two of his favorites (especially "Take It Easy" and "We Didn't Start
the Fire"). The idea was to turn the humdrum morning commute into a
backyard barbecue. He thought about bringing beers but Ellen talked him
out of it. A cooler of Bud Lights. He patted himself on the back for having
come up with the veggie idea—taking the initiative of removing one
discomfort from the workday and replacing it with deliciousness and
good times, two things Lord knows everybody could all use a little more
of. You have to make yourself happy, Tim believes. No one will do it for
you. People get stuck in these ruts. It's in human nature to get into a routine no matter how unhappy it makes you and stay there. It's very hard,
it takes a lot of energy to keep yourself out of these ruts. Tim felt he was
the man to shake everyone awake. A Fun Coach. That was the title he
gave himself. He plans one day after retiring from the army to have a

career in motivational speaking. He didn't hesitate to call the person whose turn it was to bring the veggies and dip on the night before to remind him or her. He did it with grace, in his opinion. And early enough so they'd still be able to run out to Giant if they had forgotten. He was very smooth about it. He'd call and say, —Hey there, [name of person]! Tim Eucker! How the hell are you? Ha-ha, I know what you mean! [Maybe make a joke here, something relating to a humorous anecdote from that day's commute.] Oh thank you, it's nothing really—comedy is in my genes. But, listen. I just thought I'd call to let you know that we are *really* looking forward to your veggies and dip tomorrow. Our imaginations are going nuts, we were all talking about it today. Yeah, yeah. I mean, it could be anything. Broccoli, cucumbers—who knows? Your basic ranch dip or a feisty peppercorn—ouchie momma! ¡*Ay caramba!* Or none of the above. Something we've never even *considered* before! What will it be? No, no, don't tell me—don't tell me—being surprised is the best part!

Then he'd go to sleep beside Ellen, staring at the ceiling with his hands behind his head, licking his lips, Ellen snoring, wondering if there would be cauliflower, or green peppers, or celery. In time he came to dislike Richard Batchelor as a person, to rebuke everything the man stood for as it came clear after several revolutions of the cycle that Richard Batchelor never brought anything on his day to bring in veggies and dip except a bag of baby carrots—no ranch, no peppercorn, nothing—which disgusted Tim and what made it worse was that Richard never picked up on Tim's disgust, as palpable as it was within the vehicle, even though the others certainly did, it made them uncomfortable, aggrandizing the gloom to an even further degree. In this way is Richard Batchelor quintessentially Little Rocky Runian. The warning signs of the un-self-aware Little Rocky Runian archetype share many characteristics with the known symptoms of Asperger's syndrome. In Richard's eyes, he had done well, there was nothing wrong. Tim insisted he bring vegetables, baby carrots are a vegetable. There is no discrepancy. He'd toss the bag to Tim and climb in, open his *Post,* Tim staring daggers into the back of his head. —Thank you, Dick.

—Richard please. Or sir, since I outrank you.

—You do not outrank me.

—Do too. I report to General Stephenson, you report to Colonel Wright. General trumps colonel.

Tim made a face and opened the bag and munched upon a baby carrot, pouting.

He took pride in the fact that he alone knew that the Safeway in Reston carried a tremendous veggie platter that included a sampling of seemingly every vegetable available to North America including CHERRY FREAKING TOMATOES, by far Tim's favorite. And he went to great pains not to reveal to the car pool where he scored the platter, even though they asked him every time they saw him—the Veggie Master—strolling every Tuesday out his front door to the awaiting vehicle, a hand towel over the platter (had to sneak the hand towel past Ellen) so they couldn't get a sneak peek before the grand unveiling, his face twitching from the grin he fought so hard to suppress, coming to a halt right outside the car where they could all see and yanking the hand towel off with a flourish while going, —Dun-*dun!* and watching the astonishment on their faces, climbing in with it, saying, —That's how it's done, folks! Learn from your sensei!

His platters cost $40, he was proud to say, and were fifteen and a half inches in diameter and usually stacked around eight inches tall, give or take. As a result of buying them so often he was on a first-name basis with two cashiers at the Safeway in Reston, which he went to even though there is a Safeway in Centreville to lessen the chances of being seen by members of the carpool. The cashiers secretly called him Veggie Guy. When he appeared at the end of their line they glanced up with a knowing smile, their eyes going to the platter in his hands. He would sort of lift the platter in acknowledgment of it and of them, smile-grimace back, pretend to be unassuming while idly perusing the tabloids and gum, hoping those in line ahead of him and behind him were taking notice of his remarkable veggie platter, the exquisite commercial choice he had made, a hell of a purchase, and were privately ovating him while at the same time feeling a not insignificant pinch of envy that they were not he but they, measly little they, and this was the way it always has been and ever shall be. The cashiers he considered himself on a first-name basis with were Ginnie and Ron. The way he introduced himself to Ron was, after five or six times purchasing the platter in his line and thinking it only appropriate to formally introduce himself since they both clearly recognized one another, Ron an older guy who laughed each time he glanced up while waiting for a credit card to go through and saw Tim at the end of his line but not in a derisive or mocking way but rather like they shared a good joke or like Tim was family, in Tim's view, Tim said as Ron lifted the platter off the conveyor belt and ran the platter over the scanner plate a couple of times until its UPC registered, —I'm Tim. Tim Eucker. I live in Centreville. He held out his hand but Ron didn't look up from punching something into the computer. Tim stood there with his hand out feeling an acute embarrassment washing up from the abysm of his being, the line stretched halfway down the aisle with the trash bags, a slow burn creeping into his sinuses, his face reddening, still smiling. —Shake the hand, he said through his teeth. —Shake it.

He didn't know that Ron was very hard of hearing, not to mention from Slovakia or somewhere. Ron couldn't hear shit.

But he had a name tag. Tim read it.

—Ron.

Ron looked up and saw the hand.

—Tim Eucker. I live in Centreville.

Ron blinked and extended his own hand and they shook.

The name of the Little Rocky Run Home Owners' Association's newsletter in which Tim Eucker placed his ad for the car pool is called *News on the Run*. It is delivered every first Monday to each house via the white plastic *Washington Post* boxes subscribers have attached to their curbside mailboxes which are black with a red flag, the older ones of rusty metal and the newer ones a neat plastic (no fancy wood bluebirds or anything crazy, per HOA regulations) which the people who deliver the *Post* tend to dislike because the *News on the Run* is too wide to lie flat in the box so it is just kind of shoved in there diagonally, taking up the entire box just about, and these are usually people from Manassas who for $100 a week wake up at 3 AM every morning to sit in their driveway in the dark and roll up hundreds of newspapers that have been left in their driveway in dozens of boxes and stuff each rolled paper into a narrow plastic bag then load the mountain of rolled and bagged papers all into the back of their old minivan or pickup with someone else like a child or a husband back there and driving through the ughten while everyone else sleeps, so they often just shove the *Post* into the box as if they do not see the *News on the Run* in there, shoving the *News on the Run* all the way to the back of the box like the litter the *Post* deliverers see it to be.

Vicki Donald delivered the *Post* in Little Rocky Run on Tuesdays and Thursdays for two years in 1996, telling John and Grayson that it was for the extra money but really it was because rousing at 3 AM and driving around delivering newspapers alone was more enjoyable for her than spending that time before work in the same home, sharing the same space, breathing the same air as her husband, having felt this way to a greater and greater degree since approximately 1995 when she discovered the lockbox in the back of the closet in the computer room which she picked open with a tool she bought and it was full of mash notes and a credit card with John's name on it she had never seen before.

The *News on the Run* is delivered to those who don't have a *Post* box by placing it in their mailbox, which the mailman who delivers the mail by English-style steering wheel USPS van lurching up and down either side of Little Rocky Run's streets doesn't like because he by instinct grabs the newsletter thinking it's outgoing mail and then sees what it is and puts it back, doing this over and over again, wearing him down.

Ellen and Tim last had sex early last Saturday morning.

Tim Eucker's favorite book is *Guinness World Records*.

All five Pentagon employees in their pale green military shirts, nearly light blue so pale, shirts of officers, with a black and gold patch on the flat of their shoulder denoting rank and very dark almost black pants tight as paint, everything tucked in and buttons on the shirt lined up with the line of the fly, black socks and black shoes and skinny black laces long enough for just a single knot, the cowlicked hair of the men cut every two weeks at the PX, faces imberb, teenagers on *American Bandstand*.

Tim has the gift of being engaging in conversation on any type of topic. He is able to construct conversations regardless of whether or not the other person reciprocates. The other person will feel as though he or she is reciprocating, that he or she is holding up his end of things, even though he or she might be doing nothing but nodding and making grunts of affirmation or comprehension. Tim can go solo for about twenty-seven minutes on what model leaf blower he is considering for purchase. He happens to be very enthusiastic about things like the differences between makes and models and can convey this enthusiasm orally without effort, and regardless of your previous interest in leaf blowers he can draw you in, make you suddenly very excited about leaf blowers as well. He's that type. He should have gone into sales. Maybe he will once he retires. His eyes are chronically attentive. They look directly into yours. General practitioner eyes. His vibe is sporty, Mormon. You can tell there was a time when females were attracted to him. They still are. The problems though came after the twenty-seven-minute mark of going solo on the topic of leaf blowers, for example (also the pros and cons of the coin-operated laundry business, new cars coming out, protein shakes from GNC, advances in entertainment technology, etc.), with no one in the car pool really having much to contribute to the topic and just kind of wanting to mind their own business and stare out the window or read the paper or do some work, Tim would run out of gas and run out of things to

say and there would still be another half an hour left in the commute. You
see, Tim sees silence as a bad thing. There is no benefit to not speaking. It
makes him uncomfortable. He feels it is his fault. The silence then must
be killed. A slow and steady crushing of the skull in a vise. That's how he
perceives silence. Thus that last half hour of the commute every day—the
unmoving traffic, the river of vehicles, the beige death of 66—consisted of
Billy Joel or the Eagles playing with special guest Tim Eucker on the whistle, whistling the melody in some invented key or throwing out questions
to the car pool such as, —What do you think goes through someone's
mind as they stab someone?

Can you imagine the effect that listening to a half hour of whistling
while trapped in a car stuck in sempiternal traffic has on your life?

You might think that that's what did the car pool in but it's not.

What happened was one day when it was John Donald's turn to
bring in the veggie platter he decided it would maybe be nice to vary it
up. Three months of morning vegetables was taking its toll. His piss was
beginning to smell. He was starting to see people's heads as artichokes.
And also he read on the Internet that too many vegetables tainted the
taste of one's semen. It made one's semen taste *rancid,* it said on the
Internet. Quote unquote. Having never tasted it himself, he'd never considered that his semen could taste any which way at all let alone rancid
specifically until reading that on the Internet but he'd better make sure it
didn't because now that he thought about it there was a very good chance
his semen might taste rancid. That meant cooling it on the veggie intake
a little and also purchasing pills from the Internet, available from the
same site actually, that were advertised as being able to flavor your
semen to taste certain ways, such as like strawberries or oranges. Thus
John Donald showed up one Thursday morning as the sliding door of
Eleanor's sleek easy curved dark blue Caravan slid open. Eleanor was
driving so he was last to be picked up. They all were turned, Tim Eucker
especially, licking their lips in anticipation of veggies and ranch, even
Richard Batchelor which took everyone by surprise. In the Donalds'
driveway as the morning was blue and cold, exhaust coughing from the
pipe in a thick warm cloud, lights in windows and brake lights in every
driveway as far as the eye could see, John Donald unveiled a beautifully
arranged *shrimp* platter on a circular plastic tray and high-arching plastic lid, nearly twenty-four inches in diameter and piled nearly a foot high
with more shrimp than any single member of the car pool could recall
ever seeing together in one place at one time. There was silence as John
stood there holding the platter, smiling and looking at Bruce and Tim

who was holding the Eagles CD (*Greatest Hits Volume 2*) with his finger poked through the hole ready to pass it up to Eleanor to pop in, Richard in the middle bench sulking with his long stone face, stretched-out body, skinny leg crossed over knee and arm over backrest, long dangly fingers and baby thin hair, black sock exposed and an inch of hairless white skinny leg, Eleanor up front with both hands on the wheel and radio off and her usual way too red lipstick that made her look like a fetus. John Donald waited for them to understand what he held, eyeing Tim Eucker so that he could see his face when he realized John's new dominance in the ring of platter blood sport—No, Tim, *you* learn from the sensei, motherfucker—and he wanted to see Tim's eyes as Tim blinked comprehending the simple genius of a shrimp platter. Why hadn't he thought of it? Damn it, why hadn't he *seen* it himself? John Donald waited for Tim to concede defeat, congratulate him as truly the braver pioneer of spontaneity and fun . . .

But that was not the reaction John Donald got.

There was an unmistakable glazing over of four pairs of eyeballs in faces still maintaining the well-practiced hello face of the morning professional. Oh man was it cold. The enthusiasm was dim, to put it mildly. John tried to ignore the indifference. He said, grinning big, —Shrimp anyone?

—No thank you, Tim Eucker said, putting a hand over his spare tire, and turned back to Bruce Whiting and saying, —But then again Bruce the XII-490 is pretty darn cool and exceptionally lighter. It's more of a specialized power hammer for tricky jobs as opposed to the general use you get out of something like your C-499 or your 27XLT which is Black & Decker.

—Richard? John Donald said. —Shrimp?

John Donald found he talked to Richard Batchelor differently than anyone else. He felt invasive, spoke gently and carefully, eager to be smart. Richard has a talent for bringing out the insecurity and flaws in people just by being in the same room. Richard Batchelor furrowed his brow and mouthed no and shook his head with vigor, turning to look out the window. Eleanor, ever the lady, tried to politely pretend she hadn't heard John. But he leaned up there and held the platter in her face, forcing her to make a decision since she was captive there in the vehicle behind the wheel.

—Eleanor?

—Hi!

—Have a shrimp.

—Mmm! Yum! she said, smiling. —Maybe in a minute. Thanks!

But nobody ate any except for John Donald who kept saying through mouthfuls, turning and shaking the platter with provocativeness toward the others, —Shrimp? So he ended up eating them. All of them. Every shrimp. By himself. On principle. He ate them as though he had not eaten in days. And when he was full he forced them still into his mouth against his body's great protests, using Tim's blabbering as motivation, very much overblowing the human digestive system's capacity for crustaceans at 7:30 AM. Eleanor was an annoyingly slow and cautious driver. Her day to drive was a black mar on the horizon more so even than Richard's day to bring veggies. The commute was fifteen minutes longer when she drove and they were inevitably late. They all felt derision toward her about it and about her looks and her children. They all had strong, private opinions about Eleanor. Her husband, her rank, her vehicle. Where Richard Batchelor brings out the insecurities in others, Eleanor's talent is to bring out the arcane disgust. But John kept pounding them down, four, five at a time, shells and all, making a big show of it, saying loud enough to be heard over Tim Eucker's breakdown of the plot of *Life Is Beautiful*, which Tim had seen last weekend at the Centreville Multiplex and was in his opinion, quote, *boring as hell*, —Oh! Oh *God!* Sweet *Gad! Gad!* My Lord, these are *delicious!* You just cannot *imagine* the simple glory these shrimp deliver to the palate. I mean, just—*Christ!* And I'm Catholic too! Utter fucking *Christ! Gad!* You guys *have* to try these.

Tim Eucker's rage was deep and profound. Eyeing John Donald as he talked to Bruce. Never in his life had he been so offended as he was at witnessing the desecration that John Donald was inflicting upon the veggie rule. It was rape was what it was. It was akin to rape. Veggie rape. Emotional rape. Vulgar is the word that came to mind. Sick. It was like watching some punk-ass kid with dreadlocks burn the flag right in front of him. It was sad. It hurt, was what it did. It *hurt* him. It *hurt* his *heart*.

He smiled and said, —No thank you, John. Maybe in a minute.

On 66 at the Vienna Metro station, moments after working the last shrimp enough in his teeth and getting it down, John began to feel the gurgulation of gastrointestinal revolt. His face got cold. Things were making noises beneath his spine that he was pretty sure the body isn't supposed to make. There was definitely shuffling and movement. The road began to mean infernal meshanteries. Eleanor's driving became ruthless in its methodical indolence. Traffic was a fimetic dungeon of anguish. Tim's whistling was a power drill to the side of the head. The rest of the commute was unspeakable and passed as a yearlong nightmare never to be remembered in its entirety. Most of it would be repressed in the unconscious. By the time they drove past the security post and into the thousand-acre Pentagon parking lot to park and wait for the shuttle to take them to the actual Pentagon John Donald was ghost pale and sweating tiny hot beads along his hairline. He looked malarial. Schizoid. Couldn't keep his head still or eyes open or feet from twitching. Couldn't feel the tips of his fingers. In his opinion the longest time in the world is waiting for a middle-aged woman named Eleanor with poofy black hair to slo-mo you through a parking lot when your colon is trembling and straining against its own gunpowderlike detonation. He really hated Eleanor in those long moments—really really did. He wished she were never born because if she were never born then she could not park so slowly. He had his hand on the sliding door. He pulled it open as the blue Dodge Caravan was still in motion. He heard as if underwater Tim say, —Whoa whoa whoa John. But he was already out of the vehicle and off running without his briefcase, clammy hands over his own poor spare tire, sprinting zigzag he was so disoriented, bent over, sweaty and bug-eyed, toward the nearest MP booth at such a speed and ferocity that the MP there pulled his sidearm and screamed at John to halt, and John did, doubled over about forty feet from the MP, screaming as the cars of other Pentagon workers arriving in the lot eased by him watching that he had to please please please use their bathroom please, and the MP didn't lower his gun and said, —No!

And John was weeping now and hitting the pavement with his open hand and he said, —No?! Why *not*?

—Because it's the MP booth. It's for MPs.

John whined. The MP still didn't know what the fuck was going on and was lowering his gun when John suddenly stopped crying and froze and the MP cocked his head as from it sounded like underground beneath their feet something malominous and terrible roared from the doorway into Hades. The MP pointed his gun again at him and shouted, —What . . . what *is* that?

—My fucking intestines! John managed to whimper.

Then he ran clutching his belly making a strange whinnying noise past the MP and into the booth, shouting, —Shoot me if you must! And no MP has used the booth's toilet to this day. John took a taxi home after thanking the MP who only glared in return outside the hut. John spent the next day in bed drinking first Pepto-Bismol, straight from the bottle, then, when that stopped working, ginger ale and handfuls of Alka-Seltzer. It was his day to drive. He pretended to forget to call the car pool to let them know he wouldn't be picking them up. He took a grim satisfaction imagining their confusion growing as they waited at their bay windows with their briefcases, staring out at their blue early-morning street, dressed, waiting for him to pull into their driveway in Vicki Donald's green Escort wagon that smelled like Krispy Kreme donuts. He vomited fascinating entities into a mop bucket he had his son Grayson put next to the bed before Grayson left for school. He imagined his fellow carpoolers as the minutes past 7:30 ticked off, swelling within them a childlike fear of not being on time, of getting in trouble, then realizing what they had done and becoming sorry they had refused John Donald's shrimp. For driving him to this. For their complicity in the wrong the world had done him.

They each drove themselves that morning and just kept driving themselves the next day and the next, these habits that are created so easily in Centreville, it's how things are done, and it is now how these five members of our military get to the Pentagon where they defend our nation.

Tim Eucker is forty-one years old and hasn't smoked a cigarette or consumed more than eight beers in one evening since he was twenty-two, not counting his wedding. It makes sense that he is forty-one as Ellen is thirty-eight. Most husbands in Little Rocky Run are three years older than their wives. In Officer Training School Tim was known for blowing heavy quantities of coke and his ability to stay up for thirty-six hours at a time easy drinking beers. He could get fucked up like a pro. If you'd asked him then he'd have said he'd never quit smoking, no way, can't make me. He'd never be one of those fat pussy suburban guys with no sex life and vague dissatisfaction, always mowing their lawn and jerking off. He'd die of cancer or a heart attack, he didn't care. Life was for living. Better to burn out than fade away, live fast, die young, etc. But then you wake up one day and everything has changed, including you. Your opinions about what matters and what's important are reversed. You see things totally in a different light. You find yourself going out of your way not to stand next to smokers and going so far as to complain to the waitress when the next table lights up. It's disgusting and really a bad habit, you blow your own mind by thinking one day as you mow the lawn. That's not me anymore, that's kid stuff, reckless and wild youth that is a stage and the reason is to blast it out of your system so you can focus on more important things that bring true joy like family and career. And, shit, you think now, I wasn't happy living like that back then, not *really*. I'm much happier now, being wiser with age and responsibility.

Tim tends to foray. There have been many forays, each of them excited and devout. In general but with exceptions the forays are fitness related. Mostly they involve buying things. For example, the NordicTrack that's in the basement covered by a sheet and still in brand-new condition. Tim's latest foray into good health consists of jogging. The way the forays usually work is they creep in, they approach him and wait outside him patiently as he first refuses their entry, recognizing them for what they are, waiting until he reconsiders and then striking with hell's fury. Something he even as recently as the day before wrote off as stupid and detrimental to his happiness, not for him and what he'd never do in a million years, such as jogging, which he before now would write off often in the car driving through Little Rocky Run and seeing all the women with thunder thighs and ten-year-old sweatpants huffing and puffing through their more exaggerated walk than actual technical running, equally as red-faced men with great doughy middles and pale skin and athletic socks with multicolored stripes on the top pulled up extended to their shins plodding along in gray seven-year-old gardening shoes, or those superskinny tall human skeletons with sunken faces and horror eyes like things pulled from the wreckage in micromesh minishorts barely low enough to conceal their genitals galloping along like wind up and down the hills (Little Rocky Run has tremendous hills) like gazelles with an electronic device strapped to their biceps, checking their pulse every mile with a finger to the soft upper throat. The guys who the day just isn't complete for if they don't get a run in. What's the point, he used to think, smirking at them, even getting pretty worked about it. You eat right and kill yourself running around the neighborhood looking like you're about to keel over and everyone sees you sweating and choking on your tongue, spend your life avoiding anything remotely dangerous, move out to a place like this, and you're still fat and one day you'll still die. If I run, he would think, it's to get away from something or to go somewhere. Before today he had the same thing about gyms when he'd pass Life Time Fitness on the way to Lone Star or Ruby Tuesday or taking Christopher to a baseball game or a friend's house in Virginia Run— the half brother to Little Rocky Run. Human gerbils, he'd think, glancing at the people in the wall of windows on the upper floor of the tremendous supergym on the treadmills, seemingly hundreds of them, kidding themselves and running in place, fast as they can, toiling and exerting, going nowhere. Right where they started. —Run, he'd sometimes mutter. —Run you gerbils, run.

But then he was watching Friday's Leno last night (he tapes them if he can't stay up that late) and Noah Wyle from *ER* was on and Tim was thinking how you know he sort of looks like Noah Wyle a little. Noah Wyle was smart and funny and made the crowd laugh with anecdotes about his days as a struggling actor and the way he chatted invited you in, made you mimic his facial expressions from your easy chair. Here was a good-looking wealthy young guy who had his life together, the world in his palm, famous and cool. Just like me, Tim Eucker thought. Well, except for the famous part. But Tim wouldn't want to be famous anyway. He values his privacy too much. But then Noah Wyle casually mentioned, —It makes jogging a lot easier.

In his La-Z-Boy, Tim cocked his head like a puppy.

This morning on the way in to the Pentagon sitting there in his car with DC101 on he looked around at the misery of rush hour as though he had never noticed it before, having to piss from his coffee which he drank from his portable mug, wondering what Noah Wyle was up to at this exact moment, probably curled up between two blondes in his L.A. mansion, not a care in the world, not even owning an alarm clock, nobody makes Noah Wyle wake up until Noah Wyle damn well naturally wakes, and he's probably worn out from the previous day's jog, going to run even farther today, push himself to his limits, when was the last time I pushed myself to my limits? Not since I ate an entire extra-large Meat Lover's pizza from Pizza Hut by myself when Ellen and the kids were at her parents that weekend a few months back, aunt-in-law's funeral or something, some old person croaked, when will I croak, could croak any second, brain aneurysm, blood clot in my leg dislodging, car crash, fire, freak accident, for example a tree could fall on me while I'm mowing the lawn, impossible, no trees, only little saplings still with the sticks and hose holding them up, Noah Wyle doesn't worry about his death, lives life to the fullest every day, if he goes he goes, can grow a beard whenever he wants to also without having to get the permission of an endless chain of command of United States government officials, should start watching *ER*, great show, fantastic, can never stay up all the way through, maybe brew some coffee, Ellen would get mad, not mad, annoyed, bug me about it, why are you making coffee, it's so late, kids staring at me asking me the same thing, why are you making coffee, why are you, why are you you, why are why why, Noah Wyle can drink coffee, can do whatever the hell he wants, drink coffee whenever he feels like it, what makes him so special, didn't join the army for one thing, had to, ROTC, paid for college, good career, travel, honorable, heroic, I'm athletic, I can run too, used to run all the time, Basic, OTS, I can run, I'm an attractive guy, personality for miles, even more attractive than Noah Wyle, I'm a reliable family man, I serve my country, he's a self-absorbed Hollywood hotshot, women don't like that stuff, even more attractive than Noah Wyle if I started running, maybe I'll start running, but just a little though, not go crazy like the human gazelles, not talking about Forrest Gump here, pretty good movie, Jen-ny, stu-pid is as stu-pid does, do it casually, like Noah Wyle, keep it fun, what life's all about, if it's not fun it's not worth doing, half an hour max, what's half an hour, the day's got a million half an hours in it, what's one spent running, after work, lose some weight, get a little toned, more energy, look better, like Noah Wyle, and still be able to drink a beer during *Spin City*, dumb show, don't know why I watch it, Ellen likes it, Michael J. Fox, bet he runs, Alex Keaton, Doc Holliday, great movie, hilarious, maintain my identity, what is my identity, who am I, I am Tim Eucker, what is that, does it mean anything, in the great scheme of things, I am Timothy Edward Eucker, TEE, T-Bone, T-Dawg, the Timster, Tims-terooski, Timsters president Jimmy Hoffa, where is he, cool customer, great friend, Giant Stadium underneath it, freethinker, uproarious sense of humor, immense people skills, a people person, lieutenant colonel in the United States Army, $57,000 a year, whom the men want to be and the women want to be with, has traveled the world, seen a million faces, rocked them all, I'm wanted, I've had some good times man, I could die right now, car could explode, some electrical problem I don't know about because I don't know about cars, can barely change a flat, Noah Wyle, Tim Eucker, who saw Springsteen once in concert, five years ago, no ten years ago no fifteen years ago, Lordy, fourteen, 1984, in Detroit Rock City, Ellen and I, before married, first dating, she flashed him, I put her up on my shoulders and she flashed the Boss, something I think about a lot, when I have a hard time, Springsteen has seen these, Springsteen has seen these, made love in the car on the side of the highway after, Ellen on top, in the driver's seat, the headlights from traffic in her hair, my bottom lip in her teeth, "Dancing in the Dark" tape playing, I can still jog, sculpt the bod a little, still be the Timster who drinks a beer and sometimes stays up for Leno and gets the jokes, plows everyone's driveway on Bluestone Place with his Bobcat compact ultramini bulldozer which he had built to spec, just for the hell of it, because that's the kind of guy he is, fun, out-doorsy, grease monkey, youthful, adventurous Tim T-Bone Eucker: sol-dier, father, husband, man. I'll feel better, have more energy, do the things I've always been meaning to do, join a softball league, run for something, school board, mayor if there's a mayor in Centreville, don't think there is, only Mayor McCheese and he's not going anywhere, won't be a runner, not one of those people for whom running is a lifestyle, running is life the rest is just details, seen those shirts, maybe get one of those, wear while running, those people who run twenty miles a day, look like Holocaust people, mental illness, like drug addiction, I'll be a man who runs, just do it for me, like how Noah Wyle does it just for him, two guys making it through this crazy world, we should meet, a whole new world probably out there that I will discover, the world of endorphins and maxed-out energy level and a full tank of gas in the old libido, I'll be nineteen again, more sex with Ellen, sex drive so high it will make me plan things like weekend getaways, maybe a Springsteen concert, surprise her, then afterward pull over on the side of the road, pop in "Dancing in the Dark," no she won't like that, yell at me, why are you stopping, what are you doing, what's wrong with the car is something wrong with the car? Yeah there's something wrong with the car baby. What, what's wrong with the car? Well, for one thing I'm not screwing your brains out in it. Now we're talking, I'll start running, an hour or two a day, do some hills once or twice a week, sign up for a marathon, half marathon, get a weight set too, start eating better, organic, alfalfa sprouts, won't be long before I'm cranking out eighteen miles easy per run, make it a lifestyle, quit drinking, cold turkey, pour out the unopened Bud Lights in the fridge down the sink, call the kids over to watch, tell them to watch their old man, remember this boys, never forget this, this is something called willpower, imagine how easy life would be if I could run twenty miles without it being a big deal, a trip up the stairs would be nothing, won't need to drive anywhere, just jog places, get rid of the car, save money, jog to work, no more traffic.

He was whistling as he entered the Pentagon this morning, a jogger, the morning of a jogger, a day in the life, he even walked like a long-distance runner, he believed, the legs that had propelled this humble man over hundreds of miles of the earth's terrain, conquering its harshest inhospitalities. The other Pentagon employees he passed were seeing a man who runs. The little Arabian guy or whatever he was at the newsstand listening to the radio beholding the runner. He took the stairs to his floor—no elevator for the runner!—and made the decision as he heaved his way up, plodding like his black officer shoes were made of cement, not to mention to anybody, not his coworkers and certainly not Ellen, what he had decided, recognizing that he has a history of foraying full throttle out of the blue only to burn out with equal spontaneity, which explains the kayak in the basement next to the NordicTrack, and also the Soloflex down there too, and the half dozen or so ab workout doohickeys, and the time he decided to learn how to play the guitar and bought a $7,000 Gibson Les Paul and a vintage Marshall Stack and took one lesson in which he learned how to tiptoe his way through a very dinky version of *Ode to Joy* using just the two littlest strings then never touched the guitar again, it sat in the corner of the living room where he'd set it up until Ellen sold it one day, big fight ensued, or the time all he could talk about was taking up improvisational comedy, how it was going to change his life, that this was his calling he could suddenly see now, what did Ellen think about moving the family to Chicago if he could get a transfer there so he could take lessons at Second City with the goal of joining the cast in time, big fight ensued because she said she didn't want to take the kids out of school and move them for something like that, scoped out retail space around Fairfax County with the idea of starting his own Second City in NoVA, he'd call it Second Second City, unless there were copyright issues, visibly was trying out improv techniques he had read about or heard about somewhere on them at the dinner table, put down a $500 deposit on an improv class in DC, went to two classes, one day stopped talking about it, never mentioned improv comedy again. So this morning he kept his new life to himself, quietly twitched in his cubicle unable to get any work done because all he could think about was running. Routes, regimen, equipment, upcoming races. In the afternoon he was looking up shoes on footlocker.com with a herculean order of work piled up all around him like skyscrapers of paper inanities when Ellen called saying blab la bla about the drain. He got rid of her without mentioning his new life as a runner. He came within one click of purchasing some seriously awesome Sauconies that looked like shoes from the future and cost $219, which indicated that they were state of the art, top of the line, implementing all sorts of science technology he didn't understand to create the ultimate and healthiest running shoe experience, basically a day spa for the instep. But he somehow found the willpower to withhold making the click and closed out the window and turned to the work awaiting him. Cool off, T-Dawg. Make this real. Don't make it just another of your forays. Make it permanent. Legit. Ease into it. You have sneakers already—you can use those for now. *Don't buy anything.*

Half an hour later he found himself in Sports Authority pushing two shopping carts and a handbasket all overflowing with three pairs of shoes including those same Sauconies, three pairs of micromesh ultrahigh running shorts (black, red, and green), two Nike headbands, two pairs of Nike wristbands, two packs of six pairs of athletic socks with multicolored stripes on the top, a pedometer that also tells you the time and tempera-

ture that cost $46, a pace monitor that you strap to your biceps for $39, a
small AM/FM radio you can clip to the waist of your shorts and has head-
phones for $23, a flashlight, a canteen, Oakley sunglasses with UV pro-
tection for $103, four gray Hanes T-shirts and four red ones, a micromesh
long-distance-running tank top with something called moisture protection made by Nike, a hat, two jock straps, three Ace bandages, four rolls
of athletic tape, a can of bug spray, Band-Aids, BenGay and Icy Hot,
baby powder and three sticks of Old Spice High Endurance deodorant
(from the CVS across the street from Sports Authority), suntan lotion,
sunblock, Neosporin, a Denise Austin Power Yoga VHS tape, a crapload
of Gatorade and PowerBars and some gel you're supposed to eat for
energy, granola bars, pocket heat packs, a tub of powder to make protein
shakes from, batteries, a jump rope, boxing gloves, two fifteen-pound
dumbbells, weights you strap around your ankles, a Thigh Master, a new
ab workout doohickey, and on the way home he stopped at the Colonnade on Union Mill Road and went in the Giant there and got two two-
pound bags of carrots, three pineapples, four pounds of potatoes, four
cantaloupes, fifteen apples, a ton of grapes, a Mack truck's fuel capacity of
skim milk, low-fat Jell-O, a small pond's worth of orange juice (no pulp),
more PowerBars and Gatorade, two handfuls of Met-Rx bars, a couple
cases of POWERade in every available flavor in case it was better than
Gatorade, and a whole bunch of other shit he doesn't even remember
picking out, and then he went home.

    He walked out through the garage to his driveway with the radio
clipped to his waist, pace monitor strapped snug around biceps, micromesh
running tank top, headband, wristband, kneepads, shoes, socks jacked
high as they'd go, water bottle in one hand, pedometer clipped to other side
of waist. He started to stretch but his neighbor across the street, Steve
North, the former NFL placekicker who missed the game-winning field
goal in the Super Bowl eight years ago, was mowing his lawn even
though it was dark out. So Tim slunk into the two-car garage and stretched
behind the closed door, waiting until he heard Steve North's mower stop,
waited another few minutes to be sure, and then he was running.
Ephedrine pills, weight-gain powder, vitamins A, B, C, D, and E, a multi-
vitamin: a runner. Running is what it is. Running is the key. He started out
in a sprint, down Bluestone onto South Springs, speeding up whenever he
passed another runner or dog walker, especially if they were female, and
whenever a car passed. Sixteen minutes later he was back in front of his
house on Bluestone, Ellen's Grand Cherokee in the driveway, bent over
with hands on knees and legs tingling and thick white shit hanging from

his lower lip halfway to the ground, spitting and coughing and making a
high-pitched wailing noise.

Ellen opened the front door to see her husband lying there in the
front yard. She walked down the front steps and stood over him and said,
—Did you get Drano?

—Oh. No. Oops. I forgot.

—So you're a runner now?

—I don't know. I thought I'd try it. Nothing serious.

—How'd it go?

—I'm pretty out of shape. I'm just easing in to it. Nothing too hard-
core. Just some light jogging to get the endorphins flowing, you know?

—Nice socks.

—Thank you, they're running socks.

—I can see your genitals.

—You can? Tim said. He didn't move or try to look. He couldn't.

—Please go inside before the neighbors see you or some kids. What
if some kids saw your genitals? Did any children see your genitals, Tim?

—I don't think so. I didn't know they were out.

—They're out. I can see them. Go inside now please. Now. Did you
get my Almond Joy I hope at least?

It was at that moment, nearby, that Grayson Donald kicked the
stepladder away.

DC101—101.1 FM

This music is created in static by people in structures far away from
Northern Virginia with clothing and moralities severely different from
those that wouldn't draw eyes in Northern Virginia, the owners of the
stations—the safety of watching from afar is to put you and people like
you in moods. It is produced not in moods but in adept knowledge of
moods and what triggers them, words and phrasing and intonations and
guitar distortions and cymbals, a tilting of the head at the existence of
states of emotion that neither the music makers nor the music listeners
have experienced. The safety is in tuning in and allowing young loud

rabble who did not go to college to get their degree with tattoos and unwashed clothes to perform things they have created alone in rooms instead of doing their homework, thinking of other songs created by others alone, in rooms, on drugs, in places less clean than NoVA, and somehow less successful, where the listeners could not imagine living or what failings in one's personality or life could lead one to live in such a place, though distantly curious almost enviable of places with pasts and names and mental images that are summoned when mentioned.

Windows up and air-conditioning on, gas tank full with supreme and running smooth from the latest lube, in blue cotton shirt with tie and khakis because you work and that is what is worn to work. The music and fast food and haircut with short sideburns and a goatee trimmed neatly with a Braun electric beard trimmer. Then allow yourself to understand that you are a shared soul. It is there for you to ponder in idleness. You know it means something if you were to think about it hard enough. You consider that some people get this angry or despondent enough to write words like this, and what their lives must be like then, a foreign universe, of pain and the world closing in, to think about ending it all. Then you stop thinking about why people commit suicide because you get to your office parking lot and are looking for one of the good spots right along the sidewalk, which you have had the fortune to obtain only once in your life and still remember it clearly, proudly. You cut off the engine because now is time to exit your car, and the music cuts off in midsong because you must be at work and walk across the lot after bleeping your car locked and glancing back at it, keys jingling in your hand, your car, your life, the NoVA sky.

This is DC101. A safari expedition in an office park that you can whistle along to, there enough so you are able to not care about it.

This is music, the modern sound just before the millennium ends. The representative today of fuck you is DC101. Irreverently disregarding music theory or skill in favor of sleeping late into the afternoon and drinking beers and sleeping with women and being unemployed. Emotion over training. You wish you could understand it. Sometimes—every so often, in your car, going to work and smelling good, imagining rebellion—you think you might.

It lets you feel the spark that is in all of us urging us to drop out and shoot poison into your veins and fuck but without missing work.

Without actually wanting to die.

Music that makes you feel, at a moderate volume.

That you can turn off when you get there.

13762 Bluestone Place— Second Entrance

Christopher Eucker who is eleven woke this morning with the unsired fear that what if he didn't get into Harvard or Yale but ended up at a lowly state college like James Madison University with the mediocre, the possibility was real, something could go wrong, he didn't know what, but what would he do then, stuck in some normal and humdrum life, what if he didn't grow to over six feet tall . . . He stood in the shower he shared with his two brothers using his loofah and Gillette Wild Rain–scented body wash then Vidal Sassoon rejuvenating shampoo and conditioner he had his mother purchase from his stylist at his last appointment, a water-proof AM/FM radio that sticks to the wall, a shower caddy with a mirror on it that he had his mom order from a catalog that came in the mail, and then he plucked his unibrow using the tweezers his mother purchased for him from People's on 29. He and his friends call unibrows fribbles and point at boys and girls such as Sofia Hassan who have hair between their eyebrows and yell at them at random in the cafeteria or hallway, — Fribble! Then he blow-dried his hair and doused it in a heavy amount of Aquanet that he had his mom buy last time she was at Giant, having recently emptied his last can. Spent forty-five minutes trying to decide between the Lakers sweatshirt and the Gap button-down shirt that cost $42. The Lakers sweatshirt cost $58 and this fact has gotten around the entire sixth grade and a good chunk of the fifth grade and even a small number of seventh graders at Rocky Run Intermediate, generating whis-pers of envy and nods of approval on the blacktop and in the gym, orange carpet with the basketball court lines dyed in, where they gathered for an assembly—a magician, or one time there was a guy who had all these keyboard synthesizers that made sounds like cars honking and kids laughing and for Christmas that year Christopher got a $300 Casio with a sound bank of over one hundred different sounds that he played once or twice—mostly scrolling through the different drumbeats and pushing Fill over and over, since he stopped taking piano lessons after the fourth one in favor of the trumpet which he played once and now sits in his closet somewhere underneath an old Rawlings bat bag and a bunch of magician equipment—the Casio now resting upside down along with its accompanying stand and stool in the basement on top of the Soloflex.

The Lakers sweatshirt is not available at Fair Oaks Mall or even Tysons Corner—it is available only from the catalog that came in the mail from which Ellen ordered it after Christopher dog-eared the page and circled it and wrote his size and LAKERS and left it on the kitchen table with a Post-it on it that said *Mom—Can I have this? Thanks.* So it could be assured that as long as he kept the catalog a secret no one else in sixth grade would have or be able to obtain the same one. It's a Starter, a men's large, even though it looks ridiculous on him, like he's the kid in *Big* after he's all of a sudden turned back into a kid again, the bigger the better, like the high school kids, like black people who are the coolest. Starter is a respected brand and the Lakers are a respected team because they have Shaq and Kobe Bryant. But the main problem here this morning was that Christopher couldn't be entirely positive whether he had last worn the sweatshirt last Friday or last Thursday. The difference was paramount. He checked his notebook. He keeps a notebook—a $24.99 hardcover journal that his mom ordered for him from the Scholastic Book Club catalog, from which he always orders the most books in the class—in order to keep track of what garment has been worn and when. It's arranged by the week. He has formatted a page for every week of this school year. This system prevents him from wearing the same thing twice in one week which would bring an inescapable barrage of scorn and humiliation from his friends. Such a slipup would ruin his life. But this morning there was a problem—a discrepancy in the record. There was no listing for LAKERS SWEATSHIRT BY STARTER at all last week. Thus there was panic this morning. He stared at the record for a long time, blinking his eyes, looking away then back again. He must have read it a dozen times. Adding to his anxiety was what might have been a zit above his upper lip, even though he wasn't sure if he was supposed to be getting zits yet since Mr. Jackson said in sex ed class that you don't get zits until you're thirteen, around the same time you get pubes. Christopher was ashamed to report that he did not have a pube yet but was certain he would be the first to get one. Nonetheless he snuck into his mom's bathroom after blow drying and hair spraying and dabbed on concealer to cover the zit up.

He rubbed his Gillette stick deodorant on his chest and in the creases of his elbows then sprayed Polo Sport he had his mom buy at Hecht's at Fair Oaks onto his neck and rubbed it on his face. She was calling for him now to come downstairs to go to school. He threw caution to the wind, closing his eyes and praying as he put the Lakers sweatshirt on, holding the neck hole wide apart with his hands so as to not touch his molded, toxic head. It was still so new that its inside was soft and fuzzy. He hummed along to "Dope Show" by Marilyn Manson playing on DC101 through his triple-decker Samsung stereo with dual tape decks, removable speakers, CD player, and digital bar thing that bounces in rhythm to the music, remote control. It cost $300. He got it for his birthday last year. He checked himself out in the full-length mirror. His jeans pegged. His Champion socks matching. He touched his hair and it crinkled and bounced back. He went downstairs, palms sweating, throat tight, and stood inside the door putting on his Samba Classics.

He didn't sleep beyond a few fitful hours last night. How could he, with the new Gillette Wild Rain body wash hanging so nearby in the bathroom he shares with Brian and Michael, hanging in the shower upside down from the caddy by the hook built into the bottom of the bottle, where he had hung it last night, full and unopened, when his mom brought it home from Giant last night, he was bowled over with joy, he didn't even know this kind existed. It would make him happy. There wasn't a lot in his life he had to look forward to as much as using a new body wash for the first time. The crystal mist, water hitting the bottle, dousing it, small droplets forming on its now glistening surface. The feel of the new shape in his hand. And the first emergence of the substance—the source of all things—coiling onto his loofah, revealing its colors and nature like a newborn, and soaking into the lace, foaming upon his being like the old beard of an ancient sea, a new fragrance going up his olfactories in pinches of hearty pink flower petals, then rinsing the loofah and hanging it by its rope, placing himself beneath the water allowing it to wash him from head to toe of the white ylem that cloaks him, then stepping back, dripping and pink, boy wonder redivivus.

South Springs Drive—
Second Entrance

After dropping the kids off at Twin Lakes Elementary this morning, Ellen Eucker drove a steady 12 mph down South Springs Drive, coming to a complete stop at a stop sign, feeling the need to either pee or eat chocolate, saw a high school boy trudging along the sidewalk in the opposite direction wearing oversized khaki cargo pants and smoking a cigarette. He had the hunched posture that boys get when their bodies grow too fast for their brains. She watched him, her hands on her steering wheel—Why wasn't he in school? Who were his parents? Who taught him how to talk? Jesus, didn't they monitor him? *Doesn't anyone give a damn that he's not in school and smoking cigarettes?*

She made a solemn oath over the cassette playing in her tape deck—the *Footloose* sound track—not to ever let her boys walk in such a manner. Not to let her boys become like this. The sight of smoke billowing from between his fingers, pouring out of his lips, transporting nicotine and spreading cancer. It fueled her alienating abhorrence of this child. It was weak and stupid, just plain stupid, smoking was. Did he think it made him look manly? It didn't. Not to mention it smelled horrible and was otherwise just plain unattractive. She pressed on the gas and idled by, and the boy who looked half asleep glanced over as he exhaled a lungful of nocuous vapor, and they met eyes. His were an abysm, boiling cauldrons of woe. She became frightened looking into them and suffered an intense discomfort that caused her to speed off without further thought, holding her breath, her heart pounding and a coolness spreading throughout her flesh. She exhaled only once she got far enough down South Springs that the boy was out of sight in her rearview mirror from which hung two fuzzy soccer balls. On the back bumper of the Grand Cherokee were several bumper stickers—a powder blue one that said SYA WILDCAT FOOTBALL, a red one that said I LOVE MY TWIN LAKES ELEMENTARY BEARS, one that said I AM PROUD OF MY BOY SCOUT. In the rear window behind the tint was a yellow sign attached via suction cup that said BABY ON BOARD. The Bears is the official mascot of Twin Lakes Elementary, although it's never used beyond the paperback cover of the yearbook produced at the end of each school year, seeing as an elementary school has no sports teams or marching bands, etc. She pulled over along the curb in front of a house on South Springs and searched for her cell phone in her purse resting on the console between the passenger and driver seats that held two Shania Twain CDs, another Garth Brooks, a Faith Hill, Frank Sinatra *Duets*, and U2's latest one still in its plastic, and also a Paula Abdul cassette and the case for the *Footloose* tape and also the sound track for Disney's *The Lion King*. She held the phone thinking who to call, dialed 911, doing—in her mind—the Right Thing, letting the law handle itself, as she has seen them say on *Cops*, a show Tim watches but she hates, and it rang once before they answered and Ellen told them the situation, holding her hand over the mouth of the phone for some reason, speaking her words very slowly and softly like she was tied up in a trunk, said, —There is a boy smoking a cigarette who is not in school. The dispatcher listened then asked her if she was kidding, and when she said no she wasn't, the dispatcher hung up on her.

—Unflippinbelievable, she said aloud to herself, staring at the phone. She called back, using her angry voice, which she reserves for the office of Twin Lakes and her insurance provider, and the dispatcher—this time a different one—said, —911 what's your emergency? And Ellen said that she had just called but she was calling back, you see, is the thing, because she was hung up on, and the dispatcher asked her again what her emergency was and Ellen told her the situation then added, —You know, what if I was being raped and you hung up on me? What if I was being raped?

—*Are* you being raped?

It was a black woman, Ellen could tell. Not that it mattered to her.

—Well, no, but there is a, a *juvenile smoking a cigarette and playing hooky from school!*

—I understand that.

—And he looks . . . Well he's dressed in such a way that is rather antisocial, I'd say. I don't judge people on their looks and I don't mean to sound paranoid or discriminatory because I have an open mind about how people dress. Don't judge a book by its cover. That's my thing. But you just never know in this day and age. You just never know. Especially when people dress in such a way that says they *want* you to think they're trouble. And if he's the type to skip school, I'd say he's trouble enough to be of a concern. What else is he capable of doing if he is capable of just *not going to school*? Is he on drugs? Is he mentally ill? We don't know. Is he impulsive? Does he have no self-control? We don't know. I don't know, I don't think I'm going too far out on a limb when I say this person who obviously has little regard for authority shouldn't be allowed to just wander our community unsupervised like this where there are children playing, for goodness gracious's sake. Who knows what kind of person this is. He gives me the creeps. I'm not judgmental but I have good sense of people and he gives me the creeps. It would be nice if someone were to find out whether or not he's mentally ill and why he's not in school. I'm sure his parents would like to know he's not in school. I know I would. He needs a haircut too. Maybe someone could bring him to a barber. Look, what I'm saying is this person probably needs some help in his life that he's just not getting. He needs to be loved. That's all. And I don't think it's fair to be made to feel afraid because of it. I don't know. All I'm saying is that as a citizen of my community, *I don't feel safe.*

Ellen listened but the dispatcher didn't answer.

—Hello? Hello?

She took the phone away from her head and looked at it then put it back to her head and said, —Hello?

She listened for a moment longer to the silence on the other end then ended the call. She was infuriated, her eyes huge, jaw trembling, teeth grating. She managed to steady her hands long enough to call Tim who didn't answer. Then she called her neighbor across the street, Donna, and told Donna that she didn't have time to explain but to keep her kids (she has a two-year-old and four-year-old, a boy and a girl, respectively) inside and away from windows, and Donna called Sally, who called the other Sally, who called—among others in her book group—Judy Stanley, while Donna pulled the curtains closed and brought her kids to the base-ment of the house whose blueprint matched exactly that of the Euckers' home and watched her kids watching television on the big screen down there and eating Twinkies and Fruit Roll-Ups and remembered one day in college her junior year at Radford when spring had just begun, eating so many shrooms she thought her face was melting off and then later, when she came down enough to believe his penis wasn't an evil enchanted creature from a fantasy world, screwing her boyfriend at the time in her room, letting him put it in her butt even though he'd tried before and she'd always stopped him, and when he pulled out after coming in her butt she shit all over him, herself, the bed, the floor on the way to the bathroom, the bathroom, the floor of the shower, the walls, spending the next four hours as the shrooms tapered off scrubbing her own foul liquid purgaments out of the hallway carpet—which was the same color and texture of the carpet in her finished basement, and is why she always thinks of the episode when she's in the basement—before her roommates got back from going home for the weekend.

Meanwhile while the phone tree's roots snaked and vined outward and back again, Ellen still parked there on the curb on South Springs called 911 a third time and got yet another dispatcher, a white man which Ellen would never admit she was relieved about. Ellen had an abortion her sophomore year of college. It could have been fathered by any of three different men, all Brazilian cooks at restaurants in Ann Arbor. She said now in her angry voice, amped up to the next level, —Excuse me but I have been hung up on twice now and it is unacceptable to just hang up on callers in request of the police service. This is not acceptable and I demand to speak to your supervisor. It is our right as human beings who pay taxes to request police service seeing as how we pay your salaries and—

—You pay taxes? the dispatcher said.

—Yes, I do. My husband is a member of our armed forces.

—Yeah but what about you? What do you do?

—Excuse me, I am a *mother. That* is what I do, thank you very much.

And unbeknownst to Ellen Eucker all three dispatchers she'd spoken to were sitting in the same room in Fairfax leaning back in the metal folding chairs, headsets on, making faces and jerk-off hand motions to each other, stifling laughs. The dispatcher she had now, Jason Lewis, was making a masturbatory gesture with his hand, adding the flourish of pretending to spit in his hand, closing his eyes, and hanging his tongue out of his mouth, the other dispatchers cracking up. Ellen went on. Jason Lewis stopped the gesture and sat up and stirred his coffee. He nodded, furrowing his brow, pretending like a call-in radio shrink to be absolutely fascinated and intrigued as she explained why being a mother was a job. He is a big forty-two-year-old guy with diabetes and a graying beard who was chewing nicotine gum that wasn't helping, a twelve-year dispatching veteran who gets no paid vacation time and benefits that don't help him unless he like gets smeared by a tractor-trailer, makes $23,000 and will never move out of the one-bedroom apartment he rents now above a bunch of MS-13 maniacs off Germantown Road. This was nothing new for him. Another humdrum Monday morning, another fifty-hour week. After a while he cut her off and said, his eyes closed, running a hand down his face, —Okay ma'am, you've convinced me. I have decided to send a patrol unit out there now. We have a unit in the area and we're sending him over. He should be there in about two minutes.

And Ellen said, —*Thank* you, sir.

—We're also sending the National Guard and a couple fighter jets.

She ignored him and hung up and exhaled, made a grunting noise, tossed her phone onto the passenger seat. She drove away from the curb and turned onto Bluestone Place, pulled into her driveway, looking forward to taking a bath to recover and filing a formal complaint with the 911 dispatcher office if there was one. She called Donna and told her it was safe, got out of her car, gave a thumbs-up to Judy Stanley standing on her front porch next door looking concerned, holding an Easton aluminum baseball bat.

While at the door looking for the right key, Ellen suddenly stopped and went back to her car, got in, backed out, and went back to South Springs where she pulled over and waited for the cop car. She figured she'd be needed in some capacity.

After an hour and a half there was no sign of any cop car. She drove around in every entrance to make sure, traversed every street in Little Rocky Run in her Grand Cherokee, and never saw a police car, never saw the boy again whose name, she didn't know, was Grayson Donald.

When she got home she flipped through the yellow pages, looking for a number to call so she could file a complaint. Then she remembered she had a dentist's appointment in forty-five minutes so she forgot about it.

MOTHERS

Mothers in NoVA don't have the time or the energy to worry about what they feed their kids. They do at the beginning. Upon first learning there is a human being growing between their hips the commitment is there to feed them only the best food and limit the amount of TV they watch and make sure they socialize and develop good exercising habits and turn out better than they themselves did.

They think, My baby will grow up without the guilt I have of not being thin enough and being too shy to live the life I want. I will do this right, the new mother thinks, so my baby whom I love will not have to settle for anything in life but will have the power of body and mind to get after what he or she desires. Because I have seen mothers who plop their kid down in front of the TV all day and feed them fast food and soda, which is really just lazy parenting. My own parents, the new mom thinks, didn't have many friends and so I didn't have that social foundation on which to develop my social skills early on but rather I had to work and learn it myself as if it were carpentry, which of course means a lot of mistakes and awkward moments in high school and college and work.

And the new mothers feed their baby healthy at first. They peel cucumbers. They make stir-fry. But it wears them down. The baby keeps crying, is always hungry. The new mother gets to the point where the goal becomes to just shut the kid up no matter what. And so one day, in the minivan, the kid is screaming and crying and throwing a fit because the kid must be fed. The mom can't take it and stops at Burger King and that's it, it's all over. This moment occurs sometime toward the end of the second year when she has already given up on being the fashionable mother she swore she would be. Not like the other moms who look like they just crawled out of bed all the time, with big butts and and zits and short mussed hair. The new mother too by now has belly rolls and a big butt and hasn't been shopping in months. She doesn't care that her hair is a tangled frayed mess. She is able to look past this by saying to herself that the oath she took to keep taking care of herself and not be like the other moms was made in naïveté and self-absorption when she thought how she looked was important. But now that she's had a kid, she tells herself, she knows it's not important, not as much as taking care of the kid is. And so her chapped lips and sweatpants are a sign of maturity and enlightenment almost, in the new mother's view.

Most of what is eaten is eaten for taste with little regard for what it does or doesn't do to the body. The food eaten most often leads to ill mental health and feelings of fatigue. It is processed, an artificial mock-up of real food. It smells like food, looks a bit like food, tastes kinda like food. Good enough. It is cheap and quick and tasty enough to shut your children's mouths.

That which is pleasing to the immediate senses is what is given preference: hamburgers, mustard, salt, sugar, ketchup, grease, goo, glop, shrink-wrapped meatlike substances. Standard brands that are reliable to be tasty and delivered on time with little hassle. Red and blue Domino's, orange and brown Burger King, yellow and red McDonald's, orange and green 7-Eleven.

Little Rocky Run with a car is heaven on earth, a sad flight from discomfort, a devilish dash from suffering. The kids suffer so little they get fat and learn to rely on the brands that fatten them as they grow tired and bored. The food so fast there's too much time left over. They grow up with tummies stuffed and washing machines tumbling the dirt from their clothes and vents pumping cool air and minorities or inbred redneck women from Manassas cleaning their homes, nothing on TV which is a machine to entertain, nothing to do but stare out the window thinking about how there's nothing to do. The most commonly expressed complaint by the children of Northern Virginia is that they are bored. They tell their moms, their brothers, each other. They get so bored they cry. They stomp their feet, demanding something happen. The boredom is so intense it takes shape inside their guts, crawls up their vertebrae, makes them twitch. They hate the carpet, they're so bored. They wake up decades later as overworking, full-scheduled adults, remembering in shivers how bored they would get as children. They take action to ensure they are never bored ever again.

The boredom is part of life and one must learn to deal with it, like they deal with wild bovine mooing in the streets of India. The kids stay horrifically bored into high school. The common complaint becomes that their town sucks. They loathe themselves because they're so comfortable. They watch TV and get depressed, feel inadequate. No one is proud of being from Centreville. If asked, they will say they're from DC. Being from Centreville is shame. It means nothing to say it. They call it Centrehole and talk of how they can't wait to leave. It is fashionable to hate Centreville. If you don't echo the hatred of Centreville when others profess theirs, there is something wrong.

The people of NoVA make many choices in their daily

lives and with food they choose feel good now, feel bad later. The fake food that tastes delicious and fills up the hole in the belly rots the brain until you see sour and are bored, the body tires, you hate yourself for being lazy and fat, too bored to find something to do because whatever you find will be boring and you'll still hate yourself. The blood moves refuse up and down the corpse and the colon heats up and spits. Cells mutate and skin gets soggy and breaks out into zits, your eyes dim, you think only negative, you hate how you sit. You eat when you're not hungry because suddenly you want taste and you get taste for fifteen minutes then you shit it all out in a burning liquid. You have the money to do it without worrying. This is your choice, the deal is complete, it is what you want.

By Grayson Donald

17653 BATTLE ROCK DRIVE— THIRD ENTRANCE

From: snorth7532@earthlink.net
To: gdonald81@yahoo.com
Sent: Monday November 2, 1998 20:17 EST
Subject: RE:

Grayson,

Thank you for the email. Not that I am so hard up for human contact that receiving an email sends me into fits of gratitude. But I acknowledge receipt of your email is more what I mean. We say thank you to mean that. It's a good way to begin a response that you never thought you would get.

I get tons of emails like yours and never answer of course. How do you people get my email address? You all would make fabulous detectives. Or "y'all" is what they say here. You come out of nowhere with information on how to reach me. Is there a secret society of you? An Underground Ex–NFL Placekicker Location Network? The UENPLN? The minds and pens of this culture of ours have the ability to take ordinary men like me and turn us into inflatable masked creatures who stomp around the stratosphere. Then prick a hole in them when it's time and watch them deflate. It's their childish world and people like me are their toys.

To answer your question of, "How did it feel?" I get asked this wherever I go. It's now and has been for the past 7 years of my life become what is said to me by strangers. My inbox right now is full to capacity with emails like yours. My number is unlisted. Yet my voicemail is always filled. Did you think you would get a response? An actual explanation after I haven't said a word to even those ESPN shows who come knocking every month with their black backdrops and symphonic mood music in the background over grainy slow motion replay footage, asking me how did it feel?

Thousands of emails, literally. Word for word exactly like yours. What are the odds today I'd think, What would happen if I picked one of these and responded? The temptation is stronger than you would imagine.

By the way I know the slow motion replay of what you're talking about is why you felt compelled to search me down for answers. You've been influenced. You and I have nothing to do with each other's lives. I have no importance to you. It didn't happen in slow motion in real life. That might be hard for you to believe. I don't remember it in slow motion or in looped footage shot from beneath the goal post, the night sky, the ball sailing just wide. For me, I see it like you would playing that carnival game where you throw a ring around the neck of an empty milk bottle. It's close but bounces off and you smile and say it's rigged then go off and get a hotdog and forget about it.

Not to play it down. It was a tough field goal, you forget—
40-something yards. The slow motion makes it look like a
chip shot. No such thing.

We got paid a lot of money to be in the game in the first
place. If you win, you only get more money. Did you know
that? What is the difference? What changes among the
winner and the loser, really?

How did it feel?

I wasn't some schmuck plucked from the stands to try and
win the Super Bowl with a field goal as time expired. I was a
pro. This was my career and the devotion of my adult
professional life as a man. Imagine having one chance where
you have to succeed or fail in what you do. A culmination of
everything you've worked in your career for. Does it exist?

My muscles were programmed. I didn't have to think. The
hardest part about training yourself to calmly kick an oblong
inflated brown synthetic leather ball through big yellow
sticks 40 yards away in front of 80,000 psychopaths whose
very emotional well-being and self-worth depend on you
not missing (Do you have that at your job?) is training
yourself not to think. Your muscles have memories unto
themselves and you have to let your muscles do what they
remember.

Have you ever stood alone on a great big expanse of grass at
night under lights as 80,000 human beings with their own
romantic heartbreaks and favorite foods who each paid $500
at least to be there screamed at you? Plus they say nearly a
billion more watching you on TV from all over the world—
that's the planet, Grayso baby, not just the country—in their
living rooms where they spend their free time. The big planet
you live on and see pictures of taken from space now turned
inside out and circling around only you? How did it feel?

I mow my lawn at night in the dark in my quiet
neighborhood in the middle of the earth. I make a peanut

butter and jelly sandwich before I take the bottles to the recycling place. All the while I know that I am being thought of by somebody, somewhere, who I have never met and will never meet and where I have never set foot or heard of.

How did it feel?

South Springs Drive— Second Entrance

Smoking is for kids is why—when you're a kid you mistake buying cigarettes and turning the pack over and slapping it and tearing off the cellophane and lighting it and standing outside with smoke coming out of your nostrils and flicking the butt into the street for tough or cool, as an f-you to food health and you think, we'll die anyway one day one way or another so why not enjoy your life now while you still have it? And kids think they look appealingly dirty with a cigarette dangling from their lips as if it's a dangerous or difficult feat to accomplish, standing by yourself spitting at your feet tapping ash and exhaling plumes. They think they look like James Dean. It's a childish thing to do, it turns out. Only children are fooled into believing it's tough or cool while everyone else thinks it's either filthy, pretentious, a waste of money, or a combo of all three. Maturity is realizing no one respects you for smelling like crap and always being out of breath and avoiding anything physically exerting (such as this). Or looking at your watch noticing that it's been two hours since you last had a cigarette which means you must drop everything and slip outside and stand there sucking on cotton and tobacco and who knows what else for ten minutes so you can function. Oh and also stopping at 7-Eleven for smokes every time you leave your house, your face and brand known to Swetmil there behind the counter. Panicking when you realize you have five cigarettes left and it's six o'clock in the evening and you have to put your shoes back on and go back out to the store for cigarettes. Stopping at the ATM to get cash so you can have cash to buy cigarettes. It's a sham, forgery, an ass raping by the tobacco companies who have themselves a perfect product—the product of all products that their customers don't only want but physically and emotionally need to buy and consume and buy more of and will pay whatever price you ask.

Then one day around twenty-three or twenty-four when you live with your girlfriend and are seriously thinking about marriage in the future and for the first time you both finally have jobs in the fields you studied in college, and you've begun getting a haircut once a month and buying new, normal-looking clothes, and are embarrassed at your appearance in your college photos (pretentious and assuming), your real life starting to come into focus, and one day instead of going to 7-Eleven you go into CVS and get a box of nicotine gum. You begin to smell it on smokers and look down at them as weak and postulant juveniles, even the adults, who haven't yet had the life experience of figuring out that smoking is for kids, and that figuring this out is growing up once and for all, part . . . of life . . . and a . . . very important . . . milestone and . . . *fuck* . . . god*damn* . . . I have to just . . . just slow down a bit . . . this hill is a . . . motherfucker . . . a real fucking . . . oh shit, okay . . . that's enough . . . I'm turning around . . . that's enough for the first day . . . turning around and if only I can make it back to my yard before I puke . . . uh-oh here it comes . . . uh-oh, oh boy . . .

THE PATH—FIRST ENTRANCE

There's a path students of Braddock Park High School take in the morning to get to school if they don't drive or live far enough away to take a bus. There is a path they walk on when they are slouched forward with their eyelids swollen and nearly closed, JanSports stuffed beyond capacity with tremendous textbooks and five-subject Mead notebooks, the zippers strained, their spines being pulled into a bow, bent forward from the heft upon their backs like a patrolling military of village peasants lunging onward in servitude. The clothes they wear are oversized and dark, overall conservative, in line with how others dress and expressing nothing about themselves, with intention. Old Navy, J. Crew clearance sale, maybe something from the surf and skate shop in Greenbriar. By high school they have likely grown out of wearing band T-shirts bought at Varsity at Fair Oaks and Jnco jeans with safety pins in them. They wear huge cotton sweaters with a horizontal stripe across the chest, the sleeves hanging down past their thumbs, a garment they can lose themselves within.

There is a path located at the end of Sandstone Court in the First Entrance, the first right of the First Entrance, that hollow small street with the wind shuddering through it over the yellow Dead End sign at its mouth. Sandstone Court runs parallel to Union Mill Road and has three pipe stems, which is when multiple houses share one driveway. Some people in Little Rocky Run call them culs-de-sac. While what others refer to as culs-de-sac are the rounded dead-end parts of streets that end with *Court,* such as Sandstone Court. Small children hear the term cul-de-sack and think it is *soda sack* and their imaginations go skittering off, taking flight with enchanted imagery.

There is a path that takes one from Sandstone Court through a small pinch of woods up to Union Mill Road which one can then cross to Braddock Park High School's sprawling tundra of a parking lot as the sun rises and one's teenage flesh revolts in sour stomach and groggy daze at the inhumanity of being awake and crossing a street at 6:50, 7:00 in the morning. The state of incomprehension never fully goes away the entire day or, for that matter, the year. Or the entire four years of high school. After graduating one looks back at his or her high school years at Braddock Park High School and remembers nothing but the feeling of fighting off sleep while trudging through the darkness, the headlights on Union Mill Road, all the cars stuck in traffic there, other kids with wet hair getting out of their cars in the parking lot and locking their door and closing it and turning to head into the building before stopping, and turning back to the car, and unlocking it, getting their backpack from the backseat, closing it again, locking it. The colors of hair and glimpses of a person's shoes under the desk, a person's backpack ahead of him in the hall. The groggy voices among the tin-can shutting of lockers. Sitting at your desk first period hunched over it, your head in your hand, snoozing. Details fleeting just out of reach, though you had them in your fist once and felt them like a winged creature flapping against the walls.

There is a path that takes one through the pinch of forest, past the small white one-story house inhabited by an Asian family with chickens kept on the side in a caged area that violates the zoning laws not to mention infuriates the Home Owners' Association because of its negative effect on property values. Vegetables grow here. The inescapable smell of manure and compost made of rotten banana peels and old eggshells. The Asian family has a son who is an Americanized Korean named Ryan Kim and is the same age as Grayson Donald and was in his social studies class in eighth grade at Rocky Run Intermediate, was caught in school with a dime of seedy dry grayish-brownish weed, if it could be called that, so his parents sent him to a drug treatment center in Reston where the staff is familiar with receiving patients Ryan Kim's age.

Anyway, there is a path that is in the morning before school and in the immediate aftermath of a school day strictly teenage territory. They accumulate here in small bunches like day laborers blown from the streets. They nod and glance at one another, bum cigarettes, kick at the dirt. It is the path where Grayson Donald goes every morning to meet his friends before school. He drives his parents' 1995 Ford Aspire to Sandstone Court and parks it at the dead end and gets out and walks up the path to his friends who are always there, bleary-eyed and stoned with cigarettes in their fingers—ready to cup them behind their backs if it is a nonteenager approaching—grinning at him as he approaches. On Friday nights in the fall when there's a home game at Braddock Park High School's sizable stadium, stern-faced Little Rocky Runians in glasses and earth-tone L.L. Bean parkas walk with their hands in their pockets alongside their wives with ear-length dyed hair, the beam of their flashlight bobbing, having planned since Monday to bring the flashlight along when they decided that yes they shall go to the game on Friday and they'd better walk because you know how parking and traffic will be, take the path through the woods on Sandstone Court through the darkness, the sound of traffic up ahead and the squawking of the stadium loudspeakers, drums thumping and the tucket of the horns. Cops with flares waving their limbs. The wife nearly tripping over a stump in the middle of the path that teenagers step around any time of day by instinct and kids on bikes steer around. Yelling at her husband ahead of her to *slow down*, Stephen, before she *trips and hurts herself*.

The path begins on Sandstone Court, a paved tongue, roots bulging beneath the dips, divots cracking, chunks splitting, leading between two homes with a larger than average gap between them and leading into the trees where it suddenly stops and turns into dirt. It looks like when they paved it they just took a bucket of tar and just poured it while walking into the woods until the tar ran out and then they stopped and went home.

Little Rocky Run's developers wanted to put a tot lot back there but the zoning board took issue with the proposed location being so close to Union Mill Road and plus the residents who live in those homes, which they purchased partially because there was a pleasant wooded backyard, threatened to throw a proper fit.

After fifteen feet the dirt path splits into two directions—left takes you to Union Mill Road and the other leads into thorns and thickets and lightning-struck trees beneath power lines that are good for sitting upon while surgically emptying a bummed Newport of its tobacco and replacing it with grayish-brownish marijuana-like material.

The path is everything. The path is the town square, a mere couple of yards into a Narnia of privacy, where whispers and smoke are blocked by the tall fences and foliage.

This morning, at 6:50, twenty-five minutes before the second bell, there again gathered five Braddock Park High School students who greeted one another with glances, grumbles, head nods. They smoked cigarettes and stood with their hands in their pockets slouched forward in baggy cargo khakis. Their smiles sordid. Muttering, spitting thick wads of mucus from their throats. The trees around them yellowing and their leaves falling. A deep blue light over all. The air cold. Jeremiah Dutton, Sean Castiglione, Katie Staunton, Andy Stephens, silent and staring Brian Donnelly, and making a rare appearance a girl named Holly Powers who normally rides with the older delinquents and was therefore somehow Brahmin. They were all watching her now stomping the butt of the cigarette she bummed off them with her tennis shoes and unscrewing the cap off a minibottle of Scope, tilting it back, swishing it around, turning and spitting it out into the leaves in a minty splat.

They were self-conscious to have Holly stop here this morning and bum a cigarette and were eager to give her one. But they were cool about it. She rides to school normally in cars driven by wrestlers with beards and Abercrombie who have beards and fight and fuck and get shitfaced at keg parties and sell kids like them dub sacks usually pinched from but what could you say?

Holly Powers went to Twin Lakes Elementary with Sean and Andy and Brian. Andy and Holly sustained a tumultuous thirty-seven-hour romance in fifth grade. They don't really know each other anymore. In the halls they might catch eyes, look away. The way it goes.

Holly left and they wondered what she was doing today, alone and walking among unwashed scoundrels like them.

Five kids who hang out exclusively with one another and hide gravity bongs behind the big air conditioner unit in the backyard and play

Nintendo 64 and listen to melodic hard-core and talk pussy and are virgins. Wondering where the sixth was.

Once Holly left, Jeremiah Dutton, sixteen, smoking a shoddily rolled joint, told Katie she could hit it only if she showed them her tits, joking at first and glancing at Sean, her boyfriend, but then persistent when Katie didn't say fuck you and just reach for the joint. He persisted until it became the rule that from now on if your name was Katie, by dictate of Jeremiah Dutton and the undersigners present hereforth, you had to show your tits in order to be allowed to smoke this joint before school today. Sean stood beside Katie holding a Coke, inhaling a Camel Light, hawking up a loogie and muttering, —Man, fuck you guys . . .

Jeremiah and Sean have been best friends for over seven years. They live on Sandstone Court. Sean has seen Jeremiah's sister's tits. Jeremiah knows this because Sean told him immediately after it happened, with a stoned grin and whispering with goety menace. She was changing in her room next to her uncurtained window that overlooks Jeremiah's driveway where they were all standing that day after school. Jeremiah was inside or something. Everybody else must have been too because Sean was the only one who saw this. He just looked up and there she was in the window, taking off her bra. Completely oblivious. They've always known she's dumb as rocks. She reminds them of Kelly Bundy. Her nipples are huge, Sean attests. Like pepperonis. Sean is half Italian, if that explains that simile. As for the tits themselves, they were magnificent. Everything Sean had ever imagined Jeremiah's sister's tits to be.

She was nineteen, blond, always getting into some guy's expensive-looking car.

A world away from them.

Katie is a year younger than they and this morning smelled to the boys foreign and intoxicating, fascinating and clean. She was the focus, her body and her laugh. As always. She was glad Holly was gone. She vaguely wondered about the absence of Grayson.

Before Jeremiah mentioned Katie's tits, Sean was thinking about how Jeremiah fought a kid named Doug Barrett here on the path after school two months ago—an actual fistfight with everyone gathered around yelling and making bets—because Doug stole Mario Kart from Jeremiah, someone said.

Jeremiah's mom, Linda, was on her way to work on 66, in traffic, with Arrow 94.7—the oldies station—on the radio, a strange news brief featuring Betty Currie, Nicholson Baker, and the Penis of the President of the United States, a news brief she was not paying attention to as she was putting on her lipstick in the rearview mirror and making a call on her cell phone to John Donald whom she would sleep with today in her car in the parking lot outside of her family practice, in between patients. Today was the rare day that she did not have to fight with Jeremiah about refusing to excuse him from school. He is failing four classes and has green eyes and red greasy hair with dandruff-matted chunks covering his eyes and cowlicking over his ears. He looks like a country mouse. He is much younger looking than anyone else and smokes the most weed of all of them. He is self-conscious about his weight even though he's anemically waifish. He looks like a good advertisement for not drinking while pregnant. He plays the most hours of Nintendo 64 by far.

Andy Stephens towers over them all. Andy is the biggest, with a beard already that is both black and auburn while his head hair is black, long, uncombed, hanging in his face, primeval, back at Braddock Park this year after being expelled last year for a year for selling his Ritalin to Ryan Kim during gym class. He had to attend Mountain View as punishment for one year, the alternative school, where Jeremiah's sister—still in the process of getting her GED—goes.

Andy was adopted by devout Mormons who had no fucking idea what they were getting into with Andy. He runs away once a month on average, has been to the rehab place in Reston six times. He's been brought home by cops at 4 AM falling down drunk with squirrel poop in his hair. He's been arrested dressed in Catholic priests' robes stolen from St. John's. He was on the lam this morning and still is. As of tonight he hasn't been to school in three weeks. He was wielding a butterfly knife with his left hand—a nervous tic. He has been sleeping on the tot lot on Springstone Drive next to Twin Lakes Elementary and it's not very comfortable. He thought he might as well see his friends and bum a jack and smoke some weed and, lo and behold, see Katie's tits it turned out.

Andy had in mind that he would go to school as he woke up on the tot lot, stood, and dusted the mulch off himself, change his life, get his shit together, be a better person. Gotta do better in school, he thinks, gotta *go* to school, do my homework, learn to love my parents, be a better person, quit smoking so much, start taking my medicine every day. They're not my parents though. Anybody could have picked me up from the adoption agency and taken me home. What do I owe them? They didn't know me, I could have been anyone. They walked into a room full of babies and pointed to one. They were childless and Mormon and ran out of things to say to each other and wanted a kid. Couldn't conceive, so went out and got one. So here I am, on a playground, birds chirping, keeping quiet, unslept and unshowered. Go to school and when 2:10 comes I'll meet my friends on the path. We'll slap hands and smoke jacks. Put them out before we go down to Jeremiah's. Can't be seen smoking on the streets. Get there and smoke more jacks. Get so fucked up we can't stand. Sit there in Jeremiah's backyard all through the afternoon watching the evening come, listen to music, make up songs, check upstairs for snacks. Play Nintendo 64, yeah, talk about going somewhere where things happen and being somebody, not like here. But first I got to go to school. I'll go to school.

Usually he sleeps in the tunnel thing on the tot lot, the part of the playground that's a little plastic tunnel, but there was water on the bottom of it this time. The tot lot is a couple blocks from his doorstep where his adoptive parents, since adopting Andy, have given birth to three doll-like white healthy blond clean Mormon children who play with dolls and toys quietly and whisper their prayers and read the Book of Mormon and glare at Andy and do the dishes like they are assigned on the chalkboard of chores in the kitchen. Two of them are already on the Junior Olympic track in their gymnastics class. Andy feels dirty and huge in his house, towering over all these excellent little Mormons. He feels like he's in the way. He feels like he will break something. He has never felt as though he really belongs here or anywhere except on the path, with his friends, smoking weed, opening and closing his knife. Inside the tunnel where he sleeps it says in red crayon, written by Robbie Cassell in seventh grade when they were all stoned, BIG RED GAVE ME HEAD. It's true, she did, Andy watched, everyone did. Big Red was a girl known for her abundance of indiscriminatory affection. She was a very popular seventh grader at the time, who has since moved away, leaving a hole and warm soft memories.

Katie moved here last year from somewhere not Northern Virginia. She never knew she could generate such attention from boys. Never considered herself one of the pretty girls. She has freckles on her nose and shoulders and some on her chest, as did Big Red.

Andy Stephens has run away this time because his adoptive mother Abigail with her big ghostly eyes said in her soft religious-calm voice *no* when Andy demanded money from her to buy brass knuckles from the knife store at Fair Oaks. No, she said, not until he vacuumed the welcome mat on the porch outside the front door below the wind chimes and beside the forsythias. He thought that maybe after this cigarette when the rest of them went to school he would walk all the way down to Grayson's house in the Third Entrance and see why he didn't show up but wait he just forgot that idea because he was high after three grav bongs behind Jeremiah's and now this joint.

Katie suddenly looked to her left then her right then pulled her Gap sweatshirt up, and her bra apparently at the same time, showing her tits to her boyfriend of one month one week's friends who like her more than Sean it's becoming clear, for obvious reasons. Jeremiah grabbed the crotch of his huge dark jeans that almost cover his shoes, put a fist in front of his mouth and went, standing on one leg, the other knee pulled up, —Daaaaaaaamn! Those are some *nice* titties!

—Oh-ho shit, Andy guffawed, rubbing his bicolored beard.

Sean was mad but wasn't saying anything. He wasn't sure how to say it, or what his reaction should be verbally. He is captain of the men's varsity diving team and member of the Future Business Leaders of America and a Supreme Court justice in the Student Government who advocates a prom for students with disabilities, in the National Honor Society, and smokes weed nearly as doggedly as Jeremiah and has a 4.0 GPA and a legitimate crew cut and Acutaned face, is friends with a few black kids even though he refers to African Americans in private conversation—mostly because of his mom and his mom's mom, both from South Carolina—as niggers, is generally looked upon as smart and likely to succeed by fellow students and parents. He has no trouble conversing with parents, saying sir and ma'am and helping with groceries of other kids' families if he happens to be at the house. He gets on Jeremiah's ass to go to school and to do his homework and to take showers, but leaves Andy alone. Volunteers for Habitat for Humanity over the summers and proudly shows his blistered hands to his friends as he complains about being so busy and worn out from working so hard. During the school year he is always having to be somewhere and complaining about it. He is transparently proud of being so busy and letting everyone know how busy he is by complaining about it.

Sean Castiglione knows a lot of people due to his ability to be friendly, especially younger girls who look up to him though in an affable broadly funny nonthreatening goofy dadlike kind of way that, alas, no girl between ages fourteen and eighteen finds attractive. Katie doesn't know why she's going out with Sean aside from that he asked her if she would and that she said yes.

He's as short as Katie. His head is too big, his body strangely stumpy. His body reminds her of a toddler pumped with steroids. This makes her giggle to herself sometimes, especially when he preens. He reeks of attention starvation. He shaves his chest and legs and armpits. She's tried her damnedest to be attracted to him. He's a boy who is not like her father. Her father lives in Portland, Oregon, and gave her up without a fight to her mom and has stopped going to AA and is probably drinking again. And she has to sleep on the floor when she visits him and be nice to whatever new girlfriend is there and listen to them late at night in the bedroom trying to be quiet.

Sean is a kid who is going places and is the kind of boyfriend you should have if you want a successful life that goes places, she admits, because life is all about choices as her mom tells her. And you are who you surround yourself with as her mom tells her. Though he is more than a little full of himself, she admits, with his shaved body and always flexing in a pretending-to-be-kidding way and wearing tank tops for the love of God, she thinks, and doing gymnastics moves on cafeteria tables while you're in midconversation with him. And the loud music he and his friends seem to like of people screaming. She doesn't know, Katie has no idea. But she knows enough not to wonder why, as she did what she was doing, thinking that who she really wanted to be here was Grayson Donald, cool air licking her nipples erect, sending a shiver down her spine, as they all looked.

The main concern is having weed. And when they don't have weed, they must get weed. It becomes—when no one they know has any—a source of serious stress. And Jeremiah and Sean have nearly come to blows over it when one or the other can't locate any or doesn't have money or otherwise can't get any weed. They'll even stop playing video games if they have to. Jeremiah's phone in his house bears unmistakable chip marks and dents that come from when one forcibly smashes the receiver into the base, or the kitchen counter, or Jeremiah's little brother's forehead. Who by the way looks almost exactly like Jeremiah, who privately knows he got his ass handed to him by Doug Barrett (who still has his Mario Kart) even though Sean told him that Jeremiah drew blood and that he'd even call it a tie.

Katie has seen many times Sean take four or five massive gravity bong hits then stand up, put on his Mossimo beach volleyball sunglasses with purple mirror lenses, check his watch, then point at Jeremiah saying, —I gotta go to diving then go home and shower and do three hours of advanced calculus then two hours of advanced chemistry and read forty pages for AP history and help my dad clean out the garage and work on my college essays and study for the SATs then sleep for a half hour and get up for school and do it all again. So you'll have to go get that weed.

Then Jeremiah will mutter, not looking away from his game, —Mm-hmm.

—Jeremiah. *Get . . . that . . . weed.* Do you understand me?

—*Okay*.

They were smaller than Jeremiah would have imagined. The tits were. And don't think that he hasn't imagined them. He has. Every night since Katie first showed up on the path after school one day in September when they were all there with a hemp necklace and blue eyes, new bell-bottom jeans, and bashfully inquired if anybody had a cigarette they would be willing to part with, slurring and eyes red rimmed and Grayson got one out to give her first. Truth be told, Jeremiah imagined them quickly this morning between falling out of his bed and tumbling out the front door.

The nipples were brighter, for one thing—the colored part around the actual nipple, Jeremiah doesn't know what you'd call it, not a dark red like in the Cinemax movies late at night but almost orange colored.

And he will never tell anyone that these were the first real-life tits he has ever seen in person. They're *glorious*.

His initial impression is that they're not big. Big titties are good, in Jeremiah's opinion. Other people approve of big titties and will agree with big titties. They weren't what he thought—not like fleshy smooth bronze cantaloupes stuck on top of the chest and hanging high like in the movies. They weren't as, he doesn't know, *defined,* or *emboldened.* Rather they were simply soft freckled rises in the chest. Slightly sloped upward.

He said what he said louder than he meant to and embarrassed himself.

They made him hyper, giddy. They'd been underneath the shirt all this time. A thin piece of fabric kept them covered—a mile between sides of the shirt. The shirt altered the universe. They'd been there in front of him all this time. *Every girl had these.*

My God, tits. In the cold dazed sad morning, like an exotic animal happened upon on a stroll through the woods: *Tits!*

He couldn't wait to tell Grayson that there were tits this morning on the path!

Katie hates her stepfather.

The way his mouth smiles at her while his eyes behind the glasses leer and burn.

She doesn't refer to him as her stepfather, nor his name: he is the Guy My Mom Married.

He's capable of destroying her. Teases her about getting fat though she goes out of her way to puke up most things that find their way down her esophagus. He pinches her waist when she is in the kitchen reaching up into a cupboard on her tippy toes for a glass, shirt riding up a little. And she flinches and says, —Don't . . . , moving away. And he chuckles and says, —Oh Christ, Katie, don't be such a . . .

He never finishes when he says this, and she never knows what she is.

—Whatever, she ends up saying inevitably, and he says, —Whatever, in a Valley Girl voice created to mock her.

He is a man who has nothing to do with her. She is a person and he is a person and that is it. Only that her mother decided to become married to him. What obligation then does she have? He is a stranger living among her. His face, the hairs on his neck. His underwear in the dryer. His stink hanging in the hot wallpaper of the downstairs bathroom. His chair in which she sat after school one day when she came home alone to watch *Saturday Night Live* on Comedy Central and he came home and looked at her in such a withering way, this person sitting in his chair, that when he muttered something about females and walked out of the room she got out of the chair and went upstairs—his stairs—to her room (not her room, it's his room) and lay on her bed facedown listening to *Sgt. Pepper*. He is the man who owns the house in which she and her mother live. A landlord. Who her mother sleeps with. Sometimes when she's alone she goes into their room and looks through their drawers. Touches the bed always nicely made. Her mother looks like an older version of her. They could be sisters. She teaches second grade at Centre Ridge Elementary. With the same way of smirking at men when she talks to them, nudging them with her elbow, whispering in their ears. Yet she is distrustful of them. She tries to screen Katie's friends. When they call the house she demands to know who it is and who they are. Keeping her home on the weekends. Planning outings and chores to facilitate this. Like a family. Katie wanted to scream at her until her face got red and her voice shredded: —WE ARE NOT A FAMILY!

She said in the car once, —I know you dislike him Katie but please try to get along. Please?

She couldn't find a way to tell her mother that the Guy My Mom Married and she would never get along. She decided this the night she was sleepwalking and woke up downstairs in the kitchen, and saw into the living room where the Guy My Mom Married was in his La-Z-Boy, set up facing away from the kitchen, watching porn on the VCR with his hands down his jeans, pumping away furiously . . .

She snuck back upstairs to her room. She wished it was her father's house. She longed for the sounds of him with a strange woman down the hall.

Sean's father is a navy officer. Sean has been groomed to go to the Citadel in Charleston, South Carolina, like his father. His father met his mother while he was a student there. His mother is a flamboyant Southern belle who has sold Mary Kay and Avon door-to-door around the neighborhood and worked in nearly every nail and hair salon in Centreville and now runs a beauty pageant consultation service out of the house on Sandstone Court which looks like one of the model homes, open and painstakingly continuous, with potpourri and pastel decor, like the waiting room to an upscale private mental hospital—professionally domestic. Every holiday she goes nuts. The entire exterior and interior become covered in craft store decor. Even Veterans Day. Last Veterans Day she draped the entire exterior of the home with red, white, and blue sheets of plastic and arranged a loudspeaker on the roof to blast "She's a Grand Old Flag" every fifteen minutes until the police came. Wait till you see what she has in store for this Veterans Day. She says things to Sean's friends when they are there digging through the pantry for Fruit Roll-Ups and Pringles of which she always has an End Days–size stockpile and these chocolate–peanut butter snacks, stuffing them in their mouths and grunting, stoned into savagery. She says these things in such a way that Jeremiah sometimes, usually when intensely stoned, believes she is attracted to him and could in the right situation and with the proper amount of alcohol indeed fuck Sean's mom, not that he ever would want to, her legs mapped with veins and face cracked and caked with powdery makeup—like a man in drag, but she says things in her loud Southern nasally twang like, —Sean was asleep naked in his room the other day and I peeked in and saw his little tiny peepee poking out. Didn't I Sean! Heee heee heee! He had a little stiffy! Did you's Sean! You did! Your little wiener was hard!

She reminds Jeremiah of Dolly Parton–meets–Roseanne from the TV show *Roseanne* that's on weeknights at 5 and 5:30 on TBS or one of the other basic cable stations that show all those reruns and bad movies.

Unfortunately, Jeremiah can tell you, she does not have Dolly Parton's tits. If she did, she would see a whole lot more of Jeremiah Dutton, he can you tell that right now.

She was the first one Jeremiah ever heard say the term *the other day,* he remembers when he and Sean were four or so and Sean's mom said *the other day.*

The other day. I was talking to so-and-so the other day . . .

Katie's stepfather's house is located in the Fourth Entrance, the newest and nicest homes, still practically gleaming from their packaging, the strips of sod still visibly defined, a big and nice home with a faux-brick façade that if you saw it and then saw Katie's stepfather, you would think that this guy has little business living in this house, with his small blue Toyota pickup in the driveway, the bed overloaded with expensive tools and a wooden fence built around the top of the bed, an accordion piece of cardboard in the windshield with a sun-bleached blonde in a bikini on it.

Her mother always takes his side in arguments.

She wouldn't be surprised if he hires illegal immigrants for cheap labor.

He doesn't drink. Not even wine. He keeps alcohol in a liquor cabinet for guests, which he never has. He doesn't smoke. He doesn't like movies. His main hobby is repairing vintage pinball machines, one of which he has in the basement. He finished the basement to resemble a 1950s diner, with booths and a counter and Coca-Cola logos all over the wall, a Betty Boop statue, a vintage jukebox that plays things like "It's My Party and I'll Cry if I Want To" and "Leader of the Pack," etc. It gives her the willies, to be honest. She never goes down there.

Her real father is who introduced her to rock and roll. Led Zeppelin, Jimi Hendrix, Pink Floyd, and her favorite the Beatles. She cranks "I Am the Walrus" and the Guy My Mom Married bangs on her door—not his door, *her* door, *her her her*—and says, —Kate! Turn it down! And she says nothing and since he called her Kate she turns it up even louder. Because it's *her* door, because *she* said so, and it's *her* name and it's *Katie*.

It's like there's always a guy over doing work on the house. Something with the wiring. Installing a security system. That's what it's like. This guy always wandering around.

A home, a family under permanent construction.

His gross, stumpy hands.

She wants to do theater this year. Be friends with the theater kids. Her people. She intends on trying out for the spring musical, whatever it is. Last year it was *Cats* and she chickened out about singing. She believes that maybe she will be an actress. She's hilarious, always cracking the boys up. She can do that thing Mike Myers does in *Wayne's World*, the thing where Cassandra is in bed on the phone and he pulls up his shirt and makes his tummy roll from top to bottom. Slays them every time. When she was a freshman she became a cheerleader because she thought it would be funny. She once came to school dressed in an awesome puke-green old prom dress she found at Salvation Army, with tons of makeup slathered all over her face and carrying a bunch of weeds in her arms like they were flowers and walking around all day like this with this terrify-

ing grin—holding it even through all her classes, including an oral presentation she had to give in psychology—going up to boys she didn't
know and asking them in a shrill, mentally imbalanced voice, —*Will
you be my prom date? Will you be my prom date?*

She burns herself with lighters. She often vomits after she eats. She
doesn't want to, and she knows it's bad, but she does. She loves food. Loves
to eat. But afterward she can only feel it inside of her, rotting in her belly
like poison. She knows of only approximately three girls who—as far as
one can know—do not puke after they eat. She has been in the girls' bathroom at Braddock Park burning herself with a lighter in one of the stalls,
puking at the same time the pretzel with nacho cheese she had for lunch,
drunk from airport minibottles of Wild Turkey she found in and stole from
the Guy My Mom Married's liquor cabinet, listening to the sounds of
Jamie Hertz—popular, big breasts, blond, wearing Abercrombie & Fitch—
puking in the stall next to her, and of Erin Conway—Goth, lesbian,
Mohawk—in the stall on the other side audibly crying as she puked up her
own lunch of spaghetti sliced into inches, while outside other girls—
black girls, Asian girls, stupid girls, smart girls, whores and virgins and fat
and pretty—were banging on all three stall doors, needing to puke up their
lunch before the bell rang.

She came back from summer vacation this year with a basketball pillow stuffed underneath her shirt. The preppy girls freaked until she gave
birth to a basketball in the middle of fifth-period chemistry class.

No one knew this morning Katie was drunk right then off a couple
eye-watering chest-burning chugs from a bottle of Jim Beam from the
liquor cabinet before he dropped her off in front of the school. He didn't
say a word that entire time and did not acknowledge Katie's presence aside
from turning off the radio as soon as she had turned it on. He didn't
respond to her when she asked him what his construction company was
working on now. She woke up this morning feeling like maybe she was
being a brat and was ungrateful and so decided that she would try to make
the effort to get along with him like her mother had begged her to. She also
decided to study more and do better in school and not smoke so much and
be nicer to her mom and generally improve herself in all aspects starting
with her relationship with Sean. All bets were off, all old vows to sadness
were broken—it would be the first day of a newer, better Katie. But the
Guy My Mom Married was ignoring her, so she gave up and got out of the
car in front of school and waited until he drove off then walked away from
the school and across Union Mill Road and down the path. Sure enough
one thing she could depend on was that her new friends and her quote

boyfriend would be there. And they were. Almost all of them. But she couldn't say she expected Grayson to be there anyway.

When she pulled her sweatshirt back down Jeremiah was standing there smiling like a singleton with his eyes half closed, rocking on the balls of his ratty old Nikes. —Nice . . . Then having gotten hold of himself and looking around at his friends and said, —Here's uh my end of the deal. Do it up.

He handed the joint to her and Andy shouted, —Smokity tikkety jabbwawho SHUT YER MOUTH! Then he sang in a choir boy alto, —Now it's time for Katie to smoke weed into her lungs and get stoooonnneeedd!

And everyone laughed. Sean laughed louder than anyone else and stepped in the middle of the circle they formed and took Andy by the shoulders, reaching up and standing nearly on tiptoe, and sang an alto choir boy note with no discernible words before letting go and laughing but no one else laughed and Sean stopped laughing and took the joint Katie was handing to him now, using his two stumpy hands to keep the thing together. He inhaled twice, sharply, and looked at the joint, exhaling through his nose onto it, brows furrowed, and said in tight weed-smoking voice, —Tastes like lemons.

Jeremiah stared grinning then said, —Oh dude did I tell you?

—Yes Jeremiah?

—I didn't tell you?

—What, motherfucker? Sean laughed and looked around but no one else laughed.

—I'm getting a car. I might be getting a car.

Sean leaned back and looked with one eye at Jeremiah. It's a look he learned from watching black men on television. Tilting his head, eyes narrow. *You crazy?* Then looking at Andy like that and pointing at Jeremiah with his thumb and saying, —What the blood's he talking about?

Andy didn't answer.

—My mom said she'd buy me a car if I passed geography, Jeremiah said.

—Oh yeah? Well then yeah you're not getting a car. Sean laughed and licked his fingers and fucked with the joint.

—Fuck you, Jeremiah whispered, watching.

—Miah, you don't go to school. You don't wake up for school. When you go to school you dip out. You have to go to school and stay the whole day and do your homework to pass classes.

—Yeah but why do you think I'm here now though?

—Because you knew if you didn't then I'd come over and smack you in the head until you did.

—No.

—Yes.

—I'm going to school from now on. Every day. No more dipping out. I've got to get my shit together. I'm going to stay after class to catch up and do extra credit. I'm going talk to my teachers to see if I can do extra credit.

—The problem, Jerry, Sean said, —is that your mom enables you. She lets you do whatever you want. You're spoiled.

—Yeah I'm spoiled. Okay. Whatever.

—She calls the office to tell them you're sick just because you don't feel like going to school. You call her at work and say call the school and tell them I'm sick and am staying home and she does.

—I'm here right now. Why are you being such a dick?

—Because I want you to stop being a loser.

—You're being a dick.

—I want you to succeed, Jerry. I also want you to take a bath.

—Fuck you.

—I truly hope you get your car and one day graduate high school. I truly do. But do you know, Jerry Berry, that before you can drive a car you have to have a license first? Do you even know what a driver's license is? You have to actually learn how to drive a car then go down to the DMV and pass a test. Do you know what a DMV is? This isn't a video game. You know that right?

—I'm not retarded, dude. I'm getting it this week. Or next week. I'm quitting smoking too after today.

—You are.

—Yeah.

—Yo, Andy said, —who saw *South Park* last night?

—Rerun, Jeremiah said, glaring at Sean.

—Still though man, Andy said, —it was funny as shit.

Katie cleared her throat before going, —Beefcake!

Andy said, —Oooh shit!

Sean said, —Of course you are, Jerry boy.

—Don't call me Jerry boy, Jeremiah said, making a failed grab at the joint.

—And are you going to start showering every day too I hope, Miah?

—Yeah, he mumbled, running a hand over his greasy head.

—Maybe get a second shirt too. You wear the same shirt every day. That nappy-ass shirt you have on now.

—I'll cut you, Jeremiah grumbled. He had a seven-inch hunting knife in his backpack which had nothing else in it.

—Okay Jeremiah. You'll cut me.

Andy said, —Yo let's dip. Oh wait, never mind.

Katie finished adjusting her bra and cleared her throat and said, —If you want to cut something you should cut your hair.

And Andy threw the roach down because it burned his lip and started punching air and swinging his butterfly knife, kicking a tree, pulling on his face and leaning back and shouting up at the sky, —MAN FUCK ALL YOU MOTHERFUCKERS! I mean, where da blood clot's Grayson at, *man*? Let's go wake him *up*!

Jeremiah muttered, grinning, eyes almost completely closed, —Orthodontist.

Sean said, —Jerry Berry, Grayson doesn't have braces.

Jeremiah thought about this. —Yes he does.

—No he doesn't.

—He doesn't?

—Um, no. He doesn't.

—Oh. I thought he did.

15683 SEQUOIA LANE— TOWN HOUSES

Amy.

Hey Amy?

Amy you awake?

Amy. Ame. Amy.

Hey Amy.

Amy? Amy.

Your eyes are open a little, so I can't tell if you are awake right now and staring at me, waiting for me to continue, or if you are sleeping. Perhaps you're dreaming about being in a contest to see who can keep their eyes open the longest, maybe on a Japanese TV show. If you're awake say hi. It's too early to be sleeping. It's only about seven I think. I'm trying to see the clock on the cable box but it's turned from when I was trying to hook up the DVD/VCR/MiniDisc/cassette/AM-FM radio/MP3 player that I went out after work today to Best Buy and picked up for $3,000. It's Sony which is one reason why it costs so much. But no one else has this, Amy, except for maybe the CEO of Sony and his family. I only got my hands on this one because you know Brian Garrison? His brother was in my unit in Hawaii and Brian is a manager at Best Buy now and ordered one for me special. No one has ever even *heard* of these things, Amy, except for the Japanese, speaking of the Japanese. Do you know what an MP3 is Amy? Ame. You just made a noise but it could have been a sleeping whimper-type noise or a noise of the affirmative regarding knowing what MP3s are or not. It's the music of the future baby in my opinion. Or rather the future of music, I meant to say. I'm a little ... well, not drunk, but ... Babe, I know you think I'm crazy. I know you think that I get too obsessed with technology and will buy whatever new shit they come up with as long as it is expensive and is made by Sony. And I know that I tend to be obsessed with the future of things in general, such as the future of football, how I'm always coming home from my job at the bank with, say, a fucking newspaper, you know, folded back to some story in the *Washington Post* about the latest Redskins free agent acquisition and showing it to you all excited and breathing hard and sometimes chewing on my nails then pacing around the kitchen table as you peruse the article as I proclaim like an old Italian man, *This* guy is the future of *football*! I know I do that and that it usually doesn't turn out to be what I say it is. But you have to understand that I believe it this time, Amy baby. You know I have been thinking of getting into the market, since we are doing so well. Or at least you are. Because, baby, honestly, I'm okay with you having such a good solid well-paying job with full benefits and the prestige of saying that you are a teacher. Even though it's just gym. But how do you think I feel, Amy, having to tell people I am a fucking security guard at a bank? When everyone here is either a lieutenant colonel or an executive of Mobil or CEO of his own consulting firm making so much money, and I get paid fucking minimum wage almost? Or telling people I am in the Army even though I haven't been a soldier for two years now. Do you have any idea what kind of pain that causes me? Would you like a beer, Amy baby? We have Bud Light in the fridge. I went out and got it while you were asleep. I came upstairs from the basement where I was on the Internet and here you were asleep on the couch after another long day teaching gym ... You've been out like a rock for a couple hours, babe. I'd figured I'd let you sleep but, since I couldn't turn the TV on without waking you up, I got bored. Being an educator is hard, huh? Like the Army where they make you get up at fucking four in the morning most days to fucking run through the fucking mud and learn how to repair Humvee engines in the dark in the rain with like no fucking sleep, people shooting at you. That'll take a toll on you, Amy. That'll make you take a nap. But unfortunately being a good soldier doesn't always translate into civilian life.

Baby, I have to tell you something. I think it has to do with why we haven't been intimate in over three months. I know this is terrible, what I'm going to say. You can plug your ears before I say it if you want or, if you're actually awake, you can say shut up now or forever hold your peace. So you've been warned. This is horrible, this is just terrible. I'm going to tell you this only because you're my wife and we can tell each other our most terrible things, right? But, baby, the thing is, ever since I got my discharge papers and started working at the bank, I can't stop these, like, *desires*. Not the kind of desires like what you're thinking. They're desires for bad things to happen. Not just bad things. *Terrible* things. For example, a terrorist attack. See what I mean? Horrible. But do you understand how great a terrorist attack would be for me? Do you understand what I could become if given that kind of chance? I'm nothing right now. I live in a nothing time and that sucks. I'm not a man. And you know what? Every time I watch TV and the show is interrupted by *duh duhn duhn-duhnn duhn!* and then the news guy is suddenly there staring at me very serious shuffling papers and saying to me very solemnly, but he's very excited you can tell, —Please excuse us for breaking in and interrupting Judge Judy here but blah blah blah . . . Well, Amy, every time this happens, babe, I get very tense and very excited because I inevitably hope that this BREAKING NEWS is the *devastating* terrible thing I've been hoping for. I lean forward in my seat and *pray* that a *lot* of fucking people have been killed in a tragic attack by foreign people who hate us. I get an adrenaline rush, Amy, I feel *good*. And when it turns out it's just some senator has croaked, I get really disappointed. That's what I was doing downstairs on the computer. I was hitting Refresh on cnn.com. For three hours. Isn't that absolutely fucking *deranged*?

My secret to you, Amy, is that I would love it if someone nuked us. Did you hear what I said? It would make my fucking life. Every night when I go to sleep and we didn't get nuked that day, I have a serious panic attack, due somewhat partially I think to my social anxiety disorder and mild depression. I toss and turn all night. I pray to God, physically, to please nuke L.A. or New York or Chicago. It has to be an *attack*. Because without an attack what am I? We have history and . . . I don't know . . . I mean, here we are between big famous historic moments like Woodstock, JFK, Vietnam, blah blah blah. The Civil War. The founding of America. Where's our JFK? Why are we important? If we got nuked that would *destroy* JFK, baby. That would *destroy* Vietnam. What do we have, generationally speaking? AIDS? Maybe a hurricane every now and then? Big fucking deal. I hold my breath, Amy, and ask God for the gift of tragedy. It will happen soon, I know it will. I can feel it. I'm not normal. I'm fucked up, aren't I, baby? Even right now, I'm imagining a disaster. You're dying right now. That's what I'm imagining. I'm at your bedside and you're comatose or dying of cancer and I'm here to tell you all sorts of dramatic things. I'm also imagining you were fucking one of your students in the backseat of your car after school today, parked at EC Lawrence Park. Baby? I'm so twisted and disturbed, right? Amy. I think this will make a good chapter in my book, Amy. What do you think? Think I should put it in my book, Ame?

I think about killing myself sometimes, Amy.

Ame? Why are you so tired? Did you go to the gym after school? Amy?

24585 BUNKERS COURT— FOURTH ENTRANCE

John Donald, stinking drunk and holding a Jack on the rocks, the ice rattling in the glass, gets into his 1995 Toyota Tacoma and closes the door and smells the upholstery, is as always pleased by the never-ending freshness of it, and this gives him the strength he desperately needs to face the Home Owners' Association meeting he can't remember how he got on the board of.

He eases out of his long driveway and then goes onto Stonefield then into the Fourth Entrance where the homes become practically estates, planted stark in the ground like landed UFOs. Here he feels weightless, shaky, his brain grasping ahead like two babies' hands.

The experience of Linda Dutton this morning in the backseat of her Explorer—the coffee on her breath, brunette roots showing at the base of her blond hair and her doughy arms, her knees by her ears—had long washed itself from his brain. You see, his brain is so ravaged by alcohol and narcissism that he has become insane, believing that he never speaks to Vicki for the reason that she is never home, and that the reason she is never home is that she is so busy obtaining her doctorate in education. And he has become so insane that he believes he will be married to her forever. And he has become so insane that he believes one day he and his son will understand one another as men. And he has become so insane that he believes he is not sleeping with Linda Dutton, the mother of Grayson's friend Jeremiah. When Jeremiah comes over to the house with Grayson, John says hello from his La-Z-Boy and chats with him as if he has not just been fucking his mother. This morning as he screwed her in her car outside of her practice, he believed himself—like Don Quixote believed himself to be slaying a giant when he was really slashing wine-skins—to be not in a car outside a doctor's office but at home, self-polluting, simply imagining the scenario at hand. Same for all the other women he had screwed over the last decade in his travels with the army before retiring. He had not screwed any of them. He had been faithful to Vicki the whole time. That's how he saw it, literally. Because he wouldn't do that. Let down his family. He was a good person, a Catholic. He wasn't perfect, but he had principles, nobility. Those were things his father did. He hated his father. All his life his father was a specter over his shoulder. His father abandoned the family, got a new one. Left John and his mother impoverished in Wyoming. John went his whole life hating him, not talk-ing to him until his deathbed. He remembered something Faulkner said. He was taught about Faulkner in English class at West Point. They read *As I Lay Dying*. He likes Faulkner. Whenever someone mentions books or authors, he thinks of Faulkner. But what did Faulkner say? he thinks. *There is only one human story and it repeats itself over and over, with more intensity each time.* Something like that. He understands it more and more with each passing year. That's the last book he's read all the way through. He started to read *Angela's Ashes* this summer but stopped after twenty-seven pages. Grayson was there with him when he met his father on his deathbed in California. Not a specter or a demon but a with-ered and sapped little man. Grayson was two years old. Sometimes Grayson looks just like him, and sometimes he looks just like his father.

Yes, one day Grayson will understand him. And he will understand Grayson. They will understand one another.

If his narcissistic need to be in the company of women and to impress the women he is with were cranked up one or two notches, he would be John Hinckley Jr.

He believes in women wearing skirts, he thinks as he drives now through the night, the only car on the road. He also believes in keeping the yard mowed and the right to life and sees the majority of people as either tragically ignorant or disgustingly selfish and self-absorbed, which is why he believes so strongly that abortion should be illegal and thinks of it as the modern-day Holocaust happening right before our eyes and just as we now look back on the Holocaust and can't believe that so many people allowed it to happen simply because it did not directly concern them, or was quote unquote none of their business, so too will the future look back on our age with shock that we did not do enough to stop the slaughter of millions of innocent lives because we were too busy, or it wasn't our business. But not John Donald. He needs to write down all he has done in the pro-life movement so the future will see John Donald *did* do something about the senseless slaughter of millions, even though it was quote unquote none of his business. They will say, Everyone let this happen except John Donald. And he will be held in esteem. A posthumous hero. He will be taught about in history classes both Catholic and secular. Because abortion is the ultimate act of selfishness, he thinks, where a human life (he has scientific stats to prove this once and for all) has to end, a child must die, so that one can enjoy physical pleasure or live as one wishes. That the pro-choicers want to keep it legal to kill someone because they chose to behave irresponsibly is why he gets shakingly irate when he's watching TV and a Hollywood liberal comes on preaching about freedom of choice. If someone is in the room with him, Vicki or Grayson, he'll go, —Oh yeah, asshole?

It makes him sick when he thinks about it, which he does a lot, but more so angry with people for being so dumb. Liberals, he believes, are dumb. Fucking *dumb*.

He believes in shaking hands firmly and in teenage boys playing high school sports and keeping their hair buzzed and being quiet or at least respectful in the presence of adult men and being able to hold a conversation with adult men but without dominating it. He believes in altar boys and male priests and Catholicism and God and Judgment Day and that women should put family first and not make more money than men but are to be flirted with and danced with at weddings while sloshed and made to laugh, especially if they are attractive, and to be pleased, and not to be employed by or ranked below.

He is retired from the United States Army four years one month and duct-tapes his trash cans rather than buying a new one and finds his son's emotional distance and locking himself in his room an act of self-ishness. He's considered removing the bedroom door in order to fix the situation once and for all.

Just like his mother. So sensitive . . .

One day Grayson—when he is grown and has more life experience, paying his own way, with a family of his own—will realize he wasn't as smart now as he thinks he is and will see how much of an oversensitive and arrogant brat he is now and apologize to John over the phone one day on John's birthday for not talking to John more and perhaps then they'll go to Mass together then go out and get drunk and smoke cigars, because another thing John believes in is smoking cigars.

He also believes in picking up your empty Coke cans from the floor of the basement and in placing the remote on top of the television when you turn it off.

He does not believe in consuming pornography as it violates a commandment, though he can't decide which one. He believes in the news and in the liberal media conspiracy. He believes Clinton is an arrogant son of a bitch, thank you very much, not to mention a draft dodger and a liar, a self-absorbed narcissistic bastard liar, with his fat face, and he has been following the Monica Lewinsky thing obsessively from its inception, feeling personal joy with every blow struck by Ken Starr, a hero, and every lie exposed. He squirmed his way out of the Paula Jones thing and the Gennifer Flowers thing, the weasel (by the way, real nice taste in women, *Bubba*!). But they got him this time. Oh, they got him. That isn't something military personnel take lightly, being a draft dodger. Or a liar. John was never in combat but the class ahead of him in West Point all went to Vietnam. He would have gone too if he was in that class. He wouldn't have had a choice. Not that he would have considered weaseling out of his duty as an American, even if he did have a choice. John takes personal offense as a serviceman (retired) to every lie that dickwad tells. In the United States military, John would tell you, truth is paramount. Especially when it concerns the commander in chief of said military. John would advocate at least privately Clinton's assassination on the grounds of treason if it wouldn't ensure that Al friggin' Gore—who is just as worse, whose senator daddy got him a cushy gig as a *photographer* in Vietnam—would then become president and he'd have to look at Tipper and her headbands while Clinton's pink babyface would be enshrined in American history as a martyr.

He believes 97 percent of politicians and newscasters wear hideous terrible ties on TV that need to be commented upon if someone is in the room.

He believes Vicki is cold and manipulating and controlling and self-ish. One reason is that she never laughs at his jokes. Another reason is that she refused to move with him to Italy in 1988 when the army offered him a very prestigious and very highly sought-after assignment there because, in Vicki's words, she didn't want to give up her career or take Grayson out of such a good school system and gamble with one on a military base, plus the psychological effects of taking a seven-year-old boy away from his friends and environment and tossing him into a land where everyone speaks another language. Who knows, it could make him a rapist, she said. And John said that's insane. Man did he want that Italy assignment. But he had his family and husbandly duties and Vicki as his wife had to be pleased or she'd abandon him like his mother emotionally abandoned him (and so he pleased her by going to West Point), so he stayed at the Pentagon pumping the three-hole punch and watching his skin turn yellow, begging for sex from Vicki once every couple of months when he got himself drunk enough in front of the TV and convinced himself the outcome this time would be different—he'd kiss her slow this time, he'd think, pulling himself upstairs, go easy, the way women like, teasing and sensual and all that, but Vicki always said no and now he doesn't even bother.

He parks along the curb outside 24585 Bunkers Court and finishes his beverage. Here the homes have pillars. *Pillars.* What the hell is a pillar *for?* Think Christ had pillars on *his* home? What would *Christ* say if he came down and saw that everyone has *pillars?* He gets out of the truck and goes to the door following the nice brick path leading through the front yard. He admires the path and wishes he had it in his yard. He knocks, Mitzy Hurkle answers holding a glass of wine (surprise, surprise), and he smiles and says hello, she hugs him with one arm, and he hugs her as well, her soft body against him, giving him a bit of a stir in his pants. *Jesus,* he thinks to himself, *really? She must be pushing two hundred pounds.* No surprise though, that thing will move at the slightest female contact, even brushing past an old heifer in the bourbon aisle of the liquor store. She leads him into a clean family room in a home where voices echo. It smells like potpourri and dinner. The furnishings are tasteful and leather. The fridge is stainless steel with that thing in the door that dispenses water and ice, something he has always wished for himself. An island in the middle of the kitchen with a trash compressor in it into which Mitzy

Hurkle throws something away. Mitzy says to make himself comfortable and asks if she can get him anything to drink, he asks for a bourbon, she says they might have that, they have whiskey she thinks, let her check, he doesn't tell her that it's not the same thing, she leaves.

He finds himself on the couch feigning relaxation with his foot atop his denim knee, stretching his arm over the back, giving his neck a back-and-forth roll, producing crunching noises, and then another, drumming his fingers, picking at his beard, looking at the painting on the wall above the new big television of an Indian (excuse me, *Native American*, he thinks, sneering) painted in oil. The, ahem, *Native American* squats over a fire sharpening a tomahawk, a scalp hanging from his belt, a nude squaw watching him work from beneath bearskin. Her boob is visible, which John checks out. There is another painting of a waterfall. This one has a light attached to the wall above it that shines onto the painting. Nice pictures, he thinks. He means that sarcastically in regard to the waterfall and more or less honestly with regard to the *Native American*. He doesn't care much for landscapes, unless they are of Wyoming. Especially when the landscape is in the home of a liberal, like Mitzy Hurkle. He can just see her picking it out at an antiques shop or something, spending thousands of dollars on it, her heart throbbing to the concept of *nature*. Oh *nature, nature*. We must preserve *nature*. The wittle fuzzy-wuzzy animals and the cutesy-wootsy bearsy-wearsies. Mitzy, he thinks—those bears would tear your fucking *head* off if you showed up at their waterfall. Wonders where his bourbon is. He has paintings too in his own family room. They're prints. Not that one can tell the difference. Some in his living room too. He admits that his living room serves little purpose other than housing the expensive furniture he can't remember ever sitting on, and a black piano that he played once the day it was delivered, and a china cabinet with things from his overseas travels. His pictures aren't of wussy waterfalls and *Native Americans* who would probably, by the way, turn ol' Mitzy Hurkle into a fucking *sieve* if she ever sashayed down to their campfire. No, his pictures are of military men—West Point cadets in a line (called *The Long Gray Line*), General Custer kneeling next to a fire the night before the Battle of Little Bighorn like Christ in the Garden of Gethsemane. There's some fucking *art* for you. That's *real* art. He wonders where everyone else is. Checks his watch.

There is also on the wall a framed orange-and-pink retro rock-and-roll bill with curvy psychedelic lettering advertising Eric Clapton and His Band Live at Madison Square Garden April 5, 1971.

—That's real, a voice says. Ed Hurkle, president, Little Rocky Run

Home Owners' Association, steps down into the family room and hands John a glass. —Scotch okay?

—Ah, thanks.

—I wouldn't have thrown that water in there but it's a school night. John says, —Oh, no no.

—It's a great single-malt that is very unique if not a bit elusive. Hopefully that still comes through with the water. I think the water actually enhances the aromas, myself.

—Ah, thank you.

—Cheers.

They clink glasses.

Ed puts a hand on the small of his back and arches it back a little. He nods toward the Clapton bill. —Yup, that's real, all right. One hundred percent vintage. I was there. I went to that. Clapton is God.

—Yeah? John says with cheer. In the moment between Ed's entering the room and now he has remembered that Clinton is going down, they've got him, they're going to impeach him, he won't weasel out of this one, the lying sack of shit, boy wonder *phony*, God bless Ken Starr, God bless the bovine Monica Lewinsky. His mood elevates with great and sudden speed. That waterfall actually is pretty nice. Reminds him of Wyoming. You should see the waterfalls in Wyoming. When he was a boy he and his cousins would jump off them . . . His female cousins the closest thing to sisters he ever had. His problem is he never had sisters . . . Ed has a manila folder in his free hand that he's holding from the open end. Nothing is written on it, the edges are not frayed or bent. The manila folder makes John happy and he looks at it, cocking his head, foot twitching atop his knee, slumped down, his red face fuddled and begrutten. Ed's wearing a forest green turtleneck and Mitzy, publisher and editor in chief of *News on the Run,* has entered now with her wineglass refilled with cabernet sauvignon and sits smiling in the love seat opposite John and John turns his face toward her with his head still cocked, and his eyebrows raised, as though he expects her to speak or is listening to something in the other room.

—Yep, Ed says. —I must have been, oh shit, how old was I, twenty? Was I twenty? Twenty. Twenty years old. He laughs and shakes his head.

—I knew everything, of course. I was dating Mitzy's younger sister, as a matter of fact. We were engaged.

—Ed, Mitzy says.

—It's called candor, Mitzy. I believe in candor. It's only polite. For example, how much weight have you put on since I married you? See? Candor.

Mitzy rolls her eyes at John, and he feels Ed's curse word like a flag-waving stiff, self-conscious. It says, I curse.

He has known the Hurkles since they lived on Moss Glen Road in the First Entrance, when they were parishioners at St. John's, before they stopped going. John has never gotten a straight answer about why, but he holds them in not a small degree of contempt. This is the fourth time John has sat on this couch with Mitzy staring at him while Ed's talked about the Eric Clapton poster and the concert, which he is recounting song by song using his fingers for help as John imagines Mitzy performing fellatio.

—Rock and roll, Ed says. —*That* was *rock and roll*. It was real *music*. *Art*, you know? It was *pure* and competent musically and I don't know. It had *purpose* and *said* something. It was a real magical time. Vietnam and all that. I don't think our kids will ever understand that those times were so different from their time. I still have all my records.

—He does, Mitzy slurs. —He had the storage closet in the basement converted to be absolutely optimal for preserving LPs. It's like a library in there, but of records.

Ed shrugs and says, —It's exactly seventy-six degrees and there are four anti-dust filters cranking full blast around the clock. No moisture or anything. It's absolutely optimal. The *CentreView* wants to do a story on it. I have over two thousand.

—Wow, John says.

—Yeah.

Mitzy goes, —We try to get Brian to listen to them, but you know how that goes.

Ed says, —He didn't live through the magic of our times. It was a magical time. It was.

—Sure, John says, knowing what comes next out of Ed's mouth and mouthing the words along with the tall gray-haired man with a hefty gut:

—They'd rather listen to their own music, which is fine, of course, except for it all comes from ours. I just wish they had some sort of, of, of *perspective* in which to place their gangsta rap and their heavy metal. Some, some, some *context*. Acknowledge its flaws and derivativeness. That's all I ask. It's frustrating. It really is. It makes me *sick*, actually. It's such an angry culture this has become. Bitches and hos. *Murdering* people.

—You can't even understand the *lyrics*, Mitzy says as Ed takes a breath.

—Hearing what comes out of his room sometimes and how he rolls his eyes when I suggest he listen to James Taylor just once.

—I don't even know what Grayson listens to, John says.

—Just once, Ed says. —See what *real* songwriting looks like. Poetry, subtlety. The, the, the *endurability* of the *human spirit*. You know, you love them, you give them all you got, and then they listen to crappy music.

—Noise, John says. —Grayson listens to noise.

—It's *terrible*, Mitzy pleads to John. John's son is hanging from a basketball hoop right now. Ed has chronic back pain and is a civilian engineer for the navy and has been married to Mitzy for thirty years and makes $175,000 a year after taxes. They have a beach house on the Outer Banks in North Carolina where they spend two weeks per summer.

—In seventy-one, John says, —I was a West Point cadet about to graduate and get married and go off to Ranger School.

He pauses to let *that* sink in. He continues:

—I guess I missed the whole sixties thing. We used to beat those kinds of people up. When we'd go into town. We saw Janis Joplin at a bar once. She had a bottle of Southern Comfort in her back pocket and went home with my roommate. He cut off some of her pubic hair when she was sleeping. Probably still has it. Terry Rogers.

Ed smiles when John talks to him, his mouth open a little, head back, a smile John finds irritating and distracting, a pretense at listening, patronizing.

—I liked the Beatles, though, I guess, when I was a kid, I suppose, John Donald says. —Before they got political and grew their beards and started taking drugs and, you know, before they . . .

Ed is staring at John and so is Mitzy, waiting for him to finish, both their faces like that, Ed's head shaking slightly, quick.

— . . . got weird, John says, then quickly sips his beverage.

—But so much *violence*, though, Mitzy says.

—The Beatles were violent? Ed says, cocking an eyebrow and agitating his drink in a gentle circular motion.

—No, well, no, that's not what I meant—

—All we need is love? he says, laughing with incredulity.

—No I know—

—I love you yeah, yeah, yeah?

—Yeah I know but—

—All I am saying is give peace a chance?

—No I know, that's not what I meant, but John Lennon of course *was* murdered now that I think about it.

—Helter Skelter, Ed says, nodding, thinking. —Manson.

—You can't control how some wack job responds to your music, John says.

Mitzy says, —But what I meant though when I said so much violence though was *rap* and all that. I mean, have you heard some of those lyrics they sing? It's absolutely unbe*lievable*.

—Sure, John says. —Shoot people you disagree with and you'll be just like me. Nice way to solve your problems, huh?

—What no one wants to acknowledge, Ed nearly shouts, —is that the first rappers were bluesmen.

—Just the violence though and the *vulgarity*. It's gotten so *bad*, Mitzy says, her wine sloshing in its glass.

Ed reaches toward her elbow. —The rug.

—No I know but where's the line? You know? I really question the value of what's being put into kids' heads. It's *really* gotten *bad*.

John says, —Some minority kid growing up in Southeast DC with parents who aren't married and no positive male influences in his life, idolizing gangbangers. Disrespect women. Use the female body as an object for pleasure. Great message.

Mitzy says, —Though you can barely understand the *lyrics* half the time. They *mumble* and *scream*. Would it *kill* them to *enunciate* and take a *singing* lesson? Half the time you can't even understand what they're *saying*. And half the time they're not even in *tune*.

John says, —There has to be some responsibility.

—Hello? Muddy Waters? Ed says. —Hello? Robert Johnson? Hello? They called it talkin' blues. Rap is just talkin' blues except in talkin' blues they actually played instruments. Though I don't know if Muddy Waters and Robert Johnson themselves actually ever did talkin' blues.

—That kind of, Mitzy says. —Just those kind of . . .

—There has to be some responsibility on the part of these people, John says, and Mitzy furrows her brow with drama and opens her eyes wide and says from the top of her throat, —Yeah!

Ed goes, —Though they could talk about the same things they talk about without being so, so, so *explicit* and *coarse*. Folks, let's face it. They come from places where, excuse me, but sex and, and, and *violence* are very prevalent. These people are very underprivileged and, and, and, *undereducated*. And this is what they see on a daily basis.

John mentally rolls his eyes and thinks, Liberal. He's a liberal. Physically, he nods and makes an affirmative sound with his mouth closed.

—Bluesmen talked about a lot of the same things, Ed says. —Murder. Crime. Sex. Except they did so using subtlety and, and, and, you know, *nuance*. You had to listen and, and, and, *think*, and, and, and, use your *brain*, to understand what they were actually singing *about*. You had to *think*. It required critical *thinking* skills to get it. Ed curls his fingers in the air on either side of his head as he says *get it*. —But otherwise you could just enjoy the tune and dance without being bombarded by vulgarity. That's the art.

—But just some of those lyrics, though, Mitzy says, furrowing her brow and shaking her head, eyes wide.

Mitzy Hurkle, tenth-grade English teacher, South Lakes High School in Reston, expert on Faulkner's *As I Lay Dying* and owner of eighteen Vonnegut first editions (eight alone *Slaughterhouse-Fives*), graduate of University of Wisconsin, writer who hasn't written anything, derider of *Catcher in the Rye* (overrated, melodramatic, in her opinion), taker of Zoloft now after first 80 mg a day of Prozac then double that of Wellbutrin, then a ball-bustingly high dosage of Paxil that got so high she can't remember exactly what it ended up at, then an off-label cocktail of all three all proved ineffectual. Survivor of an early menopause in which she ate an average of four pounds of chocolate a week and cried four—once, seven—times a day and gained fifty-three pounds she hasn't yet found the time to shed. Second chair clarinet Fairfax Symphony Orchestra, cooker of, in her opinion, the most surprisingly mischievous (her words) beef stir-fry in the Mid-Atlantic, devoted watcher of *Antiques Road Show*, an astute and aware collector herself, and of *Oprah*, loyal member of the Book Club. Noticer of lawns on the route from Union Mill Road to Bunkers Court that need mowing, and there are a lot. Here with her husband Ed who once, back when camcorders first came onto the market, taped themselves in their intimate venery. The results were horrifying. Ed after first resistance gave in to her demands that he smash the tape and the camcorder with a Stanley hammer in the basement on a Hefty trash bag used as a mat then carried the bits out to the grill in the backyard and made some VHS barbecue, very very well done. Ed's back is in too bad a shape for any kind of activity like that anymore, even if either one wanted to, which they don't. They're almost fifty, find themselves exhausted at the end of the day, it's not something they have the urge to do anymore. The activity in concept feels like croquet. Fun in theory but in actuality something in which they aren't ever really in the mood to participate. Speaking of which, an expensive set of croquet mallets serves as *very* hot arachnid real estate in the garage. Which speaks well to that analogy. There's also a pool table in the basement, which they also hardly use. Their son Brian uses it more than anyone. You could say he's a pool enthusiast. They're more interested in antiques, food, rearranging their furniture, their retirement funds, and making damned sure Brian keeps knocking his grades out of the park and is prepared for the SATs in six months so he has a shot at Yale or Columbia or at least the University of Virginia on early decision next fall.

Mitzy is really getting impatient for the rest of the HOA to arrive so she can bring up what has been eating away at her since the last meeting here two months ago, which is that Mike Horton over on Foggy Hills Court in the Third Entrance has a *basketball hoop*, one of those Huffy portable Plexiglas backboard pour-water-or-sand-in-the-gray-plastic-base *basketball hoops* on his *curb*, in direct violation of the HOA regulations. And he has boldly ignored all six written requests typed out in Microsoft Word and printed on HOA letterhead on the Hurkles' family computer, with 1,246 pornographic images, JPEGs and GIFs, more than half of which are of Middle Eastern girls who look barely eighteen, buried way down deep in the bowels of the hard drive, and hand-delivered to the Hortons' mailbox by Mitzy herself on her way home from school at 4:00. She knows from thorough surveillance and research that Mike Horton is at work still at 4:00 and Claudia is with the kids at football practice since the last week in August and until the first week in December. The written requests say to move the basketball hoop to the top of his driveway which is where HOA regs explicitly state is the only allowed spot for a basketball hoop, or to remove the hoop entirely, adding as of the fourth request to take down the hideous plastic pink flamingos Mike Horton has stuck in his lawn like a flock of hell precisely, Mitzy Hurkle believes, in order to give Mitzy Hurkle an aneurysm, knowing she drives past his house every day thanks to Lance Hogg (pronounced *hoag*, Lance isn't shy to tell telemarketers who ask for Mr. or Mrs. *Hog*, as in pig). Lance Hogg, Mitzy knows from her sources, idolizes Mike Horton. She knows with the utmost degree of certainty that Lance Hogg—whose wife Donna works under Mitzy on the staff of the *News on the Run* as an ad sales associate—is leaking information about Mitzy's drive-bys to Mike Horton. She is careful to maintain a decent speed and not slow down or look over when passing her recon target, so that if anyone sees her she wants them to think she is someone either with business farther on down the street or is a lost nonresident who made a wrong turn or perhaps is checking out the neighborhood because she's considering moving here.

Mitzy every day at school when she looks up to see it's almost 2:15 and the kids will be gone soon tells herself she will not drive by the house today and will not get herself worked up about Mike Horton today but she somehow before she knows what she's doing always ends up on Foggy Hills Court, coming to like a blackout victim just in time to see the hoop and the flamingos and get stewed. Lance Hogg, Mitzy has learned from Lisa Anderson, Mike Horton's next-door neighbor to the other side, has taken a leave of absence from his job at Mobil to monitor Mitzy's monitoring full-time. He comes out every evening at 6 PM as Mike Horton walks the dog, a golden retriever, past Lance's house and updates him in cryptic covert mutterings about Mitzy Hurkle's latest activity. Lisa Anderson, an HOA board member and staunch Mitzy Hurkle loyalist, found this out from Lance Hogg's cleaning lady whose sister, also a cleaning lady, does the Andersons' house and two other families named Anderson in Little Rocky Run and to whom Lisa Anderson paid $50 for the information. Mitzy had a very vivid dream last night of a portable basketball hoop, adjustable height, a Huffy with a tinted black Plexiglas backboard and a teal-lined bank box, black rim, white net, hobbling after her down an infinite dark cave with Eric Clapton posters on the wet rocky walls and overgrown grass coming through the mucky floor tangling with empty condom wrappers and rejection letters from the admission offices of Yale and Columbia and UVA and even, to her dread, Virginia Tech. She dreamed she fell and was wearing her work clothes, an ankle-length shoulder-padded rayon floral print dress from Hecht's, and the basketball hoop morphed into a veiny black tremendous male sex organ and set forth upon her despite her screams.

—What they don't understand as a matter of fact, Ed is saying, having refreshed all their beverages, filling them all to the rim and not adding water or ice to the single-malts this time, —is that when rock and roll was still *fresh* and music *said* something, the quote *vulgarity* of it, Ed making air quotes around the word *vulgarity*, —that our parents objected to and called the devil's music which my parents by the way never did and I don't know where they got that everyone over the age of twenty-one back then did call it the devil's music. But the, air quotes again, —*vulgarity* that the kids found so exciting and liberating had a, um, you know, *purpose*. How about that? The *vulgarity*, again with the air quotes, —had social implications. It *said* something, damn it.

Mitzy goes, —Not like today.

—No, not like today.

—Now.

—Now it's—

—Yeah, Mitzy says, gesturing toward Ed.

—It says *nothing*.

—Nothing.

—Except what it says.

—Not like ours, Mitzy says. —Ours *said* something.

—Now it's just vulgarity for—

—Vulgarity's sake.

—Right.

—Yeah.

—It's a business now, Ed says. —It's all about money. It's not art. It's not rock and roll even. Rock and roll was art. It was a product of passion and, and, and, not business.

—Not commerce, Mitzy chirps. —*Art*.

—As if life's all about money. Great message to the kids.

He and Mitzy are standing side by side before John who is just watching them in the pose of now almost irreverent relaxation on their leather sectional, which cost $3,000. It blends in nicely with the wallpaper, the sectional. The wallpaper is a calm earth tone with prints of cookie jars and gingerbread men and dried roses and butter churns. There is a vintage microscope on the bookshelf in the corner. Also on the bookshelf are the Vonneguts and three *Great Gatsbys* in paperback, various editions. A bunch of Steinbeck and Hemingway, Alice Walker, four of the same kind of *Invisible Man*, one *Angela's Ashes* in hardcover with the Pulitzer silver thing on it. Plus a plethora of other novels and books. There is an actual butter churn on the floor in the corner and an antique horseshoe set and wagon. All the furniture is dark and the wood is burned looking and looks like it was chopped out of a tree felled yesterday. A very large VHS collection is in a display case beside the TV. An enormous inflatable red exercise ball with same-colored raised latitude lines on it is in the corner.

—In *our* household, Ed says proudly, —we have *full* say over what kind of entertainment is consumed as well as over what kind of activities occur. *That's* the rule. Not to sound like my own father, God rest his soul, but my house, my rules. Thankfully Brian was never interested in the drug thing and knows the importance of academics. You know, they don't want to hear it but you know the fact is there *really* is such a thing as bad influences. If you don't like it, well *excuu-uuuse meeee*! Being a teenager is a *very* impressionable time. We *know* this. We've *been* teenagers.

John drums his fingers, twitches his foot, nods once, looks off at Brian Hurkle's school portrait, framed and large, from it must have been at least five years ago. He looks like his father.

Mitzy says, —Their brains are still developing. Like, physically. Like, the *brain* chemicals.

—Just because it's cool doesn't mean it's necessary. I can't believe I'm saying that but, I mean, when I was seventeen . . .

—You knew everything, John says.

—No, I didn't know everything until I was twenty, Ed says with one finger raised, then laughing and looking at Mitzy. Mitzy kind of smiles. John doesn't laugh. Ed is the only one laughing. His face gets red he laughs so hard. —I didn't know everything until I was *twenty*! He gets hold of himself. —But I'll risk not being cool and disappointing my twenty-year-old self if it means my kids are better for it. So I'm not cool. Oh well! Guess I'll just have to be not cool and be a good, responsible *parent* instead.

—What's cool about drugs and murder? Mitzy says, brows furrowed, eyes wide.

—Sometimes what's cool is actually doing the *not*-cool thing, Ed tells John who sort of nods.

—Someone please tell me, Mitzy says, spilling wine on the rug, —what is so cool about *drugs* and *murder*?

Ed reaches for her elbow. She looks down at the rug. Ed puts down the folder and goes with his drink to the kitchen for paper towels. The other members of the HOA board arrive, all bearing wine and other bottles of calefacients, and the bottles are opened, drinks are poured—Steve North, who smells like freshly cut grass (to Mitzy's approval) and whom John watched cackling from his La-Z-Boy eight years ago as Steve flubbed the most important field goal as of 1998 ever in professional football. No one has ever asked Steve about his playing career though he's been attending these meetings for six years. It is not clear what has brought him to Little Rocky Run. It's like he's in witness protection. He has no known wife, no kids. He lives alone in his big white house. There is a rumor that he was raised in Northern Virginia. But he went to school in North Dakota. His veneer is a fragile stink that keeps everyone away. They hold him in the reverent holiness of the Dalai Lama. Also there is Donnie Warren, also a former NFLer, ex–Washington Redskin, three-time Super Bowl champion, tight end, one of the original Hogs, recently retired at age thirty-six because of his knees and now working part-time as a security guard at Braddock Park High School where his son is a freshman. Donnie

Warren is with his blond wife and is a hulky mustached slab of a guy with all three Super Bowl rings shimmering on his hands. They look like they weigh ten pounds each. One of those rings came against Steve North's team. Tyler Nickerson and Marsha Roman who compete with each other for dominance of the Little Rocky Run real estate market also arrive. And half a dozen other couples. They all stand around the living room drinking, chatting. Ed squats before the great fifty-eight-inch television, trying to get the new DVD player to work, fiddling with its remote, which is a complicated and tiny-buttoned gadget that appears to glow in the dark, the way its buttons are colored. He adjusts his glasses and squints through them and grumbles, —Now hold on just a minute here . . .

Someone says, —DVDs? Those will never last.

Ed says, —No, now, hold on, I wouldn't say that. Wait until you see you the picture. It's perfect clarity.

Mitzy hears from where she is on the other side of the room and shouts, —And you don't have to rewind!

—That's what they said about LaserDisc.

—What's wrong with LaserDisc?

The guests are otherwise quiet and polite, loosening as they imbibe. They chat about their children's performance in soccer and school and agree that reading is more important than it has ever been. They discuss their health and the health of their children. Someone's child has been sick with the flu that has been going around. Jim Manahan on Battle Rock had brain surgery to remove a tumor, someone says she heard. John sits there in the same spot he's been sitting, pretending to be concerned with the sole of his shoe so no one will make eye contact and essay to engage him in conversation. He breathes through his nose and drinks, glancing out of the corners of his eyes at people because he has the feeling he is being talked about. He stinks of booze and looks one hundred percent methystic. But in his insanity he believes he looks comfortable, stately even. A West Pointer. A former Ranger. A man who has trained snipers. An officer. Who overcame the challenges of his impoverished upbringing by a single mother in a rural state to do incredible things with his life. Like Clinton. *Oh God*, not like Clinton. *Not like Clinton.* Clinton's lower lip, Clinton biting it at the podium before a sea of women voters, giving a thumbs-up, Clinton standing beside Hillary that ball-breaking harpy, Clinton getting blown by a twenty-one-year-old in the Oval Office. *Clinton lying. Lying!* Now, now, knock it off, John . . . look cheerful and nice, like the West Point Catholic you are . . . He attempts to assume such a demeanor . . . In his taplashing though he only looks like a dog who's eaten something disagreeable . . . Don't want them to think because he's sitting alone not talking to anybody that he thinks he's better than any of them . . . Want to assert humility . . . They'll think he's a snob . . . He looks around with his eyes half closed, taking a sip of scotch, trying to figure out who among him practices contraception, who voted for Clinton, who's liberal, what the women looked like when they were twenty-one, what they look like getting DOGGYSTYLE FUCKED AND FACIAL . . . He has an incredible urge—almost a need—to say something to get the women worked up . . . Poke fun at them in such a way that it is funny how they react . . . They talk about churches and teachers, homework, college, bikes, Knights of Columbus, youth sports, home improvement projects, weather. John thinks about what he always thinks about among them, which is the cabin in Wyoming, along a river stocked with trout, eighty or a hundred miles from the nearest neighbor, nothing to do but fish and shoot a shotgun out over the water and sit on the porch smoking Swisher Sweets and drinking cheap beer in cans, pissing in the bushes, sitting on the Internet, meeting lonely divorcées and flying them out for romping sleepless weekends then sending them back home, reading newspapers and laughing out loud as he turns the pages, shaking his head, thumbing his nose at the world.

One day. One day soon.

Speaking of the Internet, he needs to check his e-mail. He can feel the buildup of unread messages in his in-box like something sticky on his hands that needs to be washed off. Glances at his watch. It's been over an hour since he left his house. That long already? He becomes overcome with the physical urge to sit before a computer. To adjust the swivel chair and shake the mouse and double-click on the Explorer icon and wait for it to open then type an address into the location bar and then hit Enter and stare as the screen goes white and the status bar appears empty but zooms full as, first, the title of the page shows up at the top of the window and then graphics and text appear—text first, then graphics—blurring into focus, appearing one at a time inch by inch and rearranging themselves, then hitting Stop before the whole page loads because all he needs is the boxes that say Username and Password, filling those with a fluttering of the fingers on the dirty gray-white keyboard, a responsive instinct, muscles trained. Like things crawling up his spine he feels it now, a pressure on both sides of his skull. He must know and see and receive and wait. Fast, now, the immediate.

—What do you think, John? Ed says, nodding toward the TV where a bootleg DVD of *Saving Private Ryan* is beginning in ultrahigh definition, the sound dynamic and textured. Ed obtained the DVD from a CIA field agent in Bangkok he knows from work. John is in the minority here in that he has never seen the movie. As soon as it begins they all start *oohing and aaahing* at the picture and the quality of the film in general. He doesn't think much of Spielberg. Or Hanks. What do they know about war? Bunch of phonies. John doesn't think much of movies in general because all he can see are asshole Hollywood liberals playing make-believe. He watches the screen. War. Forrest Gump pretending to be landing at Normandy. And soldiers are being massacred on the beach, limbs flying off, gunfire, explosions, heads bursting in brain and pink, young soldiers his son Grayson's age just screaming as they die. —This movie is great, Ed says. —Can you believe how great this movie is, John?

Everybody's watching him, and his foot twitches. —No, I can't. Wow.

—Very realistic war footage, huh? Ed says, eyes big, saliva on his lips. —Look at this right here. Right here. Watch. BLAMO! Wow! You're a military guy, aren't you?

—Yup. Yup.

—Marines wasn't it?

—Army. Yeah.

—That's what it's really like, huh.

John realizes that he is the only military man here. Or woman. That makes him some sort of authority.

—You bet, he says. —You bet.

Someone says, —I read they had a whole team of World War II experts and army people consulting. So it looks exactly like you're actually on the beach of Normandy.

—I read that too, someone else says.

—It's a brilliant movie, Ed says. —Watch this. Watch. Here it comes. BOOM! Walked right into that one, huh? Good Lord, look at all those fucking guts. He's *twitching*, isn't he? He's fucking *twitching*!

—Is that his arm or his penis? Mitzy says.

—He's in so much pain he's fucking *twitching*! Ed shouts with glee.

The boomers move closer to the television, crowding around it with their drinks, murmuring with pleasure. They gasp and cheer when another bomb strikes, when more death is given to them, exclaiming at the ruining of flesh and at the woe.

The boomers eventually disperse from their carnage and John says hello now to Jim and Lonnie Gallo, the Gallos, a couple about a decade older than he with two grown daughters, sitting down on the couch

beside him and turned to face him, smiling like televangelists, prepared to
undertake discourse with him. One hundred percent certified, grade-A
cafeteria Catholics. He's witnessed them with his own eyes showing up at
St. John's out of the blue and pilfering donuts from his Coffee and
Donuts without paying.

—So how are you enjoying the retired life? Jim Gallo asks John.

Lonnie says, —It must be nice having nothing to do all day.

John just smiles at them and nods and agrees. He remained sitting
this past Sunday at the 9:30 AM Mass when it was his and Vicki's pew's
turn to rise with piety and stadium-shuffle to the aisle where the usher
stood—Louis Taylor whom John knows from the Knights of Columbus—and stand in line to receive the Body and Blood of Christ. He
averted his eyes and moved his knees so others could shuffle past him,
averting their own eyes and going out of their way to appear as though
they were not judging him—not even noticing him—for not being in the
proper state of grace necessary to be able to receive the Eucharist. It was
shameful. He knows well how shameful it is to not get up for Communion. You stay seated all by your lonesome, the only body in the long
wooden pew, small and solitary, your head bowed and eyes closed as if in
prayer but really hiding yourself because you know that you are screaming to the rest of the congregation that you—YOU—have this week
done something to violate God's law to a degree severe enough to put you
into the state of mortal sin—the worst state one can be in, being stained
in gooey black dung, marked for hell if you were to die before getting to
Confession. It shows that you not only committed this act that you committed but also that you did not go to Confession last evening to confess
it and be forgiven of it. Which would mean that either you are not sorry
enough for committing the act to make the effort to go to Confession and
reconcile the rotten deed or that you committed this horrible act last night
after the hours of Confession, or very early this morning, a Sunday, the
Sabbath, you committed a mortal sin on the Lord's day, which is supposed
to be devoted to the loving and worshipping of God. Perhaps you committed the act even on the way to Mass just now. How repulsive. What
could the act be? you can feel them all wondering. Children staring at you
from across the congregation with their huge unblinking eyes wondering
what you did on the way to Mass just now. And then Vicki and the rest of
the row returning from receiving the Eucharist, their hands folded, and
stadium-shuffling back into the row, John moving his knees again to let
them by, and pulling out the padded kneeler, kneeling, squinting their
eyes shut and moving their lips in prayer. Perhaps adding him to their

order. *And please bless the soul of John Donald for whatever wretched, disgusting act he performed on the way to Mass just now—maybe in his car in the parking lot!—that put him in the state of mortal sin. And protect my children from him too please.* And you suck on your teeth and think about how the crotch of your dress pants makes it look like you have a boner when you sit, but then remember you're supposed to be praying for forgiveness. *Oh my God,* he prayed, *I am heartily sorry for having offended thee. And I detest all my sins because of your just punishments. But most of all because they offend you, my Lord, who are all good and deserving of all my love. I firmly resolve with the help of your grace to*—right then he interrupted himself and opened his eyes. In his madness he could not remember what it was he had supposedly done. What was he asking forgiveness for, exactly? He had done nothing wrong. However, he remembered Catholic school. You have always done something wrong. You should always ask for forgiveness. So he finished his act of contrition. *I firmly resolve with the help of your grace to sin no more and to avoid the near occasion of sin. Amen.* He crossed himself and opened his eyes and looked around, checking out the women.

Often during the day when he has nothing to do he'll be looking out the window and will see the neighbor girl across the street—Lauren Manahan, who just graduated high school last spring—emerging from her front door just as a car pulls into the driveway driven by a girl or boy her age. Down the concrete porch she'll go, often this summer wearing a thin dress with a bikini underneath, over the concrete squares two or three inches apart on a white path of gravel that John watched Jim Manahan lay two springs ago, to the driveway, her ponytail bobbing, smiling and waving as she scampers to the passenger side and stands kind of hopping with her hand on the handle waiting for her friend to unlock it, her teeth and legs and the arch of her back, her thighs. And he will find himself with his hands on the glass of the window, mouth open and eyes unblinking, face smooshed against the glass, fogging it with his breath, groaning, —Oooooohhhh . . .

He's nearly been in accidents driving down Union Mill Road on the way home from talking to an owner of an auto repair shop or used car dealership about placing one of the twenty-five vending machines John purchased after his retirement in their waiting room—his grand post-retirement business idea—so far no one has said yes and there are twenty-five vending machines sitting in the garage as well as dozens of boxes of candy bars and bags of chips, which Vicki steals and eats—because the Braddock Park High School girls' cross-country team will come frolicking down the bike path out of nowhere in a sudden glittering horde, impossible for John to look away from.

It's their bodies. Something about a female body. A young female body. Not young like little girls or anything like that but biologically appropriate young women of legal age. Like a switch gets flipped. It makes him happy. He can't look away from it. Even older women. As long as they are beautiful. Like Linda Dutton. Not like Mitzy Hurkle or the majority of the women in Little Rocky Run, Vicki sure as hell included. Their bodies baned by motherhood, spoiled by gravity, their flesh hardened by their cold neuroticism, their voices callow and mean, without humor, all their hair chopped off, their insides scraped, voices raspy and deep, veins on the top of their hands, the bottom of their arms wobbly, always frowning, wrung dry, achy, eyes expressionless and bloodshot. He sees them as men with breasts, more or less, their penises inverted into vaginas that are then dried up, dressed in clothes from the women's department, answering to women's names, yelling at John to take out the trash.

In the manila folder are applications to be the second owners and residents of the newly vacant home on Stonefield Drive in the Third Entrance (divorce), being handled by Tyler Nickerson after very tense negotiations and late-night sweaty backroom dealings that serve as a landmark for how far real estate agents are willing to go. There is a process for buying a house in Little Rocky Run and it involves more than putting down a payment and getting a mortgage and signing something—you have to also fill out an application the size, Mitzy has noticed and remarked upon to nobody, of a standard public state university application, but instead of an essay about a time you had to persevere or something, you have to write an essay on why your family is right for Little Rocky Run, one thousand words maximum, and which no one on the association can remember actually reading.

There are spots on the ten-page form to fill in the family's religious denomination and income—fill in the bubble next to your range, and the list ranges from $15,000–$25,000 to over $100,000. Most submitted applications arrive with the highest range bubbled in—what sports the kids play and how old they are and where the parents graduated from, with what degrees, in what, what kind of lawn mower they have, any carpentry skills the husband possesses (this is a trick—leave this one blank or write N/A), etc.—like a super job application.

Stapled to the top page of the stack that makes up the application is a

Polaroid of the family taken by the realtor's assistant when the realtor showed the family the house.

Also applications include pictures and copies of registrations and maintenance histories of any of the applicants' cars, and printed-out background checks and descriptions and vet histories of pets, plus notes made by, for example, Tyler Nickerson's assistant about the overall *feel* and vibe of the family and how they smell, dress, anything they might have said or were overheard saying that in the assistant's mind raised a red flag, such as one rejected family three or four years ago who were a lock for a yet-to-be-built house on Laurel Rock in the Fourth Entrance whose wife/mother the assistant witnessed whisper to the husband/ father on the way back to Tyler's car after the walk-through, —The front yard right there would be a perfect place for the statue.

Today there are six applications for consideration. John Donald is looking through them along with everyone else. He's starting to suffer the effects of Internet porn withdrawal. He's twitching, fiending. But he's holding up. They examine each one the way people look at pictures of someone else's vacation. John's leaning toward going with this one he has in his hands now, the . . . Gershwins, it says. The father, it says, is a lieu-tenant colonel in the army coming from Germany for a Pentagon assign-ment. Poor son of a bitch, John thinks happily. And the father filled out the application judging from the handwriting, which, blocky and childlike, John is pleased to see, looks very much like John's. He used a blue pen too, which gets extra points from John because John likes blue ink better than black. It says this man is a Republican ("die-hard" it says, quotes and underline his). He doesn't look taller or much better-looking than John, which John likes. Nor does he have any noticeable traits that suggest a high level of arrogance or selfishness, which John also likes. His wife has a nice little body, he can see from the Polaroid. Good tits, bright smile, blond. He wants to meet her, make her like him, fuck her. The daughter looks seventeen or so. She is blond too, a prettier version of her mother. He wants her to laugh at his jokes, like him, think fondly of him. The son is twelve or thirteen and has a sane haircut and his shirt's tucked in. He is smiling broadly with the oblivious do-good glow of a private school boy, Catholic school John hopes, maybe, and he gets giddy here, even an altar boy perhaps.

He's thinking up possible scenarios in which he could pork the wife, whose name he sees is Jane. That's the only negative point earned so far because the name Jane reminds him of Jane Fonda. Hanoi Jane. Sworn enemy of West Pointers in the late 1960s. In moments of particular irritability, he still gets visions of her on the tank with the Viet Cong. He wonders if this Jane has an e-mail address and how he can get hold of it. He's brought up that the applications need to include a space for an e-mail address in this day and age—so he can send women like Jane e-mails so that they can like him and perhaps become attracted to him and let him fuck them—to no result. He stores the mental image of Jane and her tits for later, passes the application along, and gets the next one. Total nightmare. A white guy who looks like a game show host, soft and obviously not military and most likely fucking *Presbyterian* or something. And, to his utter dismay, the wife is *black* and not even all that attractive (as if, John thinks, black women can be very attractive). And *no fucking kids. No kids.* He passes it on almost immediately to the Gallos. He does the same with the rest of the applications passed his way, without looking at them. He is starting to sweat. His throat dry and constricting.

When they vote, everyone's eyes closed, John raises his shaking hand for the Gershwins, peeking by barely opening his lids to see that everyone else is also raising their hands. No one else is peeking, he is relieved to see. The prospect gives him a full-blown erection as he thinks about helping Jane and daughter move in and fucking the daughter from behind in the moving truck while Erin eats Jane and then blowing his load all over both their faces as they kneel before him, playing with their tits, cheek to cheek, then eating his come off one another's face. He's chewing on the inside of his mouth by now, scraping his fingernails on his palm, tapping his foot, and he can't quite think of anything but he *has* to get home immediately and open Explorer and check his e-mail and then cnn.com and then TeenAnalJizzQueens.com. He *needs* to sit in the chair, he *has* to have his hands hovering over the keyboard, watch the pages load the status bar fill, he *needs* to ejaculate, he *needs* to go *home.*

He stands to leave, waving a general good-bye to the room. —Aw, you're leaving? Lonnie Gallo says.

—Yeah, better go now before Mitzy gets me as drunk as she is.

Lonnie smiles and he laughs and looks over at Mitzy to see her enjoy his joke too but she is not laughing, nor is she even looking at him. Oh fucking great. Pissed her off. Now she's going to punish me by pretending to ignore me. Even though in truth Mitzy between the din of the room and her conversation with Donnie Warren did not hear him, nor is she aware—in her intoxication—that he has even gotten up to leave. John Donald is not on her radar whatsoever. He kind of shrugs at Lonnie as though he is helpless. Then he calls to Mitzy over the chatter of the room in a faux-petulant tone, like a boy being forced to apologize for stealing a candy bar, —Sorry *Mitzy*. Just kidding *Mitzy*. But she still doesn't look at him. John shrugs again at Lonnie. —Well, I tried. Tell her I'm sorry but, Gad, reacting this way to a little joke is very, very silly.

Lonnie smiles and waves and watches John turn back to Mitzy once more, turn to the Gallos, shrug again, then go, turning once he is gone to her husband Jim and saying to him, —Did you get any of that?

—What?

—What was he saying?

—Hmm? I don't know. Couldn't hear.

It's profoundly difficult for John to tear himself away from the situation in the shambles in which he believes he has left it, but his addiction drives him to speed-walk out of the house and through the front yard to his truck which he gets into and drives home, going forty-five the whole way through the streets of Little Rocky Run, laughing with disbelieving frustration at Mitzy Hurkle and her lack of humor and oversensitivity. Parks his truck in the right side of the garage, goes inside, puts his keys on the table, and pours a drink so fast he gets bourbon all over his hand. Wipes it on his jeans and nearly breaks his neck on the dog who is standing under his feet, says fucking hell dog, and bounds up the stairs two at a time then past Grayson's room where the light is off now and the music is silent and door open, a black abyss, a note on the made bed folded once and unread. John doesn't look in but keeps going, sprinting now, to the computer room where he uses his hands to pull himself through and collapses into the swivel chair and shakes the mouse frantically until the screen comes to life with a quiet hum. He octuple-clicks on the Explorer icon until it opens into a white window and he's biting his knuckle and making weeping noises, stomping his foot, using his fist to hit the thin drawer that slides out for the keyboard but not hard enough to break it. Doesn't connect to the home page, gets an error screen instead, PAGE CANNOT BE DISPLAYED, a dog-eared square with a lowercase *i* in it, and below that it says, *The page you are looking for is currently unavailable . . .* , then beneath that a column of unhelpful tips that he ignores and blue underlined links that lead to no cure, hits Refresh, nothing, hits it again, nothing, hits F5 which refreshes the page, nothing, and each time the screen blinks but nothing changes, the PAGE CANNOT BE DISPLAYED, his face blank like a monkey hitting F5 on automatic, rapid-fire, smashing the key, face blank and two and a half inches from the monitor, colors blurring and dust particles individual and his eyebrows standing up and reaching for the static, a field of invisible hair that coats the screen. Checks the cable modem, all lights are on.

Unplugs the thing that resembles an oversized phone jack and plugs it back in, unplugs the plug in the back of the computer and plugs it back in, reboots and waits seven minutes for it to completely load up and tries again to the same result, cursing under his breath, nearly in tears, heart pounding and tongue twitching in his mouth, feeling like a little boy and breathing hard through his nose, covers his face with his hands and lets out a crazed but subdued screech and whines into his palms, —Nothing in this house ever fucking *works*.

John feels bad for offending her, but is it his problem that she misrepresented herself as someone who can take such jokes in stride? No, *his* problem is that he did not grow up with sisters. Now he wishes he had. It would have taught him how to deal with women. It's silly for her to react like that. He's disappointed in her. He knew she's a goofy liberal, but honestly. This aligns her in his mind with all humorless people on earth—the majority of them, really—such as Vicki for example, and Grayson who can be exactly like his mother. At least as sensitive. More so. What weird people they all are. He doesn't get them. He never will. All their neuroses and hang-ups. He wasn't trying to piss Mitzy off. In fact, he was using a version of Mitzy's own self-description. Earlier she said something about feeling woozy when Ed offered her another refill. He was just trying to make her laugh, or at last get a reaction from her. At least Lonnie Gallo responded appropriately. That woman is a gift. She brings people together. She is a sister. Sisters are priceless. Life is short, and this all seems so stupid to him. But if Mitzy wants to be a drama queen and cease contact like this, then fine—he'll oblige her. They won't talk. They'll ignore each other. He'll stop going to HOA meetings. What choice does he have?

He checked Explorer again but still no connection. He went downstairs for another bourbon and came back, sat in the chair staring at the screen, his rage exacerbated.

24585 Bunkers Court— Fourth Entrance

Brian Hurkle lay horizontal on the couch in the basement of his home on Bunkers Court, HOA meeting under way upstairs, skinny but hairy legs crossed, white socks, hand down the front of his khaki cargo shorts that he wears around the house no matter the temperature or season, phone to ear, head turned to the large television tuned to MTV where the *Tom Green Show* was on, Tom Green riding a cow through a grocery store, remote on Brian's chest, a couple empty Coke cans on the floor. Beside the glossy wood entertainment center housing the large TV and surround system and DVD and VCR and CD player was an overstuffed, unopened navy blue Eastpak weighing around forty-eight pounds with the decorative brown leather diamonds. Brian's socked toes curled and the cordless phone's antennas poking awkwardly into the long skinny small cushion that goes against either armrest on a couch that he uses as a pillow. 7:17 PM. Ate just enough baked ziti upstairs with his parents Ed and Mitzy to satisfy his familial obligations toward the 6 PM family dinner. His parents—his mom especially—are total Nazis about sitting down together as a family for dinner at 6 PM every night. Brian Hurkle hates baked ziti and barely ate any because he wasn't hungry. Mom ended up throwing away half the pan of ziti afterward. He had the sightless eyes of a phone talker now, the mindless grin of a person speaking to someone who isn't there. He was saying, —Uh-huh . . . yup . . . yeah . . . uh-huh . . . yeah . . . okay . . . no . . . yeah . . . uh-huh . . . I love you too, babe . . . uh-huh . . .

The basement is carpeted wall to wall with a thin brown carpet and finished with white blank walls, a single big room save for the square white support pillars in the middle and a bathroom in the corner and the door to his father's record humidor. Also in the basement is an all-in-one home gym that resembles a killer android at the end of the movie when it has been blown up but still lives and is chasing after the battered hero and the hero's battered love interest, with a butterfly press and a pull-down bar, and leg thing, etc., etc., padded seats and backs and spongy handles on the bars, all working off the stack of sliced metal weights in the middle, unused from the looks of it, and a blue fitness ball and a couple jump ropes, a punching bag hanging from the ceiling, a Thigh Master and free weights of a variety of sizes and a bench press, chewed-up Nerf footballs, a non-functional put-it-together-yourself miniature electric race car track with stickers that make it glow in the dark, a bucket of old action figures, a Nerf bow and arrow without any arrows, a deflated Pogo Ball, an aerobic trampoline upside down with a hole in it, a plastic Redskins helmet for a kid, an old AM/FM cassette radio, springy grip handles for exercising your hand, an old TV with a UHF dial, junk strewn about, and lingering reminders of vows to change and improve that vanished with the purchase.

A pool table in perfect condition and straight shiny sticks lined up in a complete perfect row on the wall rack, three chalk cubes on its little shelf, balls in a triangle on the felt over the little dot, polished and unscuffed and all numbers facing up and in stripe-solid-stripe-solid order, eight ball in the middle. After school today Brian Hurkle who is in the same precalc class as Grayson Donald (Ms. Meade, first period Mondays, Wednesdays, and Fridays) at around 2:30 engaged in fervent gynics with his girlfriend Havva here on the table. This was a blatant violation of the strict rules set by Ed about how to use the pool table. Ed cherishes objects and religiously adheres to their correct usage and maintenance. Havva's bare fanny over the side pocket leaving a red circle on her lower left cheek would be an example of *incorrect* usage of the pool table. Both naked with socks on and seventeen years old and red faced, listening for the sound of the electric garage doors rumbling to life above them. Then on the weight bench for a little while. Then on the floor with her head on a stuffed Pluto. He came and got off her and hobbled bare-assed into the bathroom where he flushed the rubber and wiped off with toilet paper as she wandered over to the couch to change the channel because it was *Win Ben Stein's Money* and she doesn't like that show. Though she was cold she didn't pull the knit blanket draped over the back of the couch over her. She lay there smiling at him when he came back out, patting the space beside her. He smiled back and slid into the small space and felt agitated and irritable as she wrapped her legs around him, feeling a scratchy wetness on his hip, her breath on his neck. The agitated and annoyed feeling didn't go away until she finally got dressed and went home before her parents got mad, and he as always pretended to be sad and pout which she liked.

There was a test today in precalc, a pretty big test, and Grayson Donald wasn't there, which Brian Hurkle noticed because Grayson Donald sits in front of him and sometimes during tests Brian can see Grayson's paper over his shoulder and as Brian Hurkle finishes way early he likes to then after coming back from Ms. Meade's desk to turn his test in keep himself occupied by looking at Grayson's test and seeing how many answers Grayson's getting wrong that Brian Hurkle knows he himself got right.

Sometimes he watches as Grayson writes the correct answer then, before turning in the test, goes back and erases it and writes an incorrect answer, goes back through his work and alters it in order to appear like he has made common, easy mistakes.

But now the feeling was back. Tonight was another night, the same as every night since after school back in April when he first asked her out and she said yes and she became his girlfriend. Then followed a month of official going out in which they accomplished first the make out, then the bra off, then him touching her you know what, then, the next week, her touching his you know who, then her going down on him, then him going down on her, culminating in her not saying no when he whispered in her ear on the same couch, just as naked, a blue spring day fresh as daisies, —I have a condom if you want to.

She didn't immediately say no, didn't stop him from getting the condom out of his backpack then opening it and rolling it on just like he'd practiced and prying her legs open and bracing himself over her and sticking it in. He lasted a couple of seconds and when he got back from the bathroom as the toilet chortled she had a pen, told him to come here, wrote *I love you* on his chest, around his right nipple.

The second time, a week later, was somehow more flobbing, more quickly culminated, and overall more embarrassing than the first time. For the third time, the next week, Havva heard from her friend Dawne that you're supposed to use lotion and it's better, and so Havva pulled a tube from her purse after he rolled on the already spermicidally lubricated Life Styles and slathered kiwi-apple-scented Bed Bath & Beyond pinkish lotion over his jacketed member before he proceeded. This resulted in a nasty chunky cheeselike infection that brought Havva to the gynecologist where she was told very nicely about something called K-Y Jelly. That third time Brian Hurkle remembers looking up at the mirror that hangs over the pool table his father bought two years ago for five grand and seeing himself between the thighs of a girl, an actual naked *female*, holy shit, and he gave his wide-eyed flush-cheeked reflection a thumbs-up and mouthed to it, Oh my God I am having *sex* right now!

—What are you doing? she said right now in his ear over the phone, a Persian girl. Glamorous and fashionable. Big tits, nice ass. It took three months of very dedicated pursuit and perseverance to close the deal on

her. The pursuit included a lot of similar phone calls and walking with
her and her annoying friends to class, going fucking roller skating with
them for God's sake, etc. They met in Spanish class. Brian sees himself, a
3.9 student with four AP classes and Student Life editor of the yearbook
and a pretty good member of the cross-country team and capable lifeguard in the summer and who wears J. Crew and has a good haircut and
works a cash register at Galyan's—a two-story sporting goods store in
Fair Lakes that has a rock wall—as someone with uncommon intelligence, superior breeding, good looks, and better luck. Someone who can
bullshit a history essay and still get a low A and who can work his parents to let him stay out past curfew. He is someone who sees what he
wants and has the skills and know-how to obtain it, is how he sees himself. He went to Buffet this summer. He is popular enough but still gets
along with Goth and punk kids. He gets along with everybody. He likes
punk rock, reads Hunter Thompson. Eats mushrooms at Dave Matthews.

Everybody wanted Havva, which is mostly why he put up with basically following her around for three months hearing about what actors
were her favorite and how she couldn't decide if "Too Close" by Next was
sexist or not and who her favorite on *Dawson's Creek* was and why,
without so much as a peck on the cheek. He is proud to note that he now
gets a lot of nasty glares, when he's with her in the hallways, from guys
who think she's into them. He sees them out of the corner of his eye while
he makes out with her against her locker, secretly touching her hello-hello
over her panties from under her skirt, making her twitch like she's being
tickled. That's the way she is—flirtatious but untouchable. Well, for
everybody but Brian Hurkle. Sucks for them. He likes to watch her from
across the cafeteria in her black stretch pants when she doesn't know he's
watching her. All the guys with no chance ogling her in discretion or flirting with her. She thinks they're just being friendly (she's pretty naïve, or
at least likes to come across that way) or maybe she likes the attention and
knowing they want her. Brian likes to watch this all the while thinking, I
took her home yesterday and took off her panties and screwed her until
she screamed. I took her virginity. Mine was the first dick she blew.

—Hmm? he said.

—I said what are you doing, she said.

—Right now? Watching MTV.

—What's on?

—Tom Green.

—Me too. It's so funny, she said.

—Yeah. It's a rerun, though.

—I haven't seen it. Ha-ha, did you see that?

He said, —Yeah.

—I can't believe he just did that. Oh my God. Eeeew that's so gross. Can you believe that?

—I know.

—What is that? she said. —A pony?

—It's a cow I think.

—I think it's a pony, she said. —Eeeeww.

—It's a cow, he said. —Ponies don't have udders.

—Can you ride a cow, though?

—A small cow I think you can, yeah. It's at least some sort of bovine. See? What do you think he's sucking on? Those are udders.

—Wait hold on.

—Okay.

There was silence on the other end and Brian, staring straight ahead expressionless, let the phone drop out of his hand onto his shoulder, mouth open a bit, drooling down his bottom lip on purpose and groaning. He pulled his hand out of his pants and smelled it. It smelled like latex and like Havva. An exotic spice or something. It never fully scrubs out of his skin, her smell. No girl's hello-hello has ever smelled like hers. And he's seen and touched a lot. Well, depends on what you consider a lot. Somewhere around seven. He thought about her friend Dawne who hates him. He thought about earlier today, spreading her ass cheeks apart and looking at her asshole and the tiny black hairs around it and thinking, *This is Havva's asshole.* His dick sliding in and out below *Havva's asshole,* out of *Havva's vagina,* glistening, and all of them glaring at him, the condom stretching at the tip like an extraterrestrial creature, *Havva's face* as she looked back toward him screwing her. Pushing down on her small lower back with his thumbs, hands wrapping almost entirely around her waist, like a puppet, her gasping breaths, making her arch like in the pictures on the Internet, pulling her hair. She said like she always says, slow, whispering, but matter-of-fact, —Do you like being inside me?

Sometimes he answers but today he didn't, telling her he was going to come and then she said, —Come, come . . . , which almost made him laugh but he didn't because he was coming.

Then they lay curled together on the couch. He told her four times (in response to her asking) that he loved her. She said, —We have *good* sex, don't we?

—Yep.

—I bet other people who have sex don't have sex like us. Lindsay

Baker and Jason have sex but I know for a fact it's not like the sex we have. They only do it missionary and don't make a sound. She told me. But *we* have *good* sex. Don't we have good sex?

—We do, we do.

—Do I look good having sex?

He smiled and said definitely, running a hand up and down her back, you look like Carmen Electra. He thought, She heard that somewhere— *good sex*. On TV or in a rap song or an interview with Pamela Anderson Lee on cable. *Good sex*. They were satisfied that their sex was good sex and looked good, and that their sex was *hot*. What is to be obtained is good sex. He hoped she told her friends in front of lockers or in line for lunch, shopping for clothes at American Eagle, that she and Brian have *good sex*, that he was what they call good in bed. He hoped his teachers overheard.

And now the phone, down between the cushions of the couch, said, —Hello? Brian picked it out of there and lifted it to his head and said, eyes on the TV, —Hello.

—Hey.

—Hey.

—Did you miss me?

—Of course, babe.

—Say it.

—I missed you.

—How much?

—This much.

—How much is that?

—Well, I'm holding my arms out. If you could see me my arms are out as wide as they go, Brian said. One hand was under his head, armpit ceilingward, and the other hand was down his pants again.

—Do you love me?

—Yes I love you very much, babe. Do you love me?

—Yes.

Brian said, rolling his eyes, making a jerk-off motion, holding the earpiece away so he could hear what John Norris was saying about Tool, —How much?

I appreciate John Norris, he thought. Not many people do, but the guy's a pro, you have to admit.

—I love you more than anything in the entire world, she said. She kissed the phone, saying, —*Mwah*. Do it back.

Brian kissed the phone and went, —*Mwah*.

—Good, she said. —What did I miss?

—Nothing. Commercials.

—What's wrong?

—Nothing. Why?

—I don't know. Seems like something's the matter.

—Nothing's wrong, babe. I'm just a little tired. And I have home-work. My ankle hurts for some reason too. I think it might be sprained.

—You want to get off the phone with me, she said.

—No I want to put ice on this stupid ankle. It's broken I'm pretty sure. Or tendinitis.

—You hate me and wish I was dead so you don't have to talk to me anymore.

—Babe. Stop. My foot's shredded from standing behind that stupid cash register all the time for one thing. That's why. You should see like the fucking calluses on the side of my toe.

—Hey babe? Um, hold on. There was silence and then she said, whispering, as a door closed, —Okay. Um. Today? When we . . . you know?

—Yes, my tulip?

—This has actually been bothering me a lot and I'd like us to talk about it.

—What is it, my beautiful buttercup, my goddess?

—Today you, um, tried to, you know, uh.

—What, my Persian rose?

—Put it in the wrong, um, *place*.

—Oh my God, Brian said. —I *did*? Oh my God I had no idea, angel. You're serious? I. Seriously, baby. I'm so embarrassed.

—Yeah.

—Honestly. Really. I seriously was *not* trying to do that at *all*. It must have been an accident. For real.

—But from now on? Just ask me first, okay? And use plenty of lube and work the, uh, area with your fingers first to relax the muscles. You should be able to get two fingers at least in before you put your . . . *thingie* in.

—What? Where'd you hear this?

—Loveline.

—Oh hey, I meant to ask you this before, Brian said, —but what was the Spanish homework?

—143. Activity A and B. And write a paragraph about your family in Spanish.

—Mm.

—Just next time if you could just, you know, ask me before we try anal sex? You know?

—No, honestly, babe. It was a mistake. Seriously. It was not my intention to like sneak it on you. I'm not like that. That's just such a fucking creepy like disgusting thing to do. That's something fucking Trent Batchelor and his asshole friends would do to like freshman girls. I'm not like that, babe. I'm not that kind of person. Those guys are fucking moron closet fag wrestler losers. Not that I'm homophobic.

—And go slow. The key is to be gentle.

—Baby. Havva. I'm serious, though. I am *not* the kind of guy who would do that. He thought, I'm shift supervisor for fuck's sake. I close down the fucking *store* sometimes. I have a fucking *key* to the fucking *cash office*.

—Carrie's done it and so has Lindsay Carlington because she's saving herself for her virginity. I mean for marriage. Did you know Carrie like had an abortion?

—Nuh-uh.

—She did. Last summer. It was Ben. I think it's an abusive relationship. She needs help. You can't tell anyone. She needs to get away from him because I think he might kill her or like take her hostage one day. He hasn't actually hit her but I think he could. He almost has. Oh I love this song. In this commercial. *Check it out now! Funk soul brotha! Right about now! Funk soul brotha!* Who do you want to go prom with? Chris and Jen or Carrie and Ben? Or Lindsay and Jason and Jeremy and Geoff and Brian and their like *freshman* dates.

—Babe my love first of all those are your friends not mine. Second, prom is like five months away. Or six.

—*So?!*

—I'm just saying.

—*You don't want to go to prom with me?*

—What? No—

—*Fine*, I'll go with someone *else*!

—Babe—

—I'm just kidding. But we need to start planning now. We have SAT prep class and we have to study for our AP tests and then take SATs and then AP tests and join clubs for our college applications and then do our college applications which oh my God what if I don't get in anywhere and have to go Nova? What am I going to do? My parents would kill me. Then not to mention school and homework and I have to get a job at Starbucks or Sephora to start saving money for food and books and clothes at college. I can't dress like this in college. Should I join a sorority you think? I've heard good and bad things. What are we going to do if we don't get into the same school? Could we do long distance? They never work I heard.

Brian thought, Well, when *I* go to college I'm going to fuck twenty-four hours a day. I'm going to fuck girls way hotter than you. The kind of girls on MTV Spring Break. Blond chicks all tanned and oiled up. Threesomes with big-titted blond college chicks. Foursomes, fivesomes. I'm talking massive orgies of hot college pussy. Drug- and alcohol-fueled weeklong binges of sex. A pyramid of ass. The Great Pyramid of Pussy. I'm going to stack them all up one on top of each other and fuck my way to the top and blow my load from the summit. Wads of my jizz flying through the air, splattering all over chicks' faces and butts and tig ol' bitties. Hot tub romps, tennis court screws. Sweetheart small-town chicks and raunchy big-city skanks. Black chicks, white chicks, Latina chicks. Panties will hang from my ceiling fan, bras out my window. Tits, tits, tits. I shall eat nothing but pussy and tit. I will live off sex. A Furor of Fornication. A Circus of Cunnilingus. The Perfect Storm of Stimulation. We're talking Fuck-o-Mania I thru IV, baby! Live on Pay-Per-View! Main Event: Brian Hurkle Fucking Hundreds of Horny Hot Chicks. It's going to be absolute and gooey Sodom. Blow job homework, X-rated tutoring sessions, lesbian anal sluts at keggers. The World Sex Series. The World Fuck Cup. The Olympics of Orgasm. The halls will echo with the cry of Oh Brian, oh Brian, oh yes, oh yes! The sky shall rain with sex! My prick shall never be dry, my balls will never be full at Fuck Me and My Sorority Sister University!

—I don't think we should break up, Havva was saying.

—Absolutely not.

—We have a connection, right?

—We do.

—This isn't a silly high school relationship like Lindsay and Jason. Ours is, I think, you know, real.

—Absolutely.

—Hey, she said, —change it to Comedy Central.

—Okay. Hold on. Brian did nothing then said, —Okay. What is this?

—*Kids in the Hall*. This is awesome. I squish your head!

—Yeah. Ha-ha.

—Hey look on E!

—Okay, he said, not moving.

—Howard Stern's so gross. God, he's so sexist.

—Yeah, I find him pretty offensive.

—Babe, you have the perfect penis.

—Yeah?

—Not too small, not too big. Too big is painful. Yours is the perfect size.

This gave Brian a jolt. What? What does that mean? How would she know? Was she not really a virgin? Could there have been a way that he really wasn't the first one to fuck her? He felt a ruthless stab of panic in his ribs as he imagined someone getting to her before he did. It's entirely possible. Making out naked, sticking it in a little before stopping for some reason. Either she stopping it because she was taken by surprise. Or the guy going limp. Or the parents—her parents or his parents, depending on where they were—coming home. Drunk at a party with upperclassmen before he met her. Some darkened bedroom. The black mulch of bushes in a backyard by a pool, under a summertime full moon. It transpired quickly from a slim possibility to a near certainty. She hadn't bled. She hadn't seemed too uncomfortable or in that much pain. How would he know if she had lied to him? There was no way for him to. Would anybody else know? Did the whole school know except him and laugh at him behind his back, especially when they all saw him holding hands with her, kissing her, thinking he was really the first one to hit that? Did the guy who fucked her first watch and nudge his friends and point them over and they all laughed as he smirked and described her anatomy, her grunts and whimpers? Was it Gary Needler? He bets it was Gary Needler. If it was anyone it would be Gary Needler. She used to talk about him when he first met her. He's seen Gary Needler in the halls looking at her. She's always been vague about Gary Needler. He should find out about Gary Needler. What was Gary Needler's dick like? *Too big?* Oh God . . .

—Hello?

—Yeah.

—Did you hear me?

—Yeah. How do you know I have the perfect . . . you know . . .

—It's just a fact.

—Yeah, but what are we comparing it to here?

—Nothing. It's just a fact. Everyone knows. Too big hurts. Too small? Sorry. I need to feel *something*. I mean, like if you were like two inches that would be a problem. We would have a problem, I'm sorry. You know? But I like your penis, babe. You have nothing to worry about. It's perfect. I want to try it without a condom sometime. Carrie says it's awesome.

—Uh, no way. Not after you know what.

—But I can barely *feel* you, babe. All I feel is the condom. Carrie says wearing a condom during sex is like eating food with the wrapper on or something. I want to *feel* you. I want to try it on E too. Carrie knows someone who can get it. Do you want to? It's thirty dollars. But once you do it on E it's so good that you can only enjoy sex if you are on E. So I don't know. We should stop doing it so often.

—What? Why?

—Because we'll get sick of it.

—I don't think that will happen. I'm not doing it without a condom, though. No way. It's just not worth it. Not unless you're on the pill which you're not. So forget it.

—I would but it's like forty dollars a month.

—Ask your parents. Lie to them about what it's for. Say it's for clothes or something.

—It *would* make my boobs grow. Carrie got fat on it. That's why she stopped taking it. Would you still love me if I was fat?

—Sure. Though of course I'd suggest an exercise regimen. Being overweight just isn't healthy.

—Would you work out with me? she said.

—Yup. We could begin to live a very physically active lifestyle. I've always wanted washboard abs.

—You really think I look like Carmen Electra? she said, lowering her voice again.

—Definitely, he said.

—Did you see *Undressed* last night? Where they shaved? Down there? We should do that.

—Definitely.

—They sell wax at CVS. You can just shave it but I'll wax. Let's do it on Wednesday night and then I'll come over after school on Thursday and we'll, you know.

He fears more than his own death the thought of Havva having sex with somebody who isn't him. An older, smarter, better-looking guy— with sideburns and an orange Abercrombie & Fitch hat sold frayed and faded, in college, with more friends and a more active social life than Brian—kissing her, unhooking her bra, pulling off her panties, wrapping her legs around somebody better, then lying naked on another couch in another basement beside a better-built guy with a dick that's too big, someone willing to not wear a condom. It makes him physically ill with anxiety. His chest burns at the thought. His head aches. He becomes dizzy, his hands clammying up, heart racing.

Soon her mother will be heard in the background, her low sexy voice like a Persian Kathleen Turner, and Havva will tell Brian to hold on and he will hear her say like a bratty princess to her mom, —*Okay. Fine. Hold on. I am.*

In an average, standard phone conversation, no matter what the nature or the duration, Brian is told to hold on at least six or seven times due to her mother interrupting. The interruptions usually occur, much to his psychological distress, only when he is in the middle of saying something he really wants to say, most often after he has just sat through a long and meandering monologue by Havva in which he said nothing for ten or eleven minutes. He could call to say six words to Havva and he'd have to say one word at a time, each one interrupted by her mother. He understands though, as her parents are Iranian. He perceives them as traditional and conservative compared to Western parents. He believes her mother interrupts all the time because she does not like Brian or anyone else sniffing around her daughter as her daughter is too young to marry thus has no business with males. And even if she were, they would let them fraternize only if he were an Ivy League med student or hotshot young lawyer or whatever. They left Iran for the U.S. during the Islamic Revolution in 1979, when they were in their twenties. Her father was in the royal family under the shah in some unclear, indirect way. Brian gathers he was sort of the equivalent of a duke or something. Or his father was. Both he and Havva's mother were liberal, secularists. They fled for their life in 1979 when it became clear the revolution was for real. They were executing people like her father. Some of his relatives. They found his brother's headless body on an overpass. He still fears for his life. He's very secretive, even to Havva. He comes and goes, disappears, shows up again. Is on the phone all night in his office, whispering in the dark. The air in her home has the odd ions of conspiracy. The shades are always drawn, the phone number is constantly changed. Brian can never remember what it is. Havva is technically a princess, or something somewhat similar. Her original name when she was born in Pennsylvania after they came over on work visas, eventually obtaining their citizenships, was something other than Havva Khabbazi. She doesn't know what it was. Her parents won't tell her. Her parents moved here and had all their names changed because they believed she was in danger of being kidnapped by fundamentalists who had made it inside the U.S. She also has two birthdays. One is her real birthday, which only she and her family celebrate and acknowledge, and one is her official birthday, the one on her driver's license, a fake birthday that her father was able with the help of conveniently located United States government officials he knows to have her official records altered to contain. She has an altered birth certificate, altered Social Security card. She cannot say for certain what it is her father does for a living. Brian privately believes he does something to fund or aid the Iranian secularist resistance. Arms trading or something. Moving money around. Her family has a palace in Iran, she says. It's where her father grew up until his family was forced out of it. Soldiers with machine guns now stand around in what should be her living room. It's a museum now—a local relic of the dark secular days. Tourists wander through what should be her bedroom. Her father makes it seem to Havva like one day in the near future there will be another revolution, a reverse revolution, and the Muslim fundamentalists will be overthrown and the monarchy will be restored, and Havva and her family will go back and reclaim their palace, live in it, take their proper place as the royal family they are. Brian's not sure how much of this is legitimate and how much is Havva being dramatic and grandiose as is her nature, but either way the idea turns Brian on a great deal, screwing the hell out of an Iranian princess.

Havva eventually, if she can bark off her mom, will say to Brian, —Okay. I'm back. Did you miss me?

And they will keep going like this late into the night then he will fucking finally be able to hang up the phone, happy because he can rub his hot red flattened ear back to life and be left alone to watch *The Simpsons* reruns on Fox and then do homework.

An Essay Turned in Yesterday by Grayson Donald for Eleventh-grade GT English Class on the Topic "What Is the Meaning of the Symbol of the Green Light in *The Great Gatsby*?" on Which He Has Yet to Receive a Grade Because His Teacher, Mr. Moad, Is Not Sure if It's Some Sort of Joke or What

The significance of the green light in *The Great Gatsby*, a novel by F. Scott Fitzgerald, is uncertain. It is also uncertain what the F in F. Scott Fitzgerald stands for. What is certain, however, is the significance of dish towels in Northern Virginia.

Most dish towels in Northern Virginia are kept on the handle of the oven door. They are draped over the lengthwise bar so that the resultant halves hang equal, ready for wet hands. This is true no matter the color or size of the dish towel. Most dish towels are made of a thin rough cotton, almost a reusable paper towel. This material is not very absorbent. One will find that those who do not keep their dish towels on the oven handle keep theirs on the refrigerator door handle, which is vertical. You can tell a lot about a person by where they keep their dish towels.

Every resident can testify to the inconvenience and unsatisfactory performance of both methods of dish towel hanging. Husbands from the dirt roads of Loudon to the luxury high-rise condos of Arlington have individually, on many more occasions than they would desire, experienced the stress that comes with attempting to dry their hands on a dish towel hanging from the handle of an oven door. Bending down just enough to be awkward in order to reach below the oven handle, tugging on the front half so gently that what you are doing is merely suggesting that the striped rough cloth make itself a wee bit more available, causing the dish towel to fall completely off the oven handle into the hand drier's possession.

After utilizing the towel, the utilizer must now, before he can go about his day, struggle with folding then replacing the towel in the same way it was before he dried his hands on it. This is hard. It is especially difficult for men. Guiding a dish towel back into the narrow space between the handle and the oven door is much harder for a man's thick clumsy hands than women seem to realize. It's man's primal instinct not to fold the dish towel first but rather to force the whole thing in at once, using the fingers to shove. Men, if allowed, would keep their dish towels on the counter, in a lump, like a dead animal.

In their lives, Northern Virginia men must fight their instincts. Mostly they do.

The typical NoVA resident will once, sometimes twice a day, often while in traffic or struggling with the objects themselves, as described heartily above, find him- or herself wondering who decided such a thin nonabsorbent material would be the best choice for a dish towel. Most dish towels hardly dry one's hands at all. Rather one always finds himself after successfully replacing the fallen dish towel on the oven handle wiping his still damp hands on the butt of his pants in order to completely dry them.

Residents of NoVA touch their own butts for the purposes of cleanliness many times a day.

Try to get through twenty-four hours within twenty miles of the Beltway without touching your own ass.

Good luck to you.

Go to the Giant in Centreville. It's in the Colonnade on Union Mill Road, with the Shell and the Kentucky Fried Chicken and the Outback and the Starbucks and McDonald's and the Blockbuster and a bunch of other things. Let the automatic doors open for you with a whoosh and a whir of air. Step in like boarding a spacecraft. Grab a cart, poke around. Squeeze the apples. Examine the cabbage. Decide on a toothbrush. Mentally whistle along with the Muzak. Grimace-smile when you come head to head with another shopper's cart and allow them the right of way. Suck on your teeth and squint at the soups. Move your cart out of the aisle when a woman with a baby needs to pass. Look like you're shopping. See all those other shoppers schlepping carts stacked way over the top?

See them?

They, each one, touched his or her own butt today. Lots of times.

They have washed their hands with a refillable bottle of scented liquid Dial kept along the edge of the kitchen sink. They have given their hands two or three shakes into the sink. Then they have attempted to dry their hands on a rough incompetent dish towel rife with stains and bacteria that stays wet literally hours after the last wiping. They have put the dish towel back then bent to pick it up off the floor after it's fallen. They've thought that somebody needs to come up with a better dish towel and also a better way to hang them. Then, their hands still wet, going from the kitchen toward the television, looking forward to sitting down on the easy chair (if they are male) or sofa (if they are female) to watch the news, they have touched their butts. This is how people clean their hands in Northern Virginia.

The significance of the green light in *The Great Gatsby* will always be a mystery to mankind. The significance of dish towels in Northern Virginia, however, is a mystery no more.

So long, ass touchers.

Greenbriar High School to George Mason University

Vicki Donald in the car. She left school, drove to Mason, taught class, went home, got dinner ready, ate a little of it, baked ziti, headed back to Mason to attend her other class. MY OTHER CAR IS A BROOMSTICK. KEEP YOUR LAWS OFF MY BODY. AGAINST ABORTION? GET A VASECTOMY. KEEP ABORTION SAFE—KEEP IT LEGAL. PRO-CHILD, PRO-CHOICE. These were the things Vicki was told as she sat in traffic on Braddock Road toward Fairfax on her first trip to Mason. Standard fare as far as bumper stickers go as one approaches Mason. Vicki clicks her tongue and says a prayer for each one she sees. *Dear Lord, May you enter into their hearts and allow them to feel Your love so that their minds may change . . .* Vicki was never these kids' ages. The age where you can be idealistic. It is the age where they have been raised in NoVA and now go to college in NoVA. The boredom at its peak. The theory of the world. The boredom turning into guilt. She drove with her hands on the wheel of the Escort wagon at eleven o'clock and one o'clock, unable to understand how people can be so self-absorbed and selfish that they believe not in God but in a life in which all that matters is the pursuit of pleasure and the doing of only what is in accordance with your own desires, avoiding suffering and responsibility at all costs. Seeing no value in suffering. Even if all they are avoiding is the guilt of the Caucasian middle to upper middle class in America. They must be so unhappy. She feels sad for them, the people with these bumper stickers. *Dear Mother Mary, Please enter into their hearts and bless them.*

She herself feels lazy just sitting in her car. Every day after school walking across the Greenbriar parking lot, she remembers like a forgotten obligation the guilt and dread that will come with being immobile for the next thirty minutes—forty minutes if traffic is especially bad, roadwork for example—it seems there is always roadwork—as she sits in her car, sitting down, not speed walking somewhere or battling the ergasiophobic wills of twenty-five teenagers for control of her classroom, or tending to some catastrophic emergency of public education. Not studying, not grading, not writing, not planning. Doing nothing. Steering.

Lazy. Gaining weight. Watching out for crazy drivers. Saying the rosary. The biggest source of the dread which creeps over her like a disease as she moves across the parking lot to her Escort—and speaking of, she has for the last several months had the constant feeling of an oncoming cold, that hot pressure between her eyes, a lethargy—is that being in the car forces her to think. The meditation of driving. She doesn't like to think, too many things to think about. The outcome of these things to think about is not a buried treasure chest she wishes to disinter. Too many inconvenient truths locked within it. A Pandora's box. She wishes sometimes there were no truths. Only Masses and meals and work. The world—the universe—is all one great big truth. It's ugly. It hangs over her like the fist of God. When it comes down she will be squished by it. And one day it will come down . . . So she rushes about, keeps herself frazzled, in order to prevent the fist from coming down, with her husband wrapped within it, a damaged disaster of a man. Yes, stay up, stay up fist, trembling with restraint, keep me away from his beard, his little boy eyes, voice saying hello to me from the computer room as he wipes away the evidence. She knows for a fact what he does in there. And what he's done. For a decade she has known. Other women, other women's bodies. But she has admitted it to herself only when she found the lockbox. He doesn't know she knows. Which poisons the air of their home like gasoline fumes. Making it easier for her to stay away. How awful it must be for Grayson to live in it. What a failed mother she believes herself to be. She will apologize to him one day and he will forgive her. *It was not your fault, Mom—it was that asshole's fault.* He is a smart young man, he can handle it. He will need to. In order to become a man.

Nearly two years ago, after finding the lockbox, she purchased from Best Buy in Fair Lakes software that lets you spy on your spouse or child's e-mails and monitor their Internet activity. She never used it to spy on Grayson's e-mails. She will swear one day to him that she never, never did. And he will believe her. *I believe you, Mom. I love you, Mom.* Every day she comes home and gets dinner ready. Then she goes to the computer room to work on her papers. First she checks the software. She keeps an eye on the shadows in the hall. Holds her breath so she can listen to the ticks and whispers of the home. The poison wafting around in the air. But she never, never checks on Grayson's activity. And she sits there scrolling through the URLs, the things typed, the images downloaded. Seeing what he has chosen to see. It is like putting on his flesh and entering his mind. The man she thought she knew. Her best friend and love of her life. For twenty-five years her life has been his life. And they have had nothing else but Grayson. And she reads the obscene, wretched words. They do not shock her. They are vulgar, obscene. But she is not disbelieving when she sees them. She is disgusted and disappointed. As she is when she sees the images and reads the e-mails. It is interesting and exciting—like a drama. A soap opera. They are—each image, each URL, every letter of every e-mail and ad placed on those sites—a self-contained package of lies and truths intertwined and coiled like strains of plague. And she reads his e-mails to Linda Dutton. And to his high school sweetheart in Wyoming. And all the other women. Most of whom she's never heard of. And he kisses her on the lips. He smiles, drunk, and says, —Hi Momma. The truth and lies of the package so simple and complicated that still she does not know what to do about it. You marry someone you are entering an eternal covenant. Not just a lifelong one—an eternal one. You make a vow to God that it is until death do you part. Not just as long as it makes you happy or until it gets difficult. That is not a marriage. At least not one recognized in God's eyes. She has gone to therapy to try to convince herself what to do. She has tried medication. Sessions with Monsignor Crosby have helped. She has cut her hair, gained weight, joined Life Time Fitness, lost weight, gone shopping. She has tried joining a book club with fellow teachers at school. She tried becoming a fan of women's college basketball. But nothing has helped like work has helped. Always so much to do. Things to worry about. She'll go forever if she's allowed—if no one stops her. Just go and go, work work work, keep on going as she is because it works, doesn't it? She is alive, isn't she? It could be worse, couldn't it? It can always be worse.

Things are fine, if you compare her life to the lives of women around the world. Goodness gracious, some women have it a hundred times harder. African women for example. Women in those Middle Eastern countries where they have to wear black sheets over themselves and get raped by their husband's father on their wedding night.

Brake lights and street signs and 66 on-ramp—forever.

She can hold on. If she can hold on. Life will end and your soul shall be measured. And the wheat shall be separated from the chaff.

Her Heavenly Father shall return to reclaim her. He shall call her daughter and he shall love her as no one has loved her.

A half-empty Diet Coke in the cup holder beneath the radio, country station on, a Three Musketeers wrapper on the floor of the passenger seat next to her canvas tote bags with her books and papers. Her whole life, everything she has.

She can't look at pictures of herself pregnant with Grayson. She has taken all those ill-lit photographs and hidden them away. The hard cube boxes open like Easter eggs.

But do you think he does not see you? Your father sees you. Your mother and he watch you, your teeth ripping chunks off chocolate bars and chewing with your mouth closed, your head bowed and shoulders stooped. You cannot leave. And John watches you. He will watch you always. And what do you know of what God thinks? Can't you see that your apologies are drowned in the church bells clamoring over these ancient Southern swamps?

LEE HIGHWAY—FAIRFAX

Fairfax where George Mason University is is best when wet, after the rain, in the evening, in the springtime.

The confusion of the intersection where 29, Lee Highway, jettisons off without warning, the stoplights vague arrows that point at a fifteen-degree angle, and if you don't know it's coming you find yourself driving head-on into oncoming traffic.

Honk horns and stand still in the middle of the lane with signal on and leaning forward over the steering wheel waiting for a break in traffic or for somebody to brake and wave them in, to which they wave by raising a hand as they make their move, saying to themselves, —Thank you. Thanks.

Korean grocery stores and Russian video rental places, a Hooters, nurseries, arts and crafts stores, chain restaurants and chain bookstores and electronic outlets, fast food places, auto repair shops, gas stations.

A world of Miller Lites and vodka crans and Marlboro Lights and hip-hop.

Fairfax is a place on the way home, existing only in evenings in moments of exhausted stress and bleary-eyed weakness, in an air-conditioned vehicle with the windows up and the radio on or a six-disc CD changer pounding away from the trunk of a black car with tinted windows that looks like a spaceship driven by apparently an eleven-year-old, the woman in the car next to the eleven-year-old glancing over with her hand covering half her face, alienated and uncomfortable at hearing another's music.

They answer their cell phones that ring in an electronic replication of a landline phone and tell them where they are, where they're going, what they are doing, and what they plan on doing, tonight, tomorrow, next year.

What they want to buy and what they've seen and how it was.

MS-13

In Fairfax. At the bus stop, going to Fair Oaks Mall. Me—Sergio aka Gato—and my clique.

Looking like a bunch of wetback housepainters fresh off the turnip truck.

Gloria keeps glaring at us and is quiet.

But Julia is squeezing her arm & saying to just shut up and chill or they'll do to you what happened to Raquel last night.

Let them think that, even though that's not a possibility.

Fear is a powerful thing.

Once we get to the mall I can use the fear Gloria has for me to get us some money so we can eat.

& get over this hangover & get some smokes too & get a room at the Holiday Inn tonight.

Can't look at Julia without seeing our baby & seeing Julia's face after I slapped Julia's face with my ring still on and all bloody.

FAIR OAKS MALL

What you stop noticing after a while about Fair Oaks Mall—which is either in Fairfax or Fair Lakes, depending on whom you ask (locations here are never in any one particular place—see for example my neighborhood of Little Rocky Run, which is in Centreville and Clifton)—what you stop noticing over the years as the mall becomes ingrained into your soul is the constant sound of water falling inside the mall. It can be heard everywhere within the mall except within the stores themselves where instead of the sound of water the background is infused with pop music featuring bland cheerful people performing what is basically musical lobotomies on all that are unfortunate enough to fall victim to hearing it. The sound of the water falling feels like it's always just behind you, making it hard to hear the person you are with if they are speaking in a normal speaking voice. Thus most shoppers strolling through the mall are more often than not shouting at one another, literally screaming and hollering, stripping their dialogue down to three or four key words, gesturing to their ears, shaking their heads, shrugging their shoulders. It is the language of rock concerts and old people. They all race about shouting, slightly panicked as if trying to find their way out of a collapsed structure after an earthquake.

The reason for the sound of falling water, which makes being in the mall feel like spelunking in an underground cave in a South African rain forest—maybe or maybe not the architects' intention—is that there actually are waterfalls here, located in the middle of the mall on the first floor, the mall having been built in the late 1970s or early 1980s, that era of aesthetic withershins when things such as indoor waterfalls seemed, without explication, like a tasteful design choice to commercial architects.

Fair Oaks is a two-story mall. It is big compared to Manassas Mall, which is essentially a one-story shack. We Centrevillians laugh at the mere mention of Manassas Mall. A punch line of a mall in a punch line of a city. The only favorable asset Manassas Mall contains is a Cinnabon.

But however Fair Oaks is minuscule and hopelessly limited when juxtaposed with Tysons Corner Center. Indeed, Fair Oaks Mall becomes Manassas Mall when compared to that monstrosity. Thus, for its main demographic—thirteen-year-olds—Fair Oaks is the mall of choice for small quick trips—such as for a particular CD—and general lollygagging. It is perfect for a thirteen-year-old child of NoVA when in the throes of another fit of aimlessness and maddening, ravenous boredom in which only the entering of a mall, the circumforaneous wandering amid others of your kind, or the buying of a CD (usually more like the stealing of a CD) can cure the disease. Tysons Corner Center, on the other hand, is where all serious clothes shopping is done. And in NoVA, all clothes shopping is serious. Tysons, as it is referred to in the vernacular, is a hulking terror of a mall in Vienna and Reston and Falls Church or wherever it really is. It lies off the Beltway, that vast puzzling orbit. There are signs on the Beltway that indicate which direction you are going by telling you that you are or aren't heading in the direction of Tysons Corner Center. Tysons offers a spectacular, superior shopping experience—sans waterfalls. Its more than 300 stores make a mockery of Fair Oaks's 190. Often a Fair Oaks devotee will shop at Tysons for some reason and afterward will find himself or herself unable to come within a one-mile radius of Fair Oaks Mall for over a month afterward. Perhaps it is the Barnes & Noble. Or the sixteen-screen multiplex. Perhaps it is the upscale Tysons Galleria, located right across the street and featuring J. Crew, Chanel, and Ralph Lauren among very many others.

The waterfalls of Fair Oaks are one of the best parts about this place—which I will miss—if you are a little kid. Aside, of course, from KB Toys. These miniwalls of water in constant frozen motion, overflowing from the penny-filled fountain in the middle like the overflow from a giant champagne glass pyramid pour. The overflow is thick and lengthwise, running forty, forty-five yards long. One who was raised on Fair Oaks Mall knows it is coming as the sound of rushing water grows louder. A child knows that the wall of water is at perfect child-hand height. He can stick his scrawny tanned arm out to make an airplane wing that pokes through the wall of water and he can then walk like this along its entire length, cutting a gash in the wall, ruining the space-age perfection of it, enjoying the harsh sensation, the mom allowing this and carrying new shoes and shirts in a big white heavy-paper JCPenney bag. And the child can then continue on like this—as I am now demonstrating, for the last time, my arm not scrawny anymore, my hand not a child's but not with black hairs on the back of it like my father's, not tanned but pale—until the end of the waterfall. At which point the hand is soaked—there is nothing like a soaked hand in the middle of Fair Oaks Mall—and can be wiped off on your butt.

These floors are the color of earth and bare and hard. My feet walk upon them. One of the last things they will walk upon. My footprint left there forever in the dimension of God. And the ceilings light but vaulted to an incredible height. Sounds bounce around up there like small nails spilled from a box. The clicking of my shoes. Once upon a time, years ago, ten years ago, Fair Oaks was ultramodern and huge. It was a structure that astonished. Its fake plants and real dirt and glass elevator going up and down the tube in the center of it. The fountain. Kids tossing in pennies and wishing for the ability to fly. The strange brown block things in the middle of the walking parts that house the fake plants and are made of a pebbly blend of plastic and maybe cement such that their surface resembles ice cream rolled in crushed almonds or walnuts or whatever nut it is they roll the ice cream in after placing it on the cone to create a Nutty Buddy, my favorite ice cream which was available in the cafeteria at Twin Lakes Elementary. They had chocolate on them. It was vanilla ice cream on a cone, rolled in nuts, then covered in that chocolate that hardens. The strange brown block things are flat in some spots it seems specifically for sitting on. But most other places the surface is angled to a point which makes sitting on them a motherfucker. But people do it anyway, kids mostly. They endure the discomfort of a giant point up the butt. Maybe they were designed this way in order to keep us moving, shopping. A commercial Bataan Death March. As far as benches are concerned, these sharp giant basically potholders that poke you up the butt and provide little room to set your Icee between sips or to spread out your Arby's are all you get. Other than the three or four legitimate, padded benches—maybe it's a federal law that a mall must have at the very minimum three or four real benches—which are mostly located at the tops of the escalators at either end of the mall and almost always occupied, as they are now at around twelve o'clock noon, by old people with canes and big black sunglasses who come here to trudge around and around in hunched-over circles, their hips grating, their bladders bulging, not buying anything, staring off at nothing, the culmination of all their time alive on earth, their entire lives designed around retirement, this is what they have toiled for, this is success, and now they wait for time to finally wear itself out . . .

MS-13

The night before last night at the Breezeway Motel on 29 in Fairfax.

A knock on the door and there was Raul.

Oh shit! Like a fucking ghost in the night!

He came inside and told us about prison.

It's a fucking summer camp he said.

You live better in prison than you do out here he said.

It's a joke he said.

Can't wait to go back he said.

& then I was wondering if he was here to kill me.

If he heard I got a visit from the cops and didn't believe that I didn't tell them shit.

Everybody was acting strange. Even Julia who was being distant and weird.

You can't trust nobody.

My breathing got tight.

I felt dizzy & hyper & couldn't sit still.

Best I could do was sit there silent and be ready to attack.

& kept a beer can full in my hand thinking it was the only thing I would be able to smash them in the face with if I had to.

& made sure to always be by the door for if I had to run.

After awhile everyone was drunk and stoned and fucked up and Gloria was sucking Raul's dick on the bed as the rest of us watched Coming to America.

Raul couldn't get hard and told me to come here & I got nervous but didn't act like it.

I said what & he said hold her down, I want to do something.

I had a good idea what Raul was planning on doing.

If you knew Raul you would too.

I didn't want to seem like I knew I was greenlighted.

I wished I had my machete with me.

So I went over & held Gloria down who was naked & saying no no.

& Julia and Raquel smoking cigarettes and telling Pedro to turn up the TV.

& I was so happy that I wasn't going to be gutted that I was laughing so hard when Raul squatted over Gloria as I held her down

& the shit oozed out of Raul's asshole

& coiling onto her nose and lips.

& her eyes closed tight, squealing.

I was embarrassed I was laughing so hard.

& I think they all noticed and were laughing at me for laughing like a lunatic & feeling like a little kid because of it.

Even though I told Gloria the night before I love you and that one day I will get money and we'll run the hell out of Fairfax together to where no one's heard of MS-13 and don't know what the tattoos mean. & we'll go to Canada & build a house there & live in it & have 20 babies & go to Mass & bring our families from El Salvador & never worry about nothing like Raul or motel rooms.

Raul left after that & I didn't get gutted which was good.

FAIR OAKS MALL

A blending of dimensions and worlds, a crashing of realities, undermining the bubbles constructed with care and maintained with meticulousness, those of subdivisions like Little Rocky Run and the schools that fuel them and distract the children, house them for the day, give them something to do. The school you go to and the house you live in and the parents and kids along the way. This is the universe.

24585 Bunkers Court— Fourth Entrance

November 2, 1998

Michael Horton:

This is to inform you that for the third week in a row you are still in quite serious breach of HOA Regulation 74C. This plenipotentiary regulation is clearly detailed in your Home Owner's Manual and, like all regulations, needs to be respected and followed to maintain the asthetic of our neighborhood, Little Rocky Run; but also the property values and peace of mind of your neighbors and there homes.

The breach in question, as I am sure we all know by now, is the basketball goal on the curb in front of your residence at 31098 Foggy Hills Court. One might even say with qualification and without argument that itis nearly on the street. There are eyewitnesses who can testify with verification that they have seen the basketball goal on the street. I am not alone in having to be the bad guy and enforce the regulations and guidelines for homeownership, you can tell from that last sentence. I will not divulge which fellow residents have verified witnessing the basketball goal on the street. It is not fair to them as they are only trying to cooperate with the maintenance of the integrity of our neighborhood. A sense of continuity and curbs rid of basketball goals is something we as community residents count on to enjoy in Little Rocky Run.

I am not being a "killjoy" or a "party pooper" here. I love recreation and athletics. Health is very important. I find

nothing healthier than children enjoying the game of
basketball; especially as a former athlete myself. I certainly
am not being a "certain derrogatory word for females" that
rhymes with "witch;" as it has gotten back to me that by
which you have taken to referring to me.

Being a teacher and writer who holds others in firm respect,
I will not mention the vulgarity here. I will if it comes to a
legal trial. I do not think vulgarities are necessarily "bad"
per say, but in circumstances such as these they are certainly
unnecessary. One example of a situation in which a
vulgarity would not be considered "bad" would be in art.
Though the art must be making a point and be done in skill
and training.

I am not a "prude" or "uptight." I try to find better words to
express myself than common euphemisms and vulgarities,
"four-letter words," though many of them are not four
letters. However, I will not change the channel if, during a
show such as a primetime police drama or a movie on HBO,
a character utters "d—" or "son of a b—."

Compoundedly, I enjoy *The Simpsons* very much. The biting
hip satire of this animated show is one I always catch on
Sunday nights and allow my children to watch as well. It is a
very smart program that accurately satires the suburban
American family experience. Its characters are sympathetic.
Its humor has many levels to it, therefore children do not
get the more racy, "grown-up" jokes. But they still find the
show entertaining to watch. The best satire is that which
reveals truth.

Rather the florilegia is rather an issue of regulations, Mr.
Horton; maintaining the integrity of a community that we
all pay a lot of money to be a part of and labor strenuously
to enjoy. It is also an issue of safety, Mr. Horton. That is the
"crux" of the matter.

We all came of age during the "60s," Mike. We Boomers
experimented during that radical and exciting time. We

protested an unjust war; rebelled against the restrictions of our parents' culture; developed our own idea of "America": the true idea of American that Thomas Jefferson and Abraham Lincoln set forth. I went to Woodstock. I do not know if you knew that.

In addition, I have read every book by Kurt Vonnegut (speaking of satire done right; *Slaughterhouse-Five* is my favorite; such a biting, revealing exposition of the terrors of war!). I saw Janis Joplin at a small concert hall in New York City in 1968. My husband Edward owns many, many rock and roll records. Do not tell my son, but both Ed and I experimented with marijuana as college students. We are not proud of it, but those were the times.

In additionally, we supported Robert F. Kennedy's presidential campaign. Edward even canvassed for him as a high schooler. I was too young, being 13 and more interested in "The Beatles."

But in all my reckless times as a youth, I never hurt anyone else. I understand you have an issue with authority. We all do, as children of that radical confusing time, the "60s." But those were the "60s." It's one thing to rebel and maintain your individuality. But it's another to place other's well-being in danger. You must find a balance and curtail your struggle for identity before it puts others in harm's way. Certainly your "lack of respect" does not extend to the point where you desire for children at play to be injured, maimed, or killed by your family's maverick discrepancies, namely your illegal basketball goal?

Its heart made up of the family, Little Rocky Run is a community built on safety. Safety for its residents and the residents of its children alike. Such a joy it is to watch children at play in its streets! Cars respecting the 25 mph speed limit and stop signs placed through, halting for a group of children to merrily cross to retrieve an errant ball. Watching the children grow and learn and becoming successful! Working hard and reaching their dreams!

Fair Oaks Mall

A good chunk of the kids you see at Fair Oaks Mall at any given time are stoned or drunk or have just stolen something or said something horrible about somebody else or lied to their parents in some capacity. They are teetering on the edge of a nervous breakdown because their hemp necklace might be gay. Most of them don't consider themselves attractive, even if they are. In which case—girls especially—they are hated for being attractive and they are lonely.

There is a hierarchy of respect from high school seniors on down. A quiet self-consciousness.

There's the underground parking lot, below JCPenney, which is where my mom parks when she comes here. I park in the regular aboveground lot. It is tremendous in its own right but there are rarely close spaces. I parked today near the Bennigan's. In addition to Bennigan's there is Ruby Tuesday, Chi-Chi's, Sbarro, and many other restaurants. I have eaten at all of them. My favorite is Chi-Chi's because they have somehow figured out how to fry ice cream. There is no traditional food court in the mall. Rather the restaurants are placed here and there in the outer wings, accessible via their own entrance. Also scattered at random are Auntie Anne's pretzels and places like that. An Arby's, my favorite fast-food place by far. I could have eaten there today but chose not to. Instead I will stop at Giant on my way home from sticking my hand in the waterfall and buy my very own frozen baked ziti which I will take home and put into the oven and eat and dispose of before my father comes home.

A couple jewelry stores, a leather goods store called Wilson's that has leather jackets and suede purses, Sam Goody and the Wall for CDs—Sam Goody is bigger but the Wall is cheaper—and a couple toy stores, department stores again, the Gap, Banana Republic, Abercrombie & Fitch, shoe-stores, John B. Hayes which is a tobacco shop where you buy Zippos in junior high and try to buy cigars by saying they're for your dad who is off buying something for your mom. And there are canes in there too and pipes which kids buy sometimes to smoke weed out of. I have one—a corncob one I bought when I was in seventh grade.

Fair Oaks is a rectangle hallway that expands like a wide-open avenue, dwarfing and endless and loud. And it bursts through its walls and extends out to the Fair Lakes business parks and shopping trips nearby, satellites of the mall, Best Buy where Bryce Gauthier—whose wife Amy will one day leave him—purchases Martin Lawrence DVDs and where my mother bought the software and to which Jeremiah once submitted the lone job application he has ever submitted—still sitting there behind the Customer Service counter gathering dust—and Toys "R" Us where Andy used to work as a maintenance man wandering around with a mop cleaning up toddler puke, and Galyan's where Brian Hurkle works—who looks over my shoulder in precalc—and Red Robin where his girlfriend Havva—who was not a virgin—this past summer worked with her friend Dawne. And it goes on and on, with nicely manicured hedges and smooth parking lots. Plastic exteriors curved and colorful with hotels and conference rooms and shiny-faced young men at the front desk who go home after their shift and shoot meth into their ass and masturbate. Birds flying over all pooping upon it. And there's a Taco Bell where my friends and I piled into my car and drove to the day I got my license. All of us higher than those birds. And the ground is sprouting more of it by the hour. You can watch it grow. See it shoot from the earth and engulf it at superspeeds.

The dog pound where we picked up Barkley when he ran away and he had pee on his paws and howled the whole way home. I try to under-stand that I will not see him again after today. And I start to cry, watching my hand break the water, the water hot in my eyes, thinking about how I won't see my dog anymore after today. A little kid on the other side of the fountain doing the same thing is looking at me. And I look back at him, bawling. And we stare at each other for a while until his mom drags him off.

Those long-gone souls all driving along in their cars and thinking nothing and hopeless in their ease thus buried under and passed over by redemption.

31317 Marblestone Court— Third Entrance

From: gdonald81@yahoo.com
To: info@washingtonpost.com
Sent: Sunday October 3, 1998 17:09 EST
Subject: Proposal—Smithsonian

Dear Sirs,

My name is Grayson Donald. I am a junior at Braddock Park
High School in Centreville, VA. I live in Little Rocky Run. It
is a nice neighborhood. The mascot of my high school is the
Wildcat (rowr!). I am 17 years old. How long have I been
writing this letter for? It feels as though it has been over an
hour now but I only have written a couple of sentences.
According to the clock on the computer it has only been
three minutes. The reason for this is because I am very, very
stoned right now due to taking four gravity bongs this
afternoon behind my friend Jeremiah's house.

Sirs, I write you today to pitch a story of epic proportions. It
concerns the Smithsonian, that hallowed institution of
historic junk. The Smithsonian is known far and wide. Its
junk is revered, a national treasure. People come from
Iowa—where they certainly have more than enough junk of
their own—for the sole purpose of beholding the junk of the
Smithsonian. Oh, the Smithsonian, hallowed be thy name.
The Smithsonian is all. Everything is the Smithsonian.

The Smithsonian. The Smithsonian. The Smithsonian. The
Smithsonian. I cannot stop typing The Smithsonian.

The Smithsonian. The Smithsonian. The Smithsonian.

However, this story I propose to you, sirs, would expose the Smithsonian for what it truly is: a sordid den of child molestation. Yes, there is rampant child molestation occurring every day at the Smithsonian. It's true. I have sources. My sources tell me that certain perverted, deranged men hide in the stalls of the women's bathrooms, waiting for little girls to be sent in alone to urinate or poop while their parents wait outside. And when one falls into their trap, they strike. They tell the little girl they are a police officer and not to tell anybody about this or they'll be arrested. Then they molest the little girl.

I also have it on good faith from a reliable source, a person close to the situation, who tells me that very recently a male was hiding behind the escalator poking little girls in the butt with an HIV-infected needle. Did you know this? And people in Iowa still brings their kids all the way to Washington, DC to see the Smithsonian's old junk? Fairfax County Public Schools still bring their students on field trips to the Smithsonian when they are as young as fourth grade?

Also, do you know that there are plainclothes detectives and security personnel at the Smithsonian occupied on a full-time basis, tasked with the sole purpose of finding child molesters hiding in women's bathrooms? I will not tell you how I know, but I do.

And that the District attorney has not prosecuted even one of these cases because the victims are always visitors from Iowa who came to see all that old junk in the Smithsonian and it would be a headache for the parents to have to come back to Washington, DC and deal with a legal case? Is this something you are aware of, Washington Post?

I could write about this issue, sirs. I am an excellent writer, as you can tell. I am in GT English this year and know man, many adjectives, adverbs, and participles. I also know the significance of the green light in The Great Gatsby, by F. Scott Fitzgerald.

I bet this has happened here in Little Rocky Run. I could open a journalistic investigation. I bet there are girls in Little Rocky Run who have been poked in the butt with AIDS needles at the Smithsonian on field trips with their school. I could ask around, follow leads. That be what I do, what I am. Many people in Little Rocky Run would buy the Washington Post if this story was in it. Please say yes. Please please please. I'll accept any amount of compensation, as I know that I am not a veteran. It would be an invaluable service to the community. Maybe we could print the story in Iowa so people would be warned and reconsider the value of their own museums back in Iowa.

I look forward to hearing from you on this matter of child molestation at the Smithsonian.

The Smithsonian. The Smithsonian. The Smithsonian. The Smithsonian.

Sincerely,
Grayson Donald

P.S. The Smithsonian The

Smithsonian The Smithsonian The Smithsonian The
Smithsonian The Smithsonian The Smithsonian The
Smithsonian The Smithsonian The Smithsonian The
Smithsonian The Smithsonian The Smithsonian The
Smithsonian The Smithsonian The Smithsonian The
Smithsonian The Smithsonian The Smithsonian The
Smithsonian The Smithsonian The Smithsonian The
Smithsonian The Smithsonian The Smithsonian The
Smithsonian The Smithsonian The Smithsonian The
Smithsonian The Smithsonian The Smithsonian The
Smithsonian The Smithsonian The Smithsonian The
Smithsonian The Smithsonian The Smithsonian The
Smithsonian The Smithsonian The Smithsonian The
Smithsonian The Smithsonian The Smithsonian The
Smithsonian The Smithsonian The Smithsonian The
Smithsonian The Smithsonian The Smithsonian The
Smithsonian The Smithsonian The Smithsonian The
Smithsonian The Smithsonian The Smithsonian The
Smithsonian The Smithsonian The Smithsonian The
Smithsonian The Smithsonian The Smithsonian The
Smithsonian The Smithsonian The Smithsonian The
Smithsonian The Smithsonian The Smithsonian The
Smithsonian The Smithsonian The Smithsonian The
Smithsonian The Smithsonian The Smithsonian The
Smithsonian The Smithsonian The Smithsonian The
Smithsonian The Smithsonian The Smithsonian The
Smithsonian The Smithsonian The Smithsonian The
Smithsonian The Smithsonian The Smithsonian The
Smithsonian The Smithsonian The Smithsonian The
Smithsonian The Smithsonian The Smithsonian The
Smithsonian The Smithsonian The Smithsonian The
Smithsonian The Smithsonian The Smithsonian The
Smithsonian The Smithsonian The Smithsonian The
Smithsonian The Smithsonian The Smithsonian The
Smithsonian The Smithsonian The Smithsonian The
Smithsonian The Smithsonian The Smithsonian The
Smithsonian The Smithsonian The Smithsonian The
Smithsonian The Smithsonian The Smithsonian The
Smithsonian The Smithsonian The Smithsonian The
Smithsonian The Smithsonian The Smithsonian The
Smithsonian The Smithsonian The Smithsonian The

Smithsonian The Smithsonian The Smithsonian The
Smithsonian The Smithsonian The Smithsonian The
Smithsonian The Smithsonian The Smithsonian The
Smithsonian The Smithsonian The Smithsonian The
Smithsonian The Smithsonian The Smithsonian The
Smithsonian The Smithsonian The Smithsonian The
Smithsonian The Smithsonian The Smithsonian The
Smithsonian The Smithsonian The Smithsonian The
Smithsonian The Smithsonian The Smithsonian The
Smithsonian The Smithsonian The Smithsonian The
Smithsonian The Smithsonian The Smithsonian The
Smithsonian The Smithsonian The Smithsonian The
Smithsonian The Smithsonian The Smithsonian The
Smithsonian The Smithsonian The Smithsonian The
Smithsonian The Smithsonian The Smithsonian The
Smithsonian The Smithsonian The Smithsonian The
Smithsonian The Smithsonian The Smithsonian The
Smithsonian The Smithsonian The Smithsonian The
Smithsonian The Smithsonian The Smithsonian The
Smithsonian The Smithsonian The Smithsonian The
Smithsonian The Smithsonian The Smithsonian The
Smithsonian The Smithsonian The Smithsonian The
Smithsonian The Smithsonian The Smithsonian The
Smithsonian The Smithsonian The Smithsonian The
Smithsonian The Smithsonian The Smithsonian The
Smithsonian The Smithsonian The Smithsonian The
Smithsonian The Smithsonian The Smithsonian The
Smithsonian The Smithsonian The Smithsonian The
Smithsonian The Smithsonian The Smithsonian The
Smithsonian The Smithsonian The Smithsonian The
Smithsonian The Smithsonian The Smithsonian The
Smithsonian The Smithsonian The Smithsonian The
Smithsonian The Smithsonian The Smithsonian The
Smithsonian The Smithsonian The Smithsonian The
Smithsonian The Smithsonian The Smithsonian The
Smithsonian The Smithsonian The Smithsonian The
Smithsonian The Smithsonian The Smithsonian The
Smithsonian The Smithsonian The Smithsonian The

Smithsonian The Smithsonian The Smithsonian The
Smithsonian The Smithsonian The Smithsonian The
Smithsonian The Smithsonian The Smithsonian The
Smithsonian The Smithsonian The Smithsonian The
Smithsonian The Smithsonian The Smithsonian The
Smithsonian The Smithsonian The Smithsonian The
Smithsonian The Smithsonian The Smithsonian The
Smithsonian The Smithsonian The Smithsonian The
Smithsonian The Smithsonian The Smithsonian The
Smithsonian The Smithsonian The Smithsonian The
Smithsonian The Smithsonian The Smithsonian The
Smithsonian The Smithsonian The Smithsonian The
Smithsonian The Smithsonian The Smithsonian The
Smithsonian The Smithsonian The Smithsonian The
Smithsonian The Smithsonian The Smithsonian The
Smithsonian The Smithsonian The Smithsonian The
Smithsonian The Smithsonian The Smithsonian The
Smithsonian The Smithsonian The Smithsonian The
Smithsonian The Smithsonian The Smithsonian The
Smithsonian The Smithsonian The Smithsonian The
Smithsonian The Smithsonian The Smithsonian The
Smithsonian The Smithsonian The Smithsonian The
Smithsonian The Smithsonian The Smithsonian The
Smithsonian The Smithsonian The Smithsonian The
Smithsonian The Smithsonian The Smithsonian The
Smithsonian The Smithsonian The Smithsonian The
Smithsonian The Smithsonian The Smithsonian The
Smithsonian The Smithsonian The Smithsonian The
Smithsonian The Smithsonian The Smithsonian The
Smithsonian The Smithsonian The Smithsonian The
Smithsonian The Smithsonian The Smithsonian The
Smithsonian The Smithsonian The Smithsonian The
Smithsonian The Smithsonian The Smithsonian The
Smithsonian The Smithsonian The Smithsonian The
Smithsonian The Smithsonian The Smithsonian The
Smithsonian The Smithsonian The Smithsonian The
Smithsonian The Smithsonian The Smithsonian The
Smithsonian The Smithsonian The Smithsonian The
Smithsonian The Smithsonian The Smithsonian The
Smithsonian The Smithsonian The Smithsonian The

Smithsonian The Smithsonian The Smithsonian The
Smithsonian The Smithsonian The Smithsonian The
Smithsonian The Smithsonian The Smithsonian The
Smithsonian The Smithsonian The Smithsonian The
Smithsonian The Smithsonian The Smithsonian The
Smithsonian The Smithsonian The Smithsonian The
Smithsonian The Smithsonian The Smithsonian The
Smithsonian The Smithsonian The Smithsonian The
Smithsonian The Smithsonian The Smithsonian The
Smithsonian The Smithsonian The Smithsonian The
Smithsonian The Smithsonian The Smithsonian The
Smithsonian The Smithsonian The Smithsonian The
Smithsonian The Smithsonian The Smithsonian The
Smithsonian The Smithsonian The Smithsonian The
Smithsonian The Smithsonian The Smithsonian The
Smithsonian The Smithsonian The Smithsonian The
Smithsonian The Smithsonian The Smithsonian The
Smithsonian The Smithsonian The Smithsonian The
Smithsonian The Smithsonian The Smithsonian The
Smithsonian The Smithsonian The Smithsonian The
Smithsonian The Smithsonian The Smithsonian The
Smithsonian The Smithsonian The Smithsonian The
Smithsonian The Smithsonian The Smithsonian The
Smithsonian The Smithsonian The Smithsonian The
Smithsonian The Smithsonian The Smithsonian The
Smithonian The Smithsonian The Smithsonian The
Smithsonian The Smithsonian The Smithsonian The
Smithsonian The Smithsonian The Smithsonian The
Smithsonian The Smithsonian The Smithsonian The
Smithsonian The Smithsonian The Smithsonian The
Smithsonian The Smithsonian The Smithsonian The
Smithsonian The Smithsonian The Smithsonian The
Smithsonian The Smithsonian The Smithsonian The
Smithsonian The Smithsonian The Smithsonian The
Smithsonian The Smithsonian The Smithsonian The
Smithsonian The Smithsonian The Smithsonian The
Smithsonian The Smithsonian The Smithsonian The
Smithsonian The Smithsonian The Smithsonian The
Smithsonian The Smithsonian The Smithsonian The
Smithsonian The Smithsonian The Smithsonian The
Smithsonian The Smithsonian The Smithsonian The

Smithsonian The Smithsonian The Smithsonian The
Smithsonian The Smithsonian The Smithsonian The
Smithsonian The Smithsonian The Smithsonian The
Smithsonian The Smithsonian The Smithsonian The
Smithsonian The Smithsonian The Smithsonian The
Smithsonian The Smithsonian The Smithsonian The
Smithsonian The Smithsonian The Smithsonian The
Smithsonian The Smithsonian The Smithsonian The
Smithsonian The Smithsonian The Smithsonian The
Smithsonian The Smithsonian The Smithsonian The
Smithsonian The Smithsonian The Smithsonian The
Smithsonian The Smithsonian The Smithsonian The
Smithsonian

The Smithsonian

BEST BUY—FAIR LAKES

Brian G. went to Arby's at Fair Oaks Mall for lunch where he ate a very
large roast beef sandwich called the Montanan with a large side order of
curly fries that he alternated between dipping in little cups of ketchup and
barbecue sauce in a booth, alone, by the window. He watched people pass
back and forth, and they watched him, and he was a guy eating in a
window in a mall. One of the people passing back and forth was Grayson
Donald whom he did not know nor did he have any reason to know. But
Brian G. is the guy who aided Vicki Donald with her purchase of the
Internet-monitoring software, even though technically he works in the
car stereo department but he was walking by and saw her unattended and
since customer service is number one and since there was no computer
software associate in sight, he swooped in, answered her questions best he
could, took the commission on the sale. It's team-player assertiveness like
that that has made him manager of his department. Brian G.'s food now
was on a plastic brown tray with a paper place mat that had a pretty sim-

ple maze on it, in his opinion. He came very close to dropping his food as he carried it from the station with the ketchup and straws and napkins etc. to his plastic booth because he had his extralarge Mountain Dew on the tray too and it offset the delicate balance almost but he recovered quickly, thwarted disaster, slid in to the booth safely, aware of being watched by the middle-aged black woman with braces behind the counter and a mom across the dining area in another booth with her toddler.

He has a goatee that he keeps short by going over it five days a week with a Norelco cordless beard trimmer with a 2 guard and using shaving cream and safety razor (Schick Mach 2) for the rest of his face, an ingrown hair on his neck red and nearly glowing, gets paid $11/hour and sales commission as car stereo department manager at Best Buy in Fair Lakes, was hired while still a cashier at BJ's Wholesale also in Fair Lakes before Best Buy opened five years ago by a guy who was a few years older than he was and seemed cool and whose name he forgets but who said he would be working under him and have a good time. But when he started at Best Buy he asked about the guy and no one had ever heard of him and he never saw him again. They said they never heard of him but their faces got a tightened, closed look in the eyes that said don't ask us any more questions. Helped unpack boxes of merchandise and set up the displays and break down boxes and built CD display cases and organized the back warehouse part a little, took out a lot of trash, hung gift cards along the registers that had not been plugged in or programmed yet, that hot summer of newness, high spirits, lunches to McDonald's with other new hires—they all were new—and chatty and friendly, able to be who they always wanted to be. Spent a week alone inserting what in the retail industry are called fixtures, those little metal arms on which small petty things like batteries and gift cards and wall jack adapters hang for people in line to look at while waiting to check out and maybe decide they need because they're only a couple bucks. He is proud of knowing that these tiny purchases made on impulse account for more revenue than most people think.

His work shirt is a blue collared polo-style shirt that says BEST BUY, with the yellow price tag logo, almost waffle-meshy fabric with a change in fabric around the cuffs of the short sleeves, must be tucked in according to uniform regulations. The teenage high school sales associates, he thinks, seem to have the biggest problem with this, but threatening them with pay cuts seems to do the trick. Every morning he tucks his shirt in before his full-length mirror that he still hasn't hung up on the wall and so it leans, making him look tall, which he likes, because he is not tall, merely 5'8¾". He often feels dwarfed by other men, even if the other men are no taller than he is. He doesn't know why. Tucks his shirt in quickly each morning in his one-bedroom apartment with laundry and air-conditioning, pool, gym facilities, day care, in the Newgate neighborhood in Centreville, always catching the digital alarm clock that makes ocean waves if you set it to that which he bought from here at Best Buy with his 25 percent employee discount and the clock whenever he looks at it in the morning always says 7:54 it seems like.

Today he took his lunch break at 2 PM as usual for a nine-to-six shift, got back at 3. On Saturdays he usually does the eight-to-five shift, gets Sundays and Thursdays off, unless there is an emergency or someone doesn't show, which is more often than most people think. Not everyone is as responsible as he is, in his opinion, especially high school kids who don't need to work like he does, since they don't pay rent or bills like he does. He takes not a small amount of pride whenever he pays rent or bills or thinks about paying rent or bills.

Decided on the way out to his 1996 Pathfinder for lunch that he would not go to Burger King or Taco Bell today as usual but instead acted on the craving for Arby's he'd had all morning, and he enjoyed parking in the Fair Oaks Mall lot and going in through the heavy glass doors, held for him by a high school kid who was probably skipping school, with helmetlike hair with glasses and a plaid J.Crew shirt who didn't say anything when Brian G. thanked him and whose name was Grayson Donald.

Went to Arby's, ordered, paid, waited, almost dropped, sat down, ate, crumpled up the foil-like wrapper with its bits of reddish-gray beef that'd fallen out from the overstuffed (but delicious, new) sandwich, dumped his tray into the trash, set the now bare tray on top, wiped his hands on his butt, thought about starting to jog on his lunch breaks from now on instead of eating shit like he just ate, left Arby's. Got back into his car, feeling, if anything, the pride of being at work, drove back to Best Buy, parked in the same spot, sat in his Pathfinder with DC101 on low, for three minutes. Called Bryce Gauthier, Brian G.'s brother's boy from the army, told him that the Sony DVD/VCR/MiniDisc/Cassette/AM-FM Radio/MP3 Brian G. had ordered for him using connections only a Best Buy manager has had come in this morning if he wanted to come by and pick it up later. Went back into Best Buy through the electric automatic sliding doors, smiling. He was aware of being watched, judged by customers. He was a worker, employed and productive. Clocked back in by sliding his plastic photo employee ID card into the scanner in the break room with thirty-seven seconds to spare on his break, giving him a significantly sharp warm burst of pleasure as he made his way back to his post.

24585 Bunkers Court— Fourth Entrance

Parents who move to Little Rocky Run do so with the intention of letting their children play in the front yard with other little boys and girls. But knowing they can do so safely. That their children can go over to the next-door neighbor's home to play with the little boy there or attending a "sleepover" knowing who will be supervising their children. That they all share a common morality, often, but not necessarily, based on a belief in a higher power, be it Jesus Christ or another deity from another part of the world. After all, we embrace diversity and encourage understanding of others' beliefs.

People like you, Mr. Horton, to be frank, are what masticate away at this. Your cynicism and ill regard for others cast a long, dark shadow over the neighborhood. Frankly, you desanctify Little Rocky Run.

Where is the line? Must something awful happen for you to get the message? Must a young child learning to ride his bicycle, out for his first cruise without Daddy running along beside him cheering him on, propping him up, tears welling in his eyes, be <u>murdered</u> when a basketball goal tips over and <u>crushes him to death</u>?. Or <u>permanently</u> <u>paralyzing</u> him? <u>Then</u> will you be "happy?"

Imagine if you will, this scenario: Two teens are walking home from a tough day of school. They're seniors in high school, mere months away from graduation. They are discussing the evening's homework assignment or the upcoming "Prom." One of them sees a basketball hoop on the curb in front of a house. He says to the other, "Hey, 'know what? I think I am going to see if I can reach the hoop of this goal." (You know how "logical" teens can be, I am sure. To utilize sarcasm, a method of satire.) And then this teen jumps and, hey, how about that, he reaches the hoop!

"Nice one, man!" his friend exclaims cheerfully.

The teen hangs from the hoop to show-off for his friend who is amused and impressed. But he becomes nervous and uses his judgement to realize that this is not a good idea. After all, as it displays a lack of judgment on behalf of teens who are supposed to be striving to earn the respect of their parents and community as well serving as examples for the younger children.

"Hey, maybe you should come on down from there," his friend says warningly.

"Sissy!" the teen jeers tauntingly.

But before his friend can act, the basketball goal collapses on top of him. It breaks his neck. The hoop smashes into his skull with a sick cracking sound, splitting it open. Blood and brains emerge in a pink goo that spreads slowly around the sneakers of his friend. He knows the teen is dead.

Another life with so much potential snatched from us so young.

Or the teen merely breaks his arm on the fall and you then are liable from a legal standpoint. You face a lawsuit and financial ruin along with possible incarceration. Your superiors at your work do not want to be associated with someone in such legal pressure. And they are coming under much negative pressure. So they then decide to let you go.

Your wife moves out because you are failing to provide for your family, taking the kids with her. Months pass and she files for divorce. You have to sell your home and move into a small apartment in an unpleasant neighborhood in Alexandria. Your wife remarries a man who is able to support her and her children. There are no photographs of you in the new house or any physical trace of you. Your daughter grows up away from her father and becomes pregnant before her 17th birthday. The father is a 24 year old homeless man. She drops out of school. The baby's father is abusive. Your son gets in to drugs and steals to support his habit until he is arrested and placed in jail. This goes on his permanent record and no colleges are willing to accept him. You are robbed one day in front of your apartment by gang members and beaten very badly. Or worse.

These are very negative images. They are tough contentions to swallow, I know. I apologize. But this is reality. This happen every day. Watch the evening news. Peruse the newspaper. The fact is, this is the condition of the world in which we exist today. It does not make sense to hide from reality.

BEST BUY—FAIR LAKES

Brian G. keeps his dish towels on the handle of his oven door. He is twenty-eight years old, has a hairy chest, went to Braddock Park High School and graduated with a 3.4, worked at BJ's Wholesale after school and during summers except for the two that he was a lifeguard and saved a four-year-old girl from drowning. Switched to full-time at BJ's after graduating, during his year off from James Madison University that ended up being forever, doesn't recognize the humor in the name BJ's.

Folks mill about picking up plastic-vacuum-wrapped things and looking at them and dropping them into their handbaskets. Stay-at-home moms, exasperated as usual, speaking to the employees who are red-eyed slack-jawed with shaved heads like they . . . do . . . not . . . understand . . . English.

Brian G. advanced to assistant manager of the television department after four months at Best Buy and, after only another seven months, was promoted to manager of car stereos after the old one was arrested for pirating Adobe Photoshop. Went to Arby's for lunch on a Monday, the day a Braddock Park High School student named Grayson Donald committed suicide. He now sees this dude he went to high school with checking out hip-hop CDs named Chris Jenkins who was caught jerking off at lacrosse camp he heard in ninth grade. Brian G. goes out of his way not to make eye contact, grins widely now at another man in a Best Buy shirt, manager of cashiers named Greg, goatee, khakis. Brian G. shakes Greg's hand with both hands—one on Greg's forearm—and says, —What's going on?

Greg says, —Working for a living.

—What's the sales totals look like so far?

—We're cruisin', nigga, Greg says. —Big time.

—So are we at, uh . . . what was it . . . ?

—What.

—The, uh, the sales goal. 102. Are you saying we're at 102?

—Pssh, Greg says, rolling his eyes and looking around, then making a jerk-off motion, —Nigga, we eclipsed 102 an *hour* ago.

—102 by two o'clock? That's in*sane*.

—I know. And we're still rockin' and rollin', man. *Big time.*

—Nice, baby. Brian G. says, giving Greg thumbs-up. —That's what I like to hear!

Brian G. is known as Brian G. because there are eleven other Brians employed here at Best Buy Fair Lakes, three alone in management. Brian G. likes to imagine customers watching him talk about sales goals, his eyes bright, with an athletic physique, hair and goatee trim, khakis unwrinkled, confident, like a quarterback. Brian G. calls guys he doesn't know Man and Bud. Nigga if no black people are within earshot. He feels watched every second of his shift and every breath of his life. That's because he is. In fact, Brian G. remembers now a moment a few weeks or months ago on a day actually eerily similar to this one, not that that's a rare occurrence, in which there was a high school kid hanging around in the CD section, this weird skinny kid staring at Brian G. with big eyes and glasses as Brian G. helped a customer with a subwoofer and then seeing this kid again after work that day in the Bertucci's parking lot in Centreville where Brian G. was picking up his takeout, and then again in the parking lot at the Colonnade in front of Giant where Brian G. had stopped next to pick up his allergy prescription, condoms, and a twelve-pack of Miller Lite bottles then going to the Shell station there to fill up his Pathfinder with premium and to buy a pack of Marlboro Lights—in fact what he wants right now more than anything is a cigarette even though he just smoked one—and anyway he saw the kid the next day in the same spot in the CD section, staring at him again, and this time Brian G. saw him leaving the store with a Korn CD stuffed into the front of his pants (*Follow the Leader*, the newest one) and the security bar had been ripped off the CD and lay on the floor where the kid had been standing and for some reason Brian G. didn't stop the kid or signal to the loss prevention guys hanging out by the door checking people's receipts but instead he let the high school kid go and in fact now that Brian G. thinks about it—his belly full, enabling optimal thinking capabilities—that was the same kid who just held the door for Brian G. on the way in to Fair Oaks. Brian G. gets the heebie-jeebies now but overall tries not to think too much about this.

The song "Cumbersome" by a band called Seven Mary Three is what is playing on the satellite radio loop pumped in over the PA at a background-level volume from wafer-thin screened-over speakers in the ceiling. Songs people know, by artists they've heard of. He whistles along, grin-grimaces hello to a cashier he doesn't recognize who, he notices, isn't at her station despite the high volume of customers in line at the registers. But before he can act he is distracted by a middle-aged man with a beard in a khaki ball cap and tucked-in flannel shirt who is looking at PC-mounted digital cameras, seeing to his chagrin that no employees of this department are in sight.

—Anything I can help you with today, sir? Brian G. says, hands behind his back, mouth grimacing, dimples slighter than he thinks. The man, who is John Donald, looks bewildered by the attention but says he's fine. Brian G. kind of tilts his head and goes, —Great. Okay. Well, if you need any help with anything, give me a holler.

He wants to slap the guy on the back but stops himself and walks on, whistling. He feels nothing short of blackened derision for that cashier, who is now out of sight. She disgusts him. He wants to find her, give her the Alec Baldwin speech from *Glengarry Glen Ross*, which he bought from here with his 25 percent employee discount. The whole speech. All seven minutes of it. Even taking off his Timex Ironman which cost $54 with his 25 percent employee discount and dropping it on the counter before her, saying, —See this watch? It cost more than your car.

Brian G.'s wife is twenty-one pounds overweight and wears makeup by the handful. She has a baby that isn't Brian G.'s and receives child support from the father. They've been together since junior year at Braddock Park High School. She got pregnant when they were on a break. She is a graphic design teacher at Braddock Park High School and she smokes Marlboro Ultra Lights, knows everyone's name at T. T. Reynold's, has an expired membership at Life Time Fitness. So does Brian G. Her hair is dyed blond and she waxes her pubic area, has a tattoo of a Chinese symbol right below her bikini line, goes to Mystic Tan twice a week. Every evening when they get home from work (she is always home first, in her Pathfinder that her parents gave her) they watch the *Whose Line Is It Anyway?* rerun from that day, recorded on the VCR that Brian G. sets every morning and bought from Best Buy with his 25 percent employee discount. They drink Miller Lites and eat Bertucci's takeout that he picks up from the Centreville location, near the Sweetwater Tavern. Brian G.'s friend Brian Floyd's little sister works there at that Bertucci's. Sometimes she hooks him up if her manager's not around. Brian G. thinks she has a crush on him. After they eat Bertucci's, Brian G. and his wife take bong hits, put the dishes in the dishwasher, and Brian G. plays with his wife's kid if her kid's there, watches TV, plays Xbox if she lets him, fucks his wife maybe, goes to sleep.

He likes "Cumbersome." Catchy tune, pretty rocking.

He likes music, loves music, can't live without it. He's always listening to music, like twenty-four hours a day. He doesn't know what would happen if he didn't have music.

Brian G. is in his own opinion a victim of either social anxiety disorder or moderate depression and is waiting for himself to come to the point in his life where he chooses to seek treatment, wonders when that will be. He fears something, has an implacable tension about a looming disaster but he doesn't know what it is. He feels a fleeting elusive guilt over Vietnam and WWII. Like his brother's boy Bryce Gauthier does. In fact Brian G.'s brother Johnny feels the same way—they have talked about this. Brian G. enjoys almost more than anything in the world when there's Breaking News on TV, but he is always disappointed when the Breaking News isn't a sign of like World War III beginning. He also might be anorexic and notices in himself symptoms of early stages of OCD. He's slept with fourteen girls but tells anyone who asks like forty or fifty, he lost count. He wishes he had a bigger penis. He desperately waits for meaning or purpose to happen to him. He has owned seven different video game systems since Nintendo, including Game Boys, counts off in his head the number of orgasms he gives Beth when they have sex, which occurs two or three times a month, pathetic, in his opinion. He lives and dies for the Redskins and going into every season he sees no way that they will not win twelve to fourteen games this year. He goes into a legitimate funk for the entire week when they lose, which is often. He gets tense when he hears on TV that a couple has sex five or six times a week.

They've taped themselves doing it. The tapes are in their VHS collection with her baby's birthday parties.

Brian G.'s becoming increasingly addicted to the Internet lately. It's the first thing he does now when he comes home. During *Whose Line Is It Anyway?* as he eats his Bertucci's, monitor turned so Beth can't see, he is usually looking at pictures of skinny girls he finds way more attractive than Beth with cocks in their assholes. He's recently discovered a rich full pleasure in posting phony singles ads from women on online dating sites then masturbating to the responses he gets from suburban dads or divorcees who send him pictures of their badly lit erections or flexed torsos in bathroom mirrors. One of the dads who responded once—not that he would know this—was the customer he just engaged in the PC-mounted digital cameras aisle, John Donald, who didn't include a picture or any identifying information in his response, only that he wanted to put his, quote, dick between Brian G.'s, quote, ta-tas until it, quote, spit.

Brian G. finds himself at work lately keeping an eye out for any faces he recognizes from those responses so that if he does he can rush off to the employee bathroom in back and jerk off. He can jerk off very quickly, in like ten seconds. Numb wang or no. He jerks off at least once a day by routine, usually at work, in the employee bathroom. Brian G. is twenty-three pounds overweight and uses his left hand and used to be in a band that opened up for Modern Yesterday once, at T. T. Reynold's. At one time he thought he was put on this earth to establish a retail entrepreneurship like Arthur Blank or the Wal-Mart guy. He's always envisioned himself in the future as extremely rich, happy, and envied.

Brian G. has no tattoos but had his ear pierced during his lone year at James Madison University. He also got a girl pregnant there and she had an abortion, he paid for it with the credit card that his mom gave him for books and food, which he also used to pay for a pet python.

MS-13

Raul found out about her going to the FBI about Raul chopping off Lorenzo's hands even though Lorenzo deserved it.

He came to me and told me it was me as leader of the clique that had to do something about it.

He said make sure Raquel has no idea we know.

He said make sure she feels safe and comfortable.

So last night me and Raquel went on the bus to see Godzilla which I thought was overdone and full of plot holes but altogether a fun little thrill ride.

Raquel thought it was silly and stupid b/c the Godzilla was so fake and stupid looking.

Everybody has their opinion I suppose. Raquel is more of a comedy fan anyway, shit like Adam Sandler or Chris Rock.

On the way out of the theater discussing this I told Raquel I wanted her to give me head around back.

& we went back there where it was secluded and dark, behind one of the big dumpsters

& I was telling her I love her and wanted to take her to Canada and have babies and build a big house and I'd work hard

& Knowing what was about to happen

& getting hard.

& she was jerking me off

& then Pedro and Chester showed up behind her with a machete and a knife

She heard them and turned around.

I held her by the throat so she wouldn't be able to get away.

Pedro and Chester stabbed her over and over.

She made a gurgling choking sound through the hole in her throat,

& blood bubbling out of it then shooting like a fire hydrant!

Her hand still on my dick which started spurting come.

The fingers of the other hand went flying off somewhere because she put her hand up.

Then in the car Raul got from somewhere out to the mountains & to the river.

I was in the backseat with her body wrapped in dropcloth and blankets

& I peeked under her shirt to see out of curiosity what those fat girl titties looked like now.

They were all torn to shit and still pumping blood out a little.

I kissed her on the forehead, licked her blood off my lips,

& whispered so Pedro & Chester wouldn't hear and make fun, Goodbye Raquel.

& Stroked her hair and looked out the window.

Chester was driving.

The radio was on, DC101

& I told Pedro to give me a cigarette and to change the radio to the Latino station.

Best Buy—Fair Lakes

The men who built this did so quickly, via template. There is a team designated for such purposes. They, this team of nomads, travel up and down the East Coast building Best Buys and Wal-Marts and Home Depots. They are like a band of cantors. Steinbeck immigrants and odd-duck carnies. The West Coast has its own team, as does the Midwest and so on. They erected this one like a barn raising, using pulleys and manpower to heave-ho the giant cutout walls that arrived on the back of a flatbed truck with them, a helicopter hovering over it all with the tremendous square roof dangling by basically a very strong rope, and a paunchy balding man with wraparound Oakleys wearing a blue polo-style shirt tucked in, hard hat, goatee, khakis shouting through a megaphone at them all. It took about three weeks to raise the Best Buy, in total. That includes knocking down the trees and tilling the land or whatever is done to land. Paving the parking lot. The parking lot seems to have happened overnight or by freak of nature because no one remembers seeing any steamrollers or tanks of tar. One day there was a rocky sylvan plat between Fair Oaks

Mall and Toys "R" Us and the next there was a Best Buy with a gleaming parking lot still humming with the smell of freshly laid tar and the employees at their stations and the merchandise on the shelves as if it had been there for generations and it is you who are newly arrived.

MS-13

Bus comes, we get on.

Pay our fare in mostly dimes and nickels that we spent the last two hours asking people for outside Borders.

Driver pretends to ignore us.

Walk down the aisle not making eye contact with nobody & sit down in the back. Other riders mostly niggers asleep as usual.

Gloria sits next to me, asks me what's wrong & I shoot her a glare so full of hate that she shuts up.

I have been thinking of her with shit all over & the memory is so fresh like it's just happened & the same emotions like it just happened.

& Chester says Hey and points out the window his head is leaned against, tattoo behind his ear of MS-13

& we all look at this fucking hot Spider that is red and souped up and with a system so fucking juiced that it practically bounces off the road

& I try to look inside to see what the driver looks like and if he is Latino b/c I suddenly have to know if he is Latino.

But the windows are tinted thick black and no light passes through.

We are all silently respectful of it

& the light changes and it zooms off, tires squealing, roaring like a wild animal

& I am 16 years old & Gloria 22 & Chester and Pedro 15 I think & Raul is 19 & Julia 14.

& I am seriously considering getting a new tattoo on my knuckles in full color this time professionally done

& I am wearing Nike sweatpants and a Tommy Hilfiger t-shirt and one leg of my Nike sweatpants is pushed up revealing a white Adidas sock hiked up

& my shoes are Nikes

& I ask Gloria what she thinks, GATO across my knuckles in full color, one letter per knuckle, paid for in a tattoo parlor with cash and the tattoo artist tipped afterward with a $100 bill

& she looks at my hand, takes it in hers and says while caressing it, Yeah I can see how that would look good.

& the bus bouncing

& traffic behind & next to & in font of us

& zooming along through Fairfax and Fair Lakes

& Julia says, I gotta go to Sam Goody because I want the new Usher CD and I want to check out the new Alanis Morissette on the listening booth thing b/c I like that song Thank U

This irritates me

I want to tell her no Alanis Morissette allowed but I get distracted b/c there's a Washington Post from today under my feet which excites me at first but it's only the book review section something by some fucker named Michael Dirda

& I look at it and read it

& imagine him in his kitchen in his bathrobe pouring coffee and reading books—probably McLean or Rockville, MD

& sitting at his computer sipping his coffee in his finished basement as his wife makes baked ziti upstairs and his little dog yaps in the perfectly mowed and watered backyard

& this must be nice

& I make the decision that when we get to Fair Oaks Mall we will go shopping and check out some books at the bookstore

& new clothes

Tommy Hilfiger or Abercrombie and Fitch most preferably and FUBU—new shoes too especially Nikes or Timberlands.

& I also would like some more Polo Sport as mine is running low.

Maybe to kill time later we'll steal a car in the parking lot and crash it somewhere

& break into some of the condos near Fair Oaks and see what we find

& fuck a middle aged white lady or a small boy who lives there or whatever.

I tell myself to calm down further.

Somebody has written COCKSUCKER over an advertisement for Sylvan Learning Center of all things

& I point this out to Gloria who sees it and clicks her tongue in disapproval and goes, That's real rude, to vandalize like that, you know?

Best Buy—Fair Lakes

Saw a skinny white kid who worked there breaking down a great big box in the world music aisle. The kid must have been eighteen or nineteen with a shaved head and pubelike facial hairs growing from his chin, wispy shadows on either side of his head that could've been mistaken for sideburns. Broke down the box not by slicing away the packing tape with a box cutter then allowing it to collapse then folding it but by setting the box down and taking two steps back and leaping upon it with his foot, smashing it. And when this only succeeded in crushing a section of the box he did it again, and again, and again, until the box was a mangled pile of cardboard. Then he wiped his nose and picked up the wreckage in his arms. Brian G. approached him, a boy with a tattoo of thorns around his forearms, freckles, Best Buy shirt too big and coming untucked. He touched the boy by coming at him sideways then placing a hand on his stomach and on his back as if to hold him still as he said into his ear, —Let me have your attention for a moment. So you're talking about what? You're bitching about that sale you shot, some asshole who doesn't want to buy, someone who doesn't want what you're selling, some chick you're trying to fuck, and so on and so forth? Well, let's talk about something *important*.

The kid tried to pull away from him but Brian G. held on tighter. —Put . . . that box . . . *down*. He didn't. —Boxes are for closers only. Do you think I'm fucking with you? I am not fucking with you. I'm here from downtown. I'm here from Mitch and Murray. And I'm here on a mission of mercy. He looked at the kid's name tag. —Your name's Andrew?

—Yeah.

—You call yourself a salesman, you son of a bitch?

—What? No, I—

—See this watch? He held up the Ironman.

—Yeah.

—It costs more than your car. Know what car I drove to work today? A BMW that costs eighty thousand dollars. I made nine hundred and seventy thousand last year. You can't play in a man's game. Because only one thing in this life matters, Andrew, and that is getting them to sign on the line that is dotted. You hear me, you fucking faggot? The kid was squirming, the hairs of Brian G.'s meticulous goatee nearly brushing his big lobes which were pierced with big black gouges covered by corporate mandate with Band-Aids. The boy was stoned out of his skull trying to figure out what the fuck was going on, and at that moment had thirteen CDs (Deftones, *Around the Fur*; Snot, *Get Some*; Tool, *Undertow* and *Aenima*; System of a Down, *System of a Down*; Incubus, *Enjoy Incubus* (already has *S.C.I.E.N.C.E*); Downset, *Do We Speak a Dead Language?*; Rage Against the Machine, *Evil Empire*; 311, *Music* and *Grassroots*; Pink Floyd, *Animals*; Rahzel, *Make the Music 2000*; Henry Rollins, *Come in and Burn*) and four DVDs (*Dazed and Confused, Billy Madison, A Clockwork Orange, Friday*) stuffed down his baggy cargo khakis which hung so far down off his hips that it looked like it he had no butt, Brian G. noticed, and also which had little holes all over the crotch and thighs from incendiary weed bits blowing out of the bowl and from dropping his cigarette on himself while sitting down. Brian G. said, —The good news is, Andrew, you're fired. Oh, do I have your attention now? The bad news is you've got one week to get your job back, starting tonight. And you can start with getting your ass to Computers to help the gentleman who is looking at PC-mounted digital cameras. A-B-C, Andrew. Always Be Closing. Because it's fuck or walk. You close or you hit the bricks. Think they come in to get out of the rain, Andrew? They don't walk on the lot unless they want to buy. Look at them. They're out there waiting to give you their money. Are you going to take it, Andrew? Are you man enough to take it?

—Y-yes?

—It takes brass balls to work retail. Don't like the abuse? Leave. Get mad, Andrew! I can go out on this floor with the materials you've got and make fifteen thousand dollars in two hours. Go and do likewise, Andrew. A-B-C! I'd wish you luck but you wouldn't know what to do with it if you got it.

He patted the kid on the back and took the box from him. From afar, from the point of view of John Donald who was looking over watching this from Computers, it looked like the two were having some sort of terse, covert homosexual lovers' discussion in the world music aisle. John Donald found this both abhorrent and alluring. The kid wandered off toward him and Brian G. watched him go, saying to himself, —And to answer your question, pal, of why am I here? I'm here because Mitch and Murray asked me for a favor. I said here's the real favor: Follow my advice and fire your fucking ass because a loser is a loser.

Then he carried the cardboard off, passing it off to another employee to take to the compressor in the back.

BRADDOCK PARK HIGH SCHOOL

Lunchtime, Braddock Park High School cafeteria, a wide-open room of no particular shape, though if forced one could say with passable accuracy that it resembles something kind of like a rhombus maybe. Heels click on the hard tile floor and voices echo into a callithumpian aural blur. Bodies are dwarfed by the immense institutionality of this room of mass feeding. Faces are given an unhealthy tint, darkened around the eyes, the fluorescent lighting, tubes flickering in their sockets up in the ceiling panels. Girls shiver, their gray teeth chattering, crossing their goose-bumped arms over their chests. There are reflections up ahead of you on the floor wherever you go, but the reflections are of you and always keep their distance from you, like the moon. An army recruiter standing in uniform inside the entrance next to his display, trying to catch kids' eyes. Across from him is one from the navy with his own display, smiling with blankness, pretending to ignore the army recruiter. They are trying to sell them their fathers' lives. Tell them things about military life they know are untrue. False promises. At the front of the cafeteria the line to get soft pretzels (with nacho cheese for an extra 25¢) or inch-long spaghetti—covered in a chunky dark red sauce that comes in big plastic bags from the distribution center and all the cafeteria ladies have to do is heat it up—feeds into one doorway and exits out another. A stream of students passing through the cafeteria to the gym or trailers on the other side. The walls are cinder blocks slathered in rubbery white paint. You can still see the dimples of the cement, the gobs of paint dried in the thick cracks between blocks. The walls up near the ceiling running the length of the cafeteria and continuing out into the school lobby are painted green, orange, white, yellow, and navy blue, for no particular reason as, if you remember, those are not anything close to Braddock Park High School's colors—powder blue, black, gray, and white. Long folding tables, the same kind that were used at Coffee and Donuts at St. John the Apostle. Circular ones here and there. Blue plastic chairs with silver legs and little wobbly circular feet. The students sat with their backpacks hanging from the backs of chairs and self-arranged by grade, race, and general personality. All sat with those who resembled them. They wanted to look across the table and see themselves looking back. The voices they wished to hear were none but their own. It would ensure their existence, confirm their legitimacy as humans. As little does when you are a teenager. They used to serve lunch on pink Styrofoam trays. Nowadays they serve lunch on trays made of some reusable substance the color of newspaper turned to mush in the rain. Not many people actually eat during lunch. They might pick at a soft pretzel. Lick off all the huge salt grains and leave the rest. Drink a Veryfine Fruit Punch or Coca-Cola product from the machines. More so than eating they copy homework for the next class, manufacture and distribute information, long from afar for sex and love, plan fights, sleep. The overall sound is of sleepy bees in a wettened honeycomb. An agminate of hormonal, sleep-deprived bodies fully grown yet still restrained, stretching from wall to wall like refugees of an airborne toxic event, drinking and eating nonnutritious semiedible matter.

This one was the earliest of the three Omega lunch periods in a day at Braddock Park High School. It was 9:57 AM. One of the assistant administrators, Mr. Hayden—who once was the varsity football coach before he was promoted after taking the team to States and bringing home the hardware, the human growth hormone miniscandal not a hindrance—he holds a bachelor's degree in kinesiology from Longwood College—has been lobbying Sam Cahill, the humorless principal of Braddock Park High School, referred to by students and faculty only as Principal Cahill as opposed to Ms. Cahill or Mr. Cahill because his or her gender has never been officially confirmed, to create a seventh lunch period, which would start at 9:28 AM, for the sole reason (which Mr. Hayden doesn't say out loud) that Mr. Hayden is tired of having to wait all the way till 9:57 each morning before he is able to swing by the cafeteria and grab a delicious soft pretzel with nacho cheese to bring back to his office.

Sitting at the round table way off on the fringes of the cafeteria with some other males who resembled them, Sean Castiglione, Jeremiah Dutton, and Brian Donnelly sat hunched over their trays picking them apart and licking the salt off soft pretzels and each sucking down his third or fourth Mountain Dew of the morning. They seemed bent in conspiracy. A cabal planning its takeover.

—So like. Basically like what I was doing all weekend was I made a decision last week to, like, embrace technology, you know? So I spent all weekend like embracing the modern technology, you know?

—Yeah dude. Sweet.

—Ya'll know who I'd fuck in like a hot second? Blythe.

—Oh my God yes dude.

—I heard she has herpes though and gonorrhea of the throat.

—Dude you can't have gonorrhea of the throat.

—Dude, yeah you can, because my cousin had it.

—Your cousin's a slut.

—Yeah she is.

—Your *mom's* a slut.

—Har har, fag.

—Dude. Don't say that.

—What.

—Fag. It's not cool.

—Oh, dude. I'm getting Deftones today after school.

—It sucks. I heard it. The new song is on DC101. It sounds like the fucking Foo Fighters.

—For real?

—I saw Deftones in San Diego. Oh my God, did I tell you this dude?

—Nah.

—Yeah, but, uh, you saw them at Warped Tour while we saw them at Nation and we saw a dude on crack fall down and he had like newspaper on as like underwear so we're cooler.

—Mm.

—It was tight as shit though. Seriously. Chino fucking lost his shoe when he did a fucking flip into the crowd and it fucking hit me right in the fucking face. His shoe, I mean. I swear to God. It hit me right in the fucking *face*.

—Chino shouldn't have shaved his dreads off. Now he looks like Sugar Ray.

—You've told us this before like eighty times. And we still think you're fucking lying.

—I swear to God. I'll wear it to school tomorrow.

—You're a fucking fag.

—I'll punch you in the face if you say fag again dude.

—Ow. Shit. It's infected I think. Can you see it? Is it bleeding?

—Ew, nah, there's like greenish-white shit coming out. Ew. Ew! It looks like poop!

—Poop?

—Where's Grayson?

—I cleaned it though. Does that mean it's not clean? I cleaned it like eighty times.

—I'll kill you for saying fag again. I'll beat the fucking life out of you.

—What are you eating if your poop looks like that?

—Your mom. Every night.

—Whatever, I'd eat his mom. His mom's fucking hot.

—Shut the fuck up. I'd eat your sister. I'd fuck your sister in a second.

—Oh my God dude yes.

—I might take a little just maybe a bit longer than a second. But seriously though, I'd fuck *your* mom and *your* sister.

—More like you'd fuck his brother. Or his dad. Or one of the Flex Kids.

—Whatever yo. Give me a cigarette.

—Hey did you do the math homework? Hey. Yo.

—Yo, I dare you to like fucking eat this.

—How 'bout you suck my dick?

—Did you do the math homework though?

—Five bones.

—You don't have five bones. What do you have.

—I have five bones.

Then came the thing with the homework.

The sensation of sudden and violent loss. The alarm. There was no horror more vulgar, no news more breaking or urgent, adrenaline bolts shooting up and down the body's veins through the limbs, throbbing the fingers, sucking out the heat from the toes and sending it to the cheeks . . .

What happened is—well, first of all there is no bell at Braddock Park High School. But that's not due to some progressiveness on the part of administration. Even if such progressive notions did foster in the skulls of people like Mr. Hayden and Principal Cahill—and believe me, they don't—those ideas would have to stay there since nothing gets put into action in Fairfax County Public Schools unless it is a mandate faxed in by memo from the superintendent's Kremlin, er, office. And for a dictate to be faxed, the idea must first be studied, tested, weighed, its costs calculated, put to vote, tested again, weighed again but this time in cascading form, presented to the board, begged for, revamped, rolled out, unrolled out, subjected to brainstorms, then to idea showers, looped back upon offline, put through a participatory performance network, aggregated into interactive critical-thinking allocation interface, and finally rerolled out in a multidisciplinary, top-down curriculum integration endeavor.

But anyway, the reason Braddock Park is without a bell or any other sound indicating the end of the class period aside from the ones at the beginning and end of the day, is this: Since there are thirty-one hundred students in the school—designed by its architects, who usually build prisons, to house a maximum capacity of fifteen hundred inmates—I mean, students—the classes must change in a tiered schedule. One half changes on one schedule. They're called the Omegas. The other half changes on another schedule. They are the Alphas. This is necessary because otherwise during period changes there would be thirty-one hundred fourteen- to eighteen-year-olds flooding the confines, six or seven times a day, running rampant in every unsupervised direction. It's two schools in one, then, as the citizenry has procreated with a vigor and enthusiasm too powerful and efficient for the infrastructure provided them. Their loins cannot be suppressed. They spurt and spit the gunk of life in massive quantities, never missing, breaching the levels of the rooftops and drowning the sprawling commercial centers. The walls of the public education facilities are blasted through and bowled over, filling the new homes blossoming from out of the untilled soil like mold. It is a Chinese rabbit free-for-all of reproduction, new children falling from the sky like confetti in a parade, the matuary of Fairfax Hospital like the DMV of a third-world Latin American country in civil war. If you are an Alpha and your sister is an Omega you might go the whole year without seeing one another at school. You will never be made aware of the existence of half of your graduating class. You can become forgotten. Floating on your own orbit like an unimportant piece broken off a spacecraft. Lost to the cosmos forever. Separated and not swung back for.

The junior is on the Omega schedule and was staggering along toward AP Micromanagerial Arts and Systematized Third-Generation Time-Phase Theory in a hallucinogenic daze from having time for only an hour and a half of sleep last night due to his homework load and being woken every half hour by a nightmare having to do with dropping his college applications the hour before the deadline into a big blue steel USPS mailbox only to remember he forgot to stamp them; oversized forest green polo shirt from J. Crew with the fold lines still and the chemical odor clothes get when they spend a long time wrapped in plastic, skinny, baggy cargos, having just successfully conducted a social interaction with a kid his own age named Brian Hurkle who was his best friend in sixth grade and who, though they've had the same advanced and GT and AP classes in the same schools ever since, he has not spoken to or made eye contact with since the end of sixth grade. The conversation, if it could be considered a conversation, consisted of merely his asking Brian Hurkle if the oversized plaid shirt he was wearing was from J. Crew and Brian Hurkle, who was in a hurry, saying yes. The junior got head from Big Red in seventh grade on the Pot Lot on Springstone, the first time he smoked weed. He drives a 1997 Ford Explorer. He likes that Marcy Playground song. He looks and talks exactly like Brian Hurkle and Grayson Donald except for the hair. He does not know Grayson Donald. He lives next door to a fourteen-year-old who is in eighth grade at Ormond Stone Middle School named Seung-Hui Cho whose sister is currently a junior here at Braddock Park and is in fact in this junior's upcoming AP Micromanagerial Arts and Systematized Third-Generation Time-Phase Theory class and is also in fact walking by him right now with her books against her chest oblivious to what is taking hold of the junior and next year Seung-Hui Cho will be a freshman here and after he graduates high school (not from Braddock Park but from the new high school, Westfield, which is in Centreville and will open to accommodate the mass expansion of population) he will attend Virginia Tech. Wondering, the junior was, as he trudged along carrying forty-two pounds of books and papers etc. in his Eastpak backpack on his back, both shoulder straps, inside of which somewhere is a Texas Instruments TI-83 graphing calculator for his Advanced Calculus BC class that his mom bought for $86 from Best Buy in Fair Lakes, wondering if he should play flag football in college at Yale or start a fraternity or go to Harvard and get on the *Lampoon* so he can write for Letterman after graduation, or if he should make porns or skip college or hitchhike around the country and follow Kerouac's route in *On the Road*, and drink himself to death under an overpass while writing a great poetic novel in all-night bursts of intoxicated grammarless truthful exultation, exposing the phonies and corruption of Western culture in the process, but make it be about his life and his experiences, to be discovered and praised after his death, so he'll be a legend. He wondered if his wife should be brunette or blond, big breasts or nice ass, or if he's homosexual and if he should become an organic farmer in Africa and save AIDS babies on the weekends or if he should act or become an MTV VJ or start a band. In which case he would choose tough-tattooed-living-in-vans-eating-dogfood punk rock metal but with passionate poetic lyrics about the underbelly of the human experience. But he would find a way to make a lot of money off it down the road so he could have a nice house and get laid and be respected. Or he could be a stripped-down acoustic bard folksinger, witness to the social injustices and pathos of our day and evils of American capitalism, the terrors of its greed, its racism, its poverty. This, thought the junior, would also necessitate living in squalor somewhere at least for a little while just so he can say he did. Perhaps in a self-storage unit in Wilmington, DE, or a storefront in Portland, OR, because those cities are not as dangerous as, say, NY, meaning there aren't as many black people who scare him, frankly. He would have to break up with his girlfriend to do that though which also scares him shitless. But the question was this: Could he break up with her and still have sex with her until he finds someone else? He thinks he could. Why couldn't he? He worked on the campaign for the Democratic candidate for state representative, is genuinely nervous about the election tomorrow. But he can put it on his college application regardless of whether the candidate wins or loses. He was stressed out and hungry, finding nothing to his liking in the pantry before leaving for school this morning when it was still dark out, since his mother bought the wrong kind of donuts again from Giant and he was sick of Pop-Tarts.

He was near the top of the stairs, Brian Hurkle gone, Grayson Donald gone, when he was hit with the sensation that caused the incident. The last thing he remembers is that Lisa Evans was in front of him, blond, skinny, hot, wearing a high tight skirt and panty hose, but he had heard she was *a prude, her legs attached at the knees* was the way it had been put to the junior. The junior was sneaking a peak and imagining fucking Lisa Evans in a three-way, his girlfriend cheering him on as he fucked Lisa Evans. He noticed through the pantyhose way up high on the rear upper thigh a scratch on her skin, or a scar, something severe that he couldn't look away from. And that's when he suddenly pulled up dead, when he got to the top of the stairs right then, that's when the feeling plowed him over, or ran off with something very necessary to his emotional balance, breaking the rhythm of the class changers moving like a hardening flow of lava, as he suddenly remembered—and why just now, and why just here?—that he had completely not even forgotten to do but like erased entirely from his brain the *existence* of an assignment for AP Micromanagerial Arts and Systematized Third-Generation Time-Phase Theory, taught by Dr. Powell, a three-page thesis, due today, in ten minutes, on the, quote, capitalist bureautheories of the American oil industry, without going over the three-page limit or it's as good as not even doing it. The paper was to be 95 percent of the semester grade. There would be no extensions, Dr. Powell said the day he gave the assignment, the first day of school, the last time he mentioned it. Sean Castiglione, whom the junior knew, said as he passed him, —What da blood clot? but he didn't reply or notice, he was feeling his future taken from him, sweat now on his face and arms, saw the world spinning by and away, fading black then illuminating, blasting off, leaving him in a chilly cold with only fear. Kristin who works at Best Buy in Brian G.'s car stereo department after school stopped and asked him if he was okay but he didn't reply or look at her. A girl who was in Grayson Donald's Spanish class who asked him once about the conjugation of *poder* stopped too and leaned in and as did others—dozens, everyone on the second floor at the time changing classes, meaning probably close to a thousand people—opened their eyes wide and dropped their jaw, gasped at what they saw. —Oh my God. More people stopped due to the others' stopping, and they began screaming. A remedial math teacher named Ms. Mueller came running, cleared the students out of the way, and peered in close to the junior's face, her eyes betraying her fear, and said, —Honey, oh my God are you—? She tried her best but she couldn't continue. She turned and vomited. Someone else was heard shouting, —Please help! Someone help! Go get someone, quick! Another person, a girl, screamed, —Oh Jesus! Oh Jesus oh God!

MS-13

You forget sometimes, on the bus, speaking your native language, that no one else knows what you're saying

& you can say whatever you want as loud as you want.

In our life you get used to waking up on motel room floors amongst cigarettes

& joints

& the smell of cleaning agents in the carpet

& the smell of bodies cooking naked together in drugs and fast food

& body fluids in the early afternoon.

Stale breath and unwashed armpits

& backs sweaty w/ lint and crumbs stuck to them

The TV on full blast, the mirrors you can't stand looking at, opening the heavy starched curtains that seem to be made from wood covered in corduroy onto the highway and sunshine

& traffic

& FAIRFAX.

You learn it is possible to become a wild animal.

Your daily concerns eating and fucking and protecting yourself, prowling around.

You find yourself trained to wake up first so you don't have to sit on the edge of the bed or lean against the doorway waiting for someone else who's gotten up before you to piss or shit.

You learn girls when they spend enough time in close enough quarters, sharing beds and getting fucked together and using the same toilets and soap, they start getting their periods at the same time.

& don't care about making an effort to cover their bloody tampons up in the trash can or wrap them in toilet paper

& so when they're all bleeding it looks like a bunch of mice were fucking massacred.

You learn the warm loose feeling of fucking a pussy that two dudes have just come inside of before you, what three dudes' come smells like mixing together inside a pussy, how it fills a whole room.

That there is freedom in being invisible and speaking gibberish.

That white people at the mall are so willing to give money to brown people who look like they've crawled out of the sewer that you hardly have to do more than go up to them and ask

& this is especially true for well-dressed and smart-looking white boys, swim team kids with high IQs.

B/c they want to be you or think they understand you

& they think they are helping the world

& they want to show themselves they aren't racist

& they think all that separates us from them is skin color and heritage and how much money their parents have.

But that's bullshit because there's something more, way more, separating us, they will never understand the depths of the rift between us

& how we have nothing to do with them.

And you learn how far $80 a day can go between 6 people even after a motel room and beers & weed & smokes & food

& speaking of food you learn how little food the human body actually needs (one $1 hamburger a day) but also what malnutrition as a daily thing & starvation over long periods of time does to your mind body & emotions.

You sweat a lot, first of all, feel light pale empty, find your attention directed strictly on where are we going

& how do we get there

& your body screaming like a baby for attention, strictly immediate things, while the possibility of thinking of anything long term or deeper in the way of the Big Picture of GOD and THE SOUL & HUMAN EXIS-TENCE makes you nauseous

& exhausted

& like you want to puke on the bus or curl up under the seat

& cover yourself with the Washington Post

& die.

You learn, killing a person, something very profound about human life that you will never learn any other way and find impossible to explain to anybody who has not killed another person.

A lot of people, it's no big deal if they die or disappear.

No one misses them and their absence from the earth has no effect on anything.

You learn that stabbing someone to death is much more respectful and meaningful and feels better afterward for you than shooting some-one, and this is important, this makes a difference and is something that matters.

You learn that it becomes a comfortable thing to rely on your dis-connectedness & unreliability.

That body odor is a subjective thing, especially when it comes to your own.

You learn the importance of family.

But your family can be made up of anyone you choose

& that just because someone is your sister doesn't mean you can't fuck them or throw their body into a river

& same goes for your brothers.

That it is possible to take every argument, every question of right and wrong, and twist it so that it fits your needs, and this is a perfectly acceptable way to live your life.

That what matters is not me but MS-13.

That pretending not to know English gets you a long way

& gets you out of paying for a lot of things like refills and whatever.

B/c if you don't know English people just don't want to deal with you.

You learn what it feels like to be so high you feel inside out
& in a womb

& so you lock yourself in the bathroom pretending to be pissing just so you can check your bellybutton

(seeing your HUGE tattoos on your belly—GATO—and MS-13 and JESUS and EL SALVADOR and a picture of Jesus on the cross, bleeding & Mary)

to make sure there is no umbilical cord.

& the reason you have locked yourself in the bathroom and locked the door to check is not because your clique would laugh at you for being so high you think you have an umbilical cord but you've locked yourself in the bathroom because WHAT IF YOU HAVE AN UMBILI-CAL CORD?

GEORGE MASON UNIVERSITY

While she on the other hand firmly believes that men in a marriage should think only about their wives when it comes to sexual matters, and that if they don't then that is a problem. They should not be aroused by other women's bodies, on TV or in magazines or movies or real life. That is the point of making wedding vows, for now and forever, she believes. She considers it infidelity for husbands, her own included, to have private deep-down desires for other women's bodies, no matter how private or secret. She was never *told* otherwise. She was never given the *opportunity* to observe differently, never had the *experience* or overheard any conversa-tions to suggest that men are basically perverts. She never knew any males growing up besides her father, having attended an all-girls Catholic school in the early '60s, and not allowed to date, had no brothers, no friends had brothers, no male cousins, etc., and none of her girlfriends dated either or knew any more about the opposite sex than she. And so she was left with only assumptions and what she saw on TV and movies, and she of course used these assumptions to fill in for what she didn't know or understand. Men had to be like her, she figured, but with penises and facial hair and bigger muscles. She assumes that when men like her husband John swear when they are caught leering at other women's bodies that they are responding to a basic animal instinct they were born with and there's no harm in it that they are lying to themselves. She believes they are rationalizing their own inability to control themselves and are effectively *choosing* to leer. Men are babies, for the most part, she believes. They are pushy. They are slaves to their own urges. They lack willpower and the ability to think of anyone else but themselves.

When her husband was stationed for a year in Thailand a year before Grayson was born and she chose not to go with him because she had just gotten her first teaching job and was settling in to her career and didn't want to bail on her new job, which would have looked awful on her résumé and the word would have spread through the school system about her, she assumed that he spent the year apart from her, on the other side of the world, in a city full of underage whores and cheap sex shows, where white men with money are treated like gods, the same way she would have spent it—alone, working, sweeping the floor of his shoddy on-base apartment, going to Mass, jogging, asking passersby to use his camera to snap a picture of him in front of famous landmarks, writing letters to her and making quiet, tinny long-distance phone calls back home to her at odd hours. Thinking of her, his wife, and his love for her. Barely holding himself together until they could be together again. Abstaining from touching himself of course even if it would have been while thinking about his wife and her body. And that when any local women in thin dresses hardly clinging to their girlish bodies, no matter how attractive they were in the dusk on the street, fanning themselves, or touching his arm and asking him to buy them a drink at the officers' club, where he went only when he had to because the general he was working under ordered him to—he would kindly but firmly explain that he is married and Catholic anyway and not interested, thank you.

She's never lived alone, never been without a father or a husband. She was a virgin when she was married, swore lifelong commitment before God and family, had a baby, moved to Northern Virginia.

CHILDREN OF NoVA

Starting at puberty, kids in Northern Virginia start going around muttering like a mantra that they hate Northern Virginia and can't wait to leave.

Parents love their kids, give them everything they can afford, love them so much they can't bear to watch them suffer, even for a Coke or a new graphite baseball bat. Then the kids grow up and can't believe it when they discover the cost of stereos and clothes and vacations, things that once appeared before them like magic. But they still want them so bad it goes from wanting to needing.

They go from air-conditioned houses to air-conditioned cars to stores with air-conditioning cranked and in between they sweat and it's gobs and pounds shed.

MS-13

Images of Raquel looking at me right before Chester jabbed his knife into her throat

& her eyes

& her tongue when she opened her mouth to scream or ask WHY but nothing came out.

As we are pulling up to FAIR OAKS MALL.

MEDIA GENERAL CABLE

Thirty-seven percent of homes in Little Rocky Run at 6:26 PM November 2, 1998, have at least one TV tuned to Channel 4 news, NBC, and 100 percent of homes have Media General Cable, soon to be bought out by Cox Communications. If the TVs are watched, they watch the news. A twelve-year-old girl is missing from Loudon, a man is shot in his car in Anacostia, a pit bull has killed a twelve-year-old boy in Rockville, a fifteen-year-old Alexandria boy has been struck by a freight train, eggs can kill you, day care people hit your kids, there is a rapist loose, the Redskins are very optimistic about the way things are going and are insinuating that the new third-string quarterback they acquired for $9 million over four years is the final piece of what has seemed till now to be an unsolvable puzzle.

BEST BUY—FAIR LAKES

John Donald left Best Buy without buying a PC-mounted digital camera and felt a distinct awkwardness as he passed through the checkout aisle—the store's designed so you have to pass through a checkout aisle to get to the exit—avoiding the eye of the bored Asian girl in the blue polo shirt and khakis staring through him from behind her register.

He noticed he is an old man, doughy and not funny and gray.

Kept his head down and hands in his pockets and told himself he'd wait until at least tomorrow—twenty-four hours is a good period of time—to give himself ample time to chew over the purchase before actually buying a PC-mounted camera for which to take pictures of himself sitting before his computer for online dating profiles or flirting with women on the other side of the country, different countries. Often, he's found, women are more likely to e-mail you a picture of their bare breasts, rears, or vaginas if you are willing to first send them a picture of your dick, either flaccid or erect. Breaks the ice.

He congratulated himself as he whooshed through the electronic doors for having the self-knowledge and willpower to hold off on such a pricey purchase—$140, for the cheapest one—until he had chewed it over and maybe had done some research and compared prices and asked around for inside information about which camera has the best light filtration and contrast and which gives you the least grainy shot, best bang for your buck durabilitywise, etc. Though then again he also knew from past experience that there was a hefty chance that the rest of his day would be consumed with obsessing over whether or not to make the purchase until he would be finally driven, like an alcoholic—which his father was but which he does not believe himself to be—back here to this parking lot tonight, two minutes before closing, to buy the camera.

He feigned whistling as he stepped off the sidewalk, past an employee in a blue polo shirt and khakis smoking a cigarette and staring off at nothing, smile-grimaced, and raised a hand to a souped-up Honda Civic that slowed down to let him pass even though, he noted, pedestrians have right of way.

What was basically a twenty-yard-wide crosswalk, yellow diagonal lines, etc.

He experienced self-loathing for thanking the driver—whose bass-thumping rap music he could hear from here and was probably a teenager though he couldn't see through the tinted black windshield—for stopping. The self-loathing caused him to dislike himself for wasting so much time indulging himself on the Internet, sitting without mind in front of a humming box being fed information faster than the brain was designed to accept it, news about the world going on outside, things done by people not sitting at home in front of humming boxes, updated nearly in real time. Too much news is bad, he thought. It's not good to know everything. Too much progress, he thought, is a scary bad thing. Though he wasn't sure exactly how and was glad he was not being pressed to explain it. Some things you just know. Just a hunch, a gut feeling of something inside himself and us rotting away. Of the human race clearing its throat and draining the last of its coffee and waiting for the next silence to stand up and say its good-byes. Plus the anonymity of it makes it too easy to control communication and how others perceive you. You find yourself saying things you never would to people in face-to-face conversation and it makes you when away from the humming box antisocial and paralytically self-aware, with no time to sketch your words before delivering them, afraid of being discovered. It's a terrible thing, the Internet, he thinks, because everyone gets full control whether they deserve it or not. It's passive-aggressive. And, damn it, he decides, it's time to change. He decides there and then that he will *not* buy a PC-mounted camera nor will he go online *at all* anymore, starting *now*. Right now. He will cancel his ISP account, erase the porn from his hard drive, disconnect the third phone line they had installed for the modem, stop self-polluting to thoughts of Linda Dutton or thoughts of anybody but Vicki, train his brain to re-eroticize her to him, reconnect with her and Grayson. Yes, instead of reading about the world and literally sitting around jerking off, he'll experience life more, in all its small joys—walking with his wife down the beach, giving Grayson advice, discussing the philosophies of Thomas Aquinas with him over beers on the deck, going on fishing trips smoking Swisher Sweets like they did when Grayson was a kid. Still is a kid. He doesn't know his son, he realized then. *I do not know my son.* That has to change. It will. It will. I'll break the cycle. It ruined me, John thought today, not having a father. Mom was a nut, controlling, religious, loony, obsessed with constipation, always shoving laxatives up my ass thinking I was constipated, and it wouldn't have hurt to have had a father to keep her in check. He'd shave his beard and get a haircut, start running more, every day, get back into shape, start the next half of his life. Start up Coffee and Donuts again. Get the pro-life table up and running again. Go to Knights of Columbus meetings more often. Resume counseling pregnant women at the Crisis Pregnancy Center. Attend Mass every day of the week. Confession weekly. Repair the ol' soul. Do a little soul maintenance. It's been through the wringer these last couple of years. Boy, it's been a tough time. Not that I'm blaming anyone but myself for neglecting it like I have. Buy a new pickup truck. Reintroduce the wolf into the southeastern United States. Run for office like was supposed to be his destiny when he was class president of St. Michael the Archangel Catholic High School in Cheyenne, Wyoming, and headed to West Point, personally selected by Wyoming State Senator Martin Gable (R). Start local but work his way up to national. Maybe be a senator. Who knows? Or work on the staff of one. A campaign—help put someone into office who can repair all the mess Clinton's made. Restore dignity to the United States presidency. That's what we need—or *I* need. Dignity. That will be my general theme. Dignity. Do it all for Grayson. Give him a father. A real father. Someone who loves him. Break the cycle of indignity that has plagued the family. He thought, He's growing so damned fast, if I'm not careful I'm going to lose him entirely.

John jingled his hand in his pocket for his keys this afternoon as he approached his 1995 Toyota Tacoma, excited about the new life awaiting him, thinking about stopping at the Wal-Mart or Fair Oaks or Galyan's or Sports Authority or somewhere else to get new running shoes and athletic attire. He was happy for the first time since he could remember. He was ashamed for his years of reclusive inactivity and for drinking too much and doing his part to let his marriage disintegrate. Though Vicki more than did her part, indeed she had a far bigger one than he—never being home, being, in his view, so career obsessed and controlling and not going with him to Thailand right when Grayson was born, separating him from his family for that entire crucial first year of his new baby's life—the worst thing you can do to a man, the *worst*—then keeping him from going to Italy, effectively squashing his military career. But they could work on all that. Yes, they had so much work to do. It wouldn't be pretty but it would be for the—

His train of thought was interrupted when a Ford Explorer drove by with a Clinton/Gore sticker and one bumper sticker that said PRACTICE RANDOM ACTS OF KINDNESS AND SENSELESS ACTS OF BEAUTY and another that said MAY THE FETUS YOU SAVE BE GAY, causing his stomach to cramp. *You fucking liberal bleeding-heart liberal jerkoff Democrat anti-life liberal fucking stupid draft-dodging lying coward liberal asshole selfish fucking nitwit* ... He fought back the urge he gets whenever he sees such bumper stickers, which is to chase after the vehicle and toss a brick or heavy rock through the window. Because they were gonna get him, finally, he'd been praying for it for six years, ever since he first saw his arrogant cocky smirk and red bulbous nose, phony compassion. *Just an honest local boy from rural Arkansas who done made good.* What a liar, what a cheater, what a dirtbag. He started laughing in rage at Clinton and the driver of the Explorer. *They've got him. They've got your precious sweet little president now. We've got him. Ken Starr is gonna nail him to the wall. Culture of death. Godless Secular Society of Stupid where babies must die so their mothers can live as they wish and Truth is ignored.* What a hero. Pro-life. Ken Starr's pro-life. Conservative, Catholic, a West Point graduate. Just like John Donald. Slick Willy might be able to grin and charm his way out of Paula Jones and Whitewater and Vince Foster, but you know what? You want some bad news? He can't scam his way out of the noble grasp of Ken Starr. Know why, you dummy? Because you cannot escape Truth. They're gonna get that son of a bitch, that fatty fucker, and then who knows what's possible for me after that? They're gonna get him, gonna get him and his she-devil wife. Hillary, the fat-ankled ice queen, probably hasn't been fucked in years. No wonder he porks those ten-beer wolf dates: His wife's pussy's got teeth. IMPEACH CLINTON . . . AND HER HUSBAND is his favorite bumper sticker on his truck. He hoped the driver of that Explorer saw it and went into a whining pinko tizzy over it. He laughed thinking about it. Probably cried. For the *children*. Probably hurt her *feeeeeeelings*. He started his truck and looked in the rearview and checked out the tits on a black teenage girl walking by, putting her hair up. Turned up DC101 and said happily to himself, —Oh yeah, baby, you'll be pregnant and on welfare in no time with that body, honey, don't you worry. Pulled out, drove off, got home, went to his computer and checked his e-mail, looked at porn, masturbated a little, then a lot, hours and hours, stayed there until his wife came home, went to the HOA meeting, pissed off Mitzy Hurkle, ran home to look at more porn.

BRADDOCK PARK HIGH SCHOOL—
CAFETERIA

—Dude know what we saw this morning on the path?
  —What?
  —Titties.
  —Nuh-uh.
  —Whose titties?
  —Oh no one in particular.
  —I know whose titties.
  —Whose?
  —No one's.
  —Nuh-uh.
  —Man, fuck you guys.
  —Dude whose titties. Seriously.
  —Oh, I don't know . . .

—Come on.

—A gentleman never tells.

—Whose titties, dude?

—And I also won't say that she also blew us all while her boyfriend Sean watched. But I also won't say she didn't.

—No way.

—Miah, how about you shut the fuck up.

—Were they nice?

—They were tight.

—Damn.

—Um hold on. Eighty-six. Eighty-seven. Eighty-seven cents. I have eighty-seven cents. Oh, and I'd fuck Katie, by the way.

—I wouldn't, yo. I have higher standards ever since Sarah sucked my dick.

—Sarah told me she blew you because she was drunk and mad at Jeff for dumping her for not putting out.

—I don't care, yo. She still blew me. Fucking ho.

—Stupid slut.

—For real.

—Man, what the blood clot.

—Hey, but if someone gives me five bones, or if maybe everyone chips in and comes up with five bones, then, yes, I will eat this.

—Fucking disgusting.

—You have to chew it. You have to swallow it.

—Your mom swallowed it.

—Hey what's up with you and what's her name?

—Who?

—You know.

—I don't know what you're talking about.

—Whatever. I heard you fingered her, yo.

—What'd her pussy smell like? How many fingers did you get in?

—Yeah chewing and swallowing. Also known as *eating*, retard.

—Fag.

—Whatever.

—I swear to fucking Christ.

—Anybody know where Grayson is? He was burning me this Pennywise album that was from France or like Germany or something.

—Yeah real funny. Homophobia is fucking hilarious dude.

—Pennywise fucking sucks butt.

—But what.

—They used to be awesome but their new album fucking blows.

—No way. Their new album is the best one ever. It's so dissonant.

—It's what?

—Dissonant.

—What?

—Dissonant.

—Whatever. It's gay.

—Grayson's a fag.

—Yeah, he is.

—Oh, dude, did you see that like Pennywise video motherfucking Robbie has? The one where fucking Fletcher puts like beads or something, or like a necklace or some shit in his fucking nose on one side? And like inhales and shit until it comes out the, like, the back of his throat? And he fucking reaches the fuck back and, like, fucking like grabs it and like, is all like, fucking flossing his fucking like, his fucking throat and his nose with these like, fucking beads or a necklace or whatever? And then pukes?

—Nuh-uh.

—What the blood?

—Oh dude.

—Whatever.

—I'm seeing them though at Nation in fucking like April. Wanna go? They're uh . . . They're playing Nation at, in April.

—Fuck yeah dude. Let's start *doing* shit like that. Let's start *doing* shit, you know?

—Yeah yeah.

—Nah man I don't mean fag like gay. I meant fag like *stupid*. Like, —*Don't be stupid*. You know? I'm not homophobic.

—My uncle's gay or whatever, yo. So fucking shut the fuck up, okay?

—Anybody know though? Where Grayson is?

—Just don't call people fags. It's worse when you mean *stupid*. That means you think of fags as stupid. I knew this gay dude Rob at camp in middle school and he was one of the coolest fucking guys I ever knew.

—Whatever.

—You wanna know who I kind of don't hate when I hear it on the radio? Blink 182. Oh God, I'm so ashamed!

—Yeah. *Whatever*. Because homophobia and hate speech is so *awesome*, dude.

—Blink 182 fucking sucks monkey butt.

—Blink 182 gives me gas.

—Yeah, you probably like Hanson too. Fag.

—Dude. Seriously.

—Whatever. Fag.

—Stop.

—I think he's sick.

—He killed himself. He's dead.

—Who wants these?

—How would you kill yourself if you like had to? I'd shoot myself in the butt.

—Mr. Brody tried to touch my ball sac today.

—Oh dude guess who I saw when I went to Red Rocks on Saturday? Ms. Lee. She was fucking trashed and was trying to make out with me I think.

—You should have fucked her.

—I'd like shoot myself? Like in the head? But like at a pep rally? Or during lunch? I'd stand on a table or something? And like blow my head off with a shotgun? You know?

—Blood and guts and fucking brains and shit all over the fucking Abercrombie kids.

—And the like the fucking cheerleaders and shit?

—Girls screaming and shit.

—Like in the "Jeremy" video.

—Pearl Jam fucking sucks now though.

—*Ten* changed my life. Seriously. It's soooooooo goooooooooood dude.

—He died of AIDS of the rectum and testes.

—He's dead of a boner to the domepiece.

—Look at Katie Halloway. It looks like she's giving her fucking Diet Coke a fucking blow job.

—Yeah she does.

—She has fake tits. Did y'all know that?

—Fag. Faggity faggity fag fag faggity.

—Fuck you.

—Fuck you, fuck you, fuck you. *You're* cool. I'm out.

—Hahahahahaha.

—Hey man you got a joint? Be a lot cooler if you did!

—Oh dude have you seen that movie?

—Livin! L-I-V-I-N!

—Hahahahahahahahahaha!

—You eat pieces of shit for breakfast?!

—HAHAHAHAHAHAHAHAHAHAHAHAHAHAHA!

—I came here to fight and. No no. I came here to drink some beer and fight some motherfuckers.

—And I'm all out of beer.

—HAHAHAHAHA!

—Mom! Kitty's being a dildo! I know a special kitty who's sleeping with mommy tonight.

—HAHAHAHAHA! Oh shit!

—You eat pieces of shit for breakfast?!

—Fuck you, fuck you, fuck you. *You're* cool . . .

15683 SEQUOIA LANE— TOWN HOUSES

What I'm saying is Amy is that I FEEL things that the common person doesn't feel. I'm serious. It's solitude, it's being sensitive to, like, the inner life. Like today on my way home from work, in my car. I'll have the radio on and it will be playing Semisonic or "Crush" by Dave Matthews, and I'll be like transported by the song and by the sounds. Not physically I mean but just, like . . . Okay, you for example hear a piece of music like that Third Eye Blind song, right? And you find it catchy and so you sing along with it. Because it *sounds* good, right? If you're awake now say "right."

Amy? Ame. Hey Ame.

Look, when I'm saying this I'm not trying to put you down in any way, baby, but I'm rather trying to only just express myself as a person, okay? A *person*. So I can end once and for all this, like, *charade* that is my life. All I want, Amy, is just to go ahead and be happily married to you like I'm supposed to. I owe it to myself, and to you, to be happy. That's something we are supposed to earn for ourselves. It's a goal to achieve, Amy, like a raise. I just want to love you and totally stop thinking about other girls all the time. I mean, baby, come on, you know how guys are. Let's get real, right? Let's be honest here and face the facts. You're a very down-to-earth realistic person with no illusions, especially after your mother fell off her bike, right? I'm sure you . . . okay, look, you cannot honestly like tell me there is no other dude, no other male human being, no actor, no coworker, no R & B singer or something who you look at with just this basic irresistible physical attraction sometimes and just want to fuck him really hard, with his fucking balls slapping against your ass, but nothing more than that, right?

Right? Ame?

Or maybe a girl like Pamela Anderson who you would have a lesbian experience with? If given the chance? After all, all girls are a little lesbian, right? Like Howard Stern says. Let's be honest here. It's only natural to want to spread your genes around as far as possible before you die. Because, baby, we're animals. That's all we are when it comes down to it. I think it's important that we are honest here. I want to be honest with you about myself and happy because we're married for the rest of our lives.

But what I'm saying is, and I am saying something by the way, baby, I mean I do have a point here, but what I'm saying here and why I'm talking to you here pretty damn drunk now and with Lindsay on her way and you asleep . . . What's becoming more and more clear is that today, coming home from work where they let me go home early again, I felt transported into the future.

There. I said it.

It's weird, I know. It was *so* weird, and I can only imagine how it must seem to you hearing it from me. But baby, it's true. It was like a spiritual existence outside of myself. I was listening to "My Own Prison" by Creed. My eyes as I was driving sort of blurred on the lane line, whatever it's called, up ahead. And as I drove I just stared off into the distance and felt, all of a sudden, for like a brief second, as though it was the future. And I was cruising along in a George Jetson–mobile instead of my Camry, and the earth was just this fucking paved *sphere* with all these *buildings* and plastic *walls* and *biodomes* and *machines*.

This is something I don't believe many people have the sensibility or intelligence to experience, Amy.

Ame?

But that is my whole point. At work, baby, at the bank, like in the military too, babe, I have to act normal. You know? Watch people stand in line, pretending to be looking at their deposit slip. Putting their hands in their pockets and taking them back out. Staring up at the top of the wall. Shuffling their weight. And I have to be aware if any of these people standing in line are planning on robbing the bank today.

I have to say hello to the tellers in the break room and be friendly to

Jason the vice president. He finds me being in the military fascinating. He's like fascinated by me. He's like a little kid, it's funny. Obviously, baby, this guy would *never* make it in the Army. And so he always wants to talk about it. Guns, snapping people's necks, bombs, who we're planning on going to war with after Kosovo. As if I, as a soldier, have like secret information. He thinks we're planning a war with China but the government just isn't telling anyone and how it'll be World War Three. His eyes light up because he's excited about watching World War Three on the news. And how it'll be crazy because China has nukes, he says. And he's almost grinning and licking his lips talking about how fucked up and on a massive scale a war with China would be because all these other countries would jump into the fray and we'd blow the *fuck* out of the world and really get to bring out our top secret apocalyptic FUCK YOU IN THE ASS bombs, as he calls them, that bring forth all sorts of biblical hell onto those who dare fuck with us. And he talks about how the best thing about a war would be how he will get to protest it and start a war resistance and wear a green army jacket and grow a beard and smoke dope and all this *shit*—he has it all planned out, Amy. He says he will make documentaries about the antiwar movement and have a huge antiwar concert–slash–drug orgy. He has all these ideas from watching shows about the sixties on VH1.

I'm serious, Amy. Ame? Hello? Baby?

He asks me every day if I've heard anything about any terrorist attacks in the works that will provoke us to go bomb the shit out of someone and start a war so he can go get an American flag tattoo on his face and put a decal on his car. He says he looks forward to getting misty eyed during the "Star-Spangled Banner" before the World Series and the fucking Super Bowl. And help his neighbors bring their groceries into their house. I don't know what that means, this is just what he says. Help his neighbors with their groceries. He says he'll walk around shirtless with his flag tattoo on his face helping people with their groceries. And maybe holding a ladder if someone is up scooping leaves out of their gutter. Who knows what the fuck. He's a fucking fruitcake.

And then he's told me before, another time, about how he has a shed in his backyard in McLean . . . and how his shed on his great big wooded property is full of canned foods and gas masks and solar-powered TV and like twenty American flags and bumper stickers that say things like SUPPORT OUR TROOPS and IT'S A CHILD NOT A CHOICE and STOP THE WAR and BOOKS NOT BOMBS and, like, video cameras for the antiwar documentary and a hand-cranked radio and a bunch of those posters on sticks people carry in protests and bongs and all kinds of shit. Please let there be a war, he says, babe. Please hurry and cause mayhem to happen. And every day he asks me what the latest news is and I tell him I don't know and his face drops. He gets this totally lights-out look in his eyes and he drops his head and says, Oh. You know? Amy? I fear one day after I tell him this that he will fucking fire me. Is that, like, possible?

How am I supposed to go through life transporting myself one moment, and the next tolerate people like that? You know? Does any of this make sense? It doesn't, that's the point, that's the fucking point of what I'm saying. Aren't I the most fucking deranged person you've ever met? Can you imagine someone would be so fucking *weird* as me, Amy? Jesus, Bryce, what a fucking *nutbar* you are. Right? Right, Amy baby?

Watch, I'll do it right now. Ready? You awake? All I have to do is, well I won't tell you exactly but watch. Watch.

See? There. It happened.

I felt the flash and had the feeling like I was outside myself and I could see humanity for what it was, these like mutated creatures floating around on this rock in outer space. I'm going to write about all this in my book, by the way. I think it will say a lot about me and I might decide to sue the military for post-traumatic stress disorder.

Wait.

There. Did it again. Boom. Boo-yah. Fuck yeah.

It's so weird, huh? Don't tell anyone please babe about . . .

There's the doorbell.

Lindsay's here.

Amy? You should wake up for this. Amy? If you want to stay asleep you can stay asleep. I have the camera rolling so you can watch it later. I just thought you'd like to be awake for it.

Amy?

BEST BUY—FAIR LAKES

Brian G. likes staff meetings. He calls them twice a month. The car stereo department has eight employees: four full-timers, four part-timers, and one all-the-timer (Brian G.) (and in truth, as the store manager who gave him the position can tell you, Brian G. has the job only because no one else wanted it). The staff meetings take place at 7:30 in the morning on Saturdays. They are unpaid, mandatory. He takes roll. He brings Krispy Kreme. He saw somewhere that communication is an important part of good leadership. He prides himself on getting the best out of his employees, pushing them to their limits. He tells his department the sales goals for the month, often lofty and intimidating, and tries to convey his enthusiasm about reaching them, clapping his hands, saying it's tough but not impossible guys, because anything is possible if you put your mind to it. As if the enthusiasm is inside them, in their blood, waiting to be found, without reason or cause. Usually, however, if they are enthusiastic about anything it is the meeting ending so they can go home and go back to bed.

Tells them their eye contact needs improving and walks up and down the line—he has them stand in a line, army-style—testing their eye contact, one at a time, mini staring contests. Says customers have left comment cards—waving quickly comment cards that Best Buy has up at customer service but that he has taken the time to not only premeditatedly take as he leaves the day before the meeting but also to scribble on in his car in the parking lot before coming in for the meeting, waiting until 7:33 to come in so they will be waiting for him (more executive that way, more professional)—have left comment cards saying they had a great shopping experience except for being really disappointed and emotionally hurt by _____'s (name he leaves intentionally withheld) lack of enthusiasm and failure to greet them upon their arrival in the car stereo department and make them feel at home and comfortable and loved, and that they had to (here he lowers his voice like in a scary story) seek out the help of the sales associates of another department, and that this terrible experience has left such a bad taste in their mouth that not only are they having trouble sleeping at night and awful acid reflux that even handfuls of Rolaids don't kill and not only did these customers choose not to buy their car stereo here at Best Buy on this trip but they vow to go elsewhere to one of the like hundreds of places around here where one can buy a car stereo and to suffer through the lesser shopping experience and higher prices these hundreds of places offer—like watching their ex-girlfriend move on to a total douche bag who is awful for her, is the emotion Brian G. is aiming to stir up—and to never return to Best Buy in the future and to tell all their friends to do the same and why.

All this on one comment card.

Then Brian G. waves the open comment card that is off-white and looks like a greeting card except not made of glossy paper and not as thick, but not long enough for anyone to see that it's nonsense scribble and looks around at his employees, his eyebrows raised, silent, moving his gaze up and down the line of donut-munching red-eyed associates, a powerful way in Brian G.'s point of view of letting them know this comment could be about any one of them. And that only he knows who it truly is about.

—We can always be more friendly, he says. —We can always be more helpful.

MS-13

I woke up one morning a few months or weeks ago
& Julia was still asleep in a chair in the corner.
Whatever motel this was.
There was blood and guts and purple thick shit everywhere.
There was a baby at her feet.
Like a raw plucked turkey, sucking its thumb, still attached to the cord.
I woke her up which was hard because she wouldn't respond
& I slapped her face not very hard
& shook her and thought maybe she died somehow.
Blood loss or a heart attack maybe.
& she finally opened her eyes and grunted like people do when you wake them up early
& I said Look and pointed down at the baby
& Julia leaned forward and looked down at it and looked up at me
& she said What time is it?

Best Buy—Fair Lakes

When Brian G. passed off the smashed-up cardboard box and finally got back to the car stereo department it'd been twenty minutes since he'd come from lunch and clocked back in. He rounded the corner and saw Kristin C. behind the counter where they keep the paperwork and stapler and little stickers with each sales associate's employee number on it (Brian G.'s is 0003) so that the cashier knows whom to give the sales commission to when the customer checks out. Kristin C. was standing up but her face was down on the counter in an open textbook that weighed about twenty-three pounds it looked like, her limp hand holding a Bic pen in midwriting position in a spiral four-subject notebook on its final pages and the page one-third filled but the final written word, *multinationalism,* trailed off after the last letter in a zigzag line to the bottom of the page, which was where her hand was now. She was snoring. Her back rising and falling, hair stuck to her cheek by drool.

Brian G.'s temples pulsed, his teeth sunk into the meat of his tongue which was surprisingly small if you saw it. He saw her as a fleshy lump of bad meat, begging to be tossed into a Dumpster. A group of Hispanic kids, covered with tattoos, stood nearby, ignoring Brian G. and Kristin C., talking loudly in what to Brian G. was babbling nonsensical non-English. They were practically bowing before a display of the Pioneer DEH-P77DH. He had a vision now of buying them, the Hispanic kids, three males and two girls. Taking them home and ripping open the box they're in, discarding the instructions, plugging them in, being unsatisfied, bringing them back, exchanging them for credit. He smile-grimaced and approached them with his hands behind his back and looked each one in the eye, holding it longer than usual, as he spoke loudly and with crisp good-naturedness—*Qué pasa, hombres?* Can . . . give . . . you . . . *ayudáme . . . ahora?*

(Brian G. took four years of Spanish at Braddock Park.)

The Mexican kids looked away and grumbled without commitment. Brian G. could smell them. They smelled like body fluids and cigarettes and fast food and weed. He felt fear, distance. Something was creepy about these people. He decided he was satisfied by his effort and so said,

—If you *hombres* need anything, absolutely do *not* be afraid to *pre-gunta. Sí?*

And he smile-grimaced and turned away. His smile dropped and he headed toward Kristin C. who was snoring louder than ever.

—What is your major malfunction, numb nuts? he said, poking her, to no response. —Yo. *Yo.* He shook her hard, could feel the bones beneath her skin, and she grunted and lifted her head and wiped her nose and made a face like she ate something, eyes still closed, a thick translucent rope of drool hanging off her chin, then dropped her head back down and resumed snoring, and he said, —What the blood clot, Kristin C.?

She stirred and lifted her head, said, —Habeas corpus?

—What? What's habeas corpus? Is that like some new STD or something? Actually, no, little lady, you're at work. Not only are you sleeping at work in full view of customers but what are these? What's that, *home-work? Homework?* You're doing *homework?* At *work?*

—There was no one here. It was dead.

—I don't care. You're doing homework at work. That is not appropriate, like at *all.*

The phone on the counter—a business phone that's eleven inches wide with ninety-seven or so different buttons and lights—rang and the small square red light blinking said it was someone calling from the office in back. Brian G. picked it up. It was Heather L., the morbidly obese assistant cash manager, and she said, —Brian G.?

—Yeah.

—It's Heather L.

—Yes Heather L., I know.

—How'd you know?

—I just knew.

—Well okay, I just wanted to let you know something. Her voice was barely above a whisper, deep, different from the usual nasal whine Brian G. knows. —I'm in the janitor's closet. I have brought the phone in here with me. No one knows I'm here. Is Kristin C. there with you?

—Yeah.

—Okay, Heather L. whispered. —You should know something.

—Yeah.

—Okay. You should know . . . that . . . whew, sorry, I'm out of breath. You should know that Kristin C. was seen by myself doing homework earlier as I passed the car stereo department on my way back from lunch just now.

—Where'd you go? For lunch.

—Applebee's, she said.

—Wow.

—Yeah. I had a craving. I absolutely *had* to have a bacon barbecue ranch cheddar cheeseburger in my mouth or I would *die*. Why? Where'd you go? Taco Bell? Burger King?

—Arby's.

—Whoa.

—One of those days, you know?

—Yeah. Tell me about it. But. Yeah. Anyway I just wanted to tell you.

—Thanks, Heather L. I appreciate it. But it's already under control.

—So, are you going to, like fire her? Or . . .

—I don't know. Maybe.

—Okay, but let me know if you fire her. Like, *immediately* afterward. Okay?

—Yep, sure thing.

As Brian G. hung up, he could hear through the phone Heather L. saying, —Tell me *first* if you fire her, okay?

Hung up and turned back to Kristin C., who was slack faced and staring at the floor. —So tired, she whispered.

—Yeah well, Brian G. said, —there have been reports that you were seen doing homework. On the sales floor. In full view of customers. Plus your textbook is right there and your notebooks too so don't try to lie. We can get the security videotapes too. I bet they got you in the act.

—So much work, Kristin C. said. —So tired. She wiped the thick drool off her lips and looked at it on her hand and said, wiping it with haste on her butt, —Ew.

—*Ew*, he said, mocking her.

—Shut up.

—That's gross to you? he said, leaning beside her on his elbow. —You think drool is gross? A little drool and you're all, *Ew oh my God gross get it off me!* Totally like freaking out. *Ew oh my God drool yuck! My own drool! Ew!* He chuckled and said, —If you think that's gross just wait until you start having sex.

Kristin C. looked at him. Her eyes were red, and she smelled good. Her hands were in her hair on either side of her head and her ears weren't pierced, which Brian G. liked, and she went, —Tired.

—Yeah well, guess what? Brian G said. —We're all tired. So.

—I have to read eighty-seven pages in this by tomorrow and then take an essay test on it.

—Oh no. A test.

—Yeah but Mr. O'Rourke's like the hardest teacher ever. He's like a college professor. He's so hard.

—Boohoo.

—Plus I have twenty logarithms in Calculus BC.

—Waaa-waa-waaa.

—Then I have to write an essay that's four pages on the significance of the green light in *The Great Gatsby*. Plus I haven't eaten today. And I also have to do my SAT practice guide. And my boyfriend wants to get married after we graduate because his brother died of leukemia or something? And tomorrow I have a government test too on what's the best way to implement democracy in the troubled Middle East with the lowest number of civilian casualties, keeping in mind warlords and insurgents and foreign policy repercussions over the long term. Plus my dad has basically been drunk for the last two weeks and quit his job to, I guess, write these editorials in crayon to the *Post* about how Clinton is Hitler or something. He drinks and watches *Crossfire* and porn all day, and my mom is sleeping with this guy at work I'm almost completely sure and plus I have to lead a discussion in philosophy on Wednesday that's 75 percent of our grade for the semester about the universalitarianess of the thing which we call *though*. And I have to pick a reach school and retake the SATs because I only got a 1310 because I had mono when I took them and the UVA early admissions deadline is next week and I haven't even opened the envelope the application came in plus Tech and JMU and William & Mary are due the next week but I don't know if I want to go to Tech even if I have to because I don't know if Tech can offer me what I want to do as a career which I also need to figure out soon, like as in this week. And I have to get a prom dress and reserve a limo and I'm fat and I hate my hair and I have field hockey practice tomorrow and before that I have Young Life and my boyfriend I think cheated on me with this whore named Havva because she has a vibrator and swallows and who is anorexic and did a porn on the Internet I heard and takes it in the butt I heard and is like totally evil because she has a boyfriend, Brian Hurkle, who is like totally in love with her and so sweet to her, but my friend Cheryl told me Jeff my boyfriend fingered her at this party on Saturday that I couldn't go to because I was here—fingered Havva, not Cheryl—and used a vibrator on her butt and plus my GPA so far this semester is absolutely abhorrent partially because I've been volunteering every Thursday night at a homeless shelter in DC so I can put it on my college applications because they love that shit. It's 3.9. My GPA. That's with the extra AP points thing. I think I might have ran over a cat on the way here, my voice for the past month has had this weird like quiver to it that I don't know where it came from, I'm so hungry that I'm not hungry anymore. I have a flat tire, I haven't paid my car insurance this month, the mortgage is due soon, I think I'm starting the early stages of menopause and *Oprah* has inexplicably been reruns the last week and I only slept two hours last night because I was doing homework that I couldn't do any other time this weekend because I had to work all day Saturday and yesterday and had a field hockey match Friday night and I have to memorize every stupid capital of Africa and Asia by tomorrow and speaking of Africa I need to write the starving Ethiopian boy with tuberculosis whose mom and dad died of AIDS who I signed up to sponsor even though I only did it so I could put it on my college applications and so now that I put it on my college applications I don't really care anymore but they keep bugging me, and I found out yesterday my dog has lung cancer, poor Bo-Bo and we have to put him to sleep and I realized I haven't seen him in maybe five months even though he sleeps in my bed.

—Lung cancer? Your dog has lung cancer? How does a *dog* get lung cancer?

—So tired.

—What, does he smoke or something? Ha, I'd love to see that. A dog who smokes. Ha. That'd be funny as shit.

Kristin C. looked at him with blankness like she was thinking about something else. She said, —Tired.

—Yeah well, if I or anyone else sees you doing homework on my sales floor again I'm writing you up. Is that clear?

Kristin C. nodded, put the books under the counter, straightened herself.

—It's happened before, you know, he said. —I had to fire some dickhead like two years ago. Same deal. Couldn't hack it. Couldn't manage his time. Couldn't dedicate himself. But you know how it goes. Either fuck or walk. You close or you hit the bricks. Only one thing in this life matters, Kristin C., and that is getting them so sign on the line that is dotted. He held up the Ironman. —You see this watch?

She glanced at it and rolled her eyes. —Not this again.

—This isn't the first time I've noticed this with you, is it, little lady? I've been watching you. I got a customer comment card in my office about you that someone said they saw you doing homework once instead of helping them.

—Oh shut up, Brian.

—Know what it says? It says they're never coming back to Best Buy.

We lost a customer, Kristin C., because of you. So you can see why I'm taking this so seriously. Because I mean, look, you know I'm cool, right? I'm cool. I'm not some Nazi like Greg over there in cash. I drink. I go out. I drank last night actually. Got a nice little buzz. I drank five beers. Maybe six. I don't remember. Miller Lites. That's my brand. I like Nine Inch Nails and look forward to their next album. I attend the HFStival *every year*.

—Tired.

—So are you a virgin or what?

—Ugh.

—Come on, you can tell me.

—No.

—I know why you're so tired.

—Oh do you. Why?

—From riding my dick all night.

He laughed and she stared at him until he stopped. She said, —Can we talk about something else?

—Like what.

She kind of shook her head and rubbed the corners of her eyes. And then they were quiet for a moment. They both stared out over the sales floor. He kind of hummed along to "Real World" by Matchbox 20 which was playing over the sound system. He said, —I'm trying to think of something else to talk about. He drummed his fingers in a little roll and straightened and said, —Okay. So . . . He knocked on the counter twice. And then he wandered off and Kristin C. waited until he was out of sight then went back to sleep.

Braddock Park High School—
Cafeteria

—*A four-assed monkey.*

—HAHAHAHAHAHAHAHHAHAHAHA!

—I don't know if I agree with your assessment of nihilism. Your explanation of nihilism I think is dissonant at best.

—Your momma's teeth are so yellow when she smiles all the cars slow down.

—You know what they call a Quarter Pounder with cheese in France?

—Royale with cheese.

—It's *Friday*! You ain't got no *job*! You ain't got shit to *do*!

—Hey, does anyone know the fucking significance of the green light in *Great Gatsby*?

—Tired.

—Yeah, I've thought about this before when you've talked about *Catcher in the Rye* but I'm not so sure you get it. The book. I don't know if you really understand what *Catcher in the Rye* is about and what Salinger is trying to say.

—I wish *Catcher in the Rye* was less dissonant.

—How is it fucking *dissonant*?

—I don't fucking know, dude, it just fucking is.

—What the fuck does dissonant even mean?

—It means, you know, *dissonant*.

—Your mom's dissonant.

He is not happy. He is a freshman in high school. This fact alone should be enough. But unfortunately for him he also has acne. And braces. And his mother's weak chin. And his father's flabby torso. And is short. And he gets pimples not just on his face but for some ungodly reason on his back too. Just a few points in a long litany of Job-like curses that have befallen him these last two harrowing years. He wears his hair parted in the middle, an unnatural burnt sienna from trying to dye it blond in the upstairs bathroom of his house with a bottle of Clairol, dark brown roots, as long as his father allows him to wear it. He sat alone at a table in the cafeteria drinking a Mountain Dew and picking at a soft pretzel with nacho cheese. The only other people nearby were two Mexican kids who didn't speak English and a kid from it must have been Africa because he wore one of those muumuu things that African guys wear and just sat there grinning across the table at the freshman like Eddie Murphy in *Coming to America*. The freshman's knees bounced up and down. He wore a Marilyn Manson T-shirt and had colored his nails black with a Sharpie. In his head was a noise he couldn't quiet. It wailed in a crescendo from deep out in some moonscape within him. A roaring pounding scream. Curse words, vulgar scenes of warfare and murder. He couldn't lift his eyes from the table, peeling at the spot of rubber coating on the table edge already coming off, next to where moments ago he'd—as the *Coming to America* kid watched, grinning—used a blue Bic ballpoint pen to carve the words FUCK YOU I WON'T DO WHAT YOU TELL ME. Coming to America tilted his head, trying to read it upside down. He furrowed his brow. He looked back up at the freshman and said, —Excuse me. But what is a *fuck you I won't do what you tell me*? The freshman just sneered at him from behind the hair hanging in his face and pulled his mush-gray recyclable lunch tray over his vandalism. He felt otherwordly. He wanted to die. Like he was a swine set loose upon . . . everything. A loser, a dummy. He could blast through the ceiling. And he was crying out inside. He hates his parents. They don't know him. They laugh at him. His mother wants him to go to church. Church? Church couldn't help him. God couldn't answer the cries for help coming from inside his freak show self. Nothing could fill the holes. Only pain could mend his wounds.

Coming to America now pulling from his brown paper bag (maybe the only kid in the entire cafeteria right now who actually brings his lunch) a bag of Flipz and holding them across the table toward the freshman, waving the bag enticingly, grinning, until the freshman looked up.

—What are those?

—They are Nestlé Flipz.

—I can see that. But what are they though.

—Salted crusty pretzels coated in delicious Nestlé milk chocolate. He just grinned and waved the bag like a tea bell. —You like?

The freshman shook his head and crawled back into his hole. Coming to America shrugged and opened the bag, caught sight of the Mexicans over there a few seats away leering at the Flipz, held it out to them, they took some, popped them in their mouths, said *Gracias*. The freshman is fourteen years old. In his world history class on Friday while the teacher was showing slides from his summer vacation to Egypt, the TA, Grayson, all of a sudden without warning stood from his desk in the back of the room and walked out, saying nothing, never to return, and the teacher did not stop his slide show nor did he appear to notice, nor—in fact—did anybody at all. Besides the freshman.

He may have forgotten to wear deodorant today. He put his head down in his arms and snuck a discreet sniff. No intelligence gained. Needed a closer sniff. So he pretended to reach down to tie the laces of his Vans, turning his head while he was down there in such a way that his nose went right into his pit which has a total of fourteen hairs growing out of it (he's counted). Still couldn't tell one way or the other. Ah well, let him stink. Let him fester in his pit. His pit of shit. Keep the teeny-boppers and idiots away. Here I am, alone and filthy, undeodorized, wilting and withering in a river of broken bloody dreams. Wallowing in the mire. Come and get me. Come and get my foul corpse, he thought, taking a bite of his pretzel, chunks of it getting stuck in his braces. His head still down. He heard a scraping sound and could see from the reflection of shadows on the floor Coming to America had gotten up and was walking away. Good. He cannot help him. Only Trent Reznor could understand him. Or Marilyn Manson. Perhaps Zack de la Rocha. You cannot help me. Only Jonathan Davis understands my pain. Leave me be to wallow in the mire. I cut you like you want me to. I will stay here withering like Jonathan Davis, feeling pain so immense that all the world's suffering until now compared to it will be like a big piece of birthday cake. Mmm . . . birthday cake . . . His stomach rumbled. He peeked up over his arms, saw Coming to America joining the lunch line. He looked around, glaring at everyone, chewing his delicious pretzel. Pigs. You're all a bunch of pigs. Bring it on, pigs. Then he lowered his head again and closed his eyes, covering his face with his arms like Jonathan Davis, inhaling all-purpose disinfectant cleaning solution, fell asleep.

He dreamed that he and Trent Reznor were hanging out in some grody dark room, sitting beside one another with their knees pulled to their chests, smoking cigarettes and looking around with their hair hanging in their face, sneering, eating soft pretzels and birthday cake, heroic in their capacity for pain.

—Hey, Trent Reznor said. —Hey.

He was being nudged.

—Mm.

—Hey. Marilyn Manson.

—Mm?

He looked up, drool hanging off his mouth. Coming to America standing there, grinning, the front of his muumuu held out from his body to create a large pouch in which he carried dozens of milk pouches.

—Why did you buy so many milks?

—Marilyn, you have shown me your American ritual. He gestured to the freshman and to the countless numbers of others around the cafeteria in the same pose, sleeping atop their own tables, some using their backpacks as pillows. —I am forever grateful and in your debt. Thank you, thank you.

—Uh, sure, dude.

—In return, I must show you my Zimbabwean ritual. He began

unloading the milks, placing half before himself and half before the freshman who just sat there staring at him without expression.

—I don't like milk.

Coming to America looked at him, no longer grinning. He said, —Fuck you I won't do what you tell me.

And he placed a straw before the freshman as though setting a table for fine dining.

She's always either too hot or too cold. She is always sweaty and gross or her teeth are chattering and her lips are blue. If she goes into Blockbuster or Subway in the summer she can last in there for only thirty seconds or so because of the air-conditioning. She has to carry a sweatshirt around with her wherever she goes, no matter if the region is in the midst of one of its muggy waves of preternatural heat wafting up from the Southwest. If the temperature, as Brian Hurkle well knows by now, is not exactly 78 degrees and sunny with a warm sweet breeze, her body, due perhaps to genetics or its nanoatomical makeup, suffers the effects to an exaggerated degree, demanding she be brought to more temperate environs as soon as possible and that she make insistent, repeated querimony until she is.

Today it was 76 degrees in the cafeteria, with no hint of a warm sweet breeze, and it was making Havva Khabbazi once again detest the town in which she lived. In her irritability and discomfort she could see that Centreville was not a town but a mild damnation of chills and sweats. It was a Feverland. Hotflashburg-on-Draftyville. She was in a mood today. She was wearing her forest green Abercrombie wool sweater that cost only $70—the sweater, Brian Hurkle noted, that she usually wears when she's on the rag—and her new bebe jacket that she bought this weekend for only $120 at Tysons. Last night she was unable to fall asleep until 2 AM because she was up doing precalc homework and reading for AP History and writing a twelve-page paper on B. F. Skinner (Havva kept picturing Principal Skinner) for AP Psychology assigned last Thursday. She was now using her shriveled purple hand to pick at her big soft pretzel and dip a chunk into the nacho cheese. The nacho cheese dispenses after you take your pretzel out of the rotating cube where they all hang like butchered pretzel carcasses in the pretzel slaughterhouse (*Slaughterhouse-Five*, which she read last year and understood the symbolism of, as her A on the test can attest) and slide-step with your mush-gray tray along the metal counter to the metal humming machine with a pump atop it and a sticker on the side that says NACHO CHEESE.

The popular joke among the cafeteria staff at Braddock Park High

School—hairnetted middle-aged women of minority ethnicity or of Manassas addresses—is, What do you call cheese that isn't—or *ain't*—yours?

Nacho cheese.

Havva didn't know why she was in a mood, she just was. She wasn't on her period, which she calls (when Brian's trying to get some when she's on it and she has to fight him off and tell him why) her *thingy*. She watches MTV and E! more often than any other channel. But she also will throw in a little Court TV and some *Primetime Live* on ABC now and again. She likes crime. The scandals of people. Passion-driven violence. Sex and murder. It excites her. Little in Centreville does. It is not capable of fulfilling her imagination. She is a girl of fantasy and speculation. This is why she borrows her cousin's ID to go into DC and sneak into the Spot or Dream. She tells the guys—men—who dance with her when they ask where she's from that she is from *DC*. When they ask where in DC, she makes up a location. *Church Street? Between C and D? In Northwest? Off Florida Ave?* She makes up names of restaurants she enjoys, bars she regulars. She thinks of a job—a career. She is a lawyer, she is a spokeswoman for a United States senator, she works for the chief of staff of the vice president, she is a gallerist, she is Washington bureau correspondent for *Time*. DC counts, Centreville doesn't. The men in clubs matter, the boys in her high school don't. Except for Brian of course, now with his arm around her, rubbing her back and arms which were covered in goose bumps under her sweater as usual. She likes her back but feels it needs work, as does her arm definition. She has a membership to Life Time Fitness that her mother bought her after much haranguing and she has used it once in four months. She wasn't looking at Brian. He had an erection, her hand on it over his cargo pants. She wished he would stop rubbing her arms and back and wondered who was watching her and if anyone knew that she went to DC to clubs such as the Spot and Dream and if they were impressed by her going into DC. She wondered who was attracted to her. Who couldn't live without her. Guys, girls, security guards, army recruiters, anyone. Stalking her at night in an obsessive infatuation. A little game she plays with herself when she's not particularly interested in anything happening about her at the moment.

Who was planning her kidnap and rape? He would tie her up and put her in the trunk, take her somewhere scary. But she would fight him off, beat him up, take his gun and put it on him, stand above him with the gun in her hands still bound at the wrists and her hair stuck to her face, her lip bleeding, blouse (she'd be wearing a blouse) torn showing cleavage. —You son of a bitch, she'd say. She'd spit.

She hates Centreville.

Centreville sucks.

There is a world out there that is for her. She goes to DC and pretends it is that world. She dresses like women in DC dress. Which means skirts, or tight black business pants, expensive things, perfume, makeup, her hair done. She concentrates on not looking lost. Like she knows exactly where she is going, walking these sidewalks, crossing these streets every day of her life, not waiting for the walk signal before crossing, being a woman from DC. Before she leaves her house she plans her driving route with utmost meticulousness, scouring a road map her dad had in his office which she stole, so she would not mess up and end up lost, have to ask for directions like a girl—not a woman, a *girl*—from *Centreville*.

Telling her parents she is going to Dawne's house. Or to spend the night with her cousin, who goes to the University of Maryland.

I am from DC, she tells the men. She tells them her name. And they always ask her to repeat it, leaning their ear toward her mouth, *What is it?* the music thumping, their cologne and sweat, the stubble on their cheeks, wanting her, consumed with erotic desire for her. And she repeats her names, with sultriness, like a powerful woman from DC, *Havva*, and they say it again.

They never get it right.

Havva? As in Havva a nice day?

No, Havva. As in Haavard.

They never get the joke. They smile anyway, hold her closer, offer her a drink.

In Centreville there are no men. Only dads and guys.

But girls are girls and stay girls forever.

But Brian somehow always says her name perfectly.

She was aroused even though she didn't want to be. She didn't want to be aroused. Brian touching her thigh. She tried to will it away. She tends to get wet to excess. It's like it has a mind of its own sometimes. An entity independent of her. She had a spare of panties in her purse, which she has learned by now to always have with her. She'd stop in the ladies' room on the way to her next class. She has on jumblegut roads in unfinished stretches of Virginia Run drenched the driver's seat of the white 1997 Kia Sportage her father bought her on her sixteenth birthday. She wakes most mornings in bed with uliginose thighs, feverish and anxious with a feeling between her legs—but more so inside of her, in her belly somewhere—that she cannot ignore, her skin burning, like an animal, a cat in heat, the animal she most identifies with—a skulking lady cat prowling around, curling up onto laps, purring, arching its back in need of touch, scampering off when bored. She has left dark markings on the khaki crotches of the men with gelled hair and button-down shirts in DC clubs. She cannot wear white pants. As sexy as she finds going pantyless under a sundress for Brian, she knows she cannot. Though Brian has certainly encouraged her anyway, not understanding why she won't, and she not telling him the reason, being embarrassed.

Her eyes dark and sparkle-black like a virgin sacrifice in the wild.

Her face smooth and stunning like the daughter of a pharaoh.

Her voice a girlish rasp that guts you with each vowel.

Most of the things she says to her parents, she was realizing, are not true.

She needs to be attended to. She has a way about her that makes one ask her if she is comfortable.

She shops in Georgetown. She goes to raves at Nation and Starscape up in Baltimore. She knows her way around Northwest. She knows the DJ. She is from DC.

From no certain place, out of no particular source, "If You Could Only See" by Tonic was playing at a volume just above the level of audibility.

Brian whispered in her ear, —I love you so much, baby, and she could feel him through his jeans and one day he will leave her, she knows. And why does she know that? It is just a fact. She can see it like she sees the Blue Ridge Mountains way off in the distance like the gray shadows of a triumphant history. It is scary almost, how hot it is through the fabric. How can any part be that hot? And so amorphous? It amazed her. She wishes she had one. It's alive, like hers is. And that is why it is so damned good with him.

I love you, she whispered as she made eye contact with Laura Geary whose nipples she licked in tenth grade on a dare, sitting with Lindsay Baker who had a sleepover in eighth grade where they played Truth or Dare and someone dared Havva to go into a closet and masturbate with a big massager they found and Havva did it. She watched Gary Needler who was sitting with Chris Johnson both glancing over at her. She made out with Chris Johnson once in ninth grade and touched his you know what and that summer she had sex with Gary Needler in the freezer at Baskin-Robbins where she worked that summer and where Gary still works, her butt on top of a stack of pralines and cream buckets, her bare back against the frosted metal walls, and she was so cold, colder than she had ever been, feeling no part of her body except for that which Gary Needler, sheathed in a Trojan, was within, and that part was not only not cold but flaring hot like fire, so sensational that when she closed her eyes she could see it and it was red and glowing. The rest of her had become fragmented and broke brittle into shards, their breath coming out in thick clouds. They breathed the air straight out of each other's lungs. She imagined she was being kidnapped and this was the only way to disarm her captor. She searched his face watching its every minute muscle twitch and blink for a sign of weakness and it was everywhere she looked. He has a gun, she thought. She thought about her mother. She had been kidnapped by some gang of terrorists and rescued by a CIA agent, Gary Needler, and they had fallen in love as they hid in a freezer from the gang still after her. Overcome by an intelligent and powerful lust. Unbeknownst to both of them, in the meantime in the store stood a customer interested in procuring a strawberry-and-banana shake, extrathick, "Walking on the Sun" by Smash Mouth playing over the sound system at a low level, hardly audible at all. The customer was Grayson Donald. He stood there drumming his fingers, leaning over the counter and looking for signs of life in the back. Gary was fast, spasmic. It was over within moments. Gary got possessive and kept calling her afterward, showing up at her house, leaving her letters on her car. An actual stalker—but it wasn't as erotic as she'd imagined. She broke it off with him. Tried to forget about him. It was the only time she had done it. It didn't count, it was only a couple of seconds. She didn't even bleed.

24585 BUNKERS COURT— FOURTH ENTRANCE

Basketball goals can be a lot of the fun for the entire family. Athletics are very advantageous and mitigative for children and an august form of recreation. I love athletics, personally.

I do not believe I ever mentioned it, but I played basketball
in high school. I am in no way discouraging basketball goals,
when used properly, to be placed at the top of driveways, in
line with Regulation 74C. Quite the contrary. I would like to
see more outdoor activities in our community amongst our
children.

We as parents are responsible for our children's safety. We
nurture them. We hold them when they are frightened, kiss
them when they are crying, feed them when they are hungry.
Keep them from harm. We have all come to Little Rocky Run
to provide the best environment for our children, in that
concern. Our children are the future. The future teachers.
The future presidents. They are bang-up and groovy, every
single one. Let us not take that away from them.

I call for today to be the dawn of a new day. Join me in
eradicating the difficiencies of our past. Hey, not everyone's
perfect. You know what? I'll admit it. I have made a mistake
or two in my life. Well, maybe more than one or two. (Ha ha).
Our children need us, despite our imperfections. Who else will
hear their cries? They look to us for love. They trust in us.
They love us with their entire little hearts. Are we to turn
them away? Are we to say to them, "I am sorry, Child, but I
cannot love you and care for you the way you need me to?"

BRADDOCK PARK HIGH SCHOOL—
CAFETERIA

He watched Coming to America single out one particular milk sack,
pull out a straw, bite the tip off its paper wrapper, put the straw in his
mouth and pointing it up over the freshman's head like a trumpet, blow
the wrapper off and it blasted out and feathered down atop the fresh-

man's butt cut. —Hey man, he said, swatting it off as though it were bird feces. Coming to America kind of shrugged and punctured the sack then set forth sucking down its contents at an incredible rate. The freshman watched him. Within seconds he'd consumed it all. The straw slurped and he was reaching for a new sack. —Your ritual is drinking milk? Coming to America held up a finger and drained this sack and said, a little red eyed and woozy, gasping a little for breath, —You don't just drink milk, Marilyn. You drink as much milk as you can. As fast as you can. He reached for a third sack. —Why do you do that? Coming to America said, straw poised above the sack, —To throw up. He stabbed it and drank it, staring at the freshman the whole time, waggling his eyebrows, still grinning even with the straw. The freshman watching with a new interest. In a couple seconds Coming to America was reaching for another. —You throw up just from drinking milk? —Yes. —Why? —I don't know. He started to puncture it but stopped and gestured to the freshman's share piled up between them. —Come on, Marilyn. It's a race. He stabbed the sack and the freshman unwrapped his straw and pulled a sack off his pile and did the same, missing at first but getting it eventually, and they chugged their milk, both grinning and giggling as they did so with the grotesque giddiness of deranged children, the Mexicans looking on, exchanging bets.

In her head she had the song "Flagpole Sitta" by Harvey Danger, which was the last song playing on the radio as she drove to school today in her Kia Sportage. She was very close to making a very important decision in her life: which celebrity she most resembles. Brian always told her Carmen Electra, but she had also gotten Joey from *Dawson's Creek*, probably her new favorite show. However, she was lately starting to see Jennifer Aniston, from the side at least, and in the right light, in the nose-mouth area, if her hair were lighter. She became very warm and turned to Brian to alert him to this, but she couldn't speak, she didn't know what was acceptable to say, or what anyone wanted to hear, and she didn't want to be disliked or perceived badly for saying the wrong thing. She wanted to come across as empowered, liberated, healthy. So instead she kept quiet and listened, laughed, smiled, agreed. She wished she could check her e-mail or sign on to IM. She wished she had a mirror so she could look at herself and see Jennifer Aniston in the nose-mouth area, from the side. She considered whether or not she was real. What was a Havva? What was her real name? She wondered what each of Brian's friends would look like having shadowy, sensuous sex—kissing, lace curtains blowing in the windows, candles, gasping. Jimmy, one of Brian's friends, said to him as she snuggled into his inner shoulder, —Oh shit look at Gary Needler, what a fag.

And Brian went, —Nah he's a cool guy.

—Gary Needler?

—Yeah. You just have to get to know him.

—He's in my physics class. He's a tool.

—No, you just have to get to know him.

She wants to be famous and wealthy. In some vague town-house-in-a-city way. She wants kids, one kid, a quiet life in a cosmopolitan square, a high-powered, high-paying job in a major city. In her head was "How's It Going to Be" by Third Eye Blind. She wants to be an attractive older woman with a sophisticated palate and to teach law at a university on overcast days with pigeons flying from the statues outside the hall. She wants to read true-crime novels and collect vintage photographs, attend art openings around the world, discuss politics over champagne with knighted older men. Shop in expensive boutiques and parasail in Mozambique with the wife of the prime minister. Attend black-tie events at embassies with her husband, quiet and handsome. She wants to wear sunglasses and be an ambassador, swing shopping bags down Fifth Avenue hailing a taxi while frowning, the wind blowing her hair across her face, everybody watching her. She wants to be beautiful and powerful and discuss homelessness and AIDS with officials over long mahogany meeting tables in boardrooms, host dinners at her homes in the great cities of the world. She wants to go back to Iran. Learn her real name. Celebrate her birthday on the day she was born. Live in her palace. A princess. That is what she wants to be. That is what she is.

MS-13

On my arm is the tattoo of my real name SERGIO.

I also have all sorts of shit that I don't know what it is.

I didn't pick them.

Instead had it done to me in a motel or in Denis's house by means of ink from a pen (taken from motel rooms) and sewing needles (stolen from Jo Ann's Fabrics in Fairfax City).

Back when Denis was still around.

Too drunk or stoned to feel it but also to know what they were doing.

On my left arm is MS-13, below it FANTASMAGORAS. That's our clique.

The rule is if you put your clique's name on your skin you must put MS-13 above your clique's name.

You must have tattoos, even if you think you look pretty without them.

That's the rule.

If you don't, Raul or somebody will see you

& hold you down

& tear them into you with knives

& they'll get infected like Gloria's on her ass did

& she couldn't sit down for almost two months.

Look at Chester's fucked up pink sandpapery arm that looks like it was stuck in a fire which it was.

Because Chester did it backwards. He put FANTASMAGORAS over MS-13.

Raul saw Chester got it backwards and used his silver zippo to so-called erase it.

I was there.

I was holding the pillow over Chester's face so no maids or anyone would hear him screaming.

It was nasty but interesting.

BRADDOCK PARK HIGH SCHOOL— CAFETERIA

Half a dozen empty sacks lay before the freshman. —I don't think it works for me, he said. Then he opened his mouth and sprayed puke all over the table. It came pouring out white and still cold. It hit the table and splattered in every direction, the Mexicans jumping up from the table to avoid it, one of them hooting in victory. —Aha! Coming to America said, wiping a substantial quantity off his face, —You've already figured out the next part of the ritual! The freshman started to ask what he meant but stopped himself, his face becoming overcast in a sombrous hue of horror. —No, he said. —No no no no! But resistance was futile. Coming to America lunged over the table and cast up all his lacteal accounts, dousing the freshman in yogurty vomitus, who laughed and returned the favor to Coming to America's joy. The commotion of this spectacle spread through the cafeteria like wildfire. People stood to get a look. Girls screamed, boys cursed. The two reloaded and exgorgitated anew, their faces red with laughing and puking. Their discharge melded together on the table, ran off onto the floor, pooled there at their feet. It dripped like water off the edge of the table. It was all over their clothes and backpacks. What was left of the soft pretzel was soggy. The mush-gray lunch tray floated upon an inch or so of liquid like reusable jetsam. Boy, did it stink like cheese. Mr. Hardy happened to be entering the cafeteria on his way to fulfill a not unusual craving for a second soft pretzel of the morning. The commotion sent him into alert mode. Students everywhere, standing, yelling. Disorder. He couldn't see why. This is it, he thought. This is their grand revolt. He froze, ready to run back and barricade himself in his office, let the SWAT team take care of it, but at that moment he caught the source of the disorder and, after first rubbing his eyes to make sure he wasn't seeing things, he ran irate—literally ran—over to the two in order to ... well, what exactly? Stand out of reach and yell at them until they stop or *something* because he sure as hell wasn't going to touch the little fuckers, and it happened that on his way there he crossed upon a puddle of Coming to America's puke that had streamed its way some distance along the floor and Mr. Hardy's feet went flying up in the air like in the movies and, screaming, he landed on his back in the puddle of puke right in the exact spot where the freshman was now turning to expel another sack's worth of 2 percent barf. —Aaaaaahhhhh! Mr. Hardy in reaction staggered to his feet, his entire face smothered in it, blinded, slipped again onto his back. —Aaahhhh! He wiped it off with his hands and rolled over like a pig in mud to his knees and pulled himself to his feet using the edge of a table at which sat twelve shrieking Asian girls, repulsed in bebe, everyone in hysterics of joy or disgust, often an admixture of both. Mr. Hardy staggered a couple of feet before puking himself in a chunky cascade onto the head of Trish Fields, a pretty cheerleader, who screamed, —WHY?! and turned green and puked on her boyfriend Peter Jaworski who puked on

Gary Needler who puked back onto Peter Jaworski whose mouth was open, and at getting Gary Needler's puke in his mouth Peter jumped up and ran around like a guy on fire, shrieking like a girl, everyone he came near jumping out of their seats and getting out of the way in order to remove themselves from his toxic path, until he finally stopped at the other end of the cafeteria and shat through his teeth onto the head of poor Jeremiah Dutton who had been asleep but surely was woken now by the sensation of hot slimy stink dripping down the back of his neck, and, immediately knowing what this was, he sat up and retched on Sean Castiglione, who had been cackling at the efficiency of karma, and Sean yacked on Brian Donnelly, who barfed on a lunch lady, who parbroke upon Havva Khabbazi, who exgorgitated on Brian Hurkle, who was privately turned on a little but by reflex puked on one of his buddies, and so on, the lucky ones who were not puked on not escaping as the smell of hundreds of stomachs emptying themselves filled their olfactories in an odious stench causing in them an involuntary barfing reaction, and the entire first lunch period within moments had become a foul storm of emesis, a medieval crusade battle of hand-to-hand puking, cheerleader egesting on wigger, wigger gagging on jock, jock disgorging on nerdslut, nerdslut regurgitating on Asian, Asian unloading on black, kids ralphing into trash cans and backpacks and purses, one girl running into the cafeteria line and letting loose inside the nacho cheese dispenser, the matter dripping off the cinder-block windowless walls and the flickering fluorescent tubes in the ceiling, covering the floor like some sort of leviathan bowl of soup had been spilled, and in the eye of the storm sat the freshman, laughing like he could never remember laughing, tears welling in his eyes, his face and ribs aching from it, and Coming to America belly-laughing too, wretchedness dripping off their chins, their clothes soaked.

—I win! said the freshman.

Coming to America bowed to him, unable to speak.

—This is awesome! It's just like *Stand by Me*!

—What is this *Stand by Me*?

—It's a movie. Like *Coming to America*.

—What is this *Coming to America*?

—It's *you*!

They kept laughing.

The freshman said, —You're my best friend, Coming to America.

—You're my best friend too, Marilyn Manson.

And still laughing, they reached for more milk.

17653 BATTLE ROCK DRIVE—
THIRD ENTRANCE

I was very good. As far as placekickers go, I was great. We sit
on the bench and run out every once in a while in our cute
kids' pads and single-bar helmets which we wear more for
reasons of visual continuity than bodily protection. Little
stiff midgets with shoes that don't match and scrunched-up
shoulders beside these super humans. Ever stand in a huddle
with 10 men big as trees, their eyes yellow and they're
grunting like beasts? Black men? Looking at you like you
better make this because we earned this so don't fuck it up
now, you little peckerhead?

And all my greatness in my professional life of a career,
washed away and blacklisted by one 3 second act of
incredible difficulty and extraneous circumstance.

Imagine you're a musician. A very good one. You have spent
the last decade writing great songs. These songs are the best.
You are better than anybody else writing songs over the
same decade. You're mentioned with Lennon and Dylan.
You're making more money writing your great songs than
you've ever dreamed you would make. And one day you're
writing the greatest song you know that has been written.
Grayson, this is one extraordinary transcendent genius
song. A once in a lifetime tune that will catapult you into a
layer of memory reserved for legends only. And you're in
the studio recording it. It's going beautifully. You have only
this one chance to record it. I don't know why, just imagine
that's the scenario. You do not get a retake. And your one
chance is going great. And on the very last note your finger
slips just a bit and you barely miss the last and final note.
The recording is ruined. Not only that but faceless men

barge into the studio and take all those other great songs you've written over the last decade and they burn them in front of you, and everyone forgets they ever existed. And you're not allowed to write any new songs. All because you missed the note. Your face is plastered all over the sky with the word FUCKUP over it because you missed the note. The footage of you missing the note is played once a day on TV in slow motion as a grandfatherly voice narrates it. And your name is mentioned once a day in newspapers and laughed at at least once a day by strangers because you missed the note. And then seven years later it's still happening and someone you never will see or know wants to know how it feels.

Grayson, I live my life at night in a neighborhood full of people who live their lives at day. It's a nice neighborhood outside a major metropolitan area and none of you will ever find me. It's not a part of me. I blend in.

Braddock Park High School— Cafeteria

Havva has studied her mother, sees her sharp eyes cutting into the kid at Giant loading their groceries into the back of the station wagon.

Her friends' fathers, picking her up for sleepovers when she was small. How they looked at her mother. How her mother looked back. Havva knew that he would lie awake that night thinking about her mother and what it meant for him, his marriage, his life.

But she never looked at Havva's father that way, her father who works seven days a week, dawn to dusk. Havva's never heard noises from their room across the hall in the night.

Working, rushing in and out of the house, rubbing his eyes, coffee he never drinks beyond a sip, eating over the sink, she's never seen him sitting down or dressed in anything other than a tie and slacks. Answering phone calls from Iran in the early-morning hours, whispering monosyllables, not knowing she can hear. She's walked in on him standing in the kitchen sleep deprived and delirious on Sunday morning flipping through the Men for Women ads in the *Post* opened on the counter, scanning the lines with his index finger, mumbling to himself and breathing hard, turning the pages so fast they tear. Havva's had to repeat herself three, four times nearly shouting at him before he looks up and blinks and comprehends who she is and says, —Yes, Havva?

Havva's father being picked up by a black car with black-tinted windows, freshly polished, even the hubcaps, at dawn, and not returning for days.

He won't go to a restaurant where he doesn't know and trust the owner.

Going to the window and parting the slats of the blinds whenever there is the staccato rumble of a helicopter hovering somewhere above them in the heavens.

Papers and pamphlets written in a language she knows but can't understand. Watching him jump at every knock on the door, every splash of headlights across the curtained bay window. Nameless whispering and strained yelling in the bathroom, the faucet running on full blast, toilet flushing repeatedly. TV volume maxed out, some unwatched afternoon movie on a small basic cable network, her father standing before it a foot away, staring into it as though straining to pinpoint some arcane principle. One time the phone rang and Havva answered it and it was Colin Powell and her father snatched the phone away from her and shooed her off, telling her, —Go play. She listened from the other room as her father said in his hushed harshness, —Damn it Colin, how'd you get this number?

—I'm fine, Havva, he says. —It doesn't concern you. It's just work. Don't worry about it. You're too beautiful to worry. You just focus on your grades and your schoolwork and being daddy's beautiful angel, okay, Malouse?

Malouse. Her boyfriend Brian Hurkle once heard her father call her that and asked her what it meant.

She told him.

Sweet but spoiled.

31317 Marblestone Court— Third Entrance

From: gdonald81@yahoo.com
To: shows@mtv.com
Sent: Monday November 2, 1998 15:42 EST
Subject: You suck balls
CC: william.kennard@fcc.gov

Dear Sirs,

I am writing to alert you that your show "12 Angry Viewers" is an abortion of television programming. It is exactly what is wrong with America. Its basis is mired in unbelievable moral and political corruption. As an American, and one with a brain larger than his fist—a rare thing, I know—it gives me indigestion that you have chosen to give 12 totally unqualified simpletons the power to decide which videos I have to watch. In case you're too asinine to realize it, these idiots know nothing about music. NOTHING. They wouldn't know who Bob Dylan was if he walked in to the room wearing a shirt that said I AM BOB DYLAN on it. Not to mention Maynard James Keenan. Do you have any idea who that is? Probably not, since he is talented. No, the average MTV viewer—indeed, the average music consumer—okay, shit, the average American fucking human being—has the musical taste of a middle-aged aunt. Know why? Because they have no soul. They have never experienced pain. They are bland robots going about their day. And they'll listen to and buy any fartsound that is advertised to them enough times, so long as it is pleasant sounding and brainless. For example, the latest episode of 12 Inbred Viewers, which has just concluded, was abominable to an unimaginable degree. It featured Madonna's newest pile of poop, "Ray of Light,"

winning out over the Beastie Boys, a revolutionary act that
changed hip-hop forever—not just changed it but broadened
its audience (along with Run DMC) to levels absolutely
unimaginable before them—they MADE hip-hop, or at least
HELPED to! What has Man-donna made? I'll tell you what
she's made: SHIT! That is what she has made! And billions
of dollars off morons who lick it up. I mean, Man-donna
winning over the Beastie Boys???? WHAT???? And you call
yourself MTV? More like Sellout TV.

Every time I turn on MTV I have to endure either N Suck's
newest craptastic turdfest or, even worse, that dickwad Puff
Daddy mumbling over some eighties song and dancing
around like Bill Cosby. That is, when you are showing
videos, which nowadays you simply ARE NOT. I propose
you change your name, either to the afore offered SELLOUT
TV or to What Used to Be MTV. The Channel Formerly
Known as MTV. Or how about this: EmptyV. Get it? Because
your viewers are empty, and the music you play is empty.
Man-donna is empty, N Suck is empty, the Backside Boys are
empty (actually, they're not empty—they're full of all the
jizz they've been gulping), Britney Speared-by-four-cocks is
empty. It's not music. It's products created to sell to kids with
allowance money. It makes the dull duller and the bland
blander. It taints the collective unconscious. And I'm sick and
tired of it. This is a very important issue that you need to
address. Take a long, hard look in the mirror and ask
yourself: Am I poisoning America? Because if I have to see
Usher's soulless face one more time, I will fill my Ford
Aspire with Mountain Dews and drive up to your studios
chugging them the whole way, and when I get there I will
pee a hot stinky Mountain Dew piss all over Carson Daly's
flattop and sideburns live on TR-Hell.

Thank you very much for your prompt attention to this matter.

By the way, would it kill you to MAKE SOME NEW TOM
GREENS??????? This is ridiculous. I have seen the same
episode about fourteen times since yesterday and here it is
playing again. If I see Tom Green riding a cow around a

grocery store one more time, I will be forced to kill a
Barenaked Lady. Not that I need much motivation to take out
one of those grinning technical support associates. You have
"One Week," assholes, or the mix stations playing on radios in
the insufferable office cubicles across America will go silent.

And another thing I just thought of (I am watching the
Channel Formerly Known as MTV right now as I write
this): You show way too many commercials. Your average
commercial break must be about four minutes longer than,
like, CBS's. In a half hour, only about fourteen minutes is
actual show. Why not just play commercials?
CommercialTV. It wouldn't be much of a difference.

WHAT ARE WE DOING WITH OUR LIVES??????

GET A CLUE!!!!!!!!!!!!!!!!!111

Sincerely,
Grayson Donald
Centreville, VA

MEN—UNION MILL ROAD

It's 5:45 in the evening. I watch the line of cars backed up along 66
West peeling off in red brake light freeze along the soiling wrap of Exit
52 from up 29, over the slight lull of Union Mill Road where the ghosts
of emaciated Civil War dead still sit against trees writing letters home to
their mothers. A herd of mechanical bison from this, our sonic future,
passing by the revenants nearly without sound, gliding along on air-
filled rubber and antilock braking, their mild clean engines burning premium Texas gasoline, in a long caravan row moving along at thirty-eight
miles an hour like a parade for a town in which everyone takes part, a
funeral for themselves.

Here comes Richard Batchelor in his black 1999 Saab 9-5 wagon with power windows, newspapers on the passenger seat, upholstery vacuumed, radio off, driving glasses on, his belly pudging against the buttons of his sea-green officer's shirt. He is exhausted, listening carefully for a sound he thought he heard somewhere around Exit 67—Glebe Road, in what sounded like the right rear though he hasn't heard it since, can't be sure. And here comes Bruce Whiting with a bald shiny head and thin lips and meaty jowls in his black 1998 Lexus GS 300 with gold trim and listening to WTEM SportsTalk 980 where the host is calling for the disemboweling of Redskins coach Norv Turner, their voices catastrophic, like warning of an impending disaster and the instructions you will need to know in order to survive it. Richard Batchelor in Vietnam thirty years ago shot to death a boy who must have been fourteen or fifteen years old, though it was dark and they were far away from one another, in heavy jungle, and some of them looked so young, and also his memory of the death could have been warped by the decades and skewed by the belief, solidifying more and more into knowledge as those decades did pass, that the person was fourteen and that he did in fact kill a fourteen-year-old boy, something he has never told anyone, not even his wife, no matter how hard it was to withhold inside himself when his son Trent was fourteen and then again when his other son Dwight turned fourteen. He doesn't know where he got the number fourteen, but that is what the age has become. By a habit so deeply embedded within himself that he doesn't notice himself doing it anymore, Bruce Whiting calls from the doorway to his wife his destination each time he heads out of the house, even when she is not home.

Here comes Ken Alder, who when he was in his twenties parachuted into a rain forest in the Amazon and also spent two years following the Grateful Dead, dropping acid and living off begged change and screwing stoned Cockaigne apparitions with freckles on their noses and field-tanned breasts and sunlit eyes, and now is a civilian contractor who sells duct tape to the United States Army, vowing to start jogging regularly, looking forward to dinner which will be ready when he gets home, he hopes, wearing size medium boxer shorts from Hecht's that his wife bought him in a pack of three for $11.99, driving a 1996 Mazda _____ which he bought because he has faith in Mazda's engineering.

Here comes Charles "Charlie" _____, a former Washington, DC, police officer who had to retire in his twenties because of his chronic gastrointestinal eruptions, driving a 1995 Ford _____, now a project manager at Mobil, with $37 in late fees accumulated at the Blockbuster in the Colonnade that he knows he will never pay back and has been dreading the mail and avoiding Blockbuster for seven months because of it, going so far as to consider converting his family to a traditional, some would say extreme Baptism sect that frowns upon such pop culture indulgences as mainstream Hollywood cinema (and also caffeine and artificially added flavor, which therefore would outlaw coffee and most juice too, which he would say would have to be the biggest con for him on that matter at the moment), the purpose being that then he would not have to keep thinking up new excuses whenever his three kids—seven, nine, eleven—put the heat on him to take them to Blockbuster, as they are starting to do with greater frequency and greater intensity.

Here comes Sean Castiglione's father, _____, driving home in his 1997 Toyota _____. The main thing he is not looking forward to about his plan to start jogging regularly is that you can't jog in Little Rocky Run without someone honking at you and pulling up alongside you, wanting to chat about something or someone.

Here comes _____ _____'s father, driving a 1997 _____ _____. He has out-of-control cholesterol and a mysterious and persistent itch on the right side of his forehead, and a shooting, burning pain on his upper back that so far no doctor or specialist can figure out but the neurosurgeons are pressuring him to let them operate and though he was a staunch opponent of the idea as he has a feeling surgery will just complicate things even more, opening the door to a host of new mysterious pains and difficulties, he is feeling himself start to give in simply because he doesn't know what else to do and the itching and the back pain are the only things he can think about all day.

And here comes _____, driving a ____ _____ _____, who in his twenties hitchhiked from Alaska to San Antonio then back again and also climbed Mount Everest, then got a master's degree in business from Oxford, worked for Donald Trump for a couple of years then quit to found a literary magazine there in New York, then went to medical school, served as a doctor in Ethiopia treating malnourished children, designed robot submarines for the navy, now thirty-seven pounds overweight and approaching fifty and owner of a golden retriever he named _____ after his grandfather, and he believes it to be the most beautiful and smartest dog in the world. He is on Zoloft for anxiety and drinks too much, binges on Internet porn whenever he is alone in the house, in the process of divorcing his wife who, according to his therapist, is *borderline*, because she has drained their savings buying old homes with the intention of flipping them but invariably losing interest after a couple of months and never completing the projects. His favorite show is *Seinfeld.* His car has dual rear suspension and remote keyless entry and fifteen-year warranty plus free oil changes for the first twelve thousand miles, the real deal maker as far as he was concerned. The car also came with a free pair of K2 skis. "One Week" by the Barenaked Ladies plays on CD over the stereo. His knees hurt when he walks. He makes $_____ a year and worships at St. John the Apostle Parish and suffers from erectile dysfunction and oversensitive bladder, something he hopes is not a symptom or warning sign of prostate cancer or something else festering inside his body that will end his life.

Here comes now _____ _____, driving a _____ _____ _____ with _____, and _____, and automatic _____. _____ enjoys going to Applebee's in Fair Lakes and sitting at the bar talking to the nineteen-year-old waitresses who know him by name. He tells them they are beautiful then goes home and masturbates. He is in the middle of getting a divorce. His son does not talk to him. He has a beard and prostate cancer he does not know about. He could be in his opinion a very successful stand-up comic if he wanted, but he does not pursue it for the reason that he is not interested in living the lifestyle a stand-up comedian must live, as he is happy at home spending time with his family. His wife is an alcoholic. His other son blames him for the divorce. He drives with the heat on full blast to stop the chronic itching he suffers from on his forearm, which no doctor has been able to explain. His cholesterol is high and so is his blood pressure. He has a forty-two-inch waist and now has a bag with Outback takeout on the passenger seat on top of his newspapers, and the bag is open, and he is reaching in and pulls out a fatty rib covered in obscene amounts of brownish red barbecue sauce and shoves it into his mouth like a dog bone and makes $_____ a year and his youngest son _____ is __ years old and listens to Snoop Dogg and Tupac at full blast in his room and watches *Scarface* eight times a week and plays Nintendo 64 sometimes seventeen hours a day and is seventeen pounds overweight.

And here comes _____ _____, whose sixteen-year-old daughter is secretly seven months pregnant and has thus far been able to hide it from everybody by wearing baggy hooded sweatshirts but it is getting to the point now where that doesn't work anymore, and _____ _____ who _____ a ____, and _____ _____ who has _____ of the

_____, and _____ _____ and
_____ _____ and __ ___, and _____
_____, and _____ _____
and _____ _____ and now
_____ _____ and _____
_____ and _ _____ and _____
_____ and after him is _____ _____ followed
by _____ _____ and
_____

_____ _____ _____
and _____ _____
and

_____ _____ and
_____ _____ and
_____ _____
and

_____
_____
_____
_____
_____
_____
_____
_____
_____
_____
_____
_____.

AFTER HIGH SCHOOL

Graduate and go off to JMU or UVA or Mason or Virginia Tech or Radford or Longwood and break up with your girlfriend and go there for four years and party and graduate and break up with your girlfriend and move back home then a job waiting tables at Outback then go to law

school then drop out of law school then move to Arlington, get a job, go
to shows at the Black Cat and go to parties thrown by the bartenders and
smoke cigarettes and learn about Belgian beers and talk philosophy
and start a blog and buy $250 jeans and get into trance and quote movies
and go to tanning salons and dye your hair and buy a digital camera and
show cleavage and get a new phone and bleach your teeth and lose your
phone and have to get everyone's number again and read books and get
abortions and tattoos and herpes and get engaged and get dumped and
get comed on and go over your cell phone minutes and drink Bloody
Marys and let the dishes pile up and go shopping instead of doing laundry and get confused and get unhappy and want to quit your job and vote
Democrat and get a sundress and get Direct TV and get out of the house
and take subway trains into the night, eat weekday dinners at nice
restaurants asking the waiter if you can smell the cork please, then get it
together, get a job at a strategy and technology consulting firm, get a car,
get healthy, get engaged, get married, get pregnant, get a house, get a
headache, get a C-section, get bent, get it on, get a babysitter, get a
divorce, get diagnosed, get stiff.

13762 BLUESTONE PLACE— SECOND ENTRANCE

Dinner at the Euckers'. The family of five sits around the table, silver
metal forks—from the set that Ellen's aunt gave as a wedding present—
in their right hands pronging at plates of baked ziti, left hands used to sip
milk or water or to eat buttered Pillsbury crescent rolls that Ellen made
by unpeeling a tube and pulling out a presliced cylinder of dough and
pulling chunks from it and placing the chunks on a cookie sheet then
baking in the oven at 425° for twenty minutes.

Their plates are all the same: round, some sort of porcelain material
glazed in solid primary colors with rings naturally occurring in the paint
growing outward from the center of the plate like a tree trunk's. The table
is rectangle shaped, a thick shiny woodlike material with grains so authen-

tic seeming that they divot if you run your fingernail over them. There is a seam in the middle of the table widthwise where the table comes apart making room for the extender, a chunk of the same material as the table that makes the table longer if need be and now gathers dust in the back of the closet inside the front door behind a box of Gore-Tex ski gloves and fuzzy-ball knit hats. There is a dried dot of off-white paint at the place of Michael, who must eat at the end with his back to the window or he won't eat. They all find themselves in the same places each evening at dinnertime. Dinnertime is 6 PM, so that they can have enough to eat then put the dishes in the dishwasher in time to watch *The Simpsons* at 7.

Brian the youngest cannot and will not eat any food whatsoever off any surface other than his yellow plate with a small chip on the rim. He has sat there cross-armed and starving before the green plate, as his ziti sat cold and people went to bed. Christopher the oldest isn't picky about what plate color he ends up with, though he needs his Redskins cup his mom Ellen got for free from Mobil eight years ago during a promotion where if you bought $10 worth of premium you got a free Redskins cup. Ellen was a stripper for a week after graduating college when she was desperate about not being able to find a job. The TV is on. They can see it from the table while they eat. The volume is loud enough. In the middle of the table is the pan of baked ziti with a big spoon in it, and another similar blue plate with three remaining cold crescent rolls and a tub of Country Crock with a butter knife laid across it, and a bowl that is green and is from the same plate set and is full, appropriately, with green beans which no one besides Ellen has touched.

The TV says, —Wheel . . . of . . . fortune!

Ellen groans, inadvertently stirring up phlegm that breaks up her groan. Her husband and kids notice, and she swallows the phlegm and says nothing about it, drops her fork with a heavy-handed clank and scoots her chair—that came with the table and is made from the same woodlike substance, with a green-and-white butt pad—away from the table so hard that it causes a nasty scrape that tears away a layer of the DuPont coating on the linoleum tile floor. Throws her napkin down onto her place and stomps so hard to the TV room—the kitchen and the TV room, aka the living room, are separated by a one-third wall-slash-counter that most homes in Little Rocky Run have, made from wall material and is wallpapered like the rest of the room and can be used when your parents aren't around as a seat or balance beam. Around Christmas a few years ago, Ellen tried to put a snakelike thing of white faux Christmas tree needles with white Christmas lights on it, but afterward she couldn't sleep until she tore it off and tossed it into the closet with the table extender. Stomps over to the TV so hard that all the military award plaques and framed triangle flags and framed family photos and Korean art from when Tim was stationed in Korea and Paraguayan art, etc., all rattles. She says from the bottom of her throat she can never clear of the airborne toxins and allergens hovering through her home's air (and is waiting with waning patience for UPS to deliver the ionizer she ordered on Wednesday from the Sharper Image for only $350 plus tax and shipping), —I *hate Wheel of Fortune.*

She forgoes the remote that sits atop the glass and wicker coffee table on top of a *People* magazine and the *Washington Post*'s weekly TV guide, which Michael, who was diagnosed with ADD and is on Ritalin and is eleven pounds overweight and stays up every Saturday night late into the night, hyper and wired with insurmountable anticipatory glee for the morning to come so he can rip open the large weight of the Sunday *Post*'s plastic supplement package with the coupons and the Magazine etc. to find the TV guide and flip through it and get black ink on his fingertips as he memorizes what will be on TV this week, enjoys. He gets most excited about what football games will be telecast on Fox and CBS and what the daytime movies will be on TBS and TNT and UPN, even though he will be in school. Maybe tape them.

Rather Ellen—who has slept with over seventy-five men in her life, most of them with felony convictions on their records, in fact was once when she was twenty and a junior in college engaged to a death row inmate but he was the only other person who knew about it and he was executed before they could go through with it—chooses to punch in 07 directly on the brown cable box provided by Media General Cable for $5 a month. She then stands on her tiptoes to find the Enter button, same size as the other buttons. The channel changes to local news on ABC, her favorite. She likes the timbre of the older black newscaster's voice, wise and grim and professional but warm and kind, like a grandfather reading stories to her. And there he is, same mustache and way of holding his notes. He lays her down and tucks her blanket under her chin, brushes her hair back, serves her death and woe on a spoon from a piping bowl. It goes down easy and sweet. Fires, senseless death, evil, mangled wreckage of automobiles, foreboding dastardly deceptions of men in suits speaking words she does not quite comprehend—lawyerly speak that confuses her—so she grasps for tone and emotion, the structure of their brow, their flesh, whether they seem to be good people. She likes the news and that the newscaster is always there with a fresh bowl for her. It's important to know what's going on. It's educational. The news makes one smarter. She is comforted enough by a story about a missing little girl to return to the table without stomping.

Tim wears a red, white, and blue headband and ultrahigh running shorts made from a fabric so thin he feels inappropriate around his kids. He is deeply red faced and his shirt is soaked dark in a semicircle from the neck down to the bulge of his gut. He emits the humid stink of heated body. He is finally getting his breath back but isn't lifting his eyes from his plate. He once won $300 in a cockfight in Tijuana when he was in his twenties then used some of it to pay for himself and his army buddies to watch a morbidly obese Tijuanan woman get ravaged by a donkey. He still sees, invariably, whenever he and Ellen have sex, the donkey woman's vagina stretching to horrible degrees as the donkey penetrated her. He is aware of Ellen glaring at him as she sits back down. He dabs his mouth with the square paper napkin with doilies or flowers or maybe snow on it, crumbles it in his hand, drops it next to his plate, green, leans forward with his elbows on the table, and folds his hands in front of his mouth and nose so only his eyes peek out. He clears his throat, which still burns deep in the back of it, and this causes his three kids and his wife to all look at him, but he says nothing.

Christopher who is eleven says, —I noticed today how prominent my cheekbones are becoming. I'm becoming a very good-looking male. I wonder if I'll be six feet. You're short, Dad, but I hope I grow to be six feet at least. Mom, do you think my cheekbones are becoming prominent and that I'll be six feet?

—Hmm? Ellen says, eyes not moving from the TV.

—Do you think my cheekbones are becoming prominent?

—Prominent cheekbones, she says monotonically, —are a very attractive physical trait.

—Yeah, I know. But do I have them? Or am I getting them? I have them, don't I? High cheekbones? Mom?

Brian says, —I want to play Nintendo.

—Finish your supper, Tim says.

Michael says, —I'm out of milk.

Ellen says nothing and scoots away again, dropping a forkload of ziti she was about to eat, goes into the kitchen, opens the fridge, pours 2 percent milk into Michael's empty glass.

—Fill it up all the way this time, Michael says. —You never fill it up. We need bigger glasses too. I hate when there's only like a sip of milk in the glass.

—I want hamburgers, Brian says.

—Mommy didn't make hamburgers, Tim says, looking at Ellen.
—Mommy made baked ziti.

Ellen glares at Tim as she puts the milk back.

—I don't think I'll need braces, Christopher says, touching his teeth.
—I have a natural physical perfection. I'm pretty much blessed with an
ideal body and mouth.

Michael goes, —I hate all of our glasses. Our glasses suck.

Ellen tells him to not say suck, gives him his milk, filled so high it spills
over the side as she puts it down before him and leaves a ring along the
bottom on the table. She sits down, picks up her fork, opens her mouth to
deposit ziti, and is about to bite when Tim her husband says, —Mommy,
can you get me a glass of water while you're up please? With ice please?

And she drops the fork with the baked ziti still on it, scoots her chair
back out, scraping the linoleum, picks up his glass, goes back into the
kitchen, takes a handful of ice from the automatic ice maker, drops it into
the glass, fills it with water from the Brita pitcher in the fridge, refills the
top of the Brita filter and puts it back, gives the glass to her husband, sits
down, picks up the fork and brings it to her mouth, opens her mouth, and
Christopher says, —Oh me too, Mom.

She closes her mouth and puts the bite of baked ziti down once more
and scoots her chair back, stands up, gets a glass from the cabinet, opens the
freezer, grabs a handful of ice from the ice maker, closes the freezer, goes
to the sink, turns on the water, waits for it to get cold, fills the glass, brings
it to Christopher, places it in front of him, and he says, —*Tap*? and she says,
—Deal with it, and sits down, shoves the ziti into her mouth, and swallows
it without chewing before anyone can stop her.

Michael sits on his knees in his chair, Ellen tells him to stop sitting
with his knees on his chair and to sit normal, and he ignores her and says,
—Did you hear Havva Khabbazi cheated on her boyfriend Saturday
night?

—Who's Havva Khabbazi? Tim and Ellen both say in unison.

—I don't know.

—Sit right in your chair, Ellen says.

—I think I want to be a model, Christopher says. —I'm good-looking
enough for it. Aren't I? I mean, let's face the facts here.

—Yes, Ellen says, —but we don't know anybody in that field. Which
means the odds of you actually being successful are very slim. Michael,
sit right, please. It's practically impossible. You're better off focusing
on . . . Michael? *Now* . . . You're better off focusing on doing well in
school so you can get into a good college.

—That's a given, though. I'll go to Harvard or maybe Yale and become editor in chief of the *Washington Post* or *Time* magazine and be a model and actor and lead singer or lead guitar player. The real question here, though, Tim and Ellen, is in regard to my future wife: blond or brunette? What do you think, Mom? I say blond.

Ellen ignores him and turns to her husband and points a finger in his face and says, —Before I forget, after dinner you are going to do the dishes then you will please go to Giant and get me a bottle of Drano, ultra strength, and we also need toilet paper and then *you will fix my clogged tub.*

—And get hamburgers, Brian says.

—She let Chris Something put a dildo in her butt.

—I'd like a couple disposable Kodak cameras too, please, Christopher says. —With thirty-six pictures. *Not* twenty-four. Oh and make sure they have a flash. I need to start putting together some sort of portfolio to show to agencies on my go-sees. And also I have just decided while I was speaking the previous sentence that I want to be a photographer for either the NBA or *National Geographic* and want to get started as soon as possible. So I'll need a proper, expensive camera. And a full darkroom, too, in which to work.

—What's a dildo? little Brian says.

—Michael sit right or go to your room, Ellen says. Then she says to Christopher, —I'm sorry, Christopher, but I just don't see how that will work.

Tim raises his eyebrows at Christopher, who quiets. Brian, across from Tim, is dipping his ziti into his milk, then eating it. His milk is now orange. —Mommy's right, Tim says. —Starving and being poor is no picnic. I would know. I've been poor. I've starved. I washed my clothes in my bathtub when I was at Officer Training School when I was in my twenties.

He is going to say more but is cut off by Ellen swatting at him, hissing. She sits up high in her chair with her other hand cupped behind her ear and neck stretched so far the tendons are visible, a look of great pain on her face as she watches the weather for tomorrow. No one makes a sound until it's over at which point she relaxes and exhales and says, —Okay . . . and they resume eating.

MS-13

Get off the bus at Fair Oaks in front of Sears one at a time

& Sexy white girls smoking cigarettes out front along the wall

& Pedro hits the big silver button on the wall that makes the automatic door open for tards in wheelchairs

& we go in.

We look cool and tough.

The girls sexy and tough.

& we go to the bookstore & they wait outside while I steal books

& Sam Goody to steal CDs

& then downstairs to Babbage's to play Nintendo 64

& me and Pedro and Chester try to steal one along with some games but it's a bad idea, there's no way to.

Gloria and Julia go up to white kids asking them for a quarter to make a phone call.

& I think maybe one day I will be like Raul which gets me excited and puts me into a somewhat decent mood finally.

& All is calm for now on planet earth.

& Pedro is bigger than me height-wise but not by a lot

& he has a mustache kind of that's more just darkness over his lip

& someone's old dingy Tommy Hilfiger shirt he found on a playground wet and muddy from the rain the night before.

He says to me, Gato, what was that? In the Spider. It sounded like a Pioneer DEH-P4YDH.

No fucking way, I say. Not with that sonic fragmentation. It was a Pioneer DEH-P77DH probably.

Yeah yeah, Pedro says, that's what I meant. DEH-P77DH.

Then why the fuck did you say DEH-P4YDH?

I don't know.

Say what you mean, Pedro, I say, and mean what you say.

I know but I'm gonna get one. That's what I'm going to have in my ride.

First of all, Pedro, you don't have a ride nor will you ever have a ride.

Fuck you I won't.

You'll never have enough money. Not even to buy a fucking Pinto. If you make any money you'll have to give it to Raul who has to give it to Felipe and so on. You're not living in reality.

I live in reality.

No you don't.

Yeah I do.

No you fucking don't. Know how I know? For one thing you think the *DEH-fucking-P77DH* is a good car stereo.

It is.

Uh huh.

It is, Gato.

Okay. Why.

Well for one thing, it's exceptionally fully featured.

Go on.

It fits into the vehicle without a custom install, plays CDs, CD-Rs, and AM/FM using Pioneer's legendary Supertuner III. It will control an add-on CD changer of any make and puts out 45 watts by 4 power plus Easy EQ for shaping the sound of your vehicle. Not to mention, it also includes Pioneer's famed DFS Alarm, multicolor display—

I cut him off: Multicolor display, removable faceplate, remote control, blah blah blah. So I guess you plan on driving a Chrysler then, huh? I laugh at him. What kind you have in mind? A fucking Town and Country?

Pedro looks at me sideways, glaring, and says slowly, What the fuck you talking about, Gato?

We're in front of Active Edge

& I am aware of Asian pussy eating Auntie Anne's pretzels.

I say, Any other make of car besides a GM or a Chrysler and your sonic properties will be thrown out of whack. Which you obviously know, of course.

I know.

No you didn't.

Yeah I did.

You know what? Do whatever. But don't come crying to me later when you're cruising down 66 in your bad fucking car and the higher frequencies at anything over a volume level of six fucking fall apart.

Oh yeah? You're so smart, what do you like.

The Sony CDX-R3300.

. . .

CD text clock, MP3 support. You may not be aware of this yet, by the way, and I don't blame you, but trust me, in a few years you will fucking *need* that like you need water. But that's not all. Let's go farther. Let's take this all the way home. The CDX-R3300 also has all the features you need for every kind of trip, big or small, from a quick ride to the store for a can of soup to a week-long cross-country trip with your friends. Not only will you find your precious CD-R capabilities but also CD-RW capabilities as well. How's that sound? Want some more of that? AM/FM with 30 presets, EQ3, SSIR-EZ tuner, plus a maximum power output of 52 watts and, rest assured my friend, a removable fucking faceplate for extra security and peace of mind. Run it through a JL Audio XR650-CSi 6.5 inch 2-way component system and Rockford Fosgate Power Stage 2 T212D4 12 inch Dual 4-ohm component subwoofers, and you'll find yourself with a perfect combination of high quality materials, state of the art engineering, and a liberal dose of Rockford Fosgate's notorious no-nonsense bass fanaticism. Of course, the Power Stage 2 series is ideally suited for use with Power Stage series amps but these woofers handle incredible power levels regardless.

Oh yeah? What kind of levels?

I have my finger on his chest, the bony hollow spot between the pecs

& I can feel his heart's vibrations beneath, shaking the structure of his torso.

I lean in close

& Chester is leaning forward on his feet too in anticipation of what I will say to Pedro.

I say, deliberate & slow, Up . . . to . . . two . . . thousand . . . watts . . . peak.

Pedro whistles.

Chester and he exchange looks as I resume walking.

I stare at the Asian pussy

& they have noticed my presence by now

& I make a V with my fingers and put it up to my mouth and flick my tongue at them through it.

& say to Pedro and Chester who are following me, That blows away anything standing in their path. Plus at seven hundred dollars each they'll demand the respect you shit pushers sorely and noticeably lack.

The Asian pussy make faces at each other, disgusted

& it makes me comfortable and happy

& we stop at the railing that overlooks the second floor, near the escalators, watching Julia and Gloria down below go up to a white kid standing by the waterfountain with his hand in it

& who is everything I've ever wanted from this life and to be in this world.

& I will get it.

24585 BUNKERS COURT— FOURTH ENTRANCE

Rules make children feel safe. Want to know a secret? They _like_ rules. And they are grateful for the parent who sets and adheres to rules. If we show them that it is okay to disregard rules just because we don't like them, or find it inconvenient to adhere to them, then how can we expect them to follow the rules too, when it comes time for them to follow the posted speed limit on the road? To make their house payments? To have unprotected sex? To choose whether or not to get behind the wheel after they have been drinking?

The world is based on rules, Mike. Will professors in college understand when they are told, "Well, I was going to write the term paper you assigned us but it was inconvenient for me"? Or, if they, in high school, are placed into the situation where they feel pressure from their friends to abuse drugs or have sex? To whom will they turn to inspire them to make the right choice? Their friends? Not likely. Their favorite pop music stars or actors? Don't count on it. They will remember their parents, and what their parents would do.

They will remember one day long ago when their parents were asked by the members of the community to please reconsider the placement of a basketball goal, for the concern of the safety of others. And they will remember how their parents responded.

Look, Mike, I am not trying to be a "Nazi" or "Debby Downer." I certainly am not attempting to tell you how to raise your children. But please take down your basketball hoop. Please think of the rest of us then do the right thing. Before it's too late.

> Sincerely,
> Mitzy, Ed, and Brian Hurkle
> and the Board of Trustees,
> Little Rocky Run Home Owners' Association

13762 Bluestone Place—
Second Entrance

There is potpourri in the air. And outside there are stars in the sky. The oven is on. A pair of thin green-and-white plaid dish towels hang from the handle. The Euckers' fridge is a big silver industrial-sized half freezer–half fridge. It is metallic looking, with a small cubby in the door where, once, when the fridge was new, a couple years ago, you could put your cup and push a button and your choice of crushed or cubed ice would tumble into your glass and water would fill it up but now somebody has broken it and it doesn't work anymore.

The refrigerator is Kenmore and packed to capacity with sliced deli meat by the pound in plastic bags, white and orange sliced cheese in similar plastic bags, all with a sticker that says Giant and a bar code and price, quantity, substance, etc. There are three full loaves of whole wheat and white bread way past the expiration date, fruit that has not been looked at since it was placed in the fruit drawer months ago in thin plastic bags tied closed. An opened and expired jar of what was once Pace picante but is now a solid gray furry substance. A bunch of fruit that is still good. Seven one-gallon jugs of 2 percent Shenandoah's Pride milk with purple caps. A dozen or so value-sized squeeze bottles of all your basic condiments including Heinz ketchup, Hellman's mayo, Heinz relish, etc., of all levels of fullness. A three-quarters-full twenty-four-pack of Coke and a half-full twelve-pack of Diet Coke and an eleven-twelfths-empty Miller Lite twelve-pack, cans. All surface area is covered. Not a spare inch of metal rack or solid white plastic inner-door shelf available.

One is greeted upon opening the fridge by a wall of jars and bottles, bags and packages, an endless stockpile of perishables and edibles, threatening to tumble out like a gag in an old comedy.

There is a lawn chair folded in the small space between fridge and counter that was dragged by Michael Eucker from the garage two months ago when his feet got sore and shins cramped up standing before the open fridge so long unable to find anything to his liking, light-headed with hunger at 5:15 and unsure if he'd be able to make it till dinnertime at 6.

In the freezer half of the fridge: frozen baked ziti, in cardboard packaging, two dozen or so, stacked on top of each other in perfect uniformity. Nothing else.

The pantry is stocked with value-sized bags of the Doritos flavors, even the newest Cooler Ranch, plus tremendous boxes of Lipton tea bags, two thirty-six-packs of Brawny paper towels (super rolls), a four-gallon vat of chunky Peter Pan peanut butter, a butt load of granola bars and enough Pringles and Ruffles and Little Debbie Swiss Cake Rolls to feed a bloc of Chechnyan rebels for a month. A couple of three-foot-long rectangular bricks of paper napkins with doilies or snowflakes or flowers on them. An eight-pound bag of sugar, tanks of Folgers French Roast coffee, all the crap Tim Eucker bought today, the maggot-picked bones of Dufus the hamster that disappeared from the Habitrail cage with terribly stinky damp bedding and complicated network of transparent yellow tubes in Michael's room last year. Two full unopened twenty-four-packs of Coke, three more twelve-packs of Diet Coke, eight twelve-packs of Miller Lite. One dusty case of Fresca. Half a six-pack of Zima (zomething different). Canned soup by the dozen, boxes upon boxes of Hamburger Helper. There is a compact Magnavox TV/VCR combo still in the box on the top shelf. There is despair and pathos. There is no odor, no sensation beyond the sheen of plastic hypercolored logo packages against the fluorescent lighting of the kitchen.

There is so much food and the floor and all the solid surfaces for that matter are so well swept and lemon-fresh and white—except for the hardwood of the hallway which is reflective and delicious—thanks to the maids who came last Thursday and are middle aged and Spanish speaking and who come from nightmarish poverty and incurable political corruption and who have crawled and suffered through years of indignities and often flat-out bleak and dangerous *shit* in order to leave behind their families, escape their homeland, get into America, and obtain legal alien status here, and are proud beyond the imagination of Ellen Eucker to now live in Manassas, Virginia, in dumpy accommodations and scrub toilets and mop the floors of people in Little Rocky Run that it's a wonder anyone ever finds it necessary to leave this spacious fortress for any reason aside from dentist appointments, picking up the boys from school, or to go to Giant.

The TVs and all their channels and the carpets in every room white and springtime fresh with the vacuum lines still in them. The curtains and the green trees and fence outside the window. The insulated silence of life and all that space so air-conditioned that you don't notice the seasons change or time pass.

They get their solitude in rooms in distant corners of the house, in opposite levels, can go for days without seeing or communicating with any of the family they live with.

They work in the basement. They summer in the master bath. They play in the screened-in rec room off the TV room.

They eat. They dine. They swallow. They familiate.

Their forks clink and their throats clear. They hear television.

They glance at each other's faces, their jaws grinding food, throats contracting, moving food down into their bodies.

This is what they will remember they were doing in 1998 when this moment churns itself into a globe, swirling around in space and so obvious and clear but out of reach and missed, the history of circumstances, the end of the millennium and also the future.

This is what they were doing while he was killing himself.

Time is quickly burning itself out and none of these meals will matter.

Like the weather. These years, these decades.

White space between solid lines.

31317 Marblestone Court— Third Entrance

From: gdonald81@yahoo.com
To: meowx81@aol.com
Sent: Monday November 2, 1998 09:31 EST
Subject: Fucking you

Dear Havva,

Your tits are amazing. Your ass I stare at every day at lunch. Right now you are at lunch and I should be too. If I were, I would be staring at you imagining eating your ass for lunch instead of my big soft pretzel with nacho cheese. We don't really know each other but I am obsessed with the idea of fucking you. I have horrid, unrelenting fantasies of fucking you. When you wear those jean shorts I get a big boner. When you wear those black stretch pants all I think about all day is pulling them down and bending you over a desk or some similar piece of school property and fucking you for two to three hours. Three out of five days your tits and your ass are the reason I bother going to school. I want you to blow me. Ever since 8th grade (I went to Rocky Run and you were at Stone) when I saw you at Fair Oaks with your friends I have wanted to fuck you so badly that it becomes an emotional anguish. I am Catholic (or was raised anyway) so premarital sex is a mortal sin. And I think you are pretty stupid. But these things make me want to fuck you more. I want to fuck you while you say stupid shit. I want to fuck you while you annoy me. Your lips and your hair and your tits and your arms and your pussy and your thighs are pretty much all I have much interest in. Even just watching you fucking Brian would be something I would find glorious. Provided that you were on top. Otherwise the only thing I would see would be his ass. Sometimes it tears me apart that he fucks you and I don't. Does he play Dave Matthews Band while he fucks you? Does he keep his Abercrombie shirt on? I am not in love with you. I just want to fuck you very, very badly. To be honest, I am a virgin, so I don't really know what fucking is like. I have only made out with two girls. Part of the reason is because I am Catholic. I felt one of them up and fingered the other one. The first one I burped in her mouth. Anyway, just thought I'd let you know that I stare at you all the time pretty much thinking about this and that it is scary. Have a nice day, Havva!

Your friend,
Grayson Donald

24585 Bunkers Court— Fourth Entrance

The HOA meeting having ended an hour or two ago, Mitzy Hurkle sits back in her chair and drains the last of another rum and Coke and prints the letter on her HP LaserJet at the startling rate of nine pages per minute—the wonder of technology, she almost says aloud—top-of-the-line, high-tech computer equipment she purchased with the discount made available to Fairfax County Public School employees with her level of experience. She reads the letter, feels proud of her writing ability, and, inspired by herself, opens another Word document and writes nearly an entire half a page of what she hopes will one day become a published novel that garners critical praise and prizes and sells greatly and steadily and becomes read in high school English classes for generations to come, all of which is fairly possible because the symbolism in just this first half a page alone—okay not quite technically an entire half a page since she set the font size to 14 and moved the margins an inch inward, but still—is so powerful and the subtlety is so imperceptible, just

like the great works she (thanklessly) exposes her own students to—
Steinbeck's *The Pearl,* Faulkner's *The Bear, The Awakening* by whoever
wrote *The Awakening.* She can't remember at this moment. After
accomplishing a half page almost of skillfully wielded symbolism, Mitzy
Hurkle stops in the kitchen for a snack then staggers up the stairs to the
master bedroom thinking about what she will say on *Oprah,* where,
exhausted by all her literary exertions tonight—so tiring being a
writer—she decides she needs to relax. She needs a long hot shower is
what she needs. To soak her weary, hungry bones. She undresses in the
walk-in closet, puts on her shiny bathrobe, somehow another rum and
Coke having materialized in the glass in her hand, walks the three feet to
the master bathroom with two sinks and a Jacuzzi-jet tub and a Crate
and Barrel towel rack that cost $175 and a shelf over the toilet from
Crate and Barrel that cost nearly $300 and a bowl of potpourri on the
shelf and nothing else, a picture of Ernest Hemingway on the wall,
matching bathmat and hand towels and toilet seat covers and curtains on
the window that remain forever closed, the blinds drawn. She hums
Cruella De Vil's theme song from *101 Dalmatians* which is in her head
for some reason as she chugs the entire rum and Coke, dribbling down
her chins with small black hairs she no longer bothers plucking, down
her fleshy neck, her dense pale chest and saggy boobs. She makes a brief
and halfhearted gesture of checking herself for lumps but really it is just
a pretense to wipe the rum and Coke with her hand and lick it off her
fingers with indulgence. She takes off her robe and stands there soft
and fed and vast beneath her skylights before turning on the shower—in
its own shower stall with plastic or glass doors treated in such a way that
they are nearly opaque except for primary colors—and stepping into
the shower then immediately stepping out dripping because she's forgotten to take off her glasses, then stepping back in.

The water trickles down the rolls of flesh on her arms and belly and
that long neglected expanse of woolly hair below the ever-expanding
waist. Her short dark hair clings to her skull so that she comes to resemble very quickly a family pet fallen into a river and saved and featured
briefly on the 6:00 news on NBC. She sings Cruella De Vil in a wailing
falsetto now that in her mind is moving and pitch-perfect. She is, after all,
a musician. Second chair clarinet, Fairfax Symphony Orchestra. Not to
mention also playing in the marching band at the University of Wisconsin when not staging sit-ins, peace rallies, and tutoring sessions. She
thinks of the letter to Mike Horton and considers what more can be
added—what details can be clarified, what points can be made more pow-

erful? The thinking makes her belly rumble, yet she perseveres. She thinks of her son and his girlfriend whom she doesn't like and she can't wait for them to graduate and go off to college—he to Yale or Columbia or at least UVA early decision, the girlfriend to Mason or Tech probably— so that they will break up and Brian can meet a girl more . . . well, she isn't an egomaniac or anything, but more like Mitzy Hurkle. She is quite the catch. Ed's one lucky fellow and he knows it. She's not delusional enough to tell herself that she hasn't been a victim of a little aging and gravity and a slowing metabolism, that her body hasn't . . . *changed* over the years in the ways a healthy woman can expect her body to change after giving birth and raising a child and now approaching (slowly!) fifty. But in her day she was quite the number if she does say so herself. She probably could have gone into acting, in her opinion, if she'd wanted. She had the looks and acting ability. The overall sense of drama and theater. Still does. In fact, she knows so much about film that she hates almost every movie she sees. Yet she did not pursue acting or writing or music or any of the other fields she could have pursued and excelled at—basketball for instance, she played basketball in high school. She chose teaching. She is a teacher. And mother. Far more noble and selfless pursuits. She is the most selfless person she knows. This is what she is thinking of—this just minutes ago, as Grayson Donald hangs dead about nine hundred feet away—when she hears the noise. She stops singing and stands there for a second then hears the noise again. Someone in here.

—Hello? she says. —Hello? Ed? Brian?

MS-13

Leave Fair Oaks Mall
    & go to Best Buy & fuck around in the car stereos.
    So I can give Pedro a lesson in car stereos.
    The guy there speaking to us like we're retarded.
    White & speaking Spanglish.
    Steal some shit on the way b/c the guy is speaking to us in Spanglish.
    & outside in the parking lot Raul is there.

In the parking lot with the Spider.
Smiling & lounging on the Spider.
In the back of the parking lot.
Where no cars are.
Parked sideways taking up two spots.
In a tanktop and shorts both new you can tell.
Coming towards us
& putting his arm around me
& saying Gato how's it going
& I say good Raul
& his tattoos all over his arms
& bald head
& smelling like Polo Sport.
& he says, Listen thanks for doing that thing you did
& he says, it was the right thing to do
& I say yeah no problem
& he says You're my brother
& he says You're my familia
& I say yeah you too Raul
& he says Now that you did that though I need some money from your clique
& I say what for
& he says for your dues
& I say What dues
& he says, For your dues
& I say but Raul we don't have any money. You don't let us sell drugs or anything like that so we don't have any.
& Raul grabs my arm
& holds it tight
& turns it so I can see it
& says What does that say?
& I say what does what say
& he says that fucking tattoo on your arm
& I say It says MS-13, Raul
& he says that tattoo means that you have to pay dues
& I say We've been out here all day getting money for food and a motel. That's all we have.
& he says Let me see that
& he takes all the money
& he counts it

& says this is a step in the right direction but you need way more
because the dues went up

& I need it tomorrow Gato, he says.

& he gives me a machete from his trunk

& says Go get my money.

& Raul leaves drives off in his Spider

& his system going BUMPBUMPBUMP so fucking loud

& we all watch him

& I turn to Pedro & say Sony CDX-R3300

& he says nothing.

Then we steal a car from the Best Buy parking lot

& drive the car until we're in a neighborhood.

I drive.

We park in a street in a nice neighborhood

& it's dark.

A big fucking house.

The kind I want when I live in Canada one day.

My clique waits in the car.

Front door locked so I go around back & the door there is open &
go in.

A basement.

White kid my age like the kind at the mall laying on the couch & on
the phone & playing with his balls & watching TV

& he doesn't see me

& I just walk past him to the stairs

& go up them.

I walk through the house stealing shit.

Shoving old books down my pants

& old-looking shit down my pants.

Shiny shit.

Don't know what's worth anything.

A man says from another room, Brian is that you?

& I say Yeah.

& I have the machete in my hand

& grip the handle

& stand there waiting for him to come but the man doesn't say anything

& doesn't come.

& I go upstairs.

To a big fucking bedroom.

Go through drawers.

Jewelry, cash, a wallet.

& shoving everything down my pants and into my pockets.

& I can hear the shower going in the bathroom

& going in there with my machete

& going through the medicine cabinet.

Holy shit! A fucking goldmine!

Grabbing pill bottles and shoving them down my pants.

& someone in the shower

& it's a lady

& she is singing

& naked

& I can see her sort of but it's blurry

& I'm standing there getting a stiffy

& this bathroom is fucking nice

24585 BUNKERS COURT— FOURTH ENTRANCE

—Hello?

She is in midshampoo. Lather in her hair, bubbles all over her shoulders. She opens the foggy shower door and pokes her head out and through her blurred vision she can discern a figure standing there in front of the sink among scattered debris. She squints but does not need her glasses to know that this is a boy. A teenage boy. A minority youth. She can sense one of those from miles away. She becomes angry and keeps her nakedness concealed behind the shower door and says, falling easily into her teacher voice, —Excuse me, you are in violation of pretty much every HOA regulation there is! You are not allowed in here! This is a private residence! Who are your parents? What are their phone numbers? If I call over there will they know where you are? How will they feel when I tell them what you are up to? The boy turns to her and he has a machete in his hand. She knows what a machete is. She has read about them. The boy smells horrible even through the perfumes of her bath soap. Shaved head, tattoos. They stare at one another saying nothing for a long time with the hot water running and the beautiful bathroom full of steam until she pulls her head back into the shower and shuts the door, resumes rinsing the shampoo from her hair and singing Cruella De Vil as loud and hard as she can, feeling a rage at Mike Horton and a deep craving for a piece of the chocolate cake downstairs that she bought this afternoon from Giant after school and already ate half of before dinner. She sings and washes and loathes. Then squeezes her eyes shut and opens them slowly to see the mosaic image of the boy outside the shower door and the shower door opens and he stands there holding his machete and looking at her nakedness. She stands still and he stands there for a long time and they stare at one another and his abysmal eyes and he takes a step toward her and she says, —*The Awakening*.

The boy studies her. His arms tense. The arm holding the machete tense.

—For the life of me I can't remember who wrote *The Awakening* and it's just driving me *crazy*.

Water dribbles down her face and onto her lips and into her mouth. Pours down her head into her eyes.

—I'm just drawing a blank. I mean, I teach it every year. *The Awakening*.

He says, —Chopin.

Mitzy says, —Chopin! Kate Chopin! *Duh!* Thank you!

He continues standing there and she looks away from him and when she looks up again he has turned and left with her Xanax and her antidepressants and her sleeping pills and everything else he wants. She stands still, staring at her toes on the drain on the shower floor, suds and hairs swirling around, until she is sure he is gone and then she just resumes bathing and singing what she has been singing and not getting very far before breaking down and screaming.

This is something Mitzy Hurkle will never tell you about.

31317 MARBLESTONE COURT— THIRD ENTRANCE

11–1–98

It is Sunday morning and a beautiful one at that. The sun seeps through my window. Birds sing their songs of autumn. All my truths are relevant ones. Today is All Saints' Day. See them creeping out of the ground, descending from the heavens, emerging from the forestry, their halos glowing. Last night was Halloween—All Hallow's Eve. Sean, Jeremiah, Katie, Andy, Brian, and I drove around Little Rocky Run without a specific destination. Children in costumes scampered around in the night, their parents lingering after them with flashlights. The parents stayed on the sidewalk laughing with the other parents as their children sauntered up to the doors of neighbors and rang the doorbells. The neighbors answered and dropped Smarties and Reese's Peanut Butter Cups into the children's orange plastic buckets and the children peeked inside and turned without saying anything, their parents on the sidewalk laughing and waving and saying thank you. We must have smoked 18 cigarettes each. Katie must have smoked 36 because girls always smoke the most. We listened to Tool, Deftones. The speakers maximized and the raucous din pouring forth in savage deep-boweled growls. Music of our afflictions. Those parents will never understand it. It is a strange, grating language to them. Those children will grow up to be people who never understand it. They will never understand anything.

We stopped by the home of a girl named Rachel whom Sean knows. She told us she was having a party later and that we should stop by. So we drove around and smoked a couple bowls then returned around 9:00. We stood on the porch and rang the doorbell. Rachel opened it a crack and stuck her head out. "Hi," she said. Behind her we could hear the noise of a party. Males laughing. Brian Hurkle inside in his Abercrombie shirt. Havva on his lap. Other pretty girls who looked and sounded so happy. Big football player types sitting around wearing hemp necklaces and drinking out of red Solo cups. Backstreet Boys playing. We said hello and stepped forward to go in but she said, "Sorry, you can't come in. My dad says no more people." I looked at her and could see in her face that she was lying. I also saw that she was on diet pills and that when she lost her virginity to a 19-year-old Mason student the summer before freshman year it felt like she was being split in half with a knife. I could smell the vomit on her breath. The lonely unending nights in her room, cutting herself on her butt with a box cutter. All her old skatergirl clothes fed on by moths somewhere in a Goodwill warehouse. Someone inside said, "Fuck off, fags!"

So we left. We walked back to the car. "Fuck that," Jeremiah was saying. "Remember when she used to be a fucking skater chick with a fucking nose ring? Now she's banging fucking Abercrombie kids? And letting them party at her house?"

"Man, I hate this town," Sean said.

Andy wanted to sit outside her house and tell everyone who went in there what a bitch Rachel was.

I didn't say anything.

Sean said, "Remember when she came over to my house crying because no one wanted to be friends with her?"

"And we smoked her out," Katie said.

"I smoked her out, " Jeremiah said.

"No, I smoked her out, Miah."

"It was my weed."

"But I paid for it."

"Whatever."

We went to 6–12 blasting Deftones as loud as it would go out the open windows. They were screaming, "Fuck this fucking town!" Every time we passed some children trick-or-treating we stopped and let the music roar for a couple of seconds as their parents stared at us, giving us looks, and then we peeled off. We tried shoulder tapping at the 6–12 to no success. So we drove back and parked at Rec Center #3 and got out to walk around behind it and smoke a bowl. On the way I gave Katie a piggyback ride. When I couldn't carry her any farther, I fell on top of her into the grass and wouldn't let her up. I wished we could lie there forever. After a little while I let her up, laughing. Katie wiped the grass off herself and ranked on me about how I laughed. So I picked her up and threw her over my shoulder and spun her around. Katie was screaming. I spanked her on the butt like a little kid. She was laughing and going, "Stop! Ow!" I was laughing too. I can't remember laughing so hard. Then I laid her on the ground. She stopped laughing. "You broke my cigarette," she said. I felt stupid. I let her up and apologized but only felt dumber. I wanted to disappear, drop off the face of the earth. Crawl up somewhere dark and cold and never come out. I said I was going home. They asked if they could come. I didn't want them to but I said okay.

My father was passed out in his recliner with CNN on. We all snuck passed him and down the stairs to the basement. Jeremiah said, "Your dad's so awesome. I want to be just like him when I'm old. Just chill in my fucking chair with a glass of whiskey and not give a fuck." I didn't know what to say to Jeremiah. So I didn't say anything. I just smiled at him. He said, "What are you smiling at me for?" And I said, "Nothing," and put the TV on mute and put on some music. We sat there in silence watching the flickering images of commercial television meshing harshly with our music. Jeremiah said, "Doesn't it look like it's the video for the song?" After twenty minutes everyone had to go home. One by one they got up to leave. Soon it was me and Katie. She on one end of the room and I on the other. I got up to turn down the music and sat down again. She looked at me with this look of expectation. I said, "What."

"Nothing."

We kept watching TV on mute. Now the music was off and it was silent. She said, "I must be ugly."

"Why."

She gestured back at the door through which Sean had just exited. "He said like one word to me all night."

"Yeah. He's just weird."

"Or I'm ugly."

"No you're not. If you were my girlfriend, you'd never feel that way about yourself."

"Aw."

"Aw yourself."

She came over and sat down next to me. "I don't really think I'm ugly. I'm just really horny."

I laughed a little. We looked at each other for a long time. I swallowed. It was like swallowing a rock. I could smell her. Her skin was humming for mine. My hands became clammy. My heart beating so hard through my chest I thought she would hear it. She whispered, "I have to go." She gave me a hug. We sat there on the couch together for about five minutes until she dislodged herself from me. Then she stood and looked into my eyes and plopped back down on top of me, straddling me. She buried her face in the side of my neck. She breathed through her nose. Put her arms around me and squeezed. She squeezed with everything she had and we lay there for so long. I could hear the TV upstairs.

I wished she would stay. I wished she would never let go of me. But eventually she did. She said, "I love you," as she walked out the door.

2:00—Katie was just in my room. She was on her way to Sean's. She said that if nothing happens with her and Sean by tomorrow . . . She didn't finish. She wanted me to play her a song on the guitar, so I did. I played one I made up on the spot about her. It was stupid but she liked it. She noticed a wooden beaded necklace I have and asked me if she could have it. I wanted to give it to her more than I've wanted anything, but still I made her beg for it. I said, "What's in it for me?" She looked at me for a minute and got closer. She whispered in my ear, "Tomorrow." I couldn't help but smile and give her the necklace.

11:30—Katie just called. She said, "Nothing happened. His mom kept bothering us to show me baby pictures of him. And he kept wanting to show me his diving videos and shit. And we were listening to Primus. It's kind of hard to get into the mood with Primus, you know? But you know Sean and Primus. He kept playing air bass and dancing around. But listen. Tomorrow's off. Things would just get shitty with everyone."

I laughed and said that I thought that was all just a joke anyway. She seemed surprised that I said that. She asked if I was okay and I said, "Yeah of course." She said good night and I said good night. I hung up and lay in bed and thought about everything. I made some very important decisions.

Last week in Spanish class, things got weird. The teacher was rambling about the conjugations of *ver*. I was hunched over my desk with my head in my hand, barely conscious. I had slept for only three hours the night before and had not eaten since a pretzel at lunch at 9:57. It was now almost 2:00. The room started twisting around and adopted a strange veneer. The walls pulsed, the Styrofoam-paneled ceilings drooped and rebounded. Then I felt my face go cold. I felt a pulling sensation yanking me backward like a bungee cord. Everything zoomed out until it was like I was watching everything from the far end of a long, dark tunnel. I felt so isolated from everything. All sounds were desperate echoes straining for but hardly reaching my ears. Then things went back to normal, somewhat, as I looked down at the teacher's feet, and I swear I saw something moving across the floor. It's impossible to explain. It was shadowy and elusive. As soon as I looked at it, it was gone. I looked around to see if anyone was aware of what had just happened, or was aware of me. But no one was. It was very fucked up. It was a very fucked-up day. It's been a very fucked-up year.

7145 SPRINGSTONE DRIVE—
FIRST ENTRANCE

My night begins when I get to my boy Brians house in Virginia Run. I park, finish the blunt Im smoking, check myself out in the mirror, like what I see. I get out and lock the door behind me by means of the alarm on my key chain which I insisted they include when my dad and me went to buy my Honda last year. It makes a nice beep. I ring the doorbell and stand on the concrete porch staring at the door and the knocker and the wooden fucking hand-painted sign on it that says THE PHILLIPS. Its a nice house, Ill admit. Im not gonna lie. Ive been appreciating nice architecture lately. Thats just part of maturing and growing up. Ive been mentally taking notes about what I like about houses for when Im rich and have my house custom built. I have been keeping an eye out for inspiration. I want a fucking hand-painted wooden sign on my door. I want it to say BATCHELOR or TRENT BATCHELOR. I want a fucking welcome mat and a fucking nice hardwood floor and baskets of motherfucking potpourri and all sorts of fucking antique shit around so it looks all nice and shit and feels like my parents house. In the basement I want a stripper pole and a fully stocked wet bar and a fucking wall-sized TV with surround sound and DVD and a pool table. Outside, I want a Jacuzzi and pool and full basketball court and have mad parties there with girls with tig ol bitties in bikinis playing volleyball and dancing and shit like in the fucking videos on MTV where everyone is cool and happy and everyone loving me.

I wonder if maybe I should have sprayed another couple sprays of Woods before leaving tonight, but its too late, because my boy Brians sister, who is 15 or so, opens the door wearing this fucking tight fucking Abercrombie T-shirt with her tig ol bitties in my face, tight jeans. She has grown up fast, I think, meaning her tits specifically. She looks like Britney Spears but with less nice of an ass of course. But I still want to bend that shit over a chair and fuck that shit doggystyle until she fucking passes out.

Brians sister smiles and says, Hey. By this point Im hardly able to contain myself. I want to whip it out and stick it in her mouth. But I am able to smile at her. I am able to come across as harmless, to say, Hey Brianne hows school going?

Pretty good, she says, a lot of work. Ive been real busy.

Yeah, I say, but if you keep those grades up it will be worth it. Youre smart, youll be fine.

Yeah, I guess, she says.

And I go in and my boy Brians mom is on the couch watching the news and grading papers. I wave and say, Hello Mrs. Phillips.

Hey Trent, she says, looking up, smiling.

Brians mom fucking loves me. All parents fucking love me, especially the moms. They cant resist my charm and good looks. There are a couple of moms who I could have fucked if Id pulled the trigger on it. The offer was pretty much there for me to take if I wanted. None of them have been up to my standards though. Old bitches can be pretty fucking disgusting. My standards are pretty high when it comes to fucking middle aged bitches. Its pretty rare a middle aged bitch will be hot enough to fuck. One day though I wouldnt mind just fucking one anyway, just to say I did.

I say, Mmmm! What smells so good?

She says, We had baked ziti for dinner. Theres still some left. Would you like some?

No thank you, I say, I already ate. Hows school going?

And she says Oh fine but the kids are all wound up lately for whatever reason.

Thats kids, though, I say. Whats on the news?

And she says, Kids in Kosovo in refugee camps.

Whoa, I say, thats horrible.

It is, she says.

And I say, The worst thing about all that is they are totally innocent in all of the turmoil over there. They are paying the price for the decisions of their often corrupt governing officials, things they have no involvement in. And it really is a steep and brutal price.

Mrs. Phillips goes, Its true, its terrible.

I go downstairs to the basement thinking about fucking Mrs. Phillips in the butthole. I say to my boy Brian, What da blood clot! And he goes, What da blood! and we take shots and smoke a couple bowls with the ionizer on and play a couple games of Bond on Nintendo 64. I dont like Brian too much but hes the only person I know whos still around. We make some phone calls and watch MTV and smoke cigarettes and play some more Bond and watch an episode of *Tenacious D* Brian has on tape. We find out our boy Andys parents are out of town and hes having peo-

ple over. Right now its a bunch of high school girls. He lives in Little
Rocky Run in the third section. Hes had four girlfriends and slept with I
think only seven or eight girls last I counted. He and his last girlfriend,
who I never met, fucked every day for four months without condoms.
Andy is 19 or maybe 18. I dont really know him too well, to be honest.

So we drive in my car over there, drinking 40s and smoking a bowl
and going 70, and fucking Eminem blasting, and I am nervous because my
boy Brian hasnt said anything about the new subwoofer I put in that cost
$430. We stop at Giant and pick up a case of Miller Lite, two 6s of Mick-
eys, and four 40s, all of which I pay for with my moms credit card.
Before we go in we blow a couple lines off the Eminem CD case and my
boy Brian says, That fucking subwoofer is fucking clutch dude and this
makes me happy. I feel like a man as I enter Andys house and carry all the
alcohol into the kitchen, knowing the high school sluts are impressed and
happy because me and my boy Brian are older and the only ones who can
legally buy alcohol. They are wondering who I am and want me. I put the
beer in the fridge shoving a bunch of shit out of my way and open one
and feel good and safe and confident. But I realize I need to talk to someone so that I will be seen having a conversation with somebody and
wont just be standing there like a fag. And I think about telling Brian that
I want to fuck his sister and wonder if it would be funny if I said that. But
I decide against it. There is a chance it would not make him laugh. So
instead I say, Damn I took the biggest fucking shit today, dude. And
Brian goes, Yeah? And I say, Yeah dude. And Brian laughs at how outra-
geous I am.

One time me and Brian met this bitch at Red Rocks one night. She
said she was married but she and her husband were swingers or some
shit. We went to her place in Manassas. She pulled out my boy Brians
fucking dick and it was the biggest fucking thing Id ever seen and it
wasnt even fully fucking hard. It was the first time Id seen his dick. Wed
doubled up on sluts before but Id always made a point not to look because
I aint no fucking fag. I couldnt fucking believe how big that fucking shit
was. It was a fucking hose. You wouldnt know it from looking at him but
he has a fucking two foot dick. I was dying. I didnt want to pull out my
fucking shit after that. Im not tiny or anything, but compared to that
fucking shit, who would want to pull theirs out? But she was hot as fuck
and had some tig ol bitties and was tan and blond with her pussy shaved.
She was really hot for being old (like 35 or something) and was into meth
and all kinds of fucked-up porno shit. Telling us to fuck her in the ass and
to fucking come on her fucking face and shit. I hadnt fucked in like two

fucking weeks, so I said fuck it. Shit got crazy. Her 5-year-old daughter was upstairs the whole time asleep. Some fucked-up shit. But whats it got to do with me? Nothing.

Brian and me went for two years without speaking because I didnt get him a birthday present on his 19th birthday, even though he got me an $85 shirt from Abercrombie for mine. We made up eventually. I still dont like him though. He thinks hes too good for me. He thinks hes too good for everything.

Im looking around at the high school sluts. Theyre all so young and thin. Theyre all so happy and sexy. And my dick starts fucking moving in my jeans because some are wearing skirts and I have no choice but to imagine my tongue sliding into their tiny clean assholes as I look them over wondering which one I will choose. I WANT ALL OF THEM. Andy, who is fucking shitfaced, drops a full Bud Light on the kitchen floor and it pops a hole and starts spraying a stream of beer everywhere and is spinning around and hissing, and everyone is dying, and Andy, instead of picking it up and putting it in the sink, just comes over and kicks it and takes another beer and throws it at it and leaves it there until it stops.

We play quarters and Asshole, and I win Asshole like always. Then we play flip cup, and I am the strongest player as usual. And the girls are drunk and dancing to N Sync or whatever but who cares because theyre dancing together and pretending to dyke out and are goofy and stupid like drunk high school girls are. One is all over my shit, of course, but I dont think shes hot, so I ignore her until I overhear my boy Brian tell Andy that he thinks shes hot. So I ask her if she wants to smoke some weed and for a hot second I think her friends will come too, and I think maybe a threesome will be in order. Or a foursome which would be a fucking great story to tell afterward to my boy Brian. But it ends up just being me and her in Andys parents bedroom. I change my mind about her. Shes smoking hot, not blond but big tits, nice ass. We smoke a fucking fat bowl and she comments on how good my weed is. That makes me happy and I tell her about my subwoofer. She is impressed and then we do some lines. Its her first time, I think, because she sucks at it. I pull her shirt down a little and do a bump off the top of her tits. Then were making out, and Im getting her naked, and she tans, I can tell, and shes wearing a thong, and she doesnt shave her pussy which I like for some reason. I fingerfuck her a little and she plays with my dick a bit but says, No sex, only rubbing, okay? I say, Yeah sure whatever. Of course I end up fucking the girl. The girl is too fucked up to realize Im not wearing a rubber. I hate rubbers. I never wear them when I fuck the girl. If I have to, Ill put one on so the girl thinks

Im wearing one, but Ill slip it off while Im fucking the girl. I fuck this girl in every position. I catch my reflection in the mirror over the dresser which is something I would like to have in my house one day. Seeing my reflection makes me almost blow, so I have to look away and I put a finger in the asshole and fuck the girl so hard I think Im going to pass out and after a while I finally drop a load inside the pussy which is tight as fuck.

Number 38!

Im a little mad because I meant to pull out and jerk off on her but I couldnt help it. Oh well. Shit happens.

After I finish, shes not moving and doesnt respond when I poke her a little, but I want a fucking cigarette and need to piss like a bitch and dont want to miss anything going on downstairs, so I put my clothes on and piss in the bathroom in Andys parents room which has seashell soap and a skylight and a shower with four showerheads. I weigh myself on the digital black scale and I weigh 192 and steal a Norelco cordless nose hair trimmer and go downstairs happy because my dick is wet and slimy. Theres no better feeling than going downstairs back to the party with your dick soaked in pussy juice then smoking a cigarette in new possession of a Norelco cordless nose hair trimmer. I didnt have any Norelco products before, so Im twice as happy.

Then I play Asshole some more and dominate as usual. One of the girls friends is asking everyone where she is and I dont say anything. And another one is naked in a blanket on the couch with puke all over her. Me and my boys Brian and Andy go over and write shit like WHORE and CUM DUMPSTER on her face with a marker that Andy went upstairs to get after I told him to. Then we pour beer down her throat for a little while, which is always funny. And mad heads are telling us to stop, but theyre laughing so we dont stop. Then we take pictures first of her naked then of each of our dicks on her face and sucking on her tits and putting things in her pussy like the remote. Everyones dying. I wish I brought my video camera to record this shit and watch it later on and laugh. Itd be fucking funny as shit. Put that shit on the Internet.

Then we get bored and me and my boy Brian and my boy Andy go to Red Rocks. I drive so Andy can see my subwoofer. And Im driving drunk as shit down Union Mill asking Andy what he thinks of my car, and I pass a cop and get nervous a little because Im not supposed to be driving because I got a DUI last month, my second, but the cop doesnt do anything. We get to Red Rocks, go in, do some Irish car bombs and tequila shots, drink some beers, I pay the $40 tab with my moms credit card, theres only us and a couple spics and some fucking dorks who I know from high school but no sluts, and its depressing, and someone, I think Andy, wants to go to DC so we drive to DC and go to the Spot, and I realize going in that one of the spics from Red Rocks has come along with us which is funny as shit, so me and him pound some beers and tequila shots and blow some lines behind a big speaker, and I drop another $130 not including the cover, I black out, wake up in the bathroom with puke all over me and all over the place, come out of the stall and wash up and ask some dude at the urinal if he wants to do some fucking yay, turns out hes a fucking bouncer, I get thrown out, throw my boy Brians beer on the ground on the way out, it shatters all over the place, so I get my ass kicked a little by the bouncers outside, and somehow we end up at a strip club Ive never been to where I drop another $800 on drinks, dances, a bottle of Dom P, putting it all on my moms credit card, and I give the waitress another $20 bill every time she comes over, and do a bunch of coke with some stripper in a back room then I get thrown out for going around trying to slap strippers asses, and last thing I remember about DC is getting in my car with Andy and Brian and driving off and then somehow we are at Andys again, the place is full, mostly high school kids, and I am asking everyone who the fuck wants to go to motherfucking DC, but Andy tells me we already went to DC and I say oh yeah and I make out on the couch with another high school slut, and everyones around us watching and talking shit, but nothing matters, because Im fucked up, but she wont touch my dick let alone suck it which is the point of even bothering, and I get fucking sick of trying, so then I wrestle my boy Brian in the kitchen, we slip on all the beer on the floor, break the pantry door, start spraying beers at each other until the whole kitchen and us is covered in beer, we steal some vodka and Jack Daniels and this weird peach dessert liqueur shit from Andys parents liquor cabinet, and I carry the Jack Daniels around chugging from it and puke off the deck then blow some coke, do a beer bong, have smoked 1½ packs of cigarettes somehow tonight and want to go get more, but I get distracted because the high school slut who wouldnt touch my dick is helping the girl I pounded earlier down the stairs naked and wrapped in a towel and looking fucking rough, and I start dying and the girl who wouldnt touch my dick is yelling at everyone You fucking assholes & so on. Then I am happy because Im making a Hot Pocket I found in the freezer and I cant fucking believe its only fucking 12 oclock.

The high school sluts all leave because they have school in the morning. As I eat the Hot Pocket, girls our age roll in mad deep, including Carrie, who played with my dick a little last night, and who Im trying to fuck, even though I think she has small titties and a boyfriend, I heard, at

JMU. Carries ass is banging as usual and practically begging me to spread it wide and fuck it. I go over after a while and start shooting the shit. Me and Carrie are about to go upstairs to do some blow and then probably fuck when her fucking bitchy friend Monica or Mona or some shit, who looks like a bird and had an abortion a few years ago I heard comes up to us and tries to fucking pull Carrie away by the hand and says to me Shes not interested, Trent, she has a boyfriend.

I fucked Monica a few years ago. Her pussy was the biggest pussy Ive ever had the dishonor to fuck. It had fucking meat curtains about a foot long. You could hang from that shit. I could have put my foot in it. It looked like a fucking roast beef sandwich. I had to fuck her doggystyle for like an hour just to nut. Plus she couldnt suck dick for shit. She only put my dick in her mouth like an inch and tried to use her hand to jerk me off, as if that qualified as a fucking blowjob. I WANTED IT DONE COR-RECTLY. So now because shes cock blocking me I call Monica a stupid bitch and tell her the fucking Redskins defensive line just called asking what shes doing tonight. And I find this so fucking funny, Im dying. She gives me a look, and I say Hey Monica the fucking Manassas chapter of the fucking Crips called asking about you, yo, theyre wondering what youre up to tonight. She gets mad and calls me a faggot. No bitch calls me a faggot. So then Im choking Monica and squeezing Monicas neck as hard as I can. I have Monica shoved against the wall and a picture thats hanging there falls off but misses Monica. Monicas eyes are huge from me chok-ing Monica, and Monicas making this fucking gurgling sound, and Mon-icas trying to kick me in the balls, and Monica gets really fucking close to connecting, so I take Monica down and am straddling Monica with my knees on Monicas arms choking Monicas long Big Bird neck and everyone pulls me off Monica and Monicas crying and theres blood on her neck which I dont understand. And Monica is coughing and making this whim-pering sound, and one of Monicas titties is almost out of Monicas shiny sil-ver shirt thing. Everyone, including my boy Brian, is yelling at me and saying, What the fuck dude and I say I didnt do it and theyre all saying to get the fuck out and Im saying but I didnt do that though, it wasnt me who did that and they say then who did it Trent and I say I dont know and they say get the fuck out of here Trent so I say Fuck all yall motherfuckers. I get the rest of my beers from the fridge and leave, drunk as shit, coked out of my fucking mind. I cant even walk straight. No one comes after me to stop me or tell me to come back which makes me even fucking madder, so I kick Big Birds car (a fucking Neon) hard as I can, over and over, until my boy Brian comes out the front door, holding a baseball bat, and yells at me to

cut it out and to fuck off. And I try to yell Why do you have a bat? But Im
so fucked up, it comes out like gibberish. I fall down and crawl over to the
curb and sit down and light a cigarette and yell at him Fuck all yall
motherfuckers but there is no one there.

I get in my car and peel out, trying to smoke the cigarette but I drop
it in my lap and almost fucking crash into a stop sign I run through trying to pick it up without losing the cherry. I have to close one eye tight to
see straight otherwise I see double and otherwise what I see moves up and
down and side to side. And I try to drive something resembling the speed
limit but I cant take my eyes off the road to see the speedometer because
Im concentrating so hard. Im honking the horn as I drive through the
streets of Little Rocky Run, silent and asleep, holding it down, because they
think I put that blood on her neck. Because they said Get the fuck out of
here Trent. When I think I have been driving long enough to be home, I
pull over and turn the car off and crawl out the passenger side, walk up
what I assume is my driveway because its black pavement. My vision is
like in the movies when someone is looking through binoculars, and I have
a hand over one eye now, and trip over something, realize I am not at my
house but rather am in the fucking woods, and what I tripped over was a
root or branch, and that I have been walking on a bike path. And I am in
a tot lot, I realize. I recognize it as the one in the 3rd section where I used
to play when I was a little kid and where once, when I was 14, I tripped balls
with my boys Tony and my boy Ryan and I pissed on Tonys hat, but they
both went to fucking college and and never came back but I stayed.

I wander around in circles for a little while then I sit on one of the
swings. I start swinging. I get high as shit and think maybe Ill jump off at
the top of the swing like we used to do when we were kids, but I feel like
Im gonna yack, so I stop by dragging my feet and then lean between my
legs and yack on my fucking Timberlands that cost $240, and it gets all
over my jeans which cost $67 from Abercrombie and fit me perfectly. This
fucking sucks but my mom will wash them, she can get the stain out of
anything. After I yack I feel good and smoke a cigarette and try to bump
some coke, but I cant coordinate my hand with my nose and get frustrated
and give up, feel alone and sad, decide that tomorrow Im going to go out
and get a job as a landscaper. I have a huge empty bitter feeling because Im
coming down. I always get this way when I come down. Plus from everyone saying I put the blood there and to get the fuck out of here Trent. And
I hate myself and start talking to myself, singing actually, a song I make
up about being fucking housed on a tot lot and yacking on my fucking
Timberlands. At this point I realize my fucking fly is open and my fuck-

ing dick is hanging out. I start fucking laughing. I wonder how long my dick has been hanging out of my pants. Was it out the whole time I was choking Monica? Im laughing like a little fucking kid being tickled. Im laughing my ass off and laughing my ass off and laughing my ass off, looking at my dick hanging out. But then I happen to look up. I stop laughing my ass off. There is something hanging from the motherfucking basketball hoop. I say out loud What da blood clot? I squint my eyes and stare at it with puke on my fucking lips still saying out loud What da blood clot? At first I think its just my eyes fucking with me in the dark. But theres no fucking doubt about this shit—its a fucking person. I cant fucking believe it. This shit doesnt happen in Little Rocky Run. By instinct, I reach into my pockets for my cell phone to call my boy Brian but cant find it. So I walk up to it really slowly and quietly and get real close and stare up at it with my mouth fucking wide open and I see its face all swollen and its tongue sticking out of its mouth and I touch its fucking leg but its not stiff and it has a fucking boner and smells literally like fucking shit. Then I push it a little, I dont know why, but I do. Then I say out loud, Its a dead body. And I start jumping up and down. For no fucking reason. I just start jumping up and down. I spin around in the air as I jump up and down. Im whispering, Its a dead body over and over. I jump up and down moving away from it, whispering it. I hop from one side of the court to the other, with my hands hanging limp at my sides, hopping like Im on a fucking pogo stick. I hop back across the court. I try to jump as high as I can. I stop whispering and start screaming. I am screaming at the top of my fucking lungs ITS A DEAD BODY! ITS A DEAD BODY! over and over, as loud as I can, ITS A DEAD BODY! jumping actually really high now and really fast and my cigarette still in my hand burning down to the filter and burning my fingers. I am aware of it burning me but I cant let go. My legs hurt like a motherfucker. My thighs burn. My knees roar. But I still do it, still jump up and down. I cant fucking stop. I hop along the three-point line on the other end of the court. And then along the baseline. And then around the perimeter of the entire goddamn court hopping and yelling ITS A DEAD BODY then eventually it turns into me singing that shit like a fucking kids song, ITS A DEAD BO-DY! ITS A DEAD BO-DY! at the top of my lungs, until that turns into me singing Its a dead body to the tune of the fucking Star-Spangled Banner. Im so out of breath from jumping that I can barely hit the high notes. And it takes forever because I have to pause between every line to catch my breath. And Im doing all the shrills and runs and shit. Im fucking flamboyant about it. I dont know why. I fucking realize what I am doing is pretty fucking gay and retarded. I am aware of myself doing it but its like I have no choice in the matter. This is beyond me. My body is going to hop up and down along every white line on the court, on every fucking square inch of it, and my voice is going to fucking sing LOUD AS HELL no matter what I have to say in the matter. Its just what is going to happen right now, in this moment in time, on this fucking piece of earth. Once I finish I start again. Once isnt good enough for me I need more. I keep hopping. I keep fucking singing. After I hop around the court who knows how many fucking times and have gone through my Star Spangled Banner maybe five or six times, I find myself hopping off the court away from it. I hop back up the path to my car. And then Im back in my car and fucking gasping for air and my legs are numb and Im sweating like I used to do in wrestling practice which is a fucking lot. And it dawns on me: if I get the fuck out of here right fucking now, no one will ever know that I saw it. If I leave now, I have never been here. This never happened. So I haul ass home hoping no one saw me. Im still fucking faded as fuck and barely make it up the stairs to my room and try to take my clothes off but only get as far as taking off my pants before I trip and fall into bed and I lose consciousness, birds singing outside, the last thing I am aware of.

31317 Marblestone Court— Third Entrance

His name is Grayson Donald and here he comes. He kisses the dog good-bye and leaves the house and locks the door behind him. He does not need a key. The door locks itself by turning the small button in the middle of the knob on the indoor side of the door before closing it. He tests the knob after closing it to ensure it is locked. As he tests the knob—a habit from his mother—he understands that this is the last time the hand will touch the knob. The final in a litany of occurrences in which he has come home and touched the knob, turned it to enter the house, or has touched the knob to ensure it is locked. This is the door that opens into the garage. It is empty, the garage door rails rattling from the impact of the closing of the door. On one wall the blue smiley face he drew as a target for throwing tennis balls when he was seven. Soon the reliquiae of the departed. One garage door open. A fresh oil drip pools on that side. There are two sets of garage doors to every home. One for the machine followed by one for the humans. And is it not fitting that he leaves tonight through both and in reverse order? Two, sometimes three of the big ones lifted and dropped by humming machines of their own. And just a slim gray one for the flesh, made of a synthesis of materials, operated by the hands. Wooden steps leading up to it unfinished. The knob a brass color dulled by the feculence of years of coming in from the world, its only temperature that which is given to it by flesh. Under the stairs cobwebs, the carcasses of insects, superannuated tennis ball spilth, dust protecting upon all and all palled by dust.

He has his cigarettes. He moves with the swiftness of one with a duty. Under the lights bathing the garage in the silence of this night there are tiny cracks in the concrete strip buffering the garage from the black tar of the driveway, and ants crawl upon it, and there are stray dead leaves flattened and ripped. An orange smear on the floor that he made as a child, deciding to spray-paint his shoes orange, mother opening the door upon her son envenomed in a cloud of orange fumigation, his skin and hair and clothing all dyed orange, this bedlamite oil prospector in disastrous outer-space oblasts. He tries to understand that this now is the last time these eyeballs that have grown by nature in the sockets of his skull will do what magnificent deed they perform in order to make the cracks and the ants and the dead leaves and orange visible to him. Then he leaves the garage. His legs propel him onward. He knows that these contractions of muscle and these packages of brain signals are among the last. But the muscles, the legs do not. Soon they will stiffen and whither, become the dust beneath the stairs. He has the rope around his shoulder. His father's retirement ceremony. Mother's Days. Doormen in front of expensive Washington, DC, hotels. Their uniform coilings. His mother with her purse under her arm as his father came out to meet them, pausing to allow a pretty woman to cross his path, then ushering them along in his formal wool army suit adorned in badges. Eagles and American flags, gold stars, a lightning bolt. The things of honor. Soon his brain which has been remembering this for so many years will never remember it again. And the memory will cease. It will follow the honor like two tanquams that never floated through this inherency except in mockery and deception.

The sky is black and clear, stars and moon, planets, galaxies, solar systems, the harbinger satellites of the unreachables beyond, in other worlds, living other lives, an infinitude of merciless masses spread out above you, proving God, nullifying you. See Mr. Manahan across the street pulling his rank bin curbward. He is like a child pulling a wagon filled with his filth. Hear the sound of plastic scraping the pavement. One hears it all up and down the street, wherever one goes. The sound of a legion in accordance removing the sullage and rape from their homes. All at once does it roar, ricocheting around off siding and decks, pipe stems, culs-de-sac. Mr. Manahan's face sneering in unprepossession like a harelip. The scar still bright and crimson beneath a toupee. No one knows but the boy who walks as Mr. Manahan has walked, no one but the boy can smell through the scraping the oils leaking out of his wound and wafting off across the yards stinking of death but even through the cigarette smoke does it come through so sweet and nosegay.

And here he comes—

He turns up the road. Is it not the road on which he has always been? He looks calm, like a mongrel convict among all these trampolines and ornamental wells. A son returning the borrowed things of his father. Potted griseous greenery hanging from hooks in screened-in porches, mosquitoes and flies stuck in the holes and buzzing. Wood fence gates with spouts of grass growing at the foot of them in mud. *I am of honor and I am of nothing else.* There are no yellow lines dividing traffic on these roads, streets, drives, and ways. And there is no traffic beyond a car or two drifting along betimes. They are not the cars of him but of them— whistlers and lottery players. Drinking cars, haircut vehicles. Paved glabrous deep black, the fossils of the revolution encased beneath the gunk bricks, and the curbs high with the lawns risen up off them and the colonial latticework of the front porch university flags set upon the lawns. Dear Lord is life all this? Dorm room memories and the sun bar reflecting white on the ceiling dancing off the pool water? He keeps walking. He drools as he goes. A thick slobber building up in his jaws like a canine fantod. He counts the stenciled block numbers on the curbs, sprayed there in dark green and black paint by toothless and sweaty adulterines blown in off the highway from the crank camps of Manassas, born in some ravaged nation to apparition witch-whore mothers to come here and go door-to-door selling numbers for curbs. The beds of their rusted frangibles filled with sweet damp mulch. 15365, 15363, 15361, 15359. Here and there the spots where they transgressed their stencil.

He notices which homes have numbers on them and which have numbers on the curb and which have numbers only on the mailbox and which have all three and which have none. Until they show up each summer like gypsies no one thinks about the numbers on their house. If the digits drop off their nail or fade in the sun or become covered by the wet leaves and gutter jetsam they do not replace them. He thinks about how no one thinks of house numbers until they are looking for one and can't find it, drive up and down the street cursing, squinting, turning down the radio, wondering why no one replaces their numbers.

He leans his body in such a way that the rope stays coiled on his shoulder without his holding it there. Then with that hand, still walking, he reaches into his back pocket and takes out his wallet. Cigarette hanging from his mouth, smoke going up his nose, trapping under the lenses of his glasses and stinging the corners of his eyes. He sticks his other arm through the space in the stepladder so he can carry it on his elbow, freeing that hand. He opens the wallet. Stepladder clanging against the side of his knee. He takes out a dollar bill and lets go of it. It rockabyes to the sidewalk behind him, somersaults into the lawn, gets trapped by the blades of grass, and flaps there like a wounded bird. Then he takes out another one and does the same with it. And he does the same with the five that is in there too. And then a few more singles. He does it in such a way that they sprinkle over his shoulder back behind him in his wake like he is a jolly character of miracles and blessings in a whimsical fantasia. Then there is no more money in his wallet. He takes out his driver's license and tosses that over his shoulder. He tosses his insurance card too. And his First Virginia card. And his CVS card. And a crinkled baby picture of his cousin melted into the skin of the wallet. And everything else that is in there. Then when the wallet is empty he throws it over his shoulder and it lands facedown and open on the sidewalk, a chunk of a cow's flesh, like a prank designed to expose the libertine. And he keeps going.

Cars pass him from behind, enshrouding him in the luminance of their headlights. A Chris McCandless shadow, the tramp saint of Northern Virginia, traipsing through this vacuous nugatory in which there is only one way to leave. He turns and glances over his shoulder at the last one, a red Grand Cherokee coming around the bend, and he squints into its headlights and shades his eyes, trying to see in through the windshield. As it passes he does. It's her from today, three kids in the car this time, their little crewcut heads, and she just stares straight ahead of herself as though she does not see him, and he watches the brake lights blink on and off, on and off, as it moves down the hill and rounds the next corner. He breathes in the wind it leaves and exhales it slowly. And he keeps going.

And here he comes—

He turns off the road onto the path for the last time, his heart full, feeling all the world falling away from around him. He enters a forest.

Black gum and poplar leaning gray and discinct. The schoolboy autumn crispness. All gray and brown is silver and blue beneath the moon. The moon is full. The dead leaves are full of life. A gray squirrel comes out and runs across the path and freezes there on its quirking haunches at the place he has just walked and it is silver and it is full. Its marble black eyes darting around. And the saprolite covered with earth and the undraped patches of leucosome cold but with green growing on them.

And here he comes. Face upward, eyes alight with the decision of thrilling adventure. His heart beats hard, he can hardly breathe. Old fallen sticks crack under his stepping. An unseen chantress cricket resounds like a telephone. He lets it ring. Its sound is full. It jingles and wails upon the highs.

And here he comes, coming first upon the playground where the woods clear. Its black rubber swings dangling there as if by chance. He walks not around it but past the slide, its end covered in leaves and dirt and mudwater, and under the monkey bars, their paint worn through to steel by the friction-grease of weanling hands. Cigarette butts and cans in the wood chips, empty boxes of cigarettes. Proterozoic prophylactic wrappers. He goes between the swings, parting them, and they sway in his wake, bumping one another, then they just sway on their disparate rhythms as though ridden by the unseen, their chains twinkling.

Here he comes in peace but full of hot dark things. His skin wet with a fever and his head full with the cacophony of his breathing. The air of a chimera. White spittle gathered on his lips and metallic taste on his tongue. And rageful, wild doom. Giddy. He wants to shout to all the yellow windows in the wolf homes surrounding him to pay witness to him. Here he comes, kicking up wood chips as he walks toward the court, some getting stuck in the back of his shoe, in the cuffs of his pants. Here he comes past fecaloid and mud-caked pages torn from old dirty magazines. Here he comes stepping past a child's toy. Here he comes flicking his cigarette and here he comes one evening, always and forever. Here he comes in time and space, imprinting all the things of which he and his night are full into the fixity of memory. Here he comes, in the dead season. Here he comes in the silence of eternity. Here he comes soothed in the depth of it. Here he comes, a newspaper name, a quick-burning rumor man, neutered and cast in quartz then dropped in the ocean by the science of figures. Here he comes and the ocean washes over his shipwreck. Here he comes and watch him because the truth he carries will trump your aghastment, and it will gloriate atop your sneering, and enwomb your incomprehension. Here he comes, staring down the edge of a cliff, feeling the frisson of the pull. Give yourself to it. Here he comes. Watch him. Can you see him? Are you like him? Is he in you?

He steps onto the court. He is on time and attired in accordance with the code. He walks how he was beckoned to walk. Alone as chosen. The man without a name is here as it was agreed, dressed all in negrescence, his pallescent face sunken around its bones. He sits there on a king bed of kyanite, nearly invisible in his penumbra but for his white hair. He sits with an arm upon his knee. He is the man we all know. An emaciated mythic preserved in the catacombs of always. And he knows all we have done. He waits for you somewhere as he waits for him now. You can see the bones through the flesh on the back of his hand as his fingers move, the veins blue and gray and full. He has been waiting for him to come. He is already watching him when he sees him. He nods once like the host of a grand hotel and shows his big yellow teeth and extends his grandfather clock arm out and sweeps it along in elaborate presentation. And he goes the way of the arm. The way of the funeral exultant.

And he is here.

And there he goes. He carries the stepladder to the basketball hoop and drops the rope at the foot of its green pole with the paint peeling off it in scabs like the scales of a reptile. He sets the ladder down and opens its hinge which is rusted and bent enough that he must strike down upon it with the base of his hand as though bludgeoning something illborn. Then he looks up, aligns it. The hoop from below a trap for aquatic xiphs and halieutics. The stairs between the holes in the nets. Diamonds in this swelled blackness. Engaged to this advesperate night, sworn in a vow before death and God and everyone and the millennium ending now, a thousand years of empyrean and perdition. He moves it an inch to his right and looks at it then moves it back a little then looks up at it then moves it a little forward then looks up at it. Then he picks up the rope and steps on the lowest step, pushing a little at first, brown-orange rust in its ridges. Then up he goes in the manner of the wary, keeping hold to the top of it and going slow, easing each foot onto each step, ready to assume the posture of landing if all of a sudden need be, then gaining confidence with each ascent and becoming convinced at the summit that this object will hold him and standing aright with his hand sort of out as though bargaining with aggressors, and his body straightening and his knees locking and it there above his head—the head of Simba—so close to him now, he can touch it without even trying. Rise, rise. And at this distance it becomes a different thing. It becomes made of new substance. And it is orange. And it is full.

He holds on to the net with one hand. His breathing stops and his eyes are wide, pupils dilated. The ladder rocks on its legs beneath his feet and he takes hold of the net with his other hand now too and hangs there for a moment as he settles it with his feet. Then he lets go. He starts to tie one end of the rope to the front of the rim but stops and instead ties it to the back of the rim around the bridge that bolts then to the backboard. He ties it once then ties it again. The two knots an inelegant furuncle. Then he picks a lower spot in the rope and pinches it and leans back as much as he is allowed without falling and looks up and looks down. He lets go of it and holds the spot with his eyes and descends the ladder, careful not to make it move. On the ground he still holds the spot with his eyes and steps back and tries to visualize his body hanging there. He thinks about geometry, physics. A math mind would find this instinctive. They have an easier go of such things. He wonders if someone has the facts somewhere of math minds versus language minds and the suttee rates thereof, the manners chosen. Language minds are people of the gun. Eaters of dum-dums. No calculation of space required, no figures or angles—only simple obliteration of tissue and skull. Straightforward and absolute. Wrecking the veiny walls to freedom. He wishes he thought to bring a tape measure. And a marker because now he's lost his spot.

He goes up again, with more confidence in the ladder this time. The human body was designed with stepladders in mind. He rises at the summit anew and ties the rope around his neck at what he hopes to be the spot he held with his eyes or if it is not then he hopes it is a spot that is not too high that he will be able to grasp the rim but not too low that his feet will touch the ground. With the rope around his neck he remembers antelucan mornings. Eyes still turgid from sleep, the dreams lingering in a filmy crust covering over them from the lashes. Blue shirt ironed and blue pants too tight. Standing ere the mirror in his room tying and retying a red tie. Christ impaled on the wall behind him. A reflection of scourging over a cowlick. Hands transfixed by nails. Unable to get the end to hit the tip of his belt buckle. And his ribs dirked. A gouged look of starved ecstasy pulled on his face. Either ended up down to his thighs or halfway to his chest, making him look like a goofball salesman farce. And a fat spike through his feet crossed one atop the other, splitting the bones up through the shins, the knees broken and body broken, nerves twisted, all his body twitching like an insect. This God's own son. And what of us lowborn rabble? What should we expect? We wild beasts, our fathers not kings but sons of the unclean. Of what are we to hope?

Tugs on the rope to test it, kicks away the ladder, hangs, his larynx fractures, he convulses, hands at the rope around his throat pulling on it,

chokes, right leg kicking, right eye goes dim and fogs, loses vision altogether in his left eye, vessels pop in both eyeballs and around the sockets,
from his nostrils fizzes snot, shit oozes out his rectum, dick hardens, the
rope burns through the soft baby flesh of his neck, fingers try to dig
under the rope, nails tearing the skin, come spits out into his Hanes, eyeballs bulging like something macabre and aborted, a horrid gurgle grating
from the back of his mouth, his frontal lobe turning white and withering
like bad meat, even if he were to live now he would go on wheelchair-
bound and incontinent, his heart beats once, then again, then after a few
seconds once more, then that's it, it stops, and his brain lives just enough
longer to allow it to erase itself like a shaken Etch A Sketch, and it all goes,
the heavens and hells, how to walk, the name of his babysitter when he
was four, the alphabet, cursive, the Pythagorean theorem, the brown of his
father's little boy eyes, his mother's arms, the Eight Beatitudes, the
Pledge of Allegiance, cartoons, how to drive, the china cabinet with the
xenomanic gimgraws, Sean Castiglione and Jeremiah Dutton and Andy
Stephens and Brian Donnelly and Katie Staunton, the sweet smokefruit
smell of her, blue cat eyes painted in black lines, all things with which his
mind has been marred with what seemed like indelibility in its time
rolling like a snowball through what little world he's known—all in a
matter of moments gone as though they have never been. And all that
growing the body has done since it was the minimus of God's eye in its
mother's womb, all the tears in the skin—that stupefying cloth—that
have healed themselves, the viruses and infections of which the hellbroth
blood has washed in its own doing, and the earthquake gnarlings of
puberty that mutated him so in preparation for a manhood that would
never come—all for naught. And the hour, the day, the opinions we
form, the orange township, the country that is full, the planet on which
life was granted in the murksome waters, the crawling out of the breakers with tails drawing lines in the mud, and then the food we captured and
slayed, the homes we built, the mythic crags to which we sailed off overtop those same waters that bore us, the perfecting of our savagery, the
restraint of our hungry impulsions, and the dressing and shaving of our
feral soulcases, the stocking of grocery store shelves with cartons of
milk, the evenings of dinners and television news, the checking account
overdrawals, the lessons in decency, the unanswered letters, and the
paved roads and gasoline pumps, the proposals of marriage and hours
spent in therapy with tregetours, the technology and polychrestic pharmaceuticals, all those heartbreaks spent at a desk awash in facts and discipline and gauche social intercourse, the tears of loneliness and

longing—not all for naught but all for all as they are triumphed on a whim by the soaring standards and concords of death.

His blood comes to a thick freeze and begins to darken in plum the underside of the flesh in places. He will turn first to wood then to leather then to dirt. Who are we to want for more? For the leaves shake. Bugs feed upon them. A cat hides under a hemlock licking its paws. Beneath him underground dozes a squirrel in rapid-belly repose. The clouds move in circles. They fly as high as the banners.

And the human beings are in their habitacles on their sides and stomachs. Their mouths are open and they are dreaming. They keep themselves covered. All is a human silence except for their breathing and anhelous mutterings. The wind outside the window that blows always. Hear it go. It comes down from sources behind the banners to this township and courses over Springstone Drive and up Battle Rock then through the backyards of South Springs and the gravel crunch lot of Deepwood in the middle of it all like a theme park relic. Hear it kiss the rooftops and shutters and blow through the poplars. It moves the hairs of his head. It cools the raging of him.

All at once as it blows past their windows the sleepers inside open their eyes and sit up and pull back their comforters. They meet in the hallway and go down the stairs and out the front door into the night. They take themselves from the open glad hand of memory and put themselves away forever in a dull silver lockbox to be stashed with cobwebs in the most abysmal recesses of consciousness to find their way out alone here and there, now and again, until they are sought out and plucked from their places and examined then thrown out over the cliff.

And now, finally, here they all come, a rank-and-file line of pajama-clad gingerbread men, it seems like there are a million of them, moving as though on a conveyor belt up the path and to the court and past where the body dangles and now tumbling over the edge, end over end, falling in languid motion into the unbottomed black oblivion, their blurred faces upward, their arms and legs splayed, pinwheeling, chirping, —Good-bye! . . . Good-bye! . . . as they fall. Then once the last of them has gone, a new wind sweeps in chasing out the old one and it is the last wind. It blows through the interstate and highways and blackness. And it blows through Northern Virginia, over its porch lights and stop signs and garden pollards. And it blows through us. Then whatever happenstance of science, whatever small daily magia occurs and the sky begins to lighten and birds start to sing. And it is morning.

of the night to hear your mother and father yelling, hear violent noises coming from their room, see what I saw, and want nothing more than an explanation for what was going on. Yes, I would've listened," Marcus said, looking away from his father, back toward the water.

"Well, I must have been wrong. I'm sorry," Julius said.

"You've been sorry a lot in the last twenty minutes."

"Yeah." Julius lowered his head.

"Can you tell me why you never called after you left?"

"I was planning on it, but I always stopped myself because I didn't know what to say to you boys. I was never able to think of anything to say that would make sense of me leaving."

"And what was wrong with the truth?" Marcus said.

"Nothing, now. But then, it seemed like the worst thing to say. I don't know, Marcus. I can't say what went wrong for sure over those years, all I can say is that things went wrong, and not one day went by without me thinking about my sons, about you."

"Yeah, so what?" Marcus said, feeling no sympathy for the man whatsoever, knowing that what he was saying was just a line of bull that stretched from California to Chicago over the span of two decades.

"I'm letting you know that I missed you. I'm letting you know that I'm tired of us being like this. I'm tired of being without my sons."

"And do you think I liked it? The doctors say it was breast cancer that killed Ma, but I know it had something to do with you leaving. I just know it," Marcus said, giving his father a hard stare, then standing and walking closer to the water.

"And you're going to put that on me?" Julius said. "I had nothing to do with that, and you know it. You have to realize—"

"I don't have to realize anything. You didn't see her. You wouldn't know."

"I know that she was fine when I left, and I know that grief alone doesn't cause cancer," Julius said, walking up behind Marcus.

Marcus turned to face his father. "And how would you know? What makes you the damn authority on what causes cancer?"

"Because I—" Julius halted mid-sentence. "Because . . ."

Marcus looked at him strangely. "What did you say?"

"Because I . . . I just know, that's all. Marcus, I didn't come all the way to Chicago to fight with you. I didn't come out here to discuss why your mother passed. I'm trying to make something of what we lost."

"You mean of what you threw away."

"However it went, Marcus. I'm trying to make us a family again. Do you think that's possible?" He stepped in front of Marcus, so Marcus had no choice but to look at the man. He looked at the man and tried to imagine them as father and son again. It would never happen, Marcus told himself. Then he tried seeing them as friends, as someone Marcus would talk to on occasion, someone he could get advice from. It was possible, but only if Marcus let it be possible and he wouldn't do that either.

"I don't think so," Marcus said.

Julius turned to look out on the water. "And can you tell me why not?"

"No, I don't have to give you an explanation," Marcus said. "I just don't think that's possible."

"I gave you one. I explained why I left," Julius said, crossing his arms.

"Well, in twenty years, I'll give you mine," Marcus said, crossing his arms too.

"So there's no way that we can solve this, that we can reconcile some way."

"Put yourself in my situation. I mean, really. If it were you, would you take me back?" Marcus asked.

"I don't know," Julius said.

"Yeah, right. You wouldn't and you know it. But it doesn't matter what you'd do, because I'm not taking you back. Sorry."

"I'm sorry to hear that. I'm really sorry. If you knew how many days and nights I thought about us being together as a family again. I wish it could be different," Julius said.

"Well, it can't," Marcus said, not loud enough for his father to hear.

"It's going to make things awkward between you and your brother."

"What do you mean by that?" Marcus turned to face his father.

"Your decision. I just feel it will make things awkward between you and Austin. I imagine he feels differently about the situation than you do."

"So the two of you have spoken about this. And he has no problem with it?"

"We've exchanged a few words, and I don't believe he has a problem. I really have yet to ask him," Julius said.

Marcus was glad that that had not taken place yet. "This may sound strange, but I have to ask you not to do that."

"Not to do what?"

"Ask him to take you back." Julius didn't respond to Marcus's request, just stared at him, a look of concern in his eyes.

"I'm only asking you because, like you said, it would make things awkward, and I don't think our relationship can handle that."

Julius slowly walked about the space in front of Marcus, running a hand through his hair. "I don't think you know what you're asking me to do," he said, a nervous look on his face.

"I do," Marcus said plainly.

"I don't think so, because if you knew what I went through, what I'm going through, you wouldn't be asking me such a thing. I've been waiting twenty years for this, and now that I've finally found the courage to come down here, now that I finally have an opportunity to be with one of my sons, you're telling me that you don't want me to have that. I don't think I can just give this up."

Marcus placed himself in his father's path, stopping the man. "You're going to have to. You're just going to have to."

"Why?"

"Because he's my brother, and I can't lose him to you," Marcus said.

"Well, he's my son," Julius said. "You act as though I'm trying to kidnap him. You're acting as if just because he's willing to have a relationship with me, it'll destroy the one he has with you."

"It will," Marcus said. "There are things you don't know about Austin. He can't seem to have too much going on in his life before he starts to lose control, before he starts to shut down and want to have nothing else to do with anything. There's only so much space he allots for each individual thing in his life, and that includes family. Right now, I'm the family he accepts in that space. He would never admit it, but if he takes you in, I'm out, and I can't have that, because I need my brother, and he needs me. We need each other. And now that Caleb's in prison, he's almost the only family I have left."

"After what you told me, he *is* the only family I have left," Julius said, a bit of anger in his voice.

"That's because you made it that way. You left us," Marcus said.

Julius looked dead into his son's eyes. It seemed he was searching for something that would help him understand what was being asked of him, but there was nothing. He turned, took a few steps across the rocks away from his son, and looked out on the water again.

"Why are you asking me to do this?" he said, not turning to face Marcus.

"You said you thought about us every day that you were gone. You said you cared for us."

"I did, I do," Julius said.

"Then how can you knowingly come back here and ruin what little family you left me with? It's difficult enough as it is, but if you try and reenter a life here it will do nothing but make things worse."

"But—" Julius turned to make a point.

"And knowing that," Marcus continued, "and doing it anyway, would mean you were only thinking about yourself. Just like when you left."

Julius turned away from Marcus. He slid both hands through his hair, messing it up. He intertwined his fingers atop his head, tilted his face to the sky, his eyes closed.

"I'll have to think about this, Marcus," Julius said, still in his frustrated stance. "I'll just have to think about it."

FORTY-ONE

Austin sat in his car, outside his home in his driveway. He had just returned from Marcus's house, where he had spoken to his father. Where he had spoken to his father for the last time. He had waited for Marcus and his father to return from wherever it was they had gone to talk. It seemed like an eternity and Austin found himself running back and forth to the window every time he heard a car approaching. He felt like a fool. He didn't know why, but he was worried. Worried that something might happen to his father after finally returning after all those years. The thought was almost unbearable, and he tried to keep it from entering his head again.

When they finally returned, Austin stepped outside to greet them, a smile on his face.

Both men looked solemn as Austin approached them. Marcus walked right by him, not even stopping to glance in Austin's direction.

"We have to talk, Austin," his father said, laying a hand on his shoulder and leading him down the stairs and out to the sidewalk.

"What?" Austin said. He felt his stomach turn, and all of a sudden felt dizzy. He felt something terrible was looming.

"I can't . . ." His father swallowed hard, as if the words were resisting coming out of his mouth. "I can't see you again. We can't be together," Julius said. He turned his head, and tightened his grip on his son's shoulder.

"What did you say? I didn't hear that," Austin said, worried, laying a hand on his father's arm.

"We can't see each other anymore," Julius said again, his voice stronger.

"But why not? We've barely—"

"We just can't," Julius interrupted. "It was a bad idea coming down here in the first place. I have no business here."

"You do. You do have business here. You're our father," Austin said, still holding on.

"If I was, I never would've left in the first place."

Austin fell silent. There was nothing he could say to that, because there seemed to be too much truth in the statement.

"What happened?" Austin said, fury in his eyes.

"What happened with what?"

"The talk you had with Marcus. What did he tell you? What did he tell you to make you want to leave?" Austin was splitting his attention between his father and the house. He thought of going in there, dragging Marcus out and forcing him to tell his father the truth, because Austin knew he had lied to him.

Julius shook his head. "Austin, don't say that about your brother. It had nothing to do with him."

"You're lying. I know him. He told you something that is making you change your mind. I know how he feels about you."

"Do you know how he feels about you?" Julius said.

"What difference does it make how he feels?"

"It makes a difference, a big difference. Austin, he's your family, and when the world seems to be against you, when there seems to be no one else you can turn to, your family will be there. You can always depend on him."

"And who are you? You're my family, too," Austin said desperately.

"Have you been able to depend on me, son? Have I been there for you when there were things on your mind, when you needed advice about something, when you just wanted to talk?"

Austin didn't answer.

"Well, that answer is no," Julius said. "Hell, you didn't even know if I was dead or alive. The fact is, I have a lot of nerve trying to step back into your lives like this." Julius stepped close to Austin and put a hand back on his shoulder. "Austin, I love you, son. I always have, and I always will, but there's too much going on right now for us to do this."

"But, Dad—"

"No. It's just not the time," Julius said, placing his other hand on Austin's other shoulder. "But you never know. Maybe . . . maybe in five years," Julius said, and his voice cracked a little, and he looked away at the ground for a moment, as if needing some time to compose himself.

"What's wrong?" Austin asked, deeply concerned.

Julius looked up, now with a half-hearted smile.

"Nothing son, just something in my eye, I suppose. But like I said, maybe in five years or so, things would've settled down some and who knows . . ." His father chuckled a little. But there wasn't happiness in his smile. What Austin saw was sadness. There was nothing Austin could say, the emotion he felt seemed to stop the words from coming. He leaned forward and threw his arms around his father. His father hugged him back.

Austin held him tight, didn't want to let him go, ever. But after a moment, he felt his father gently pulling away from him, and it felt too much like twenty years ago. His father was looking over Austin's shoulder at the house. Austin turned around to see Marcus and Cathy standing on the porch.

"I should be going now, son." He extended a hand, and picking up his cue, Cathy descended the stairs and placed herself at his side.

Austin just stood there, not saying a word, not making a move, staring into his father's eyes, wishing that he wouldn't leave. Julius seemed to read that in his son's face, for he said, "Austin, don't worry. Trust in your brother, your family, and things will work out fine."

He pulled his hand from Austin's shoulder, and Austin felt the void immediately, as if a part of his soul had been taken from him, and he knew he would not shake this feeling until he saw his father again, if that day ever came.

RM Johnson

Julius got in the passenger side of the car, Cathy got behind the wheel. Strangely, Austin's father didn't wave good-bye, didn't place a melodramatic palm against the glass of the car, as if needing to reach out and touch his son for the last time, didn't even turn to look at his son, not even for an instant. He just rode off.

Maybe in five years, his father had said. Austin would be waiting, he thought as he sat outside his house in his car and stared at the garage. "The garage," he said aloud. He missed seeing the thing standing before him at the end of a long day at work. It was one of the many things he missed about his life at home, his life with his family. And to think he had almost wanted to give that up.

He thought about his father, thought about what he must have gone through over those twenty years, thought about what he, himself had gone through. He would never want that for his children. Never. Besides, he had learned that the good comes with the bad; there is no other way. He would no longer compare his good times with Trace to the bad times. He would no longer even consider them that way. He would accept those times as simply experiences. Bad, good, or indifferent, they were just events that happened, that couldn't weaken but only enhance how he felt about his marriage, his children, his life.

Austin got out of his car and let himself in his house, hoping that his family would be home. He closed the door softly behind him, and found his children asleep on the sofa on either side of their mother. Trace was asleep as well, a children's book opened on her lap. He stood and looked down on them. How beautiful they were, all of them, and how much he loved and missed them. As he looked at his son stretched out across the couch, his daughter hugging her mother, his wife's hands on each of their heads, he realized what a fool he was for thinking the things he had let into his head, for questioning what type of woman she was or whether he belonged with her. They did belong together, there was no question about that, and he was more sure of it now than he was the day he married her.

He lowered himself to his knees, gently pulled the book off Trace's knees, then rested his head in her lap.

"I love you," he said softly. He took a deep breath in, then let it out, feeling safe next to her.

He felt her hand touch his face. He looked up, and she was coming out of her sleep, slowly opening her eyes. "Austin?" she said.

"Yes, it's me."

"You look tired, baby."

"I feel tired. I've been through so much," he said, thinking about his brother whom he had lost to prison. About Marcus, the brother who fought so hard to keep them together as a family, no matter what. And his father, the man he still loved and admired regardless of what had happened so many years ago. He had been through so much and all he wanted to do was be home, be with his family, and feel the love that he didn't have to question, the love that was unconditional, the love he had almost lost.

"Trace, I'm coming home. I'm coming home for good because I need you, I need my children. I hope that's okay with you."

Trace put her hands on Austin's face, pulled him toward her, then kissed him on the lips. "Welcome back, sweetheart."

FORTY-TWO

Julius sat in the visiting area waiting for his son to come out. He didn't know what to expect when he saw him and he didn't know quite what to say either, but he would think of something. He told himself he would see him and if nothing else, apologize for leaving, for possibly contributing to the mess his life became.

Caleb was escorted out, and he sat down in front of his father. Julius had never thought he would see one of his sons in prison attire— the baggy orange jumpsuit, the numbers stenciled on the breast—but there he was, wearing one of the things. He figured his son looked to be okay, considering. He could have used a shave, and maybe a few decent meals, but then again, he himself could have used the same things.

When Caleb sat down the look on his face was blank for a moment, then he chuckled, then his face went blank again. Caleb looked down at the phone on his side of the thick glass, as if wondering whether or not he should actually pick it up, if it was worth holding conversation with this man opposite him. After a moment he reached down and picked up the phone. Julius did the same and listened for his son's voice.

"I sure didn't think I would be seeing you here," Caleb said, shaking his head from side to side in disbelief.

"Your brothers didn't tell you I was coming?"

"No. I guess they didn't think it was important enough, huh?" he said, smiling a little as if amused by the entire situation. The smile quickly disappeared and a melancholy look replaced it.

"I guess not. Well, you're looking good," Julius said.

"Well, you're not. You look bad. You look sick," Caleb said, balling up his face a little.

Julius coughed. He didn't know if it was because he had to, or if the mere mention of illness subconsciously provoked the action. He coughed in his hand, examined it, and it was dry and clean. "I'm sick. Prostate cancer. I have a couple of years left to live," Julius said, looking closely for his son's reaction.

"That's messed up," Caleb said.

It was all Caleb offered and Julius couldn't tell if he was sincere or not.

"Does Marcus and Austin know?"

"No."

"Then why you telling me, and didn't tell them?"

"I didn't want them to feel sorry for me, I guess." Julius looked down at his hands. "I can tell you the truth, because I don't have to worry about you feeling sympathy for me, do I?"

Caleb shook his head, then spoke. "No. You definitely don't have to worry about that."

"Well, that's okay, because we all have to go sometime, don't we?"

Caleb didn't answer, just sat there, the phone to his head.

"You're probably wondering why I'm here," Julius said.

"Not really. I figure that you're here to beg forgiveness from me because you're dying, and you did the same of Marcus and Austin, but Marcus wasn't having it. You're here because this is your last chance, your last resort." He adjusted the phone to his ear. "But don't worry, I'm used to being a last resort." He appeared saddened, as if suddenly realizing the truth of his own statement.

"Well, I guess you got it all figured out. I was hoping—"

"You were a lousy father," Caleb interrupted. "Do you know that?" The look in Caleb's eyes was intense.

Julius always thought that he had been, but he had never actually heard it, not even from Marcus. Marcus had cursed him and pointed out all his flaws and faults, but never summed it up like that, so neatly, in one harsh, unforgiving statement.

"I know," he reluctantly admitted.

"You left us and you never came back. Never. I mean, you weren't much of a father to me while you were with us, but at least you were there."

"I know," Julius said again, not knowing what else to say.

There was a long moment of silence, then Julius spoke.

"I want to know if you can forgive me for that," Julius said, hoping the request could begin to wipe away the many years of neglect.

"Sure," Caleb said, quickly and absently.

"Do you mean that?"

"No, but what difference does it make, right? It doesn't make one bit of difference. But if you need to hear that so you can run home and die in peace, then I'll say it, even though you don't deserve it. I forgive you. There, rest in peace, Dad," Caleb said, bitterly.

"It does mean something. I want us to be family again," Julius said. "We can be a family, just the two of us. No one else has to know," he said, a weak attempt at excitement in his voice.

"What is that supposed to mean?"

"What?" Julius asked.

"Am I supposed to take that remark as you choosing me over Austin and Marcus? 'We can be a family, just the two of us,'" Caleb said, repeating his father's statement. "Am I supposed to think you finally noticed how bad you treated me, and now you want to make up for that? Because I'm not seeing it that way. I see you as some poor pathetic old man that needs to find something to hold onto before he dies, and that something happens to be me, because there ain't nobody else. The fact is, I don't need you. I don't need nobody, and if I did, I don't have nobody. I'm locked the fuck up in here and my son is gone, my woman is gone, and even if I did forgive you, you'd be gone too."

That's what it was all about, Julius told himself. It wasn't that Caleb didn't want to take him back, but that he was afraid of losing him again if he did. Caleb needed someone to be there for him just like Julius did. How ironic that the two of us, the two least likely to have anything in common, all of a sudden have so much, Julius thought. We're both desperate, condemned men in a sense, who have no one else to turn to but each other.

"Caleb, I spoke to her," Julius said, knowing the information would at least hold his son's attention for a moment.

"To who?"

"To Sonya. Austin told me where you lived and I went over there the other day. Caleb, she didn't know what to do. She had very little money, the place was falling apart, she was barely making it and she didn't know what she was going to do next."

"Why are you telling me this? Are you trying to make me feel worse about being in here!" Caleb said, moving closer toward the thick glass.

"No, no. I'm just telling you what happened. I knew you would want to know. I'm sorry if it bothered you."

Caleb settled back down in his seat, and urged him to continue.

"I looked at that place and knew she couldn't stay there, it was no place to raise a son. I told her that Cathy and I would take care of her and the child. I told her that we would move them back to California, let them live with us in our house. She could get a job. We would take care of everything."

Caleb sat there, not saying a word, a look of hate and skepticism on his face.

"Did you hear me?" Julius spoke into the phone, expecting his son to be a bit more enthused.

"Yeah. I heard you. What did she say?" Caleb asked, unaffected by the news.

"She didn't say anything right away. She made me wait a while, but she said yes. I told her there were no conditions, nothing expected of her, and she said yes. She said yes, Caleb!"

Caleb ran a hand down his face. "Thank you, I guess."

"She still loves you," Julius said. "I can tell. She didn't promise anything when I asked, but I think she'll wait for you. I really think she will."

"Well, I'll believe that when I see it."

"Caleb," Julius said. "I told Sonya, there were no conditions for her, but for you there are some."

"I knew it would be something," Caleb said, looking away in disgust. "I can't pay you anything cause I don't have no money. I can't do anything for you cause I'm locked up, if you haven't noticed, so you might as well go back and tell Sonya it's off."

"I'm not talking about conditions like that, nothing like that. I want us to make a deal. For me to do what I'm doing for you and your family, I want you to do something very simple for me. Do you think you can do that?"

Caleb grunted a response which Julius took as interest in his proposal.

"Allow me to be your friend, plain and simple," Julius said. "Allow me to write you letters and call you and know that you'll write me back, and be looking forward to receiving my next letter. I want you to walk around in this prison knowing that you have a father and a girlfriend and a son—a family that loves you, and is counting the days till you get out so they can spend time with you, and make you feel appreciated. I want you to allow me to treat and love your son the way he's supposed to be treated—like my grandson. And yes, I want to be allowed to know that when I'm gone, there is someone carrying my blood that will miss me, that will talk about me, and that will occasionally think about something I said or did. That person being you. That is all I ask from you, Caleb. Do you think we can make that deal?" Julius said. He felt his body trembling as if his life depended on this decision, a decision made by the son who really cared nothing at all about if he lived or died. The answer seemed a long time in coming.

"Why you doing this?" Caleb asked.

"Because you're my son, and I need you. We need each other," Julius said.

"I needed you a long time ago, but it didn't make no difference then. There were a lot of times when I needed you, but where were you?" Caleb said. "I might not be in here if you were around, you know that?" he said.

"I know, Caleb, but I can't help what happened back then. But I'm trying now."

"Trying. How?" Caleb said. "By trying to buy me? By taking Sonya and my son, and saying that you're taking care of them, when all you're doing is holding them over my head. Using them as a tool to make me do something you want me to do. That's what you call trying?"

"Caleb, it's not like that."

"It's not? Why you trying to take them? You don't think that I can take care of them?" Caleb said, anger filling his voice. "You don't think I can do right by my woman, still be my son's father? Is that why you're trying to take them?"

"No, son," Julius said, frantically scooting closer to the glass, as if it would somehow calm his son.

Then all of a sudden a look of sad realization covered Caleb's face, and he slowly rose from his chair, still holding the phone to his head.

"You think I've failed, don't you?" Caleb said slowly, staring at his father, fury in his eyes.

"No, Caleb," Julius said, springing from his chair.

"You think I've failed. You're trying to take them from me, because you think you can do better, and then what will I do? I'll never see them again."

"Caleb, no!" Julius shouted into the phone. And he could tell his son was panicking, could tell that this must have been his greatest fear. "Caleb, that's not what I'm trying to do," Julius said, slapping his palm on the surface of the glass, demanding Caleb's full attention. "You've got to listen to me." But that wasn't happening, because Caleb was looking around as if held prisoner not just by steel bars and cement walls but by his fears. He looked as though he was frantically trying to find a way to escape.

"Please. You can't take them. You stay away from them!" he warned, stabbing a threatening finger toward his father, rage on his face. "I can take care of them myself."

"And how are you going to do that?" Julius shouted, more at the glass than into the phone. He was shocked by his outburst, but he had to make his son understand that this wasn't a test that he had passed or failed, this was about the care of his family.

"How are you going to take care of them, when you're here?" And Julius could tell the statement hit his son like a club over the head. And Julius felt somewhat sorry for him at that moment, but it was what he needed.

"You tell me, son. What are you going to do for your family sitting behind bars?"

Caleb said nothing. His face went blank, and he dropped to his chair, as if he could no longer hold his own weight. He looked beaten, as though he had no other recourse but to listen to what the man before him had to say.

"I'm not trying to take them from you, son," Julius said, sitting down himself. "Can't you see, I'm trying to save them for you. I know I screwed up in the past, but I'm only concerned with right now. And right now, this very moment, you are in jail, and your family is in need. I'm trying to help you with that, can't you see. There is this common bond we share in that we both need each other. Caleb, we are all the other has. What do you have to lose?"

Caleb looked directly in his father's eyes. "I don't have nothing to lose, because I don't have nothing, period, and I'm blaming that on you."

"And you may be right about that, and I'm willing to bear that blame if it will bring us together as a family. The question is," Julius said, looking deeply into his son's eyes, "what are you going to do?"

Caleb looked away, and Julius could tell that he was wrestling with the decision. He knew his son was thinking that he was being tricked, that he was being used, and that he could trust no one, least of all his own father, but he would have to get over that, and this would help him. He would learn from this experience, if he accepted the offer.

Caleb looked at Julius, seeming to be looking him over one last time before he made his decision, examining him to see if he was fit to be trusted, fit to take care of his child. Caleb looked deeper into his father's eyes, and Julius could see his son's eyes narrowing some, could see the muscles in his jaws tighten. Julius felt that he was thinking back to all the days that his father wasn't there for him, all the days that he was there but treated his boy like a stranger, and Julius just knew that the day he walked out on his sons had to pass through Caleb's mind at that moment. That day he walked out, offering no explanation, not saying a word then and not bothering to say a word since, up until now. Put that out of your mind, son, Julius thought, willing his son to make the right decision. Put that bad past out of your mind, and realize what's before you, because I can only help you if you allow me to, and I want to help you so bad. That's all I want.

"I . . . I . . ." Caleb started to speak, and Julius clutched the phone tighter in his hand in anticipation of his son's answer, his heart pounding harder in his chest.

"What, son? What?" Julius pushed.

"I'll take your offer, because you said you'll take care of my son, and . . ." Caleb lowered his head, looking at the floor, "and . . . I need somebody, too," he said softly, as if almost ashamed.

Julius looked at his son and smiled. "We need each other," Julius said, and it felt as though years of regret and self-torture had been erased. He could live now, and not have to look back on how badly he had mistreated his sons, but look forward to how well he could treat this son. He felt free.

"There is one more thing I'm going to need from you," Julius said into the phone.

A concerned, almost fearful look covered Caleb's face, as if he was anticipating his father telling him that this had all been just another cruel joke.

"What?" Caleb said, guarded.

Julius hesitated a moment, feeling nervous about what he had to say for fear of his son's reaction, then eventually found the courage to speak. "If I'm going to be taking care of your son, don't you think I ought to know his name?"

Caleb looked thrown by the request. He appeared to have reservations about talking to his father, this practical stranger, about something so close to him. Then after a moment, the hard look on his face softened, and he seemed to open up.

"His name is Jahlil," Caleb said, his mouth lengthening slowly into a proud, fatherly smile. "His name is Jahlil."